CHASING FAITH

CHASING FAITH

STEPHANIE
PERRY MOORE

KENSINGTON PUBLISHING CORP.
http://www.kensingtonbooks.com

To *Jenell GiGi Clark*
who gave me the will and the passion to chase this story

To *Vanessa Davis Griggs*
who provided the opportunity and wisdom that gave me faith
to believe this tale would be told

And to *Chandra "Jackie" Dixon*
for always being there since college

Love and God's best to you all

Acknowledgments

As I peruse the page proofs for this novel on Thanksgiving Day, I am clinging to my faith that this book will be a blessing to someone. It's been a few years since I've written an adult title. The countless obstacles in my way almost made me give up this particular journey. Truthfully, only the Lord sending His great people to get me going has allowed me to continue chasing the vision of seeing this story in print. Here is a special thank you to all those who allowed Our Father to use you, to help me.

To my dad, Dr. Franklin Perry, Sr.: Thanks for teaching me how to have faith in my dreams. Life has allowed you to stand in high places, but it has also dealt you some hard blows. Your endurance through it all helps me stay my course.

To my mother, Shirley Roundtree Perry: I thought we were cut from different cloths, but as I get older I see more and more that I'm much like you. You have such a thick skin. Thanks for making me borrow your armor when this writing journey got tough.

To my special author friend Robin Jones Gunn, Beverly Jenkins, Vanessa Davis Griggs, Marjorie Kimbrough, Victoria Christopher Murray, Matthew Parker, Michele Andrea Bowen, and Lysa Terkurst: How blessed I am to know you and how better the world that you are using your gift. Thanks for uplifting me with your neverending support.

To the team that made this book possible: My agent Janet Kobobel Grant, for guiding my career; my assistants, Nakia Austin, Ciara Roundtree, and Jessica Phillips for aiding me through. Kensington/Dafina past and present editors: Stacey Barney, for seeing the vision and taking a chance; Karen Thomas for saying yes; and Selena James, for helping me finish the course. Also special thanks to Carol Mackey of Black Expressions for getting behind this title from the beginning. The collaboration of your talents on this project made it reachable to more. To God be the glory.

To my brother, Franklin Dennis Perry, Sr.'s family and friends: Your love has sustained me to keep on writing for God. Thanks for showing up at signings, telling folks about my little books, and sharing your stories with me for inspiration.

To my daughters, Sydni Derek and Sheldyn Ashli: You girls keep me on my toes. I wouldn't trade a minute of what we share. Thanks for being proud of your mom's books. If I can make a wish on a star and have it come true, so can you. Work harder and God will see you through.

To my hubby, Derrick C. Moore: Thanks for motivating me with your inspiring words you share with the world. We're always chasing more for our family, but ain't it good to see what the Lord has done with our union?

To the reader: Wanting to be in a right relationship with Christ is an awesome thing. However, sometimes we let ourselves get in the way. This story was meant to inspire you to keep on striving for perfection in Christ. When you are okay with knowing you hold no power, He can strengthen your heart and help you become all you were created to be.

And finally to my Lord: At times I went in circles trying to get this book out there. Even though I was turned around, you still helped me to head to my destiny of getting it to the world. I still have many more dreams inside of me that aren't coming to fruition as quickly as I'd like, but I've learned my lesson. No losing hope. I'll stay the course and wait on You. It is my desire that every person pursues You above all things.

Chapter 1

Venture

I'm young, attractive, and intelligent, so why am I lying here with this guy when I don't even love him? It's an early November morning and C-SPAN is blasting from the other room. I'm annoyed. I was getting real tired of the casualness of our relationship. I tried to cover my naked body with the silk sheet thrown across the bed. I moved carefully so Mr. Three Times in One Night wouldn't wake up and want to go another round.

Troy Evans and I had been seeing each other intimately, with no strings attached, for seven months. Neither of us wanted any commitment other than our jobs. We were coworkers and a darn good team, both on the job and under the covers. He was hitting thirty-three and I was almost twenty-eight. However, I now wanted more than a fling. I didn't know what it was I was chasing, but I did know Troy wasn't the answer.

As an FBI agent, I considered myself to be tough. Upholding justice was my life's work. Ever since my alcoholic dad left my mother, little sister, and me when I was ten years old, I felt I had to protect the three of us. I was the oldest, so I had to take care of my family.

My mother raised us in church, so the only father I knew was a Heavenly Father, and most times I wondered if He was even there. You know, when Mama couldn't pay the rent, when we had no food, or when I wore shoes to school that were way too small because we had no money for new ones. Where was God when my mother couldn't get folks in our small church to help her? Out of desperation she turned to a local drug dealer for a job. It destroyed her life, and not having her there for me sent me searching for love in all the wrong places. So here I am with Troy.

Troy and I found our way into each other's arms after work one day. It was early April, and I'd been on Troy's team for eighteen months. It was my tenth assignment since coming out of training—I had been an agent for almost five years. We were working a money-laundering case. We'd tracked our suspect, Rudy Roberts, from our hometown and headquarters in D.C. to New York City. Troy, another agent, and I were in a surveillance van, following Roberts in a cab. Suddenly the yellow taxi pulled over and Roberts got out, smiled at our van, and started walking briskly down the sidewalk.

Very annoyed that the guy had somehow found us out, Troy ordered, "You guys stay in the vehicle and follow me—I'm tailing Roberts."

He hurled out so fast that he didn't take a radio. When Roberts ducked down a dark alley, Troy followed him. We couldn't see either of them.

After waiting a few minutes, panic began to set in. I opened the van door.

The other agent yelled, "We need to stay put."

"We can't even see him now," I rationalized. "What if he's in trouble?"

I ducked down that same blind alley and heard a scuffle. With my gun drawn, I crept up the sidewall behind a green, industrial Dumpster. Suddenly the struggle ended.

Roberts laughed. "You've nothing on me. Get ready to die."

Taking a deep breath for courage, I walked a few paces more and saw Roberts on top of my case leader, his gun in Troy's face.

I identified myself by saying, "Freeze—FBI!" When he cocked his gun, I shot mine on impulse.

After the smoke cleared, I realized I had shot a man for the very first time in my life. I suddenly felt this awful guilt. Although I'd spent countless hours at the firing range, I was not prepared for the emotional reaction that I would have when I was actually in that situation.

"What have I done?" I mumbled.

Then Troy was in front of me, taking the warm weapon from my hands. "If you hadn't shot him, he would have killed me. I'm forever grateful—and glad you disobeyed my order and got out of that van." He smiled.

After Internal Affairs investigated for days, they concluded I did the only thing I could. Still, I was mentally drained and shaken. After the shooting I couldn't handle my emotions in the field, so my boss, Agent Thomas Hunter, decided to keep me chained to my desk, reviewing cases and talking to confidential sources, gathering evidence until he thought I was ready to get back out there.

Troy understood my disappointment. Not too long after I was benched, he asked to buy me a late meal. Since the shooting, I didn't like being alone at night, so I accepted his offer. We went to a local steak house and ate and drank for several hours. Later, Troy saw me to my door. I was slightly inebriated and he wanted to make sure that I got in safely. He opened the door for me with my keys but didn't say good night.

Troy looked deep into my eyes that hazy April night and told me I was beautiful and sexy. I hadn't heard that from a man in too long.

I pulled him close to me and kissed him deeply. I wanted to be found attractive again by a man. It had been years since I'd felt the warm hands of a strong man all over my body. No part of me hesitated as I slipped into his arms.

Though Troy made it clear he didn't want anything serious, that was the first of many wonderful, sensual nights that we would spend together. Law enforcement wasn't the kind of career that lent itself to settling down. The women Troy had dated before me didn't understand that. The long hours and spur of the moment out of town trips for weeks at a time without a decent night off weren't the kind of thing most women could deal with. He was one of the FBI's best agents, so he handled some of the biggest cases in the world. Romance came second to adventure for Troy.

At first, that wasn't high on my priority list, either, so we made a good match. We'd get together whenever we felt like keeping each other's bed warm. Other than that, neither of us had any expectations. Months ago that was okay, but now, lying next to him, I was suddenly sick of the arrangement.

As I gazed at his muscular body, toffee-colored skin, and handsome face, I thought maybe, just maybe, I was ready for more than just casual sex with no commitment. Something inside made me see this as wrong. Was it the Holy Spirit at work?

Stepping out of bed, I hurried to the bathroom. It was almost two A.M. Spending the night this time was not an option. I had too much going on inside me. Not only was I starting to hate our no-strings-attached relationship, I was also starting to despise my profession. I was honestly burnt-out personally and professionally. Our unit worked closely with the Drug Enforcement Agency, following seedy characters from state to state until we finally got enough evidence for an arrest. But each time I saw a major drug dealer get off on a technicality, it made me want another job. And watching others work on cases in the field while I was still tied to a desk didn't help matters any.

Standing at the sink, I stared at my dim reflection in the mirror. Troy often complimented me on my smooth brown complexion and warm, hazel eyes. I was just glad my eyelashes were long and thick so I didn't have to use mascara. I never wore much makeup, preferring to rely on my own natural, God-given attributes. Glamour and guns only mixed in the movies.

I really needed to redo my highlights, though. I ran my fingers through my short hair and thought about the fine man in the next room. Suddenly my insides started churning.

One part of me wondered why I was tripping. Maybe I just needed to crawl back into bed with him and get some more loving. Or maybe I needed some space. It seems like just yesterday that my first and only love, Max Cross, broke my heart. Max and I dated all four years at Baylor. I majored in Criminal Justice and he was a Business major. We met at a freshman party and were inseparable from then on. He was an exceptionally sexy man with creamy clay skin and hazel-brown eyes that made me melt. I thought we'd get married, and I was devastated when we broke up. I shouldn't have told him I was pregnant. The abortion broke my heart—and our relationship.

To get over that pain, I took on more shifts at my job at a local restaurant, Texan Grill, where I'd been working to earn money to send back to my mother and sister. It hadn't been more than three months before the married manager, Damien, and I began having an affair. I knew it wasn't right. But Damien just treated me so well—like a queen, and I hadn't been treated like that before. He bought me things and took me on trips. I didn't know what he told his wife and didn't care until the day she caught us in the act.

Over the next six months, I applied and got accepted into a training program for the Federal Bureau of Investigation. It's been less than six years. After doing well on other assignments and saving Agent Evans's life, I now enjoyed the respect of my colleagues. They started calling me "the woman with everything going on." It was true. I was good-looking, well put-together. Whatever I wore always suited me. And I'd never had a problem attracting a man. But what difference did all that really make? I wasn't happy. There had to be more to this life than survival. I felt empty and needed to be filled by something everlasting, but how could I get that. The only thing I knew was that I had to change the crazy way I was living.

I sighed and reached to turn on the faucet. That's when I saw the condom Troy and I had used just hours before. The shriveled-up thing wasn't balled up in the wastebasket, but curled up on the sink, positioned as if it had been inspected.

"What the . . . ?" I screeched out, completely lost in anger as I realized what must have happened.

Troy's voice came suddenly from the other room. "You got a problem?"

"Yes," I snapped. "What is this?"

He made his way to the bathroom, and eyed the condom beside me. "Would you calm down, baby. I'm sure it's no big deal."

"Troy, don't play. Did this burst?"

"I . . . I don't know. I'm not sure."

"What do you mean, you're not sure. You're a grown man, Troy."

Troy scanned my naked body with hungry eyes and tried to pull me close, but I held back. Didn't he get that I was pissed?

"I can open another one," he whispered. "It'll only take a second for me to put it on."

"You knew the condom broke, didn't you?" I said, scanning his guilty face and ignoring his new erection. "I can't have a baby and work in the FBI!"

"Don't even sweat that. You're cool. I'm over thirty. I've been sexually active since my teens. I've been with lots of women and never had any children. Trust me, it'll be okay. I know what I'm doing."

He tried to lead me back to bed, but I shoved him out of the bathroom and closed the door in his face.

See? I chastised myself. *That's why I shouldn't be doing this.*

Troy's frustrated voice filtered through the door. "Shut me out, then. I'm gonna fix me something to eat. I'm telling you, don't worry. I know you're fine." His confidence made my skin crawl.

When I heard him storm away, I took the only clean washcloth in the place from under the sink and began to freshen up. Emotions started to bubble up. I needed help. I needed something different. I needed not to be in this casual sex relationship.

Deep down, I felt there was only One that could fix this, so I looked up at the ceiling and said, "God, You gotta know this is not a good time for me." I shook my head. What was I doin'? He wouldn't listen to me. I'm sure He gave up on me a while ago.

But something—sheer desperation—spurred me to get down on my knees and continue. "Well, if You're still in the forgiving business, I need help. There's got to be more to this life than living and dying. There has to be more than just trying to get by. If there's a better plan, God, help me see it."

My mom used to make us pray every night, trying to lift our spirits. But ever since I had the abortion after the breakup with Max, I'd strayed away from God. Somehow I just felt unworthy of His love. But at that moment in Troy's bathroom, I needed to feel close to Him.

I emerged from Troy's bedroom fully dressed and headed to gather my stuff. Troy heard my steps and caught my arm before I picked up my bag. He pulled me to the television in the living room.

"Can you believe this?" he raged.

A news conference was being held on C-SPAN. A U.S. senator, the Reverend Steven Stokes, was addressing the nation from Atlanta, Georgia. For a brief second, I forgot that I had planned to head to my own apartment.

"Did he say he's running for president?" I asked.

"Yeah," Troy confirmed.

I shrugged. "Maybe he can win. He's a popular senator," I said, recovering from shock.

"Please! I don't care who he is. Jackson's, Chisholm's, and Sharpton's poor showings at the polls over the years should be enough to prove this nation ain't ready for a black president."

"I don't know," I said, lowering myself onto the couch. "That was years ago. Colin Powell and Condoleezza Rice have since held cabinet posts—they've changed America's outlook about having a black person in politics. Maybe the nation is ready."

"Yeah, right," Troy dismissed.

The Reverend's wife, a beige-skinned, petite lady, strode up to her husband with a bright, confident smile. She wore a navy suit, tea-length with a rounded white collar pressed to perfection. Pearl accessories added a touch of elegance. I admired her style.

Their three children followed, all seemingly in their twenties or early thirties. The eldest, Steven Jr., had a young family of his own with him. But the bad-boy look in his eye told me this guy was probably a bit of a troublemaker.

The daughter, Savannah, was a younger version of her mom. She looked to be in her early twenties. She walked up to her dad, took his arm, and gave him an adoring smile.

The middle child, Sebastian, had a muscular build that made me do a double take. He wore dark-rimmed glasses and a charcoal-colored suit and tie that made him look like an overpriced lawyer.

I didn't know them personally, but the Stokeses had been in the spotlight lately. The press loved talking about how much the family was putting Georgia on the map. I had seen headlines touting the way their community involvement had helped decrease the number of homeless people, increase the number of corporate headquarters in Georgia, and raise the state's literacy rate. I'd always felt that though we hadn't had a black president yet, we needed more politicians to keep reaching for it. And what better candidate than a family man who had been a politician and the leader of a church. Plus, I could get behind someone who wanted to work for America as president and not just push his own agenda. Reverend Stokes seemed like that type of person.

"They seem like the real deal," I said.

"Whatever," Troy grumbled, heading into the kitchen. "Wait 'til the press starts eating them up. All their dirty laundry will be out there." Troy poured himself a shot of gin. "White folks don't want a brother in the White House. They're afraid we'll get in there and make our own rules." Troy laughed to himself.

"White people aren't the only ones who vote. You'll vote for him, won't you?"

Troy chugged his drink. "I don't know anything about the man."

"He's black and he's a Democrat. Plus, he has a good track record," I said, angry at his stubbornness. "What else do you need to know?"

"Chris, if you ever meet them you'll probably see they aren't that impressive. I bet those smiles are only on the surface. Most politicians I come across are phony."

"All of them can't be bad," I said, gathering my stuff. "I imagine their life is pretty wonderful."

"Then I suggest you apply for the Secret Service temp job, guard them for a while, and find out all their dirty little secrets.

Then you'll see that the rosy picture you're talking about isn't so perfect."

I spotted my toothbrush and makeup case and stuffed them into my Gucci overnight bag. Walking back to the living room, I said, "Temp job? What are you talking about?"

"It was posted through the inner office e-mail system. Something about because it's election time, the Secret Service needs bodies to help them cover the presidential candidates," Troy said before kissing me on the cheek and opening his apartment door.

Once on the other side of his door, I raised my eyebrow, nodded my head, and thought, *Good riddance, Mr. Evans. And maybe I should look into that temp job.* It was time for a new venture.

Chapter 2

Explore

The following week was not easy. I did apply for the temp job with the Secret Service. But I worried about the possibility of being pregnant. What would I do with a baby? I simply forced myself to concentrate on work. And with many files on my desk needing to be reviewed and data entry piling up, I had much to do.

The stress of my life made me glad I would soon be headed to Texas for my college roommate and best friend's wedding. Although I had strayed away from God, Eden still remained true to the Lord. She was the only woman I was close to, with the exception of my mother and Crystal, my feisty younger sister. Even though we now lived in separate cities, when Eden asked me to be her maid of honor, I gladly accepted.

I was busy typing away at my desk. Over the last week, work had been easy. I didn't have to deal with Troy, because he was in Maryland working with the DEA on a drug case dealing with suspected trafficking to the D.C.-area high schools. I was thrilled to pieces that we didn't have to see each other. And since he hadn't called, I knew he wasn't trying to deal with me, either.

"Ware," my supervisor yelled, "I need to see you in my office. Now."

What's his problem? I wondered as I rose from my chair.

Everyone in the office considered my boss, Thomas Hunter,

an intimidating man. And he knew it. He spent most of his time sitting behind his large mahogany desk barking out orders to other people, instead of being useful in the field. Personally, I rather admired his arrogance.

I stood in his doorway, leaning against the wall, and watched him flip through some files in a tall, wooden cabinet. Hunter's jet-black hair started high on his pale forehead and extended to a shoulder-length ponytail. Plaques and awards graced every wall. The credenza held photographs of him cavorting with beautiful women in exotic locations.

I folded my arms across my chest and cleared my throat. Hunter scoped me briskly through his wire-rimmed spectacles, then motioned for me to take a seat.

"Good morning, hard worker," he said in a calm voice that contradicted his earlier tone. As I took the chair beside his desk, he settled into his large leather one behind it.

"Agent Ware," he said, leaning back, "I know you've been frustrated about not being out in the field since the shooting. Your work to date has indeed been impressive, but I've been waiting for the right situation to come along. Since you put in for that temp job, I think we'll give it a try. I have to send a qualified agent to assist with the detail of a presidential candidate. And you did save one of our agents' life. You've proven this is in your blood."

I couldn't believe what I was hearing. Hunter was actually recommending me for the job. I could have jumped around the room like a cheerleader.

"I trust you've heard that Senator Steven Stokes is running for president."

"Yes, sir, I saw he had a press conference last week."

"Secret Service said he's received some death threats."

I nodded. Presidential candidates were always threatened by crazies with deeply held political views. Adding the race issue to the equation made Reverend Stokes a prime target.

He continued, "They said typically they don't assign agents before training, but when I sent your profile to the Secret Service they chose you because the protectee wanted an African-

American and they thought by having a woman on the detail she'd blend in to many of the locations Stokes visits as well. And I really think it's a good idea, too."

"You do?" I asked, knowing that no one in the office wanted to take the assignment. I wondered what the Secret Service really thought about an FBI agent coming into their ranks.

"I don't want you to become alarmed, but . . ." Hunter said, sending butterflies loose in my stomach, "Rudy Roberts has been released from the hospital and is out on bond."

I was so relieved that the bullet didn't kill Roberts. Though having a criminal out walking the streets certainly didn't promote peace of mind.

"Roberts is a known felon with a thick rap sheet. I wouldn't be surprised if he came looking for revenge."

"You think he may come after me?" I questioned.

"You, Evans, this office, others investigating him. I know the way the case shook you up. I'm just happy to have you away from the whole thing now that we have to deal with it again. If he does come for you, you won't be here. But I don't want you to worry about this now."

Easy for him to say—it wasn't his life in danger. I didn't plan to dwell on Roberts, but I couldn't disregard the threat, either.

"I know you'll be in Texas this weekend on personal time. When you come back I'm giving you the week off before you head down to Georgia for your Secret Service training." I was shaking my head as if that was okay, but he wasn't hearing it. "Get your affairs in order. Then Monday after next you can pick up your ticket at the airport when you head out."

"Thank you, sir," I said as I stood to shake his hand.

He gave a *no problem* nod. "Just make the FBI proud."

"Will do."

I walked out of Agent Hunter's office on a cloud. Guarding the Reverend Steven Stokes would mark an end to my days of boredom behind a desk for at least six months to a year, depending upon whether or not he won the Democratic nomination.

For some reason, at that moment I remembered my prayer

at Troy's house. Maybe God had a plan for me after all. Thinking of God let me not stress about Roberts, Troy, or anything. I'd talked to God and He'd replied. Though my communication wasn't that clear, I was suddenly ready and willing to get a stronger line with the Lord. I really was on a cloud.

On the flight to Texas, I tried to keep my focus on Eden's wedding. She was marrying Dion Jones. Back in college, Dion, Eden, Max, and I used to double date. Eden was my girl. She was always there for me. I sure hoped Dion had changed for Eden's sake or she was going to be in trouble.

Ironically, Eden and I took home pregnancy tests together our senior year. We held each other's hand as five minutes slowly passed. I looked at mine first.

"It's going to be okay, Chris," Eden said with wet eyes.

"I just hope I'm the only one who has to go through this."

"Come check with me, please. I'm scared," she pleaded.

Looking at her positive result broke my heart as much as when I saw mine. The rest of the day we were in mourning.

"What are we going to do?" she asked me.

"I can't keep this baby," I told her. "But you may want a family now."

"Are you kidding?" she questioned as she paced the floor. "I haven't even finished school. Dion doesn't have a job. We can't have kids now. I want to abort."

Three days later we were at the clinic, scheduling appointments to get rid of our mistakes. We vowed not to mention this to the guys, figuring they would try and talk us out of it.

The nauseating scent of the abortion clinic and the depressing sadness that filled the faces of the many women sitting in the waiting room made it even harder. Eden and I were there for each other, but when they called us into separate rooms I had to be strong. As I placed my feet in the cold stirrups, I knew there was no going back. But when what felt like a vacuum sucked life out of me, I immediately regretted my choice.

Eden nearly went crazy with guilt. She didn't come out of her room for two days. I could hear her moaning and crying, but there was nothing I could do for her. She shut me out. And we shut out the guys by not answering their calls.

The third day after our procedures, I went to pick up some Chinese food for us. Eden loved shrimp fried rice. When I returned to the apartment, I was surprised to see her sitting in Dion's lap.

"We can have other children," he said, consoling her.

Angrily I asked, "You told him. Why'd you break our . . ."

To my surprise, Max came from behind the door and cut me off. "Why didn't you tell me?"

I was so upset with Eden. It was one thing for her to share her business with her man, but she crossed the line when she let Max know what I'd done to our child.

"Eden, how could you?" I said as I placed the food down and headed to my room.

Max followed me down the hall. I tried shutting my door in his face, but that didn't work. He pushed it open.

"Eden didn't tell me, Dion did. And when you didn't return my calls the last few days I was worried. I knew there was a chance we could be pregnant." Max said, revealing new info. "And I was ready to accept my responsibility if that was the case. But you didn't give me a choice, did you? You ended our baby's life without even telling me."

It was clear by Dion's loving support of Eden that he'd forgiven her. Max, on the other hand, couldn't forgive me. I was feeling bad enough about my decision, but his reaction made me feel worse.

"I thought you cared about me and understood what I would want," he went on. "But how could a woman who loved me kill my child?"

"It wasn't that simple," I pleaded, wanting him to hear me out.

"Well, no need to explain now. You made your bed, now lie in it—without me. We're through."

Then he just walked out on me. I'd killed my baby and my relationship. My choice still haunts me. Eden and I didn't speak

for a few weeks after that, but then she came to me with si..
ity, telling me how awful she felt.

"Chris, I never meant for Dion to open up to Max. And I actually thought Max would have been there for you. I'm so sorry. I've made mistake after mistake, but I want to make things right. My baby is gone forever. I can't lose my best friend, too." Tears welled up in Eden's eyes.

I hugged her and we were cool from then on. Truthfully, I needed her support to help me move on without the guy I loved. Unfortunately for me, Max had remained good friends with Eden and Dion. They were so close, in fact, that Max was going to be Dion's best man.

I hadn't seen Max in three years. Eden and Dion had set us up on a reunion date, trying to get us back together. We'd had a little fling, but Max wasn't ready for commitment. My stomach churned at the thought of seeing him again.

When I arrived at the Atlanta airport at five in the afternoon, I rented a little blue economy car and drove straight to the rehearsal at the United Methodist Church. I'd been there with Eden several times during my college days. Though a few years had passed, the town hadn't changed. The wide-open space was a breath of fresh air. Though I loved the city life in D.C., I also appreciated the countryside. I found the church without even looking at a map.

When I pulled into the parking lot, Eden was closing the trunk of a car. I honked and she screamed. I couldn't park fast enough.

Eden opened my door when I stopped. "Christian, you're here! Thank God. I need you. This is so stressful."

I got out and we hugged. Though we talked extensively at least once every month, it had been a little over a year since I'd seen her. She'd come up to D.C. for two weeks the summer before last to stay with me as a getaway from Dion and her job. She had been an elementary-school teacher since college, and even though she loved kids, she was ready for a break by the time the school year ended.

When I asked her about her excitement, she didn't respond. I wondered if she was having second thoughts about marrying Dion.

"We can get in this car right now and drive far away from here. Just say the word," I said.

"I can't leave." Tears flowed down her face. I hugged her, then stepped back to take a good look at her. She and I were the same height, five-foot-six, and her skin was a few shades lighter than mine. But something about her seemed a little homelier than I remembered. Her clothes were so dowdy, not at all cool. Her thick auburn hair wasn't stylishly cut, and tiny wrinkles creased the corners of her eyes and the edges of her lips.

"Okay—you're staring, Chris," Eden said as she looked away. "I know I look tore up. You just don't know how much hell I've been going through."

I grabbed her hand and made her face me. "Tell me why you look so tired."

"This is just so much. I feel smothered. I want everything to be right and it seems like everything is going wrong."

She went on to tell me that one of her bridesmaids had cancelled yesterday, and more of her relatives came into town than they had booked hotel rooms for. The flowers were going to cost more than originally expected, and she was all out of funds.

"What am I gonna do?" she asked, squeezing her head with her hands.

"You're going to take a deep breath and relax. Eden, this is your time for happiness and nothing should steal your joy." I reached down inside the car and pulled out my checkbook from my Coach bag. "How much do you need?"

"I can't let you do this," Eden said, trying to close the book.

"Like I need your permission," I said, moving the checkbook away from her. "It's not every day your best friend gets married. And with my boring life, I've got a few dollars I'm not using."

Eden was reluctant to give me an amount, so I handed her a

check for one thousand dollars. Since I hadn't gotten a gift for the couple, this worked out for me, too.

"Consider this a wedding present. And remember, nothing is going to spoil your happiness during this special time."

She clutched her chest upon seeing the amount. "You are a blessing! God will take care of you."

I hoped she was right. "Let's get you inside. We've got a wedding to rehearse for," I said.

Arm in arm, we walked into the majestic church to join the wedding party. I glanced around the room, trying to appear casual as I instinctively looked for Max. Though a part of me hated him, there was another part that at least wanted to make sure he was well. Maybe he'd come with someone—I certainly was curious.

"So," I asked when my search turned up empty, "where's the best man? Shouldn't he be at this rehearsal thing?"

Eden took a deep breath and whispered, "He'll be in later tonight. Business held him up."

Dion added, "I can't believe my best friend couldn't adjust his schedule enough to be here tonight."

I'd always thought Dion was a bit of a mama's boy. I hoped marrying Eden would help him grow up. With his wavy rust-brown hair, soft coffee-colored eyes, and skin the shade of a slightly overripe banana peel, Dion was also a ladies' man.

"Don't worry, baby," Eden said, rubbing his arm. "He'll be here tomorrow for the big day. You know that."

As Dion leaned in to kiss Eden, the wedding coordinator ordered them to move to the front. The five other groomsmen and the bridesmaids were shown to our places.

During a break, the wedding coordinator introduced herself to me as Ms. Melba. She handed me my bridesmaid's dress. The cranberry velvet was beautiful, but the style looked like something one of Cinderella's stepsisters would wear. I could certainly never wear it to another event.

As the rehearsal continued, Ms. Melba wore herself out trying to get everyone to follow her instructions. She must have had us start over ten times. Not once did we stroll down the aisle to her specifications. After a couple of hours, she finally gave up and declared the group as ready as we were ever going to be.

The wedding party piled into cars and drove to a nearby steak house for the rehearsal dinner. A cute hostess escorted us to a back room, where at least fifty people were already seated— all friends and relatives of the bride and groom. The room was nothing fancy. The décor was typical steak house: dark lighting, booth seats, and brick walls.

Dion asked for a Scotch on the rocks as soon as he sat down, and he downed one drink after another all evening. I wondered why Eden didn't seem concerned or even annoyed by it. Then I remembered that her dad used to drink a lot, and Dion's father was a heavy drinker, too. I think that's what helped them to bond while we were in college. It was something that they had in common.

Eden's dad must have felt guilty about the very thing that bonded Dion to his daughter. After everyone arrived, he got up and had everyone raise their glasses for a toast. "Sweetheart, I'm sorry I wasn't the best daddy always. But I love you, girl, and I'm so happy for you."

Eden's father kissed her cheek and bragged to the rest of us about what a wonderful wife she was going to make. Their embrace was warm, but left me feeling a little melancholy. Her dad might not have been perfect, but at least he was there.

I sat by Eden's mom, not wanting to engage in fake small talk with people I didn't know. She ordered the lamb, I decided on the pork chops, and pretty much everyone else asked for steak.

As we waited for the food to arrive, I noticed one of the groomsmen passing around a bottle of liquor under the table. By the time the meal was served, most of the guests were buzzed.

After dinner, I tried to get to Eden, but she was surrounded by friends and family, all chatting happily about her big day. Bored, I headed for the rest room.

As I approached the bathroom door, I heard whispered

voices—a man and a woman. I rolled my eyes and stood there, not wanting to interrupt someone's secret tryst, but really needing to use the toilet. I lowered my eyes and pushed the door open an inch or two.

When I looked in I stifled a scream. Chyna had Dion pinned up against the corner wall. It took everything in me to hold back.

Chyna leaned in to Dion, her arms around his neck. "Are you sure you're ready to give up being a single man?" she crooned.

When Dion didn't respond, she kissed his cheek. "Even if you're set on getting hitched tomorrow, maybe we can have a little fun tonight. I'm in room 212. Maybe I can convince you to change your mind about getting married. At least to Eden, anyway."

I could have ripped every strand of sandy-brown hair off her conniving head in two seconds. And my foot had some definite plans for Dion.

Then again, maybe there was a better plan. That fickle jerk wouldn't have to make a decision about whether or not to get married. With one word to Eden, I could stop the wedding myself.

As I started to ease the door closed, I heard Dion's voice. "Quit tripping, Chyna. You've been pulling this kind of stuff for a long time now, and it's got to stop. I'm about to get married to a woman I love, who's supposedly your friend. She cares about you a lot, you know. You just can't keep doing this. No more pushing me into bathrooms."

"Fine," Chyna seethed. "Fine." She stormed toward the door, and I quickly ducked behind the tall greenery.

Dion came out behind her and walked past her without another word. She stared after him, probably hoping he'd turn around and give in to her. Disappointed, she stomped in my direction. I grabbed her tightly woven hair and yanked as hard as I could.

She dropped back a couple of feet, her eyes wide. "What are you doing? Are you crazy?"

"No," I answered, my fist still full of her hair. "You're the one who's crazy. Dion doesn't want you. He and Eden are happy together. If you want a man, get one that's not already taken."

"Let go of me, Chris," she cried, squirming.

I opened my clenched fingers and she grabbed her scalp. "I'm gonna be watching you, girl. If you even breathe in Dion's direction, I'll do a lot more than pull your hair."

Chyna sighed and smoothed her hair. "Okay, so you caught me. But let's be clear—Dion followed me into the john. I still have a thing for the guy. If he had left me alone, those feelings probably would have stayed suppressed."

"But I heard him telling you nothing's there," I said.

She rubbed her brow. "Yeah, I heard him loud and clear on that one, too. Now I know where I stand. Eden gets the prize . . . if you can call him that."

"What do you know that I don't about this guy?" I asked, trying to hear her out.

Chyna touched my shoulder. "Stuff you don't want to know."

We held eye contact. When she let her hand slide from my shoulder to my hand, I knew she was also concerned for Eden. I looked away.

"Eden totally knows him. She wants to marry him, and maybe they will be okay," she said, tightening our grasp.

I glared at her for a moment, then nodded as we let go. She headed back to the group and I went to use the rest room.

Once I left the ladies' room, I finally got Eden's attention. "Any after-dinner plans?"

Eden grinned at me. "I'm headed back to the hotel. If I can't get any sleep tonight, I might just come over for some late-night girl talk. Would that be okay?"

"Sure, I'd like that," I said.

We drove separate cars to the hotel, then hugged in the lobby and went to our rooms. When a knock on my door woke me up at three-thirty, I wasn't a bit surprised. I knew Eden needed me.

I dragged myself to the door, pulled open the chain, and unlocked the dead bolt. But when I opened the door, there stood Max, looking ever-so-fine in a maroon turtleneck sweater and loose-fitting black jeans. What was I gonna do now? Slam the door—or explore?

Chapter 3

Uphill

The love of my life was standing at my door. For a moment, it was as if no time had passed, and then he opened his mouth and I remembered Max had changed.

"Dang, girl," he roared, "you look tore up."

I wanted to slam the door in his face. "I wasn't expecting any company. What do you want, Max?"

"I was just playing," he said, barging into the room. "Give me a hug." He wrapped his arms around my waist before I could pull away.

"Get off of me," I snapped, smelling a little nip of something other than punch on his breath.

He moved farther into the room, pushing me with him. "Hey, don't be like that. You know you still love me."

I pulled out of his arms, fiddled with my hair, and put a robe on over my flannel pajamas. "Don't flatter yourself. What do you want?"

"Just to see how you've been."

"We can chitchat tomorrow."

"Tomorrow we have to take care of our friends," he said, flopping onto the bed. "I want tonight to be about us. Last time we were together we had a good time."

I rolled my eyes. "It's three in the morning. I no longer need you in that area. I'm well covered, thanks."

"I just want to talk," he said. Unable to keep a straight face,

he added, "Well, maybe I was hoping for more. Besides, whoever you're with can't make you feel like I can."

I crossed my arms in front of my chest. "You are so cocky."

He came over to me and ran his fingers along my arm.
"Admit that it turns you on."

"Do not even go there," I said, pulling away. "I'm not gonna
play games with you. We want different things."

He stood beside me, his gorgeous brown eyes boring into
mine. "No, I'm ready to settle down now. I'm still living in New
York. Now I'm a full-fledged investment banker. I've paid all my
dues, and now I'm starting to handle some accounts on my
own. I want a family."

"You always wanted that. You just couldn't forgive what I did,"
I said angrily as I sank my bottom on the bed. I looked at him.
"Yeah, we've kicked it over the years, but I don't really want any-
thing serious anymore."

Max got the nearby chair, pulled it in front of me, and sat
down. "I love you. I was wrong. I know we need to spend some
time dating seriously, but my goal is to make you my wife. I'm
hoping your interest in the same hasn't changed."

Okay, so I was totally caught off guard. But wasn't that just
like a man? Wanting things when he wanted them. There were
so many days when I wanted Max to want me in his life forever,
but I got tired of waiting.

"Too late," I said to him as I remembered the anguish he put
me through.

He took my hands in his and spoke softly. "Honey, I have
dated many women since we broke up."

"You mean when you broke up with me," I said, slightly salty,
wishing I could have been more mature.

"That's fair," he said. "No one fills me like you used to. Most
are only interested in my growing bank account. You only wanted
my heart."

The first time Max told me he loved me, we were sopho-
mores and we'd been dating for over eighteen months. I'd told
him how I felt several times before then, but he'd always held
back.

The day he finally told me, he'd just gotten back from his father's funeral and I was comforting him at his apartment. *"I realize life is short, Chris. But mine is meaningful because I found love."*

"I know you loved your dad," I said. *"You'll always have the memories."*

"Being home and dealing with all that, only thinking of you got me through. I know I love you." He kissed me and it was like the first time.

We had many days of happiness back then. I knew when he had a headache and he knew my menstrual cycle. We were that close. I'd not found anyone since then to love me so fully, but I wasn't sure if I wanted a relationship with him again.

"Hey, did you hear me?" His gaze searched mine. "I haven't forgotten about how or why I ended things. I'm sorry, Chris. I really do want another chance."

We'd only been together for ten minutes and he was pushing all the right buttons. After all this time I was still emotionally attached to him. But no, I reminded myself, Max Cross was a part of my past, and that's the way I wanted it to stay.

"I can't do this right now," I said, looking away.

He gently guided my face back to his. "Then let's not deal with the heavy stuff. I've heard a lot about you, Miss FBI Agent," he said, smiling. "One of only two hundred black women, and there's something like fifteen thousand FBI agents?"

"Yeah," I perked up, "and actually, it's more like sixty black female agents. But I'm about to take a temp assignment with the Secret Service."

"Wow. You'll be guarding the big man?"

"Not on this assignment," I said, shaking my head. "I'll only be guarding one of the presidential candidates. But who knows—he could win and sit in the big chair."

"For real?" Max shot me a skeptical glance. "Which one?"

"Steven Stokes," I bragged.

He slumped back in his chair. "He is a high-profile candidate. Some people I work with think he's got a good shot."

"Yeah," I said with a casual tone.

Caressing my hand, he said, "Then please be careful. The more he gains in the polls, the more danger he's in."

"He's already had some death threats," I said, taking my hand out of Max's. "But don't worry—I know how to protect myself."

I strode to the door and opened it. "Look, I really need to get some sleep. I think you should go now."

Max took his time shuffling his feet toward the door. He tried to kiss me good night, but I turned from his lips. Then I nudged him out into the hallway.

Ten hours later, Max was walking me down the aisle of the church. The sanctuary was beautiful, all decked out with fresh orchids and long, glowing candles. The nearly one thousand guests in the pews smiled at us. I felt beautiful in my floor-length, form-fitting, wine-colored gown. The serious look in Max's eyes when he appraised the way I looked told me he really did regret that I was no longer his.

"I meant everything I said earlier, you know," he mumbled.

I simply squeezed his arm, letting him know I felt something, too, but now wasn't the time. When we reached the altar, I gave Chyna a warning look. She kept herself in line, and the wedding went off without a hitch. Eden was a beautiful bride. The tears she and Dion shed at the altar made it clear they were a match. I only hoped it was one made in heaven.

Near the end of the ceremony, the bride and groom had their attendants surround them in prayer. I did hope that for their sakes, God would bless their union forever. Though I was happy for Eden, I was worried about Dion's drinking. I just wanted the best for her.

The bridal party was shuttled to the reception in limos. Eden's mom had elegant taste and it showed in the lovely, up-scale Beaux Twenty Club dining room she chose for the reception. There were about one hundred round tables, each with two white silk tablecloths layered one on top of the other. The ten chairs at every table were also covered in white silk, and the floral arrangements and candles created a scene out of the pages of *Southern Homes & Gardens.*

"I love you, Christian," Eden said to me as we stood near the band. "You've been a great maid of honor."

"Yeah, right." I chuckled. "I didn't even make it to the bridal shower."

"But you helped out so much over the phone, especially with your advice about how to handle all the pressure. Nothing's stealing my joy." However, she looked away as if her joy *was* stolen.

I grabbed the hand she wasn't using to hold her bouquet. "Tell me what's got you upset. You know you can handle the honeymoon, girl." I tried to lighten her mood.

She gave me a big hug and and I felt her shaking. What was my best friend not saying? What didn't I know? As she squeezed my shoulder, I sensed a bit of fear.

"What's the matter?"

She let go and shrugged. "Don't worry about me. I can handle it."

The wedding coordinator called, "Mr. and Mrs. Jones—to the floor, please. It's time to throw the bouquet and garter."

Eden turned to oblige the request. Before she could walk away, I got beside her and escorted her across the room. She wasn't going to hint that Dion was beating her and then act as if she'd never said a word.

"Wait—is he abusive?" I asked.

"No," she said unconvincingly, holding back tears. "Everything is fine."

As quickly as she opened up, she shut down. Eden went over to her new husband, and he attentively helped her sit in her chair. I watched Dion's every movement, trying to see what was really up with him. Realizing he was on his best behavior in front of the crowd, I only hoped Eden wasn't in danger, that whatever the situation was, it wasn't what I was imagining.

As the reception got into full swing, I filled a plate from the buffet of chicken wings, shrimp cocktail, and dinner rolls, grabbed a glass of red punch, and found an empty table in a back corner where I could watch the other guests.

Within a few minutes, Max approached my table. "So, you didn't try to catch the bouquet?"

"Not today," I teased, motioning for him to sit.

He nodded and took the chair beside me. "So can we at least go out after this and really get the party started?" His eyes smiled into mine.

"I don't think so," I said, popping a shrimp into my mouth.

"Come on, say yes," he said as he ran his hand up my back.

I took a sip of punch, keeping my focus on everything but him. He was making something in me respond to all the attention. From the corner of my eye, I noticed he was checking me out. I scooted my chair away from him.

He leaned back. "Okay, I get the hint." He reached in his wallet and gave me one of his business cards. "I know you're real busy with your job and all, but next time you come through New York, call me and at least let me take you to dinner."

"Why, Max?"

"I've been telling you why since this morning." He placed his hand close to mine on the table. "One day I'm gonna get you back, my lady." He moved his hand enough to touch my fingers.

That was my cue to leave. I couldn't let Max back in. By the time I got to my hotel room, I had resolved not to waste another minute of my time thinking about Max Cross. Instead, I focused on my new assignment.

I headed to my mom's house as soon as I got back in town from the wedding. I loved November in D.C. The leaves were a myriad of reds, browns, yellows, and oranges. There was a slight chill in the air and sometimes a few snowflakes would fall from the sky. It looked like one of the paintings in the living room of my mother's house.

It was nice to be going home, and I was all the more relieved to know I wasn't pregnant. I'd taken a test the night before leaving Texas—I was still wondering why my cycle hadn't come yet. I hoped I hadn't taken the test too soon.

When I entered my mother's newly renovated, two-bedroom home, I knew my mom wasn't home. Her car wasn't in the drive. There was, however, a black low rider parked outside. My fifteen-year-old sister was supposed to be at school, but when I heard moans coming from her bedroom door, I knew she wasn't where she was supposed to be. I immediately threw my purse and keys down on the leather chair in the nearby living room.

After pounding on the door, I roared, "Crystal—girl, get out here!"

I heard low voices and scrambling. After several minutes, Crystal swung open the door, her hot-pink miniskirt and tight black tank top twisted and wrinkled. As she straightened her clothes and smoothed out her straight brown hair, I glanced past her and noticed a guy sprawled out on her twin bed, fastening his pants.

"What do you want?" my sister asked anxiously.

"Crystal, what do you think you're doing? And who is that man lying on your bed?"

"That *man* you're referring to is my boyfriend. What's it to you?" She was standing with her arms folded across her chest, a look on her face I couldn't name.

When I remained slightly shocked, she slammed the door in my face. I couldn't believe this. Once again, I beat my fists on her bedroom door.

"Crystal, you open up this door right now!" And she did.

"I'm busy, Chris!" Crystal said.

I grabbed her arm and pulled her forcefully out of her bedroom. I was about to let her have it.

"Crystal, you better act like you know better! How dare you skip school! You're supposed to be doing your schoolwork, but instead, you're here in the house, laid up with some guy—who, by the way, looks too old for you! Didn't we teach you better? How old is that guy, anyway?"

"Man, none of your—"

"Crystal!"

"He's only twenty. So what? He loves me. And I love him, too. He treats me good. He gives me presents, he takes me out. I'm tired of guys my age. So immature, so broke, so not worth my time. They're nothing like Stone. Just look at him."

Stone was a straight thug. The muscles busting out of his shirt led me to believe that he'd spent time in jail. This brother was built. A black doo-rag concealed his long, black cornrows and a chain with a huge snake charm fell limply around his neck. His lips were black, as if he'd been smoking, and it seemed like his eyes were permanently half-closed. He was obviously high. Stone wore a white tee, Gibrauds, and Air Force Ones.

I did not want my sister dating this boy—no, wait—this *man!* And from the way he was looking at Crystal, I could tell his intentions weren't pure. It looked as if Stone wanted a lot more than a kiss, and from the sound of things I hope they hadn't done more than that. I had to help her understand that this was not the kind of guy she wanted.

"Crystal, listen up. First, you're gonna take off that miniskirt and put on some jeans. Secondly, you're gonna get this thug out of Mom's house. Next, you will get your books and I'll drive you to school. It's not even noon. You can make your afternoon classes."

He walked past us without saying excuse me and headed into the bathroom. She just stared at him and licked her lips. I wanted to bop her upside her head.

"No, *you* listen up! This is how it's really gonna happen: I'm taking my purse and my man, and I'm getting out of here! And there's nothing you can do to stop me!"

Before I could stop her, Crystal had done exactly what she said she'd do: grabbed her purse, grabbed her "man" when he exited the bathroom, and headed out of the door.

"Crystal, wait!" I yelled after the black low rider.

After Crystal and Stone sped off, I stood in the doorway and remembered many days when I was Crystal's age that I watched my mom drive off with man after man the same way. I was heartbroken then, wanting more for her, and I was heartbroken now, wanting more for my sister. Us Ware ladies seemed to have a pattern of chasing after the wrong men.

A few hours later, my mother's Honda pulled into the driveway, and I went to her car door. I was relieved to see her; it had been three long weeks.

"Mom!"

"Hey, baby," she said, giving me a hug.

"I've missed you," I said.

"I've missed you, too. How was the wedding?"

"Good—Eden's a wife now, but Mom, we need to talk about Crystal being out of order."

"What?" she asked as we went inside.

"Crystal has a twenty-year-old boyfriend."

Sitting on her couch, she said, "Oh, Stone, baby? He's so sweet. He even bought a big-screen TV for us just last week."

"A big-screen television?" I exclaimed, sitting beside her, frustrated that she seemed okay with it. "Mom, what are you thinking? That's not acceptable. How can he afford a big-screen TV?"

My fifty-one-year-old mom, who looked almost sixty from her rough life, naively said, "I don't know where he got it, baby, but it plays so well."

"Mom, do you really think he can afford to buy you a big-screen TV? Look, I'm just worried about Crystal. She's dating a guy that's five years older than her. I caught them in her room today while she was supposed to be at school. I just don't want my little sister to become a teen mom or have to deal with an icky STD for the rest of her life."

"I know, I know. I don't know why that girl's been actin' out so much lately. Seems like I only make it worse by punishing her."

"So what should we do about Crystal? I tried to talk some sense into her, but she left with Stone."

"She'll come back eventually. She always does this," she said.

"You have to look out for her. I'm not going to be here to interrupt their little private sessions."

"Where you going, baby?" she asked, as if she hadn't approved of me going off anywhere.

"I'm moving to Atlanta. I took a job with the Secret Service. I'm going to be protecting a candidate for president."

"Awww no, baby!" She shook her head as she crunched her face. "I was so happy you were tied down to a desk. Now you're going to be a bodyguard. I don't think this is a good idea."

I grabbed her hand and stroked it. "Mom, I've already committed to it. I'll be fine. Don't worry. Like you taught me in life, things may be tough, but I can make it uphill."

Chapter 4

Journey

Five days later I was in south Georgia with about fifty agents I'd never met. We were all at the Federal Law Enforcement Training Center, better known as FLETC and pronounced Flut Z. It serves as an interagency law-enforcement training organization for more than eighty federal agencies.

We were all from different agencies. There were U.S. Customs Agents, IRS Agents, and agents from ATF. Me and five other FBI agents were the only ones from the Department of Justice.

As soon as we arrived on site, we were escorted to an auditorium. No time for small talk or making friends.

A man who appeared to be in his fifties or sixties spoke into the mic. "Agent Jess Phillips, folks, and my job is to take you through two weeks of intense training. I plan to find the agents capable of helping us with this crucial assignment."

The black guy standing next to me joked, "Like life will end if we don't make it."

Everyone else was facing forward as if they were in grade school. I'm not saying they shouldn't be, but I did sign up for this because I wanted a breath of fresh air in my life, not a pillow-over-my-face experience. Thankful someone else here had some personality, I chuckled.

He looked over at me and stuck out his hand. "I'm Agent Frankie Johnson from the IRS."

"Hey, I'm Agent Christian Ware, FBI, and I paid my taxes." I continued the laugh.

"I see you got jokes. You think we're gonna like this?" he asked in a hushed voice.

"Hope so," I said as we listened on.

Agent Phillips held up some clothes. "Your personal appearance reflects not only upon the center and the organizations you represent, but also upon the law-enforcement profession and the United States Government. Therefore, each of you will wear the agency-issued fatigue uniforms, in accordance with Center regulations. You must comply."

He was talking to us as if we'd just signed up for the army or something. We were all agents, trained in some specialty. Granted, guarding the president was a big deal, but no bigger than getting drugs off the streets, or convicting terrorists. He really needed to loosen up.

Agent Phillips continued, "Also, we aren't the only training program on the campus, so you'll be provided with lockers for textbooks and materials. It is the student's responsibility to provide the lock."

Before we could participate in training-related physical activity, we were going to receive a medical screening to make certain we could endure the course of rigorous training. We were also told that the use of tobacco products, and eating or drinking in the classroom, was strictly prohibited.

Agent Phillips explained that in order for us to temp with the Secret Service we had to pass the Practice Exercise Performance Requirements. There were six parts: physical efficiency, firearms accuracy, driving training, marine swimming techniques, computer knowledge, and counterterrorism training. Most of it was a repeat of the training I received to join the FBI, but they didn't care. They wanted us trained their way, by their agents.

Finally, we were done with the introduction and everyone scattered in different directions. Some to eat, some to get their training materials, and some to rest. I was in the last category. Flying from D.C. to Atlanta and then into Savannah, only to have to wait for the FLETC shuttle to bring me to the base, didn't make for a relaxing day. And even though my pregnancy test turned out negative, my cycle still hadn't arrived. I felt extra tired and that had me worried.

"So I guess I'll see you tomorrow," Agent Johnson said to me as I turned to leave.

"Oh, I'm sorry. Yes, tomorrow. I'll look for you bright and early at physicals."

"Cool—let me go get my grub on," Agent Johnson joked.

I smiled; I was glad I'd found an ally.

After getting my key, I entered the barracks. There was nothing special about my dormitory room. It held just the basics: two beds, an alarm clock, towels, washcloths, bar soap, toilet paper, sheets, pillow with case, blanket, and bedspread. It was spare, and I missed my cozy, upscale brownstone back home already.

As soon as I claimed a bed, the doorknob turned and a woman I remembered seeing in the opening session entered. I always had a habit of scoping out other black and female agents. Seeing another minority gave me a boost.

She appeared to be upset, as she struggled to get her bags into the room. I went to the door to assist.

"Oh, thanks," she said. "Suzie Winters, from ATF."

Putting her bag at the foot of her bed, I said, "Christian Ware, FBI."

"Boy, am I glad to see another female agent," she said with attitude.

"Something wrong, Agent Winters?" I probed. I didn't want to be around a sourpuss.

"Yeah, you know," she said. I raised my eyebrows, letting her know I didn't, in fact, know. "They don't want us here. Why do they let women in, only to give us an extra-hard time? And we really have it hard, being a double minority."

Okay, Suzie was overly open. The chick didn't even know me and she was assuming I had racial and gender insecurities. What was that about?

I was apprehensive at first. But then as we talked I realized there was nothing wrong with letting someone new in. At first I was put off by her "honesty," but I realized she was feeling the pressure and was reaching out. I did know what that was like. It was tough being black and female in a male-dominated business. But no one made me sign up and no one made me stay in it.

As we both sat on our prospective beds, I said, "I just don't let anyone else's bigotry get to me."

"So you ignore it?" Suzie asked.

"Oh, no. It actually fuels me to work harder." I unzipped my suitcase. "Girl, we'll have to form an alliance and help each other through this," I said, digging my roommate as I put my stuff away.

She smiled. "I'd like that. Thanks for calming me down. I feel better now."

The next day I passed the physical. After checking my stats, I was directed to the field for the Physical Efficiency Battery portion of the exam. Agent Phillips was walking alongside me. "So, you're Agent Ware, huh?" he said, almost leering at me.

"Yes, sir," I said warily.

"I know you think this is automatic for you, but like I said to everyone yesterday, if you don't pass my training, you go home." He walked away before I had a chance to respond. Suzie was right.

The next few days were spent with firearm equipment. This was one area in which I excelled during FBI training. I hit the bull's-eye every time. Whether it was a revolver, pistol, rifle, shotgun, automatic weapon, air rifle, BB pellet, or cap gun, I was best in show.

"Show off then, girl." Agent Johnson swaggered over to me. "You're making the rest of us look like amateurs. But I can't give you props in public—you know the boys would sweat me."

"And you can't mess up your rep, right?" I joked.

"Ha, ha. For real, eat Thanksgiving dinner with us. A bunch

of us are going to head off-base to a joint the locals say has slamming soul food. I won't be hanging with the wife and rug-rats, but I've got to eat and so do you."

Since I needed to study for the Secret Service scenario test, I declined. I appreciated the offer, but I wasn't there to socialize. Agent Johnson extended his hand and wished me a Happy Thanksgiving. He seemed a little sad as he walked away. I assumed he wished he was spending this holiday with his loved ones. But from what I knew of his upbeat personality, I knew he'd bounce back just fine.

When I got back to my room, Suzie had the same idea I did. "I am so thrilled I have a roommate that encourages me along the way," she said to me as she grabbed my hand. "Thank you for helping me with my aim and giving me pointers on the obstacle course. You helped me pass both portions. I'm grateful."

I swatted my hand at her, feeling slightly embarrassed. "I'm thankful for you as well. I signed up for this assignment because I needed something new. Even though they're tough on us, you're out there telling me we're just as good as the next guy. That kept me going today." I took a deep breath. "I'm running after something and I can't explain it . . ."

"But maybe you feel this job might lead you to it?" Suzie said, finishing my thought.

"Sort of. Yeah," I said, squinting my eyes. "Is that ridiculous?"

"No, I understand completely. You're believing in what you hope for, but can't see. That's faith."

Maybe she was right. Maybe I was following God on some journey that would make me whole in the end. I wasn't a strong enough Christian to make out what was going on with me spiritually. I didn't know any scripture, and couldn't recall the last sermon I'd heard. That needed to change.

During the last week we focused on driving at asinine speeds, rescue attempts from deep waters, computer hacking, and counterterrorism issues. I didn't handle those areas as well as I did the weapons training, but I held my own and passed the two-week course.

Finally, when the fifty agents had dwindled down to forty strong, we went through briefings on what was expected, skills we'd need to implement the assignment, and how to transition our training to on-the-job work. After, they gave out protectee assignments, and I was glad that mine stayed the same. Agent Johnson was also assigned to Steven Stokes's detail team. Though we'd be on different rotations, it would be good to keep that connection.

I wished Suzie well when we packed up to head out to different camps. She was assigned to protect the Republican governor of Illinois. She and I had really connected during training. I'd miss her.

"You take care of yourself," she said to me.

I handed her my cell number and replied, "If you need me, call."

"You call when you don't need me," she said, handing me her digits as well. "Now it's time to go to work." We were both ready.

Agent Johnson, two other agents, and I were each assigned to one of four groups that would be rotating to protect Reverend Stokes. Each detail had a team leader and four other Secret Service members. To make each team have six people, us temps filled in the last slot.

When I walked into a downtown Atlanta Marriott conference room on Monday morning for my first meeting with my group, the four people looking back at me were a little intimidating. They stared me up and down and gave me the feeling that they weren't too pleased to have me on their team. I knew it was the fact that I wasn't really one of them, but I didn't care, though. Three were men, one of whom was African-American, and one was another female.

Our detail leader, Agent Ben Moss, whose name was on my piece of paper, yelled for me to take a seat and then said, "You're late, Ware. In the Secret Service we don't tolerate tardiness. We were just about to introduce ourselves."

I wanted to tell him that I'd just gotten in from Brunswick.

But why bother, I thought, as I watched him pace the floor and get in the other agents' faces like a drill sergeant. It was clear that leaders in law enforcement loved enforcing power. After going back and forth for a few seconds, Agent Moss approached the other African-American on the team and barked an order for him to get up and identify himself.

The man stood at rigid attention. "Agent Randy Pitts," he stated. "From the Baltimore office." Agent Pitts was completely bald, and looked to be only in his forties. "And I'm very happy to be assigned to this detail," he added.

When Moss nodded for him to sit back down, Randy Pitts gave me a reassuring smile. Okay, so at first glance I was wrong. Maybe I would fit in just fine.

Agent Jack Sawyer from the Biloxi, Mississippi, office was the next to introduce himself. He was thirtysomething, had a bald spot in the middle of the brown hair on his head. It wasn't hard to imagine him standing in front of a trailer, holding a beer.

"Unlike Agent Pitts here," Sawyer said in a grave voice, "I am not particularly thrilled with this assignment. Personally, I think protecting this candidate is a waste of the agency's money. However, I am here and I will do my job."

"Pitts, you may sit. And from this point forward we're keeping all personal thoughts out of this assignment," Agent Moss said commandingly.

The other female agent identified herself as Kelly Regunfuss from the Boston office. She also looked to be in her thirties. She had a smile that reminded me of a teddy bear. I could not see us hanging out, but I thought it'd be cool to work with her.

The last guy, Agent Ryan Hold, could have passed for a high-school student with his boyish, freckled face and naïve expression. He was from the Los Angeles office. "I'm thirty-two, so don't let the youthful face fool you." He nodded curtly at Moss. "I've been an agent for ten years."

When it was my turn to introduce myself, all the faces seemed quite uninterested. Their blank expressions made me inwardly hope I made the right decision about accepting this assignment.

Before I could speak, Agent Moss told them who I was. The cold way he presented me made me not that interested in myself. However, I knew I wasn't there to make friends. I had a job to do. So when he was done telling them about my career in law enforcement, I waved and sat down.

For the rest of the afternoon, Moss told us everything about Reverend Stokes's schedule and habits. We each received a detailed diagram of the man's house and were told to memorize every inch of it. Then Agent Moss paired us off. He and Agent Pitts were teamed together and would mostly handle surveillance and guard steps in front of the protectee. Agents Sawyer and Regunfuss would handle coverage from the sides and the rear. That meant that their job was to respond to fire if we were under attack. Agent Hold and I were given the assignment of being closest to the protectee at all times.

"Agent Ware, this means that you do not go with your instinctive FBI training. You flee from danger—you don't run to it and try and capture the bad guy. Get the protectee out of there," Agent Moss said to me before we went through a role-playing drill.

I thought I had the *protectee mentality first* down pat. All was going well. Agent Hold and I were posted beside the dummy protectee and we were carrying him around. But when blank bullets came from my left, I immediately drew my gun and started shooting back. Agent Moss blew his whistle and everyone surrounded me.

Agent Sawyer smirked and said, "That's why I detest having to work with agents from the treasury department. They don't understand how we do things."

"Quiet, Sawyer," Agent Moss said before he got in my face and attacked me. "Ware, do you realize our protectee would be dead right now because of your little act of heroics?"

"Sorry, sir."

Agent Moss continued angrily, "You try apologizing to a dead man's family. Agent Sawyer and Agent Regunfuss were to handle defense. If you can't train your mind to remember this one task, then you need to leave now. You've got to be willing to trust other agents to cover your back, your partner's, and the protectee's."

He didn't give me a chance to respond. He turned and walked out of the room, followed by Agents Pitts and Regunfuss.

"She needs to leave," Agent Sawyer said to my partner before he exited as well.

Agent Hold touched my shoulder. "Don't mind them. You'll do fine."

I nodded. "Thanks, Agent Hold."

"You can call me Ryan," he said kindly. "If we're gonna be working together, I say let's throw out the formality."

Shaking his hand, I said, "Then call me Chris. Or Ware. I like either one. I might make other mistakes, so feel free to check me on the side."

"Would have done it anyway, but glad to hear you won't take it personally." He leaned to my ear. "Agent Moss and the others were really impressed with your background. So really, we're all honored to work with you."

The following day we all meet at seven P.M. in front of the hotel to head out on assignment to cover the night-shift rotation. I hadn't spoken to any of them that day. I wasn't feeling the best, so I slept in for much-needed rest.

Agent Moss walked over to me and said, "So I see you've decided to stay with us."

"Ready to protect and serve, sir," I said without wavering.

"Glad to hear it," he said as he motioned for us all to leave.

Moss and three of the team members climbed into a black van. I got in a black Lincoln Town Car with Ryan. We drove in silence to Reverend Stokes's Mediterranean-style stucco mansion. The lawn was perfectly manicured—so rich, edged, and green. There were tall magnolia trees, precisely trimmed bushes, and bright flowers lining the sidewalk.

I hopped out of the car, eager to see what lay behind all those curtained windows. As we approached the house, I saw Agent Johnson from Brunswick training and his detail team getting into their vehicles. Moss rapped on the door, and a short, skinny maid answered. Without a word, she stepped aside to let us enter.

A sparkling marble floor brilliantly reflected the massive chandelier in the foyer. Every piece of furniture I could see was exquisite. I felt like I'd just entered a royal castle.

Reverend Stokes appeared, tall and handsome, from his office, dressed in an expensive gray suit. Agent Moss introduced the team members, and the black man amiably shook hands with each of us.

Moss introduced me last. Stokes welcomed me formally, as he had the others. But as the team headed down the hall to set up headquarters in a back room, Stokes grasped my elbow and pulled me aside.

"I was hoping for more than one African-American on my detail," he said quietly, "but I figured they'd all be males. Pitts is what I expected, but you look too cute to defend somebody," he implied with a bit of a flirtatious attitude.

I looked him directly in the eye with an air of confidence and said, "I assure you, sir, no harm will come to you while I'm on duty."

"That's what I want to hear," he said, wearing the perfect presidential smile and then patting my butt.

My hand flew up, and I almost slapped his face, but thankfully stopped myself. If I didn't want to get tossed from this assignment, I had better control myself, and quick. But I couldn't just let this guy think he could get familiar.

Before I could respond and think of a solution to my dilemma, I noticed Mrs. Stokes standing by the kitchen entrance with her arms folded. She was a beautiful older woman. Her freshly done updo, flawless jewelry, and stylish suit made me know she was certainly an upscale lady. And that all eyes, with the exception of maybe her husband's, were going to be on her at the event. She turned her nose up at me as if I were a lowly servant, looking upset with her husband as well.

"Well, I'm not interrupting anything, dear, am I?" she asked condescendingly.

"No, sweetheart," he said as he kissed her cheek. "Come and meet . . . ,"

She cut him off and said, "Not right now." Then she ushered her husband away with a not-so-nice expression on her face as I overheard her grilling him about what she'd just witnessed.

"How could you touch her inappropriately like that, Steven? I'm so tired of your disrespect for me," she said in a hurt and angry tone.

"Quit overreacting," he said as he tugged his arm away from her. "Besides, the girl can hear you."

She turned, huffed, and said to me, "Go about your work."

As quickly as I could, I joined my team at the back of the house. I didn't say a word to anyone about Reverend Stokes's comment or overly friendly gesture, but I couldn't stop thinking about it. My opinion of him and his perfect marriage had certainly taken a nosedive.

After reading logs from the previous detail's comments in Secret Service headquarters in the back room, we went through the house, checking exits, making sure all doors and windows were locked, and made sure the security cameras that could be viewed from the van were working properly. The only rooms without a camera were the bedrooms and bathrooms. The family had to have some degree of privacy.

Moss and Sawyer set themselves up in the command post, while Agents Pitts and Regunfuss were stationed in the van to monitor the cameras. Hold and I got to rewalk the house for a final check to make sure everything was in order. He took the upstairs and I had the downstairs.

As I walked past the dining area on my way to make sure the living room was secure, I heard Mrs. Stokes's voice. "Your makeover is fabulous, darling." I paused in the hallway, curious. "That Harvard look simply had to go. You've got to be trendier if you're going to run for lieutenant governor. I'm sure you'd look great in leather."

I peeked into the room. What I saw made me stop. I'd seen the Stokes's middle child on television, but seeing him in the flesh made me tremble. Sebastian was tall, over six feet, with an amazing physique. Even through his tailored suit, I could tell his arms and chest were chiseled.

His head was shaved bald and his cheekbones popped. I didn't know if the shaved look was new or if I overlooked it when I saw him on TV. Although I usually wasn't crazy about that style, he wore it well and I was digging it. His mustache was neatly trimmed and his Rolex watch glistened in the light as he hugged his mother. I'd never seen a man show love to his mama. I nodded my approval. The brotha was fine.

The call through my earpiece startled me, and I ducked back out into the hallway.

"You need to take post next to the front door," Moss commanded sharply. "The family is getting ready to exit the house."

"Yes, sir," I said into the microphone hidden under my suit jacket.

I turned around to head toward the foyer and ran smack into Sebastian Stokes. He reached out to stop me from falling, and I could smell his musky cologne. I quickly regained my composure and backed up a few feet.

Sebastian smiled at me, a deep, sexy dimple appearing in his left cheek. Then he looked into the full-length mirror hanging on the wall between a set of gold sconces. He didn't see that I noticed his look of concern.

"Are you okay, miss?" he asked as I noticed him checking me out.

"Yes, thank you," I replied, tucking my mic back under the edge of my jacket.

He couldn't stop looking at me—I wasn't taken aback by his stare. And though it appeared the Stokes men had similar taste in women, this member of the elite family wasn't rude.

He held out his hand and I gave him mine. "I'm staring. How rude. I'm Sebastian Stokes. I must say it intrigues me to see a beautiful Nubian queen in this role."

"Well, I'm really an FBI agent. I'm only helping the Secret Service out," I said, without realizing I'd revealed more than anyone should know.

"To be trained by both agencies sounds like you're well

equipped for this task. My dad's a lucky man. Seeing someone go against what society thinks is the norm and succeed is impressive. Your name?"

"Agent Ware," I glanced away from his gaze to keep from showing how flattered I was by his remarks. I had worked hard to get where I was, and most folks resented it or acted as if I couldn't handle it. To meet someone who appreciated it was refreshing.

He kissed my hand. "Pleased to meet you."

Taking my hand away to retain professionalism, I asked, "So did I hear you're running for lieutenant governor of Georgia?"

"Yeah," he said, not sounding terribly excited about it. "I'm a long shot, but being a member of the state house of representatives has made me want to give more. I have a plan to improve our education system, improve our health-care system, bring well-paying jobs to Georgia, preserve our natural resources, protect our seniors, and improve our transportation system."

"Impressive," I said, really feeling his passion.

"Will you vote for me?" he beamed in a coy way.

"I kept hearing you say *our*. I'm not a Georgian. I live in D.C."

"Well, you would if you lived here, right?"

With a small chuckle, I said, "For sure. You don't seem like a dirty politician."

"Agent Ware, I assure you I'm not. I'd go up against my dad if he was wrong."

We both shared a laugh. Then a slight chill entered the hallway. I looked up and saw Mrs. Stokes standing at the end. "Sebastian, darling." She'd appeared without warning, which was highly unusual since I considered myself well trained in detecting the slightest sound or movement. "What are you doing?" she asked her son pointedly.

"Just talking to the lady."

"Lady?" Mrs. Stokes looked at me, her head tilted slightly and her lips curled as if she had just discovered an ugly black spider on her highly polished hardwood floor. "Come along, dear," she said, turning her back to Sebastian as she proceeded down the hall. "Your father's ready to leave."

At that moment I saw my detail leader, Agent Moss, striding down the hall.

"Agent Ware, why aren't you at your station?"

I was surprised when Sebastian stepped in front of me and extended his hand for Agent Moss. "Oh sir, that's my fault. I'm . . ."

"Sebastian Stokes," Agent Moss said in a nicer tone. "Good to meet you."

"I was introducing myself to Agent Ware and bombarding her with questions. My apologies if I detained her too long," Sebastian said, totally coming to my rescue.

"Oh, no problem. We're here to make things safe for your father. If I can answer any questions, don't hesitate to come to me."

"Will do," Sebastian said to him before nodding a polite good-bye to me.

As I followed Agent Moss out the front door, he said, "Good job, Ware, getting the protectee's son to feel comfortable. It's always tough when one fears for a parent's life," Agent Moss had completely bought Sebastian's explanation. "Next time, defer him to me or at least let me know you're being held up."

I nodded as I opened the Town Car door and stepped aside, assuming my practiced rigid stance. Reverend and Mrs. Stokes and their middle son climbed into the car without a word of thanks or even a nod of acknowledgement. Agent Hold eased into the driver's side and I took the passenger seat. Because I'd never been a Secret Service agent before, I had to admit I was experiencing new sensations and nervousness. Looking inwardly, I realized I just might really like this. After all, taking care of other people came second nature to me.

When we arrived at our destination, the Georgia World Congress Center, I hopped out first and opened the back door. Reverend and Mrs. Stokes got out of the car the same way they got in it. They acted as if I was the chauffeur, saying nothing. Sebastian, however, winked at me and said, "Thank you."

I couldn't help but smile back at him as I watched Sebastian and his parents walk into the crowded ballroom with Agents Regunfuss and Sawyer trailing close behind.

"Ware and Hold, you guys take posts beside Cool Falcon when you get inside and the other agents will mix in with the crowd. Pitts and I are in the van covering the outside perimeter."

"Cool Falcon?" I asked Agent Hold.

"All the Detail leaders handling the assignment get together and come up with a name for the protectee. Guess they named our guy," Agent Hold explained before pausing as I stopped moving. "You've got this."

Moving into position, I realized anything could happen over the next six months to a year. Who knew how far Reverend Stokes's candidacy would go. He could drop out any day, win the Democratic primary, or make it to the White House. One thing was certain: with his fine son around, I was definitely going to be enjoying the journey.

Chapter 5

Endless

My unit was now in place at the grand ballroom of the Georgia World Congress Center for a pre-presidential candidate party that was being held in the Reverend's honor. It was an all-night affair and one of many stops we'd be making throughout his campaign run to pull in votes. The event started at ten, but we didn't arrive until eleven-thirty because Mrs. Stokes wanted to make an entrance.

And she did. Lights, cameras, and all eyes in the room were on her family. Reverend and Mrs. Stokes put on fake smiles, showing off their flawless teeth as they waved to the cameras with their many years of practice.

About five hundred of Atlanta's most influential people milled about, dancing, mingling, gossiping, and helping themselves to the sumptuous buffet. With the Stokeses were Attorney Larry Thomas, Mayor Macy Jackson, WSB-TV reporter Marsha Kauffman, Congressman John Sally, and many others. Escorting Reverend Stokes to the front of the room was strategic. Hold and I could see around the room from that angle, and Sawyer and Regunfuss could clearly see every exit and entranceway from the back of the room.

Of the four Detail teams that guarded Reverend Stokes, one was off duty this week. Agent Johnson's crew had taken the day shift. We were on deck for the night detail and the other team was this event's site crew. They had come earlier to set up cameras and make sure guests were checked.

"Agent Ware, you're standing too close," Agent Moss said into my earpiece. "Step down to the ballroom's main-entrance doorway."

"Moving, sir," I said as I discreetly moved over three feet.

Sebastian tried to sneak in without attracting attention to himself. However, with his new look, everyone in the room paid more attention to him than they did to his parents. Reverend Stokes beamed with pride at the response his son was getting from the crowd.

When the first slow song of the night began to play, Sebastian came my way.

For a second I thought he was going to ask me to dance. I'd never learned how to dance, had never even wanted to learn. Besides, even though I wasn't a real Secret Service agent, I knew I was there to work, not socialize.

When Sebastian walked up to me, I moved away. My boss could see me, and Sebastian had stepped in front of my view of his dad. Guests surrounded his father—this was not the time for me to get sloppy.

"You take this seriously, huh?" Sebastian teased.

I pulled up my sleeve to show him my microphone. Then I turned and covered my mouth with my finger. He moved the mic hand out of the way.

"Just wanted to say I like it better when you smile, beautiful," he said, making me flush.

How'd he see beauty? My body was draped in black from head to toe, thanks to my short leather trench and black linen pants. My eyes were covered with none other than Dolce and Gabbana shades. Regardless of how I looked to the rest of the world, Sebastian saw something that drew him to me.

"You're the one running for lieutenant governor, not me. I have to be serious if I plan to do my job and keep your dad safe. Now, go—my boss believed your excuse once," I said light-heartedly.

He winked and said, "That was a good save . . . admit it."

"Go," I insisted, sort of wanting him to stay.

Sebastian's eyes narrowed. "If I must."

He disappeared and I went back to making sure things were in order, which wasn't an easy task. Tons of folks were very attentive to Reverend Stokes. Caterers couldn't stop offering him food. Constant flashes were emitted from a camera that took shots of everyone that spoke to him. His campaign manager stepped in every few minutes to give various updates.

I rolled my eyes, glad that they were hidden behind the sunglasses we routinely wore. We even wore them indoors so we could survey our surroundings without being detected. It was one part of the job I'd have trouble getting used to. Who wore shades inside?

An hour later, Ryan came up to relieve me for my scheduled break. His timing was perfect. Not only was I overwhelmed by my current responsibilities, making sure everyone who came in contact with Cool Falcon didn't pose any danger, but I also needed to visit the rest room.

I headed down the hall, but a mass of females blocked my way. In the midst of the group stood Sebastian, enjoying the attention. His stock went down immediately in my eyes—I didn't intend to stand there watching him gloat. My nostrils flared at the sight; a part of me was jealous. Not wanting him to see me mixed in with the fawning women surrounding him, I pushed through the first bathroom door I came to. The minute I walked in, I could tell I was in the wrong place. A man stood with his back to me, facing a row of urinals.

Then a male voice from behind me said, "I think the ladies' room is that way."

I turned around to find Sebastian grinning at me. I couldn't dare ponder why he thought this was funny—I knew I would not let newfound emotions affect me so much in the future.

I held my head high and attempted to walk around him before he spoke. When he moved the same way I did, I stepped in the other direction. Still eye to eye, I heard his shoes move again.

I squared him. "Excuse you."

"You seem upset," he asked as if he cared.

"I'm in the wrong bathroom with only a few minutes to spare, and it took me forever to get through the hall with you and all your women in the way. Of course I'm agitated. I have to pee." I walked past him, not caring what he thought of me.

"You misunderstood what you saw," he said from behind.

"Yeah, right." I made sure he heard me.

As I scuttled down the hall to the correct rest room, I wondered what it was about this guy that had me all messed up. I'd been around gorgeous men all my life. Love at first sight hadn't hit me since college, and that didn't pan out. But something about Sebastian Stokes attracted me to him with a powerful magnetic force. In my briefing, the other agents and I were told that Secret Service agents don't socialize with the protectee or his family. However, since I technically wasn't Secret Service, the line didn't seem so black for me. In fact, it was sort of gray in my mind. But after I'd caught myself feeling something, maybe I didn't need to cross that faint line.

I pushed open the ladies' room door and stepped inside. Mrs. Stokes was right on the other side, washing her well-manicured hands. When she glanced up and saw it was me, she started shaking.

"Who's guarding my husband?" she asked, panic-stricken.

"Agent Hold, ma'am," I said as I lightly rubbed her back to calm her down.

"Oh." She fingered the rhinestones on her royal blue suit. "I'm sorry, but these threats on his life are getting to be more than I can take."

"You don't have to worry," I assured her as I removed my hand. "The Agency has all of the e-mails, notes, and letters being checked as we speak. We're taking nothing for granted. We'll make sure he's safe."

She gave me a small smile. "I know I can seem a bit rude to the help sometime, but I'm overly cautious. My husband and children can be too trusting. I'm sure in your line of work you know what I mean."

"Yes, ma'am, I do—I wear that same hat when it comes to my mom and sister. You owe me no explanations."

"Good," she said, becoming stiff again. "As long as you do your job we'll have no problems."

I took a deep breath. "Ma'am, I'm here with only one goal in mind and that's to keep your husband safe."

"Well, thank you, I guess," she said with a sneer before flouncing out of the bathroom.

I wanted to be angry, but in this job I had to learn to deal with people from all walks of life. I could tell that this was definitely going to be an interesting assignment, because from what I'd personally experienced with the Stokes family, they were a trip.

Troy had told me my positive impression of these people wasn't correct. Though I didn't want to admit it, he was right. We hadn't spoken since I'd taken the job, and that was a good thing because I wasn't up for hearing I told you so. One thing was for sure: the Stokeses were a colorful family.

I was glad when Tuesday night came to a halt. At two A.M. we all retired to our respective hotel rooms in the Marriott Marquis. I would sleep well, knowing that there were no threats or attacks my first night on the job. Sebastian and I never crossed paths again. Maybe it was best that way.

The second week in December, our unit accompanied the Stokes family on a tour of the Midwest. We had stops in Illinois, Michigan, and Indiana. None of their three children accompanied us—I was glad I didn't have to see Sebastian. Like my college love, Max, Sebastian seemed to be in my head early.

In Illinois there was a presidential town hall meeting. Reverend Stokes, Illinois governor Graham Hill, and U.S. congressman Jack Daly were the three candidates on deck. Even though there were no seats, the crowd was settled. Everyone seemed attentive as the candidates were giving their opening remarks. I was glad our job hadn't been dangerous. Though the Agency had tracked and arrested several people for the idle threats they'd sent in threatening the Reverend's life, and one of his detail teams did have to call in the bomb squad after receiving a suspicious package at his residence, my team only had to deal with routine stuff.

Feeling at ease, I remembered my training roommate Agent Winters was protecting the governor. Once in place near the podium, I searched the room, hoping to see her. I was unsuccessful.

"Agent Ware," Agent Sawyer called out, into my earpiece. "I'm posted at the back of the room and there is a guy on your side wearing a red tee-shirt with a rebel flag on it. He looks very antsy. You see him?"

Quickly scanning that perimeter, I found the man in question. He was rocking back and forth while the rest of the crowd standing around was still. Agent Sawyer made it plain he had issues with a black man becoming president, so I purposely limited interaction. I didn't know him to use such an anxious tone. It appeared that one redneck could spot another.

With my adrenaline rising, I responded, "Yes, I see him—he's at my nine o'clock."

"All right, everyone remain where you are. Let's see if he settles down," Agent Moss called out from the van.

Agent Hold said, "I'm watching Cool Falcon. He's about to address the audience."

Reverend Stokes began speaking. My eyes didn't move from the suspect. Within seconds, the mysterious guy untied a trench jacket from around his waist and put it on. He then placed his hands in his pockets and pulled out a small, circular steel object.

"We can't have a black man mixing in with real candidates. It's my duty to take you out," the crazed man said as he came charging from the back of the room, waving what I could now make out was a grenade.

I wanted to take him out or at least cap him in the leg. My FBI training to go toward the fire was my first instinct, but then I quickly shook my head. I wasn't there to disarm the threat—I was there to protect the candidate. Rushing onto the stage, I ushered Reverend Stokes to safety.

"Hold, move Cool Falcon now," I said to my partner as we placed our bodies in front of the suspect.

Screams were coming from every direction as people caught on to what was happening. They cleared the area and the guy stood there alone. All of a sudden he fell to his feet.

"Suspect down," Agent Moss said, "suspect down."

About eighteen agents from on-site details for all three candidates that I knew were there, but not visible, surrounded the intruder. The person who shot him still had the gun cocked in position to fire again if necessary. When the weapon was lowered I could make out the face. I was so proud to see it was Suzie Winters.

"I know her," I said aloud as Agent Hold and Reverend Stokes stood nearby. "We were roommates at FLETC."

"Wow—thank her for me," Reverend Stokes said. "And thanks to you two as well. You put your lives on the line for real. I'm so grateful."

Ryan and I both smiled, as if letting our protectee know that he owed us no thanks. Agents Sawyer and Regunfuss took him out of the room. I was about to follow.

Agent Moss said, "Ware, I'm proud of you. You learned something in our scenario training. You protected first and trusted that others could handle the rest. Our man is safe. Good job. Take a second and speak to your friend."

People were being cleared from the event and the man was being handcuffed. I rushed over to Suzie. She dropped her gun when she saw me. An agent she knew picked it up quickly for her. We hugged so hard.

"I was looking for you," I said when we pulled apart.

"I saw you searching for someone," she said, gripping her hand to calm it.

I placed my hands on hers. "You were amazing, remembering just the right spot to get him off balance so the pin wouldn't come out of the detonator."

"I was coached by the best." She smiled, alluding to my help. "Plus, you were awesome as well, getting your protectee out of the way. Once I saw that, I had to respond."

"Oh yeah, he told me to tell you thanks for saving his life." I looked down. "And thanks for doing your job. It's still hard for me to trust others to take out the danger. You gave me faith in the system."

Placing her arms on my shoulders, she said, "See? We're both just answering our call. We must keep running after God's own heart. He'll see us through."

"Winters, we need to debrief with you," a man appearing to be her detail leader demanded, cutting off our special moment.

"Got to go. We'll be better at staying in touch," she said, before heading off to answer questions.

I knew the reality was that we might not meet anymore. However, Suzie Winters was all right in my book. She was put into my life to remind me to keep seeking my purpose. Because if I did that, eventually God would show up.

After the Midwest trip, Reverend and Mrs. Stokes took a tour of the South. The Reverend was a great candidate. He worked the crowds, hugged all the babies, and tried to shake every hand in every room. Behind the scenes, however, I heard him snap at people, talk about folks behind their backs, and promise things he'd do if elected, then later recant those promises to his campaign team.

When we were in Natchez, Mississippi, I stood at the back of a small Baptist church and watched Reverend Stokes preach to a rapt congregation.

The crowd, mainly African-Americans, was cheering him on. His preaching style was so inviting. Whether it was that or his orating skills, Reverend Stokes was always persuasive, and he always played up God.

"God's Word says," he proclaimed, "that where there is no vision, the people perish."

"Yes sir, yes sir!" someone exclaimed.

"Gotta have a vision, now!" a woman wearing purple declared.

"After working in the U.S. Senate, I realize that this country needs a serious change," Stokes declared.

"Need a change!" a man shouted.

"And the best way I can make the greatest impact is to become President of the United States. I know you all have your own dreams. What is inside of you, yearning to become reality? Don't keep it bottled up. Release it. So what if it seems impossible—with God, all things are possible."

"Yes, they are, chile!" the woman wearing purple said, shouting loudly again.

"Start working on your dream today. If obstacles appear, find a way over, through, under, or around them. If you believe you can, with the Lord's help, you will."

"Amen!" someone from the crowd exclaimed.

"Hallelujah!" another shouted.

"Come on, Springrice Baptist, and show some love for your next President of the United States."

The crowd whooped and hollered so loudly that I had to cover my ears. Cool Falcon was a hit.

I knew that with God all things were possible, and that with Him beside me I could accomplish any and every thing. The message motivated me to make my dreams come true, and not to let anything stop me. However, I still felt unworthy of His love and blessings because of my past.

I glanced at Ryan Hold, who was standing at attention next to me while we watched the protectee eat after the service. I knew his dream. He'd told me he wanted to run the Secret Service one day.

"Ryan, do you remember what Reverend Stokes talked about today?"

"Yeah. He talked about actualizing your dreams, making them realities."

Intrigued with the fact that he knew what he wanted to do, I asked, "Why do you want to run the Secret Service? Why is that your dream?"

"Well, Christian, I definitely don't think it's a level playing field, but I love my line of work. I want to run it so I can be the one to iron out the kinks," he revealed.

"Hmm."

"What?"

"No, no! It's just that I think that's a really good reason to want to run it."

We stood in silence for a moment, watching the members of the church mingle with the Reverend and his wife.

"Chris, what is it that *you* want? What is your dream?" He caught me off guard.

"I don't exactly know," I said, remaining pensive. "I want something. Does that make sense? To desire to have something, though you don't know what it is?"

"I follow you."

"I'm chasing something." I paused. "I mean, I'm well into my late twenties, nearly thirty. I don't have anything stable. I don't have anything to hold on to."

"And you'll get it soon enough. Sooner than you think. Shoot, at your age I was married with a kid on the way. Enjoy being single. Enjoy this time of development and growth."

"So I take it all is good on your end—with your family, I mean?"

"Things are okay. I've been on the road a lot since I took this assignment to guard Reverend Stokes. We're just trying to hold it together. Make it work. I love her—we're in love with each other. That's how I know we'll be fine."

"Wow, that is so totally awesome," I declared, wishing I could relate.

"How about you? How are things with your family?" Ryan asked.

"Things are okay, I guess. My teen sister is going through one of many phases. Right now, she's boy-shopping." I laughed to myself, a half-worried laugh, remembering the day I walked in on her little escapade. "I'm worried about her. She seems to be running with the wrong crowd."

"Oh, trust me, I know how that goes. I have two younger sisters myself. I worry about them just as much. I only want the best for them. We used to fight all the time as kids, and we even argue a bit now. But I still love them dearly."

"My sister is close to my heart, too." He nodded as he listened to me. "And my mother . . ." my voice trailed off. "She's okay, I guess. I honestly haven't talked to her since I first took this job."

"Wow. Why's that?"

"I don't know. I'm sort of . . . angry."

"Well, what happened?"

"Nothing really happened per se."

"Then why are you upset?" he questioned.

I turned my head toward the corner of the room. What was I supposed to say? My personal life was bothering me more than I'd realized. Ryan was still waiting for my answer.

"Chris, talk to me."

"It's nothing," I said, bringing my eyes back to meet his. "I just wish I could do more for my family. You know, I look at Mrs. Stokes, all dolled up and iced down, and I get kind of upset. I mean, why does my mom have to be the black version of trailer trash? Why did it have to work out this way for us? That's all. I want to do so much more to help them."

"Continue on your path. Keep working hard. One day you'll be able to do all the things for your family that you want to do."

"I sure hope so," I said wishfully.

Reverend Stokes appeared at events attended by both blacks and whites. Since it wasn't as necessary for the protectee to have an African-American around him, so that person could blend in with the crowd, my partner Agent Hold and I were transferred to posts in the van. But I didn't mind. Switching with Agents Moss and Pitts gave us some time to relax. Ryan and I munched on BBQ Lay's, listened to the radio, and kept encouraging each other. I really enjoyed his sense of fun, mixed with our work. He'd run the Agency excellently one day. We were brisk, but not burnt out.

After the second week's campaign trail ended, it was time to head back home. On the way back to Georgia, I was in the front seat of the car the Stokeses were riding in. The candidate and his wife spoke in hushed tones. Suddenly, Mrs. Stokes's voice rose in both pitch and volume.

"I can't believe they're having marital problems. Our son has got to learn how to compromise."

Sebastian wasn't married, and they only had two sons, so they had to have been talking about Steven Jr.

"He's just being smart," Reverend Stokes snapped back. "He can't let his wife know everything he's doing."

"Of course you'd defend him," Mrs. Stokes said, obviously feeling more than she was stating.

When we got back to the house, I inspected the premises. As I entered the kitchen, I unexpectedly found Sebastian sitting at the table eating a peanut butter sandwich. Having not seen or thought of him in over ten days, I was apprehensive about facing him. I turned to come back later.

"Well, hello there," he said, getting up. "Can I talk to you for a sec?"

I didn't respond, but I didn't head out of his presence, either.

He came in front of me, "Look, the first night I met you, you may have gotten the wrong impression."

"Maybe, maybe not. Why do you care, anyway?"

He took my hand. "I've been asking myself that same question for days. All I can come up with is that there's something about you."

"Well, that's nice and all, but I've got to get back to work."

Without hesitation, he released my hand and stepped out of my way. Part of me didn't want him to move, but I had to fight whatever it was I was feeling.

I heard laughter booming out of the kitchen—I recognized the loud voice as belonging to Agent Sawyer. His hillbilly laugh could be distinguished anywhere. What was all the fuss about? We only had a short window of time before the next detail unit took position. He should be gathering his things, not running his mouth.

As I made my way toward the kitchen, I stopped when I

heard Agent Sawyer say, "I hated having to call attention to the man with the grenade. No colored boy needs to be running for president, anyway. Maybe he could have stopped some of this steam, heated up around here."

"Hahaha!" laughed Regunfuss.

"Oh no, he didn't!" I said to myself, not able to ignore it.

What a racist comment! And who says *colored* anymore? Where does he get off, thinking he can call that grown man a boy? And why does Regunfuss condone his comments with laughter? Oh, I was too through!

"And tell me something—how does a black man live in a house like this? He must be selling drugs on the side. What do the little hoodlums call it now? Trapping?" I heard Sawyer say from my place right outside the kitchen.

"Hahaha! Trapping!" Regunfuss echoed.

"And I tell you what: these are the funniest-talking black folk I ever seen! All the rest of 'em seem like they talk like they ain't had no kinda schoolin' at all. Just straight out the ghettos and on into our world."

"What it do, my brother?" Regunfuss said as she leaned in to imitate black culture and slap hands with Sawyer.

The roaring laughter continued, echoing and bursting through the halls. I'm surprised they didn't bring everyone into the kitchen, wondering what was so funny. Their laughter was incredibly loud! I couldn't let this bashing continue. I had to stand up for my protectee and for my people.

Storming into the room, I said, "Sawyer, no more!"

"Excuse me, missy?"

"You heard me! No more! No more name-calling, no more bashing, no more laughter, no more stereotypes, no more of your ignorant stupidity! No more!"

An "oooh" escaped from Regunfuss's mouth.

"And you, Regunfuss, how dare you egg him on like that! Don't you know that if you don't stand up for what's right, you're just a part of the problem?"

She lost connection with my eyes and she looked down at the floor.

"You guys are supposed to be protecting him, but you're sitting here tearing him down behind his back. Not all black people sell drugs. Not all black people eat fried chicken and watermelon. Not all black people play basketball. Do the names Tiger Woods, Robert L. Johnson, and Chris Gardner ring a bell? No? I think it's about time you opened your eyes and released your mind from these stereotypes and pigeonholes. Before you say some of this stuff to the wrong black person and get straightened out for real."

I hoped I wouldn't ever catch him saying such nasty things again. Not in my presence, not even in my absence. My arms crossed over my chest, I stared him hard in the eye, daring him to refute, retort, or rebut. At that moment, Sebastian entered the room, first looking slightly upset, and then softening his look. He stared at Sawyer, then at Regunfuss. Then he looked at me, his face expressionless. Finally, after what seemed an eternity, he nodded slightly. The other agents began filing out of the room, hoping he didn't hear too much. I knew he did. There was dejection in his face. I could feel it. No matter what we achieved, some people still held us back.

When a little over twelve hours had passed, Sebastian and I bumped into each other again at his folks' home. I had just come in from taking the mail to the van, and he was sitting at the dining room table, going over his campaign brochure. With both of Stokes's politicians having a second headquarters in the mansion, I knew I'd need to get used to seeing him on the job.

Trying to pass by the room he was in discreetly, I caught Sebastian's attention anyway.

"Agent Ware," he called out.

"I'm on duty. I can't talk," I said, again trying not to go into the gray area.

"You've certainly been working hard," he said, stepping out in front of me. "Every time I see you, you're running. When do you get a break? I'd like to show you Georgia."

The lovebug in me did a somersault, as I could no longer keep myself from doing what I deemed wrong. "Aren't you busy with your campaign for lieutenant governor?"

"To be honest, that's just a front. My father and I are just try-ing to stir up interest for his presidential campaign. He doesn't think I'm really into politics." He leaned toward me, so close I could smell his musky aftershave. "So, what do you say?"

He really seemed to want to take me out. Apparently the at-traction I felt for him was mutual. Why not go?

"You must have meant Atlanta, right? The entire state of Georgia would take weeks to explore."

His voice lowered to a whisper. "We can cover everything in a couple of days if we put in long hours."

"Since I just finished over two weeks of straight duty, I do have a couple of days off coming to me."

"Starting when?"

"Tonight," I said, thrilled that he seemed so eager. "But I had planned on heading back to D.C. to check on my place."

"Don't go."

Mrs. Stokes sashayed into the kitchen. "Agent Ware, is this room secure?"

"Yes, ma'am."

"Well, then, you'd best get to the rest of the house, don't you think?"

Sebastian winked at me behind his mother's back as she pulled him aside and began chattering at him. I returned to the task of securing their mansion.

I entered the game room and began checking it out. The enormous room was empty and quiet. I noticed a large King James Bible lying open on a stand in the corner, and it drew me like a magnet.

"Lord, what are You doing with me? I so want to please You, but I don't know where You'd have me go," I said, as if seeing the open book was a sign.

I hadn't talked to God since the night at Troy's place, but somehow it just seemed appropriate in the presence of the open Bible. There was a longing inside of me to do what He would want, but my flesh was speaking to me as well.

"Who are you talking to?" a sexy male voice asked, not mak-ing it easy for me to do what was godly.

I twirled around and saw the man I'd been excited about. "No one," I choked out.

"Were you praying?"

I glanced at the Bible. "Yeah, I guess so."

His beaming smile lit up his face. "I knew you were a believer. This is great. So, you're not going back to D.C., right? Let's get together tonight. And don't even think about it—it's not too soon. I'm not an ax murderer. I'm normal, I promise."

Sharing a giggle, I regained a straight face and said, "I don't know. It might not be a good idea for me to be seen parading around town with the son of the man I'm supposed to be protecting."

"Who cares about that? I'll pick you up in front of your hotel at eight. I overheard my father mention where you all are staying."

"I've already told the Agency I was checking out. I've got my plane ticket and everything."

"Then go ahead and check out. I'll have my assistant call the airlines and have your ticket cancelled."

"Where am I supposed to stay?" I asked.

"Trust me," he said with a grin. "I'll see you at eight."

With a peck on my cheek, he disappeared. I stood there like a statue, the soft touch of his lips lingering against my face.

I had a date with Sebastian Stokes! The only problem was, he thought I was a strong Christian. And that seemed to be important to him. What would he do when he found out I wasn't? I guess with a mystery date planned, I'd find out.

Sebastian Stokes had class. He showed up on time and opened the door for me. With a dismissive smile at the bellhop, he put my bags into the trunk of his spotless, pearl-colored Jaguar.

What in the world was I doing? I didn't even really know this guy. Plus, this goes against the rules. But that didn't stop me from sliding in on the passenger side.

"You're so beautiful," he said as he hopped into the driver's seat.

"Thank you," I said.

"Even your name is beautiful. Christian. I love it."

"I've never liked it much," I admitted.

"What do you like to be called?"

"Most people in the Service call me Ware," I said with a laugh. "But my friends call me Chris."

"Do you have a middle name you like?"

"I don't have a middle name at all," I said. "My mother said she couldn't come up with anything that could stand beside Christian." I shook my head. "What about you?"

"My middle name starts with a K. Can you guess it?"

"Maybe. Give me a hint."

"It's a political name."

"How old are you?" I asked, figuring that the year he was born would affect his parents' choice.

"I'll be twenty-eight on Valentine's Day."

"Really? My birthday is December 25."

"So we were both born on holidays."

"Your middle name is Kennedy, isn't it?" I guessed.

He smiled and modestly shook his head. Boy, was he a cutie.

Our dinner reservation was at a cozy restaurant on Lake Lanier Island. Sebastian got us a table on the balcony overlooking the water. The sound of small waves hitting the shore, the smooth Ella Fitzgerald track, "Taking a Chance on Love," playing in the background, and the dim lights made for a very romantic meal.

When the waiters served us, Sebastian asked me to bow my head for grace.

"Dear Lord, thank You for the food we are about to receive. May it nourish our bodies. Lord, this is a very difficult time for my family and me because of the threats we've had to endure. Please watch over us and keep us safe from harm. Thank You also for my newfound friendship with Christian. In Your name we pray, Amen."

"You're amazing on your job, do you know that?" he asked as he cut into his medium-rare sirloin.

Sipping my tea with one hand and bashfully holding my chest with the other, I asked, "What makes you say that?"

"You saved my dad's life in Illinois."

"No, I just got him out of the way."

"Be modest, but my family watched it over and over on tape because we want to be aware of situations like that for ourselves."

"Oh, so you all are doing self-training," I teased.

"Yeah, because when you hear other agents joke that maybe he should have gotten blown up, it makes you want to take matters into your own hands," he said, before looking away.

Again, I felt where he was coming from. Some things weren't meant to be frivolous, so I touched his hand gently to assure him it was okay. He looked back at me and our eyes held a compelling gaze. We finished that course with lighter conversation.

During dessert, Sebastian reached across the table and placed his hand on mine. "Christian, are you in a relationship right now?"

"No," I responded confidently.

"Can a man be interested?" He smiled, showing me that sexy dimple of his again.

"Yes," I said.

That night, Sebastian checked us into a bed-and-breakfast in Macon—separate rooms, of course.

He went to his room and I went into mine. I took a hot shower and dressed for bed. All I could think about was the heat of his breath on my skin. I crawled into the full-sized bed, but knew I wasn't going to sleep right away.

I gazed out the window and could see the outline of the mountains of Georgia. All I could think about was what he was thinking.

Eventually, sleep overtook me. I slept well.

The next day we visited Savannah and rode the ferryboat. We went to Albany, and I remember being impressed by the newly built additions to the college, Albany State University. Forty miles south in Valdosta, we saw the tree lighting ceremony at Wild Adventure amusement park. We had tea in Plains, where former president Jimmy Carter was raised.

On the third day, Sebastian took me to the Château Élan, a four-star hotel on the north side of Atlanta that stood out on a patch of land all by itself. My room contained a king-sized bed with an old-fashioned quilt. There was a fireplace in the large living room area and a Jacuzzi that could fit four people.

"This suite is amazing," I said as Sebastian brought in my bag.

"So are you," he said with a grin.

Sebastian Kennedy Stokes had me completely confused. I didn't want our time together to end, but I didn't want to fall for him too quickly. He could easily break my heart, and I didn't want to give him the chance to do so.

We stood by the window, admiring the view of Stone Mountain. He grabbed my hands and held them tightly. "What are your goals? Are you planning to stay a federal agent forever, or would you like to have a family someday? I've heard it's hard to do both."

My heart froze. I'd forgotten all about the possibility that I might be pregnant with Troy's baby. I quickly withdrew my hand from his and excused myself. Tears of fear ran down my face as I rushed into the bathroom.

"Chris, what's wrong?" he asked, following me.

I stood there, staring at him, for several moments. Finally I said, "I've got to go," and quickly left the room.

He followed me as I practically sprinted down the hall. "Please tell me what's going on," he pleaded.

I turned to him, nearly hyperventilating. "I just need some time to think," I said. I walked past the reception desk and out through the revolving glass doors. Breathing deeply of the cool, fresh air, I found a woodsy area with a stream. After spending about thirty minutes with nature, I finally felt a little more relaxed. I still didn't know what to do about my situation, but at least I could return to my room.

When I got there, the room was empty. Sebastian had apparently returned to his own room. I sank onto the big couch. My body was scaring me. I was going into the second month of missing my cycle. I remembered the last time I missed a period . . . when I got pregnant in college.

My thoughts were interrupted by a loud rapping at the door.

"Christian," Sebastian said through the door, "I want to talk to you."

I let several moments pass without responding. I figured he would go away eventually. He didn't.

"Please?" he begged.

"No, Sebastian. I want to be alone."

"Let's just talk about the problem. I'm concerned."

"You don't need to worry about me. You've got a state race to get ready for," I said, and placed my head back against the door.

"Chris, trust me. If I didn't want to be here, if I didn't want to know, I wouldn't be here. But because I care about you and your well-being, I'm asking you to tell me what's got you down."

I didn't respond. Maybe he was right. Part of me wanted to just release all of these issues into the open—mainly my potential pregnancy.

"Okay," I said, unlatching the chain. "The door's unlocked."

He rushed into the room and pulled me close. "What's tormenting you, Christian?"

I didn't answer.

"Whatever it is, just tell me. We're supposed to be friends. I'll listen—I promise."

"Sebastian, I don't want to burden you. Why don't you just go home? I'll be okay."

He pulled me closer.

"Sebastian, please!"

"I refuse to leave when you're obviously upset, so you may as well tell me what's going on."

"All right," I said, letting my guard down. "You want to know what's up with me? Then I'll tell you." I paused. "I might be pregnant. I mean, I thought I wasn't, but now I'm just unsure."

He didn't bat an eye. "So let's talk about it." He took a seat in the chair next to me. "Are you in a committed relationship?" he asked.

"Well . . . I can't even believe I'm telling you this."

"Christian, nothing you say can keep me from wanting to know you. I want us to be honest with each other."

"No. I'm not in a committed relationship," I said. "I mean, I was in a relationship, but not anymore. I've always lived that aspect of my life spontaneously." I nearly choked on my tears. "Sebastian, I don't know what I'll do if I'm pregnant."

"God can help you find a way to deal with any situation."

His confidence in the power of God almost made me ill. How could he be so comfortable with his relationship with God? I silently wondered if it were possible for God to love someone like me, someone who had purposely committed the sins I had committed: ending an unborn life, sleeping with married men, enjoying casual sexual relationships. I had to tell this guy I was not the strong, put-together Christian woman he thought I was.

"I'm supposed to be a role model for my younger sister, and if she follows my path I don't know where she'll end up," I said boldly and honestly. "Sebastian, I don't know what kind of girl you're looking for, but . . . I did something a long time ago that still haunts me. How can God forgive me when I can't even forgive myself? I don't think you need to hang out with me."

"What do you mean?" he asked.

"My walk with God isn't really strong, because I have done something that is so horrid I don't believe that I'm worthy of His forgiveness. But I guess that's pretty obvious now, isn't it?"

He took my hand. "My life hasn't always been perfect, either. But God's grace covers all."

"How can you know, beyond a shadow of a doubt, that He is so forgiving?"

He looked me in the eye, his face filled with confidence. "By faith I believe that Jesus Christ was sent to this earth by God to die for my sins and the sins of the world. He's there for me all the time."

"Most of the people I know who say they're Christians are the biggest sinners I know. Every time I turn around, I see some fallen mega-pastor in the news."

"It's true—there are some leaders who profess to be Christians and don't act like it. But I leave that up to God, because they'll have to answer to Him on Judgment Day. Only God can judge what kind of person someone is on the inside."

I nodded once to let him know I understood. Sebastian just stared at me. I didn't feel uncomfortable. I felt like a lady.

"I'm very attracted to you, Christian Ware. You're a beautiful woman inside and out. You're a genuinely good person. My intuition tells me so. However, right now I'm more concerned for your soul," he said.

I looked away, unable to look into his piercing eyes. "This isn't the first time I've been pregnant." I confessed to having an abortion four years ago.

"Christian, Jesus Christ died on the cross for all the sins of the world. Even yours. There's not a single person who hasn't sinned in some way. But God promises that if we repent and ask Him for forgiveness, He will grant it. He'll even help you learn to forgive yourself."

Sebastian stayed and talked the whole night. He read a small passage from the Book of John and I sat there, soaking up God's word. It was as if someone greater was talking through Sebastian.

Sometime in the early-morning hours, I fell asleep in his arms. When I awoke, Sebastian was snoring softly, still holding me. I didn't want to disturb him, so I lay very still, enjoying the warmth of his chest through his silk shirt.

It had been five weeks since that night at Troy's place. Maybe I needed to go to the doctor to get a blood test since my cycle still hadn't come.

I was awakened by the patter of little feet and children's voices shouting in the hallway outside of my room. I wondered what time it was. I glanced at my watch to see that it was nine A.M.

When I couldn't lie still any longer and adjusted my position, I woke Sebastian. He opened his eyes, smiled, and said, "Good morning."

"You're still here," I said, smiling. "You didn't run away in the middle of the night."

He smiled. "I've got a peace that surpasses understanding. I know God can take care of anything."

"I wish I had your faith."

He held me closer. "Christian, just because you had an abortion before doesn't mean you have to make the same mistake again. If you are pregnant, you can give your child a home, either with an adoptive family or keep it yourself."

I knew I couldn't go through another abortion.

"Even if the child's earthly father won't be there for you, the heavenly Father will be."

I hugged Sebastian tightly. At that moment, he was closer to me than a confidant.

"Why don't we get dressed and go down for some breakfast," he suggested. "I'm famished." He stood. "I'll be back as soon as I get changed and cleaned up."

After he left the room, I got my cell phone out of my purse and checked my messages. Eden had called to tell me things were going great. My mom had called to see how my new job was going. My fifteen-year-old sister wanted money for a new leather jacket. Max said he enjoyed seeing me at the wedding. Surprisingly, Troy had called to tell me that he missed me. He sure did wait a while—he hasn't called in over a month.

I hadn't called, either. As a matter of fact, I hadn't spoken to Troy since that night I left him. At first, I wouldn't have minded never talking to him again; however, I knew he would play a big role in the decision I was going to have to make, if I was in fact pregnant.

I called his house.

"Hey," he said. "How's the big celebrity?"

"What are you talking about?"

"I saw you on TV saving Stokes's life."

"Oh."

"So you really applied for that temp job, and my girl got it, too. Gon' with your bad self," he teased, before changing his voice to a more seductive tone. "When are you coming back? I miss you."

I started pacing. "I don't know. Troy, I'm late."

"Late for what?"

"You know. Late. I think I might be pregnant."

"Oh," he said nonchalantly. "So, do you need some money to take care of it?"

"Troy, I'm not going to have an abortion," I said, making my way to the bathroom.

"You have to, Chris, because I'm not going to have any kids right now."

"Don't worry," I assured him. "If I am pregnant, I'll either keep and raise the baby myself or place it up for adoption."

"Well, don't count on me for any of that daddy stuff."

"I didn't plan to." I began to run my shower water.

"So you think you can raise a kid alone? You don't know what you're letting yourself in for."

His comment stung. As much as I hated to admit it, I knew he was right. I couldn't raise a kid all by myself, without a daddy figure. I couldn't support my baby. Heck, I could barely even support myself, but he didn't need to know that.

"Guess I'll find out, won't I?" I replied with an attitude.

"Hey, you said you weren't sure, right? Maybe you're stressing for nothing."

"I'm hoping I can confirm one way or the other sometime today."

"Well, call me back when you know."

I hung up without saying good-bye. Maybe I'd get back to him when I knew, maybe I wouldn't. In a way, I was hoping Troy would be more supportive. I didn't understand it: Troy could lie down with me in a bedroom, but couldn't stand up, be a man, and take care of his responsibility. One thing was for sure: I wasn't about to abort my baby.

Later that morning, Sebastian and I found ourselves at a Planned Parenthood office in Gwinnett County, Georgia. It meant a lot, having his support. We clutched hands in the waiting area. He kept smiling as if everything was going to be all right.

"You didn't have to come," I told him as we sat in the lobby awaiting the results of my pregnancy test.

"True friends don't abandon each other," he said. He took my sweaty hand. "Can I pray for you?"

I shrugged. "Yeah, sure."

He closed his eyes. "Heavenly Father, I come to You right now, asking forgiveness for past sins. Comfort Christian and let her know You love her."

I was comforted by Sebastian's prayer and presence. I got up and thumbed through magazines I had no interest in. The wait for my results seemed endless.

Chapter 6

Explosion

I walked heavily back into the waiting room with a look of despair written on my face. Sebastian got up from the chair and placed his arms snugly around me.

"It'll be okay," he told me. "You'll get through this."

I punched him in the chest lightly and smiled. "I'm just kidding. I'm not pregnant!"

He swung me around. "I'm gonna get you for that," he joked.

I clasped my hands together and looked up toward the glaring light in the ceiling. "Thank You, Lord!"

I had to set up an appointment with the gynecologist to find out what was going on with my body. The doctor thought I'd probably had light spotting that month or the stress made me miss it completely. Either way, I needed to have a full exam to assess the problem. His advice went in one ear and out the other. I wasn't pregnant. Seeing another doctor could wait.

Sebastian smiled. "So, are you really acknowledging that God has forgiven you?"

"I don't know," I replied. "Maybe."

During the forty-minute drive back to the hotel, we listened to Sebastian's gospel CDs. The lyrics spoke to my heart. Something was happening to me. It was like I was hearing a faint call, and it was growing louder and louder. I couldn't ignore it much longer.

When we arrived in front of the hotel, Sebastian placed a gentle hand on my cheek. "I'm glad things worked out—I hope you'll be smarter next time. Don't put yourself in a situation that could lead you back to that."

Being such a sensitive subject, I wanted to tell him not to tell me what to do. But I just smiled, nodded, and thanked him for his great friendship. I didn't want that moment to end, but I had to get back to work and he had campaigning to do.

Sebastian opened the car door and I stood between his arms. "I really enjoy spending time with you," he said.

"Me, too," I replied nervously. At that moment, I tried to be mature and confident, but my stomach was doing somersaults! He was standing so close to me, I couldn't help but be nervous.

He leaned in to kiss me. It was gentle and romantic.

"I'll check on you soon," he said as he handed me my bag.

I received a message from the front desk of the hotel where I was staying as soon as I entered. The clerk stopped me and mentioned that there was an emergency message for me—my mother wanted me to call her and let her know if I was going to come home for my birthday, Christmas Day. I'd be sure to call her that night. Right now, I had to head upstairs and pack. Sebastian and I were heading back in about an hour.

The drive home was incredibly relaxing. Sebastian and I talked the entire way about everything imaginable: goals, dreams, fears, life's purpose. I had enjoyed my weekend off with Sebastian Stokes, but now it was Monday and time to get back to work.

The next week was passing quickly. My assignment was to protect Sebastian's parents, but I didn't see him all week. I asked my Detail leader, Agent Moss, if I could get time off, but he denied my request. The Stokes family was planning a big Christmas Eve dinner, and all agents were required to be on duty. With it being only a week until my birthday, I made a mental note to call my mom soon.

The following day, when I entered the Stokeses' living room to perform security check, I saw a beautiful, seven-foot Christmas tree decorated with strands of tiny purple and gold plastic grapes, gold tinsel, purple and gold bulbs, and a heavenly black angel perched on top.

The room had a large fireplace, red plush leather furniture, Tiffany lamps, an original Picasso displayed over the mantel, and African masks and African artwork displayed on the shelves and walls. This wasn't the first time I had seen this room, but it was the first time I'd actually enjoyed and appreciated it. How did I miss this the first time around? I needed to take more time to smell the roses. The last thing I wanted was to become too caught up in my job.

On Christmas Eve, the smell of fresh cinnamon permeated the house. Christmas music played softly, and assistants scurried about, adding finishing touches before the guests arrived.

I had never seen so many garlands in my life. Every pole in the house was wrapped with thick boughs of holly and tiny, twinkling lights. A beautiful cranberry-colored poinsettia sat on every step of every staircase throughout the house. I couldn't help but wonder how much they'd spent to make the house so festive.

That Saturday night, I noticed an eighteen-foot Christmas tree in the foyer, covered in white lights and gold and silver balls. After leaving the tree, I noticed Mrs. Stokes sashaying down the grand winding staircase, wearing a silk, form-fitting, designer sterling-silver gown. Her sandy hair bounced up and down as she proceeded down the stairs, spiral curls caressing her shoulders with every move. She stopped halfway down and looked around. Finding no one but me in the room, she asked, "How do I look?"

Before I could tell her that she looked fabulous, she said, "Why am I asking you? You don't know anything about fashion." And she trotted off toward the dining room.

I looked down at the tuxedo-style pants suit I had to wear. Among all the holiday finery, my black slacks and jazzy jacket, white shirt, and pointy-toed black shoes seemed to fit in nicely. My new uniform was plain but I could work it out.

Swallowing my enjoyment of my new gig, I made sure I kept

with Secret Service protocol and erased any trace of a smile from my face. Then I briskly headed to Agent Moss, who was standing in the hallway. "What are my instructions for the evening, sir?"

"You'll be posted on the inside door of the dining room," he responded.

Not wanting to subject myself to more of Mrs. Stokes's snooty attitude, I said, "Sir, are there any posts available outside?"

He curled his lip. "Pitts is already stationed in the van. You'll blend in here more than the others, so I'm keeping them on the perimeter."

I had no authority to ask him to change my position. Even if I had, it probably wouldn't have done any good.

I stationed myself in a quiet corner just inside the door of the dining room. Sparkling crystal water and wine glasses and sterling silverware sat alongside elegant china plates and red-and-white linen napkins. The main table was set for twenty people; seven smaller tables surrounded it, all decorated with equal elegance. The huge dining room could accommodate about seventy-five people, so the eight tables didn't make the room seem at all crowded. I stared straight ahead, surveying the entire room, including the entrance to the kitchen.

This event was almost as big as the first Stokes affair I had attended. This party served as a double hit: familial and political. While many of the Stokes family members were present, there were also many prominent guests: the Honorable Judge Wesley Johnson, Bishop Fred Thompson, the Adams family, and the Deschazer family, just to name a few. The guests started to arrive, the men in tuxedos and Gators and the women in long gowns and diamonds. It wasn't long before they exchanged small talk that primarily consisted of gossip about various political figures. They spoke in front of me as if I were invisible. For the most part, I ignored their prattle. After about twenty minutes or so, I decided to listen in.

My ears perked up, however, when I overheard one woman tell another that she'd heard Reverend Stokes was sleeping with his secretary. She'd heard he took the woman to out-of-town conferences. "His wife doesn't have a clue," she added with a sigh.

I wondered if the gossip had any basis in fact, since I had been with Reverend Stokes for over a month and had not seen any indication of that. However, the ladies moved on before I heard any evidence one way or the other.

As the guests continued to pour in, I noticed Sebastian's twenty-two-year-old sister, Savannah, standing in the foyer. She was making sure she was presentable. She was dressed in a plain yet elegant black velvet dress. It was strapless, and fit her perfectly. A diamond choker, bracelet, and earrings made the outfit even more appealing. Her hair was pinned in a low bun, which showed off her big brown eyes and flawless skin.

Savannah sauntered over to Mrs. Stokes and asked, "Mother, what kind of man would be acceptable for me to date?"

Without hesitation, Mrs. Stokes replied, "Double degrees, wealthy family, world traveled, an entrepreneur, childless, never married, and a member of several prestigious organizations."

I found it interesting that Mrs. Stokes said nothing about the guy being a Christian.

Savannah's shoulders sagged like a deflated balloon as if she was highly disappointed in her mother's response.

"If you'd like male companionship, darling," Mrs. Stokes added, "I can introduce you to several appropriate gentlemen."

"I'll let you know," Savannah said.

"I wonder what's keeping the meal," Mrs. Stokes said. "I must check with the chef." Without a backward glance, she ambled toward the kitchen. Savannah disappeared upstairs.

Steven Stokes Jr. and his wife, Mary Anne, entered the room. It was my first time seeing the duo in person. Steven was very handsome: fair skinned, brown-eyed, and charismatic. He cordially greeted every guest he encountered. He was wearing a custom-made tuxedo that fit his lean body well. Mary Anne, in her long, pale-blue gown with a split up the left leg, just tagged along, seemingly happy. They made a handsome couple.

"I just don't understand why you're lying to me," she said under her breath, and practically under my nose. "You didn't have a business dinner and you were not working late in the office."

"You know I'm trying to help Sebastian with the campaign," Steven Jr. said, looking around to see if anyone had heard them arguing.

"Don't you blame this on him," Mary Anne said. "You know I'll ask him. He'll tell me the truth."

Steven Jr. shook his head and sighed. "Fine. You really want to know? I went out last night. There. Are you happy now?"

She didn't look a bit happy. "I can't believe you're still out there being wild."

"Well, you don't give me none no more," he seethed.

"I'll have nothing to do with someone who's got HIV, you creep."

She stomped into the dining room and he stormed toward the back hallway.

Moments later, the Reverend Steven Stokes strolled into the room, wearing a sleek black tuxedo. His handsome younger son sported a tux that looked like it was made just for him. Neither of the men looked my way. I felt like a piece of the wallpaper.

"Campaign going well, son?" I heard Reverend Stokes ask.

"Yes, sir," Sebastian said. "I'm generating lots of interest."

"Well, stay active," his father told him as they stopped near the doorway, just a few inches away from me. "Visit hospitals, nursing homes, and schools. Let people know you care."

"Schools?" Sebastian questioned.

"Preschool through high school. Even though most of them can't vote, they'll tell their parents about your visit. The votes will come. Trust me."

"He needs a lady on his arm," Mrs. Stokes said, stepping out of the kitchen.

Sebastian turned away from his mother, and his eyes met mine. He smiled and walked right up to me. "Hi," he said with a sweet grin.

"What are you doing?" his mother questioned. "Leave the agents alone when they're on duty." She grabbed his arm and pulled him away. Though she turned him so his back was to me, I could still hear them talking.

"Penelope Colon is coming tonight."

"So?" Sebastian said.

"I think she would be a fine choice for you. She's about to finish medical school at Yale, so the two of you already have something in common."

"I'm a lawyer, not a doctor. And Harvard's not Yale."

"Well, they're both Ivy League schools. That's close enough."

"Why are you so bent on setting me up, Mother?"

"If the voters see you have a serious girlfriend, you'll have an advantage in this race. Regardless of what anyone says, values still win elections."

"Honey," Reverend Stokes said, "he's not trying to win this thing."

"Well now, even though he entered the race for lieutenant governor just to stir up interest for your campaign, I think he has a great chance of winning."

"Penelope Colon is not his type," Reverend Stokes stated. Then he turned and whispered in Sebastian's ear, "Date whoever makes you happy, son."

"Thanks, Dad," Sebastian said with a smile.

"Now, don't dismiss Penelope too quickly," his mother urged. "I know you're picky, but you never know. You may like her." She turned to her husband. "Dear," she said, taking her husband's arm, "you need to start speaking with people about contributions to your campaign." Without waiting for a response, she led him toward a large gathering of stuffy-looking guests.

Sebastian watched them leave, then turned to me. "It's great to see you," he said. He tried to take my hand, but I snatched it back.

"I'm on duty," I whispered, maintaining my stance. "If anyone sees me socializing, they'll think I'm not doing my job. Or worse—I could get in big trouble."

"You're right," he said. "I'm sorry." He turned away reluctantly and joined the party.

The owner of the catering service announced that dinner

was about to be served, and the guests began gathering in the dining area. As servers entered with the first course, eager diners circled the tables, trying to locate their place cards.

It came as no surprise to me that Penelope's card was right beside Sebastian's.

Watching Sebastian laugh and interact with that girl made me realize how much I wanted to pursue a romantic relationship with him. However, with my job and his family, I knew that would be too big a mountain to climb.

As I stood in my corner, it dawned on me that I had no life. Oh, many people considered my career prestigious. And I was proud of my job. But I realized it required a great deal of sacrifice. Besides the fact that I could lose my life at any minute, I couldn't remember the last time I'd had a decent holiday. Even if I could make social plans, I knew no one in Atlanta except the family I was assigned to protect. And I couldn't really hang out with them.

My stomach churned as I smelled the delicious aroma. An hour later, it twisted even more as I watched Mrs. Stokes escort Sebastian out the front door with Penelope. Sebastian glanced at me with apologetic eyes as his mother led him out. I kept my face like stone, knowing I didn't dare let him know I was dying to be on his arm.

When my shift was finally over, I drove straight to the hotel the Agency had booked for the team. As soon as I entered my room, I picked up the phone and dialed room service.

After gorging myself on a cheeseburger, fries, and a strawberry milkshake, I put the tray outside my door, changed into my flannel pajamas, and crawled into bed.

Groaning from the stuffed feeling in my stomach, I opened the drawer in the nightstand where I'd tossed a stash of various medicines. After digging out an antacid and popping it in my mouth, I noticed the Gideon Bible in the back of the drawer. I hadn't read the Bible in a long time and something about it was speaking to me. Slowly, I picked it up. I sat on the edge of the bed and turned to the middle.

Sebastian had talked to me about Jesus interceding on my behalf to His father. Through the open Bible on my lap, I sensed that this awesome Son, Jesus, was talking to me. I could almost hear Him telling me that all I had to do was worship Him, accept the fact that my sins are forgiven, and anything was possible.

"This is crazy," I said as I slammed the Bible shut, tossed it back into the nightstand, and shoved the drawer closed.

I turned off the lamp and slithered under the covers. I've been too much of a backslider for God to be all right with me. Frustration sank in, and I uttered, "The Holy Person in the sky has not moved any of my mountains. If I've needed something done, I've had to do it myself."

I'd had plenty of obstacles to overcome in my life. My daddy left us when I was little. Growing up in a single-parent household wasn't easy. Sometimes, someone from a local church would invite us over for dinner. Once in a while the Salvation Army would call and tell us we could pick up other people's cast-off clothes. Mama said that was God's way of providing for us, but I always wondered how a loving God would let something like that happen to anyone as good as my mother.

When I was a teenager, Daddy suddenly decided he wanted to get to know his family again. But by that time, I had hardened my heart toward love and relationships. There was nothing he could say that mattered to me. Plus, my mom had already been through so much, working the drug scene, that she was done with him as well. When he came back around, my mom had a legitimate job and my dad also wanted to mooch off of that. When she told him to leave us be, I never saw him again.

Trying to stop thinking about my painful past, I thought about Sebastian. But that line of thinking brought pain, too. I wondered what he was doing. The clock beside the bed said it was two o'clock. I wondered if Sebastian was still out with Penelope Cancer, Colon, or whatever her name was.

The loud ringing of the phone startled me. "Hello?"

"Were you asleep?" Sebastian's smooth voice asked.

"No," I replied, unable to keep the enthusiasm out of my voice.

"I'm sorry for calling you so late. But I remembered that today is your special day, and I wanted to wish you a happy birthday before anyone else had a chance to."

My heart melted at the sweet gesture. No one had ever called me at two A.M. to wish me a happy birthday.

"I thought maybe we could celebrate together . . . if you didn't already have plans."

"No, I don't," I said, suddenly grateful for my empty social calendar.

"Great. I'll have my driver pick you up around five. Does that sound good?"

"Sure."

"Well, pretty lady, you'd better get some sleep. You've got a big day ahead of you."

"This place is beautiful," I said to Sebastian as I stepped into the dimly lit penthouse apartment. It had an African theme, complete with tiger and leopard rugs on the hardwood floors. Tall palm trees stood like sentinels in the corners of the main room. I felt like I had instantly traveled from Atlanta to Africa.

Vanilla-scented candles and bouquets of red roses filled the living area with their fragrant aromas. "Are there always so many flowers and candles here?"

He smiled. "Actually, I brought in twenty-six of each, one for every year of your life. And I want you to make twenty-six wishes before you leave tonight."

A tear fell from my eye. He was so sweet, and he knew just what I needed. As I started to hug him, his front door opened.

His father entered with Agent Moss. Neither one seemed happy to see me.

Sebastian stood. "What are you doing here, Dad?"

"What is *she* doing here?" he bellowed, his hands balled into fists.

"It's her birthday," Sebastian retorted. "I'm celebrating with her."

"You could have given her a present."

"Dad, I'm not a little boy. This is my apartment. I can make my own decisions."

"Your mother and I want you home for dinner. It's Christmas."

"I was with you guys all day yesterday."

"We have several very important people coming over tonight. It would be nice if you would join us."

Sebastian was in a predicament. I knew he wanted to make the night special for me, but he did have political and family obligations.

I scooped up my coat from the back of a chair. "I'll be all right, Sebastian. You should go have Christmas with your family."

"No," he replied sternly. "I'm a grown man. I can do whatever I want. And what I want is to be with you."

I melted at his words, but forced myself to do what seemed best for everyone. As I turned toward the door, Agent Moss gave me a stern look.

Sebastian started to follow me, but his dad grabbed his arm. Right outside the door, Agent Moss called to me. My heart dropped. It was never said that what I was doing was against the rules, but I knew it was implied.

"You've been great to have on this detail so far. But you're crossing the line and you know it!"

"Sorry, sir," I told him, knowing there was nothing I could say to fix this.

"I don't know how you do things in the FBI, but here, we don't get too close. What you're doing is playing with fire. I'd hate to see you get burned and cause harm to yourself, this campaign, or the Secret Service. I didn't see you tonight."

"Yes, sir," I said, before he turned to head back into Sebastian's place.

"And don't let it happen again. The next time, you're off the detail."

As I walked through the lobby to hail a taxi, I realized that I would never be good enough for Sebastian's family and this relationship could ruin my career. Whatever had begun to spark between us was simply never going to work.

New Year's Eve found us in Cleveland, Ohio, at the Cleveland Skyscraper for a big dinner in honor of Reverend Stokes. The dinner was held in a large conference room, which was on the thirtieth floor of a forty-floor building. It was decorated with red tablecloths and white napkins on round, ten-seated tables.

Sebastian had phoned me countless times over the past week, but I only returned one of his calls. He tried to convince me that we could work things out, but I cut him off and told him not to call me again. He called several times after that, but when I saw his number on my caller ID display, I just let it ring.

"Some say it can't be done," Mr. Stokes said into the microphone as he stood, straight and tall, on the platform after the dinner. "They don't think I can become president of the United States."

The audience cheered.

"But I know we will make it happen with your support."

The cheers grew louder. My fellow agents and I went on extra alert. Anytime the noise level at a function went up, the potential for an attacker to try to do something without being noticed increased.

"This time next year," Stokes proclaimed, "with your support, I will be in the White House. Together we will prove to the world that the presidency of the United States is not about the color of a man's skin, but about who is the best man for the job."

The powerful words stirred wild applause. Then I remembered Sebastian telling me that his father didn't write his speeches— Sebastian did.

Mr. Stokes sauntered down from the pulpit and I escorted him to his table. Mrs. Stokes's seat was empty. A quick call through my earpiece to Agent Pitts informed me that she was in the powder room.

Stokes shook several hands before taking his seat. When his

supporters were all busy chowing down, he leaned back in his seat and spoke to me without looking my way. "You do know that my son is not really interested in you, don't you?" he said.

I remained in position, saying nothing, acting as if I hadn't heard a word he'd said. I knew Sebastian cared. I also knew Reverend Stokes didn't want me dating his son.

"You could get in serious trouble for being involved with Sebastian," Stokes continued, still focusing on his food. "As much as I enjoy having a pretty young thing like you tagging along on the campaign, I won't have you messing with my son that way."

Before I could respond, I got a call on my earplug. "Agent Ware," my supervisor, Agent Moss, hollered, "get Cool Falcon out of there. Get him to the roof. We've got a helicopter on its way to pick him up. Move!"

Like a plane going into autopilot, I instantly went into crisis mode. Setting aside my anger at him, I said firmly but discreetly, "We have got to leave immediately, sir. There's an emergency."

Ignoring me, he started chatting nonchalantly with the constituent next to him. I grabbed his arm and yanked him out of his seat.

"What do you think you're doing?" he cried as I shoved him toward the nearest staircase.

Agent Moss met us at the stairwell.

"Where's my wife?" Stokes demanded.

"We've already escorted her out of the building, sir," Moss informed our reluctant protectee.

"What's going on?" Stokes asked, his voice beginning to show concern.

"We've got to clear out the building," Moss said, leading Stokes up the stairs. "We've received a bomb threat."

"Good heavens!" Stokes cried. "But why are we going upstairs?"

"There's a helicopter waiting for us on the roof," Moss explained. "Now, get a move on!"

Stokes finally picked up some speed. He even mumbled some prayers as he scrambled up the steps.

I heard the frantic voices of other agents shouting into my earpiece.

"All the guests are out of the building," Agent Pitts announced.

"We can't find the bomb," Agent Sawyer wailed.

When we reached the top of the stairs and approached the roof access door, the question was answered. A device with four explosives, a time clock, and three different-colored wires was planted on the door. My heart dropped.

"What do we do now?" I asked, barely breathing.

Agent Moss had experience disarming bombs, but he just stood there, scratching his head. The timer showed five minutes and twenty-five seconds.

As I looked around for another way out, I spotted a vent on the ceiling. It looked large enough for me to climb through if I could get it open.

"Moss," I shouted, "give me a boost."

He followed my gaze and quickly guessed my plan. He intertwined the fingers of both hands and I stepped into the stirrup. Pulling hard, I finally yanked off the metal facing. It clattered to the ground.

Moss boosted me higher and I climbed inside the tiny, dusty enclosure. When I saw light a few feet away, I hollered down, "Come on. This leads to the roof."

Agent Moss radioed to the other agents, then lifted Stokes into the vent behind me. We crawled on our bellies toward the light.

When we got to the end, I stumbled out of the vent, then helped Reverend Stokes out. I had never seen him so disheveled or so frightened.

"Run, sir," I screamed, pointing at the helicopter that sat in the center of the roof, its blades twirling.

Just as Stokes started climbing into the chopper, the building started to rumble. I tried to climb in behind him but the helicopter suddenly swayed and I lost my balance. I landed on the roof, and as the helicopter took off, the pilot looked back at me with wild, apologetic eyes.

I knew that only seconds remained before the explosion reached me, so I grabbed the parachute my team had stored on the roof and ran to the edge of the building. I was thrown into the air by the powerful explosion.

Chapter 7

Ski Lift

After taking a few deep breaths to settle my nerves, I released the parachute and sailed down the front side of the building. I felt myself floating gently and effortlessly through puffy white clouds in a beautiful cobalt-blue sky. The ball of fire was no longer chasing me. I was certain I would never see earth again, and I felt okay with that. A calm, peaceful feeling flooded my heart. *Death isn't so bad,* I thought. *I guess God didn't give up on me after all.*

"Lord in heaven, take me home," I whispered. "Forgive me for straying away from You. I wish I had really known You sooner, but I guess I'll have forever to sing Your praises."

Suddenly my body crashed onto the ground. People flocked all around me, crying, "She's alive. She's okay!"

I wasn't dead after all. I had floated to the ground with the parachute.

As I tried to remember what had happened, a searing pain shot through my leg. I looked down and saw that my right thigh was covered in blood.

A paramedic was cutting my scorched pant leg. I nearly passed out when I saw the bulging dark patches on my shin where fire had curled some of my skin and melted other parts away.

Agent Moss got out of the helicopter parked a few feet away, pushed his way through the crowd, and knelt beside me. This stoic man hovered over me, his normally placid eyes filled with concern. "You did a great job. That leg will heal in no time. You're a fighter. Reverend Stokes can't wait to thank you in person."

"He's okay?" I hazily recalled watching Stokes climb into the helicopter before it took off from the roof.

"Yes," Moss assured me. "The helicopter landed safely at the airport."

The paramedics placed me on a gurney and put me in the ambulance for transport to the hospital. My heart slowed as I calmed down. I was safe. I was thankful. For the first time in a long while, I felt God's presence.

After two days in the hospital, I was losing my mind. Agent Hold had brought me a stack of crossword puzzle books, and I had already completed at least ten of them.

The doctor told me I had sustained a concussion, third-degree burns on my shin, and a severely swollen ankle. He said I'd have to stay in the hospital for a few more days.

I cringed. I'd always hated hospitals. When I was about eight years old, my grandfather had entered a hospital with a headache, and he passed away the next day. No one could explain to me what had happened.

At least I was not in a regular hospital room. This place was more like a hotel suite, with pictures on the pink walls, a dresser with a mirror, a leather couch, and even a large-screen television. I felt special, pampered, and cared for.

The door to my room opened and Reverend Stokes waltzed in. "Mind if I bother you for a minute?"

"No," I said, pulling my hospital robe tighter as I sat up a bit.

He turned to my detail leader, Agent Moss, and said, "I'd like to have a moment alone with Agent Ware, please."

"Sure, sir," Agent Moss said as he nodded his head at me. "I'll be right outside the door."

Reverend Stokes walked in and pulled the door almost shut. "I sure can see why my son is so into you," he said, speaking more casually than I'd ever heard him.

"I haven't talked to your son."

Reverend Stokes patted my hand that was free of the IV. "It's okay. I've talked with him and he admits he has feelings for you. You're an amazing woman and a phenomenal agent. I owe you my life."

I felt my cheeks blush. "I was just doing my job, sir."

"I've talked to Agent Moss and he and I agree that it is not against any federal policy if you still want to see my son."

I didn't know how to respond to that. I was grateful, but I didn't want special favors. I guess it was like when I saved Troy by shooting the guy who was going to shoot him. When you save someone's life, they feel so indebted, they grant you anything. I guess this was Reverend Stokes's way of saying thanks.

He sat in the leather chair beside my bed. "Ms. Ware, God has shown me that He has put certain people in my life for specific reasons. Your actions showed me what a selfish person I've been lately. I don't have the right to tell Sebastian he can't see you or that you're not good enough for him. In spite of the mean things I said to you, you saved my life. I was wrong to judge you, and I'd like to apologize."

I was so overwhelmed, all I could do was smile. "Have you talked to Sebastian about this?"

"Oh, you can't wait to get together with him now that I gave you my blessing, can you?" Reverend Stokes laughed. "We're going to have to work on his mom, though. I don't think she'll be very easy to convince."

"Your son and I are just friends, sir," I assured him.

"That's not what it looked like the other night." He grinned.

"Sebastian was just doing something nice for my birthday," I explained. "And besides, at the time, I really wanted to talk to him about God."

"Really?" he said, his eager expression reminding me that Stokes was not just a presidential candidate; he was a pastor as well.

"Reverend Stokes, my behavior hasn't always been very godly. I mean, I believed in God, but I started wondering if He truly loved me. So much has happened in my life that made me doubt His love for me. But when we were climbing those steps to the roof the other day, and I heard you praying, I realized I need to get straight with the Lord."

"God spared your life," he said in the gentle voice of a loving pastor. "Do you believe He loves you now?"

"Yeah, I do," I told him. "I really feel God in my soul."

His face beamed. "May I pray with you?"

"Of course," I said with a chuckle.

It was a long prayer, and very meaningful. I was glad he'd stopped by to see me. Not only was I relieved to see that my protectee was safe and well, but also it was a blessing to have him acting as my pastor, too.

I awoke the next day to the smell of fresh roses. Even without opening my eyes, I knew my man had come to start my day off right.

"I'm glad you're okay," I heard his deep baritone voice whispering in my ear. "My world could not have gone on without you."

"Ms. Ware," a tight tenor voice interrupted, "I need to take a look at that burn."

My eyes flew open. Sebastian wasn't there at all. Instead, a male nurse was moving a bouquet of roses off my nightstand so he could set the portable thermometer machine down before taking my temperature.

I must have been dreaming. I closed my eyes and exhaled deeply.

That afternoon, I called my mother. I didn't mean to wait so long before I called her, but the medication I was on made me sleep a lot. Whenever I woke up it was because someone woke me up. My mom had received a call from my FBI supervisor, but had yet to talk to me personally. She had been going crazy worrying about me, but I assured her that I was fine. But she just kept crying and saying that she'd been a nervous wreck.

"You need to quit," she said. "You are not Superwoman. Just come on home and let me take care of you."

I rolled my eyes, glad she couldn't see my face over the

phone. "Ma, I know I'm not really a Secret Service agent, but I've got to figure out who's after Reverend Stokes."

"But you're injured," she squealed. "Let the Secret Service people do that. You need to take some time off to get healed."

I hated that my mother still talked to me like I was a child. But the truth was, she was right. "I'll have to do that anyway," I said. "The Agency is making me take a week off."

"Good," she proclaimed. "Shall I fly down there to look after you, or are you coming here? I can pick you up from the airport any time."

"Thanks for your concern, Ma, but I don't even know when I'll be released from the hospital yet."

"Then I'll come visit you."

"Ma, no, you don't need to do that. You can't afford to miss work. Besides, the hospital staff is taking excellent care of me. There's nothing to worry about. I'm going to be fine."

She hesitated. "You sound different, Christian. What's going on with you?"

"Nothing, Ma. Really." I wanted to tell my mother about my renewed relationship with God, but I wasn't ready to listen to her screaming *"Praise the Lord!"* and shouting *"Hallelujah!"* for hours on end. So I decided to change the subject. "How's Crystal?"

For a long moment, my mother just sighed. I knew her heart was hurting over my younger sister. I hadn't spent as much time with Crystal lately as I wished I could. She was fifteen, but looked more like twenty-eight. Her life focused on boys and money, and she'd been hanging around with the wrong crowd.

"She says she's not getting into any trouble," Mom reported, "but some of those boys she's been seeing scare me. I'm trying to switch shifts so I can be home when she gets in from school."

"Crystal has too much freedom," I said, before I realized that would just make my mom more nervous.

"Oh, Chris, what am I gonna do with that girl?" Mom asked, her voice trembling.

"Don't worry, Ma," I said quickly. "I'll have a talk with her as soon as I can."

Hearing the concern in my mother's voice made me miss her dreadfully.

Shortly after I hung up, Agent Moss came in. He asked me how I was doing and questioned me on my recollection of the events that had taken place the night of the bombing. I told him all the details I remembered, and my responses were recorded on a small tape recorder.

After he had finished his official interview and pressed the Stop button, he said, "We're all really proud of the way you handled yourself in that situation."

"Thank you, sir," I said. "When can I get back to my duties?"

He grinned and shook his head. "Don't worry. Stokes is being heavily guarded."

"He was attacked on my watch, sir," I said. "I just want to make sure he's safe until the culprit is captured."

"But you're wounded," he said. "Until you're cleared by a physician, you'll have to stay on medical leave."

I groaned, but knew I had no choice.

After my supervisor left, I was going to try to take a nap, but the phone rang. Hoping it was Sebastian, I answered it quickly.

"Your picture is all over the paper," my girlfriend Eden gushed. "I'm so proud of you."

"Just doing my job," I said.

"Are you kidding?" she squealed. "Dion says you could become famous for this. Have you had many reporters wanting to interview you yet?"

I chuckled. "They'd have to get clearance from the Secret Service, and those guys never approve that kind of thing. I'm telling you, girl, it's just part of the job."

"Well, if you refuse the media, they won't be very happy. They might even print something negative about you just to retaliate."

"That's ridiculous," I said. "Besides, who cares about the media?"

Just then an orderly arrived with my lunch tray. I tilted the phone away to thank her, then tore into my banana pudding cup.

"Chris, how are you really doing?" Eden asked. "I mean, weren't you scared?"

I put down my spoon. "Yeah, I was. I mean, I almost died in that blast. But when I thought I was dead, I recommitted my life to Christ."

"No way," she squealed. "Are you serious?"

"Yes," I said. "I feel like a completely new person, like a load has been lifted off my heart."

"Oh, Christian, I'm so excited for you," she said.

"Yeah—me, too."

"Don't you feel like there's Someone by your side now, watching over you? That's how it is for me. I feel protected and safe with Jesus Christ by my side."

"I don't know all there is to know about Jesus, and I really want to learn. But I can already feel His strength in me."

"Praise God!" she said. "I've been praying for you to get closer to the Lord."

"Okay," I said, finishing my pudding and starting on my Jell-O, "enough about me. How are you and your husband doing? And give me the real answer."

"All right, real answer." She hesitated for a moment. "Every time I turn around he wants to have sex. To be honest, I'm tired of it already. It was romantic at first, but not anymore."

"Dang, I didn't know there was such a thing as too much sex," I teased.

"You know, I shouldn't be talking about my problems while you're in the hospital."

"Hey, I asked. I want you to talk to me. Takes my mind off of everything that's going on with me, you know?"

"Well, I'd rather talk about what's going on with you," she said lightly, obviously not wanting to talk about her marriage anymore. "Have you met any cute guys lately?"

I laughed. "Actually, I have."

"You're kidding! Who?"

"Sebastian Stokes."

"Reverend Stokes's middle son?" she screamed.

"That's him."

"Oh, my gosh! I saw a picture of him in the paper once. He looked like a nerd—totally not your type."

"He's got a new style now. He's running for lieutenant governor of Georgia."

"So he's a politician? Sounds pretty nerdy to me."

"He doesn't expect to win. He's just running to beef up his dad's campaign."

"So does he like you?"

"He's definitely interested. And I can't get him out of my mind. Eden, this man is everything I've ever dreamed of. He has brains, personality, patience, and looks!"

"Sounds perfect."

"I don't know if our relationship can really go anywhere, though. His mother wants a high-society girl for him."

"Forget her. Just be yourself. You'll win her over."

"You don't know this woman." I chuckled. "She's like the wicked witch of the West."

"If you want him, pray about it. If it's God's will, it'll work out."

"You should take your own advice, girl."

"What are you talking about?"

"Maybe you and Dion can work out your sexual differences if you pray about it."

"Maybe," she said softly. "I sure wish you were going to Denver with us."

"Me, too," I said longingly.

Every winter, young black people from all over the United States got together on the slopes of Colorado for a big snow party. Not only was it great fun, but there were also plenty of opportunities to network. I personally knew several people who had gotten great jobs because of the contacts they made at the ski conference.

"Hey," Eden said, "maybe this would be a good way for you to recuperate. You wouldn't have to ski, of course. Just hang out at the lodge and talk to folks. Lots of people from the wedding party are going."

"I'm not sure," I said, although it certainly sounded tempting. "I promised my mom I'd go home and check up on my sister."

"At least think about it," she said.

I promised her I would.

We talked and laughed for another forty minutes. Just hearing her voice relaxed me. Eden was a true friend and I was glad I had her in my life.

After I hung up the phone, I decided to take her advice. First, I thanked God for my friendship with Eden. Then I asked Him what He had in store for me. I wanted my desire to match His will.

I couldn't stop thinking about Sebastian Stokes. Were my thoughts about him coming from God? Was He trying to tell me something about Sebastian? Or was I just getting excited because he was such a fine man? I wanted to hear from God. So I decided to just start talking to Him.

"Lord," I whispered in the quiet room, "it feels kind of weird talking to You after all this time. I hope You can hear me." Wanting to do this right, I hobbled out of bed and slipped to my knees. "I've lived my life so wrong. I need help. I need to get back on Your path." My right leg started pounding, but I ignored the pain.

Before I could finish my prayer, I heard the door open. My heart raced as I turned my head, hoping to see Sebastian. But instead my partner, Agent Hold, was poking his head in.

"You okay?" he asked, stepping into the room with a nice assortment of fresh-cut flowers.

"I'm fine," I said, accepting his help getting off my knees.

As he set the flowers on the nightstand, I crawled back into bed, my leg throbbing.

He pulled a chair next to the bed and sat in it backwards. "Want me to call the nurse?" he asked.

I tried to smooth the grimace off my face. "Thanks, but no. I'm okay."

"I can't believe this happened," Agent Hold said. "I sure

want to catch the guy who planted that bomb. I thought I'd lost you when I saw you leap from that building with all those flames engulfing you."

His concern touched my heart so deeply I couldn't speak.

"I never would have guessed that you were so tough," he said with a smile. "You're my hero."

We started laughing so hard my leg began to hurt again.

Then the door opened and Sebastian Stokes appeared, wearing a tailored business suit. My heart skipped a beat.

"Guess I'll be going," Ryan said, standing.

"You don't have to—" I started.

"I'll be back," he assured me. Then he grinned and walked out the door.

"You look beautiful," Sebastian said as he approached my bed.

He stroked my hair and gave me a sweet kiss on the forehead. My body stiffened with excitement.

He sat on the edge of the bed. "Forgive me for not getting here sooner," he said, his voice filled with regret. "My schedule is insane, but I made adjustments as quickly as I could so I could get here and spend time with you."

"You're here now," I said. "That's all that really matters."

When the plane took off, I couldn't believe I was sitting beside Sebastian Stokes, heading toward the ski convention in Vail. When I had told him about it in the hospital, he had immediately decided it would be good therapy for me and convinced my doctor to release me early. Since he went to the trouble of rearranging his schedule for me, I called my mom and told her I'd come to see her right after the ski weekend.

"What are you thinking about?" Sebastian asked as he saw me staring out the window.

"You," I said, then kissed him on the lips. We were still kissing when the flight attendant came by, asking if we wanted a drink. I pretended not to hear her offer. I had everything I needed right beside me.

When we arrived at the Snowy Mountain Bed and Breakfast,

it was packed with affluent black folks. As we stood in the long registration line, I heard three ladies behind us making suggestive comments about Sebastian and giggling like schoolgirls. I wasn't a bit jealous. It actually made me feel good, knowing all the ladies wanted my man.

But he wasn't really my man. Not yet.

One of the ladies came up and whispered in his ear, "Please tell me you're here alone."

"Sorry," he said, grabbing my waist.

The girl shrank back to her friends with a disappointed pout.

When our turn came to register, the desk clerk asked how many rooms we would need.

"Two, please," Sebastian said, and I heard the girls behind me start whispering again.

Sebastian carried our bags to the elevator. By the time it arrived, the girls from behind us in line joined us.

"You'll have to excuse us for looking at your man," the lighter-skinned one said as the shiny doors slid open.

"We just want to know how you snagged him," the darker one said, pressing the button for her floor.

I smiled. "He's just a blessing from God."

The girls looked at each other in shock. "Then I need to start praying!" the first girl said, and we all laughed.

Sebastian turned around, looked at us, and I could see that he was blushing.

When the elevator reached our floor, Sebastian led me to my room, brought in the luggage, and handed me my key. The room was actually quite cozy, as it contained a sitting area next to the fireplace, a queen-sized canopy bed, and a quaint bathroom.

"It's beautiful," I said with inward jubilee.

"*You're* beautiful," Sebastian said, pulling me into his arms.

He touched my face, then his hands roamed my upper body and I started to burn with desire. He grabbed my butt and moaned while his lips and tongue sent heat to my loins. Then he picked me up and carried me to the bedroom, laying me down gently on the bed. I opened my legs, and he answered my invitation by joining me on the bed. When he climbed on top of me, my bandaged leg complained. But I was willing to endure a little pain to be with this man.

Suddenly he rolled off of me and sat up. "What am I doing? I can't do this." He stood. "Christian, forgive me. I'm going to my room. I will be back in a little while to get you for dinner."

"Sebastian," I cried out as he stomped into the living room and picked up his suitcase. "I'm sorry." Before I could say anything more, he fled from the room.

I sat by the fire for thirty minutes, trying to figure out what I'd done to offend him. He'd seemed as passionate about me as I'd been about him. Why the sudden change? Then it clicked with me. This wasn't God's way. Though I'd just started following the Lord again, I knew I had a ways to go to get right in my spirit. Falling a little in the area of premarital sex didn't bother me that much. However, I felt horrible that I was causing Sebastian to compromise his values.

When Sebastian returned, he asked if I was ready to eat. I said yes, so we went downstairs to the restaurant. As we ate, we discussed what happened upstairs in the room.

"Christian, I'm sorry if you feel that I rejected you. I want to be with you so bad, but I made a vow to God that the next woman I made love to would be my wife," Sebastian uttered with compassion.

I replied by saying, "I owe you an apology. I was only thinking about what I wanted. I guess it's just hard for me to understand why an attractive, able-bodied man would make such a promise."

He stared into my eyes briefly, then lowered his head and said, "I was in a serious relationship with someone a few years ago and I loved her dearly, but she cheated on me." He looked away and had trouble finishing the story. As I stared at him, I could tell this was hard for him. Wanting him to open up when he was ready, I gently ran circles across the top of his hand.

After what seemed like an eternity, I said, "Sebastian, I respect you for your stance against premarital sex. We can talk about that whenever you want to. Again, I'm sorry that I'm just not there yet."

Smiling, he said, "If you'll let me, I want to date you in a way that pleases God. Will you let me do that?"

"I'll try. But I gotta be honest. Right now I really want more from you."

That evening Sebastian took me on a magical ride in a chartered cable car that traveled from the bottom of the ski slope to the top of the mountain. We stood at the window and looked out at the beautiful scenery under the nearly full moon.

I tried to move closer to him a few times, but he kept eluding my touch. He didn't seem angry with me, but he was certainly driving a wedge into the romance of the ride.

Sooner or later, I thought, we'd have to have a long, serious talk. But for the moment, I decided to just enjoy the wonderful ride and watch the skiers as they wound down the snowy slopes, then rode back up to the top on the ski lift.

Chapter 8

Cave

Though the view of the ski slopes from our chartered cable car was beautiful, the distance between Sebastian and me was uncomfortable. Being so close to the mountains was breathtaking. It gave me comfort, knowing that if the Lord could create such wonder, He certainly could control the heart of His own.

When the cable car reached the top of the mountain, it circled the station and began its descent. Sebastian remained silent. Since my negative attitude was softened by the wonderful wilderness, I decided to try and be cordial.

Finally I asked, "What are you thinking about?"

"Nothing," he replied, staring out the window.

"Please talk to me," I begged. "Something's on your mind. You started at dinner and I told you I'd be here to listen any time. I don't want a relationship full of strain—open up."

"I told you I'm not thinking about anything," he snapped. "Why can't you let me be?"

Stunned by his response, I endured the rest of the ride in complete silence.

When the cable car reached the ground-level station, the operator said with a grin, "You two lovebirds want to go back up?"

"No," I said firmly as I limped out, my leg in great pain after standing for so long.

When we reached Sebastian's car, he opened the passenger-side door like it was an obligation. So I kept walking right past his car.

"What are you doing?" he asked with a frustrated sigh.

I glanced back. "I think I'll just walk back to the bed-and-breakfast, thanks." I kept going.

"I can't leave you out here like this," he hollered after me. "Stop acting so childish."

"Childish?" I repeated, whipping around so quickly I nearly slipped on the icy asphalt.

"You probably don't even know how to get back."

I stared at him, unwilling to admit that he was right.

"I owe you an explanation," he said, still standing by the open car door. "Can you please get in so I can talk to you?"

I took a deep breath, then obliged.

After closing my door, he got in the driver's side. "I'm not mad at you, Christian," he said after taking a deep breath. "I'm mad at myself because I didn't tell you everything." He stared at the steering wheel. "Chris, the only reason I found out that my ex cheated on me was because she told me that she tested positive for HIV. She also told me that she had been with my brother and that I should tell him that he needed to get tested also. While I was waiting for the results of my test, I promised God that if my test came back negative, I would rededicate myself to Him and would not sleep with another woman until she was my wife. He honored my prayer and I want to keep my word."

I couldn't say anything. I was stunned. Sebastian was a man of God and I was making him falter.

He continued, "Now do you see why I couldn't sleep with you, why I couldn't break my word to God? I just don't know if my willpower is as strong as it used to be before you entered my life. I'm supposed to be helping you find the right way to God, and here I am messing up both of us. I think I need to reevaluate my feelings for you. If that's tough for you to hear, I'm sorry. I'm just trying to be honest."

"I came here to recuperate," I said, trying to remember that I was strong, "and I can do that without you." I asked him to drop me off in front of the bed-and-breakfast. He started the car without another word and we drove in silence.

When I returned to my room, I called room service and ordered a hamburger, french fries, and a slice of cheesecake. Then I changed into my flannel nightgown and started flipping through the channels on the television, finding nothing but reruns of stupid sitcoms.

I looked at the phone several times, hoping Sebastian would call. But I knew we were at a fork in the road, and I'd been too promiscuous in my life to just turn off all the heat. The way Sebastian had responded when God granted him his health was not my style, even though God had blessed me with not being pregnant. I should be taking the same stand, but I couldn't commit to that right now. Could our relationship survive?

When I rolled over and looked at the clock the next day, it was six . . . P.M.! I had slept all day. Though my leg felt better, my heart was breaking. All I could do was pray.

Okay, Lord, how am I supposed to turn off the feelings I have for Sebastian? I want to go further with him, but I know that's wrong. Please change my heart. Take away my desire to do all the wrong things.

I crawled out of the bed, took a shower, and put on some casual clothes. When I ventured out into the living room, I noticed three pieces of folded pink paper by the door. Intrigued, I picked them up.

The first one said,

9:02 A.M. I came by to get you for breakfast and knocked on the door, but you didn't answer. Later, Sebastian.

A smile curled my lips as I stared at his signature.
I unfolded the second note.

12:35 P.M. Was hoping we could do lunch, but I guess you're still tired. Going skiing with a friend. See you.

I pressed the note to my heart, then quickly unfolded the third one.

It's 5:00. Hope you're okay. There's a package for you at the front desk.

I called the front desk and they verified that they did have a package for me. I asked to have it brought up. Within moments the bellhop was knocking at my door. After tipping him extravagantly, I surveyed the beautifully decorated gift box. It had a Saks Fifth Avenue logo.

I opened the box. It contained a beautiful, black, sleeveless dress in my size, a pair of black pumps with a sexy open toe, and a satin purse. I also found a small jewelry box containing a pearl necklace and matching earrings. I was too stunned to do anything but sit down and stare.

Seconds later, I heard a knock on the door. Tossing the box aside, I raced to answer, ready to give Sebastian a huge hug. But my caller was the young bellhop. He held out a card. "I'm sorry. I forgot to give you this. It was with the package."

"Lord, what is this man up to?" I mumbled after thanking the deliverer and closing the door.

I opened the card with trembling fingers.

My dearest Christian,

I'm sorry for the misunderstanding. I don't want to lose you. I just want to honor God. I think we can work this out. Let me show you the way God wants us to be together.

I hope you feel okay. I've been concerned about you. There is a big charity ball tonight at the civic center in town. If you decide not to come, I will understand.

Hope I'll see you tonight.

> *Love,*
> *Sebastian*

I held the card close to my heart and closed my eyes, envisioning his face. I couldn't let this man get away. I had to make another effort to let him know how I felt before I ended up with nothing.

* * *

I entered the ballroom, feeling absolutely elegant in my brand-new ensemble. As I started searching for Sebastian, my cell phone rang.

"Hey, girl. How are you doing?" I could hear excitement in Eden's voice. We had spoken briefly after I received the gifts from Sebastian.

"I'm good," I said. "How about you?"

"You won't believe this," she said, "but Dion and I are at a fancy ball. I wish you were here."

"Tell me about the place," I said, amazed at the coincidence.

"A bunch of round tables are covered with red linen tablecloths and white napkins. Each table has an African violet centerpiece. There's a live band, and the lights are dim and romantic."

My amazement grew. Her description matched my surroundings perfectly. "Is there a winding staircase? And ice sculptures?"

"Yeah," she said. "How do you know?"

I glanced around the room and spotted my girlfriend not ten feet away, surrounded by her friends from the wedding party, all looking in the opposite direction. "Turn around," I said.

Eden turned, and within moments saw me waving at her. We hung up our phones and rushed toward each other. "Oh, girl," she said, giving me a hug, "you look gorgeous." She glanced back at her friends, who had followed her. "Hey, everybody, look! Christian is here."

Dion said hi to me. Max Cross, my ex-boyfriend, gave me a long, appreciative once-over. Chyna shot me an insincere half smile.

Everyone huddled around me, asking how my leg felt and telling me how fabulous I looked. Then we made our way to an empty table and filled it up. Max maneuvered into the seat to my right, while Eden sat on my left.

"Anybody know who the guest speaker is supposed to be?" Chyna asked the group. "I'm not staying if the speech gets boring." She fanned her linen napkin over her lap. "Then again, if it's somebody cute, maybe I'll just go after him when he's through talking."

Just then, Sebastian stepped onto the podium from behind a heavy curtain.

"Ooh," Chyna squealed. "He is fine!"

"Good evening, ladies and gentlemen," he said. "I am Sebastian Stokes."

"Is that—?" Eden asked me.

I grinned, then turned to give Sebastian my full attention.

"I am running for lieutenant governor of the state of Georgia. When I first announced my candidacy, most people thought it was a joke. I admit I didn't take it as seriously as I should have. But as I traveled across the beautiful state of Georgia, I realized it is filled with suffering people who need politicians to make a difference for them. I now believe this is my God-given calling."

While the audience applauded, Max tapped me on the shoulder and handed me a white cocktail napkin. On it he had scrawled

You look beautiful. I hope you save a dance for me tonight.

I gave him a smirk, crumpled the napkin, and threw it onto the table beside my plate, then turned my attention back to Sebastian.

"People come up to me all the time," my man was saying, "and tell me their opinions on various issues. When I ask what they are willing to do to correct the problem, they usually don't have an answer. Most folks seem to want someone else to fix their problems, but aren't willing to get involved personally. Some think they can't do anything because they don't have the right training or education. But my dad always told me, 'Success comes to the person who believes in himself and in God.' "

He continued on for another fifteen minutes. At the end of his speech, he received a standing ovation.

After the applause stopped, and people turned their attention to the meal that was about to be served, I saw Sebastian scanning the crowd from a corner of the room. I hoped he was looking for me. I also hoped that when he found me, it would be a moment for both of us to remember.

But before he could spot me, a swarm of women noticed him

and started buzzing around him like bees wanting honey. I considered wading through the crowd, but then I heard Eden and Dion arguing behind me.

"Why won't you dance with me?" she was whining.

"I don't want to stick around here," Dion argued. "Let's go back to the hotel. I want you."

"But I'm enjoying the ball," Eden said.

"Fine," he said. "You can enjoy it without me." Dion stormed off toward the exit. I grabbed Eden's hand to let her know I was there for her, but she jerked away and ran after her husband.

"Oh, my gosh," I heard Chyna squeal. "He's smiling at me. He likes what he sees. Sebastian Stokes is mine."

I smiled at the conceited, deluded girl. My smile broadened when I saw Chyna's excitement turn to embarrassment as Sebastian walked straight past her and toward me.

He grabbed my hands and pulled them away from my sides so he could gaze at my outfit. "Do you want to dance?" he asked.

"Why are you looking at her that way?" Chyna said, sidling up to us. "You were smiling at me."

"She's my date for the evening," Sebastian said as he led me to the dance floor.

"I enjoyed your speech," I told him as we danced to a romantic ballad.

"Thank you. I just hope some of it sticks in people's heads."

"I watched the audience as they listened to your speech. They were mesmerized. I know you'll make a great lieutenant governor and they know it, too. I believe in you, Sebastian!"

"Too bad you don't live in Georgia," he said. "At least I'd be sure to get one vote."

I smiled at his wit. But now that he really wanted the job, I wanted to help him win. He cared about the people, not the position.

"I wanted you to meet my best friend," I said, "but I think she may have left." As the song ended, I noticed a group of people waiting to talk to Sebastian. "Why don't you mingle while I see if I can find her."

"I don't want to let you go," he said, clinging to me as the next song began.

"I don't, either," I said, "but I have to share you with your adoring fans."

Sebastian reluctantly released me and started mingling. I asked around for Eden, but no one in the wedding party knew where she was. I called her cell phone, but she didn't answer. I hoped she was okay.

When the ball ended and Sebastian and I were riding back to the B&B in his limo, I told him I'd been approached by several women who said I was blessed to have Sebastian Stokes as my man.

He laughed and admitted that numerous men had told him he had excellent taste in women after seeing us on the dance floor.

He took my hand and looked deep into my eyes. "You look even better in that dress than I imagined you would. You're beautiful, smart, independent, and, best of all, God-fearing. Everything I could want in a woman."

"Are you saying I'm your woman?" I asked, then held my breath for his response.

"I want you to be," he whispered.

I knew at that moment that I loved him. And I was determined to do whatever I could to make him love me back.

The ringing of my cell phone interrupted us.

"Hello?" I said, irritated at the poor timing.

"Oh, Chris, I'm so glad I reached you," a frantic Eden cried through the receiver. "He's gone. Dion packed his stuff and left me."

"What?"

"He hit me, too."

"Where are you?" I asked her.

She told me the name of her hotel, and I asked Sebastian if we could go there. He gave the limo driver instructions. "We'll be there in ten minutes," I assured Eden. I stayed on the phone with her the whole way, trying to calm her down. Sebastian held me and listened. Just having him there was a great comfort.

When we knocked on her hotel room door, it flew open and my friend fell into my arms, sobbing. Her left eye was swollen and her right arm was bruised.

I started crying, too. Sebastian put his arms around us both and assured us that everything would be okay.

I sat on the bed and held Eden like she was my child. Sebastian made an ice pack for her eye. She cried like a baby, and I rocked and consoled her for over an hour.

"We should call the police," Sebastian said, but Eden went ballistic.

"I won't let you report this."

"Let's take her back to your room, then," he suggested. She didn't want to do that, either, but he convinced her she would be safer there.

After she took a quick shower and packed an overnight bag, Sebastian and I walked her to the limo.

When we got to the bed-and-breakfast, Sebastian told the front-desk clerk that under no circumstances was he to give out my room number to anyone. He then escorted Eden and me to my room and called room service, asking for extra ice.

After a quick meal together, Sebastian went to his room. Eden and I shared my king-sized bed. As we lay there in the dark, I asked her to tell me what had happened.

"The minute we got back to the hotel room," she said between sobs, "Dion came at me for sex. When I didn't respond with as much passion as he thought I should, he attacked me. My own husband tried to rape me. I started screaming, and someone from hotel security came and knocked on the door. That made Dion even madder. After he told the security guard that everything was fine, he grabbed my arm hard and slapped me in the face."

"Oh, Eden," I said, my heart grieving.

"When he realized what he'd done to me, he stalked out of the room. That's when I called you."

I was so angry at Dion, I felt like using some of my law-enforcement training to teach him a lesson. I wished she had at least let Sebastian call the cops.

"I don't know what I'm going to do," she whimpered. "You know, when we first got into Denver, we went hiking, and the guide showed us where the bears go to hibernate." Eden sat up and blew her nose. "I wish I could find a place where I could go and just be alone in the dark. I don't feel like I can ever face the world again."

I wanted so badly to help my girlfriend, to take her pain away. She really sounded so confused, and at the end of her rope. I could only think of one person who could help. I took her hands in mine and told her that we were going to pray. She was shocked, but she bowed her head as I began speaking to God.

I said, "Lord, I know I'm not where I need to be in my personal relationship with You, but that's another issue altogether. My friend Eden and her husband Dion need Your help. Lord, we know that marriage takes a lot of work and compromise. Eden is willing to put forth the effort, but Dion is not. Lord, he needs to be saved. We ask that You save him so that they may be able to solve their problems. Lord, please guide them through the trials and tribulations of their relationship. Please give my friend the courage to get through this."

After we finished the prayer, Eden smiled at me and looked at me with red-rimmed eyes. "I don't suppose you know of a good cave."

Chapter 9

Stone

After the trip to the ski resort, my life became drab and boring. The physical therapy for my leg was so regimented, I couldn't feel any excitement. Eden had stayed with me overnight in the bed-and-breakfast, crying most of the night. But the next morning Dion called her, and within hours they were back together, despite my objections.

Since I hadn't heard from her in two months, I decided to call to see how she was doing.

"I'm fine," she said brusquely.

"How's Dion?" I pressed.

"He's fine, too," she insisted all too quickly. I knew her well enough to know she didn't want me to continue the conversation, but I couldn't keep silent.

"How can you be doing fine with a man who abuses you?"

"Look," she said, "you're my best friend and I love you, but don't go there."

"Oh, so it's like that, is it?" I said, fuming. "I can't be concerned about my girlfriend anymore?"

She hesitated, then apologized, her voice a little softer. "He broke down and cried, Chris. And he promised never to lay his hands on me again."

"And you believe him?" I ranted. "All woman-beaters apologize and promise they'll never do it again, but they end up repeating their sick behavior. If you let him get away with it once, it'll never stop."

"Christian," she said, "Dion loves me and I accepted his apology. If we can get over this and move on, why can't you?"

"Because I think you need to leave him," I said bluntly.

"You don't understand," she said angrily, "because you don't have a husband. I'm married, Christian, and I plan to stay with my husband forever. If you can't accept that, then maybe we need to end this friendship."

I couldn't believe she'd said that. "Eden, I think we should give each other some time to cool off. We can talk more about this later, okay?"

She agreed and we ended the call. I prayed God would guide both Eden and me through this conflict.

Throughout the month of March, I accompanied Reverend Stokes and his campaign team through the northern states. Sebastian was busy with his own campaign in Georgia, so we didn't get to see each other at all, but we made it a point to call each other every Sunday and Wednesday.

Troy Evans called several times, trying to get me to go out with him again. I repeatedly declined his invitations, telling him I was in a relationship and was committed to it.

I thought Mrs. Stokes might warm up to me a little after her husband told her that Sebastian and I meant something special to each other, but she still basically ignored me. Sebastian said he figured she probably thought if she didn't make too big a deal of it, we'd end it on our own. I was determined to prove her wrong.

My first assignment after my injury was a campaign dinner in Detroit hosted by a Michigan senator who wanted to help raise money for Reverend Stokes's campaign. Security was tight since—whoever had planted that bomb was still at large.

Instead of our usual dark suits, the security agents were allowed to dress like the other guests for anonymity. I wore the black sleeveless dress Sebastian had purchased for me, my gun safely hidden on my thigh holster.

As I stood at my post near the entrance, I fought against flashbacks of the bomb blast. I felt uncontrollably anxious, constantly keeping my eye on the exit doors. When Agent Hold came up to me from behind, I almost passed out.

"Are you okay?" he asked, leading me to a chair in the corner of the foyer.

"I thought I was," I told him, holding my head in my hands.

He got on the headset and asked for water. Before I could catch my breath, Agents Ron Pitts and Kelly Regunfuss were handing me bottled water.

Taking a bottle from Kelly, I said, "I'm fine. Just having memories about the explosion, that's all."

"If you're not ready for this," Kelly said softly, "just say the word and we'll cover you."

"Yeah," Ron added. "If you need more time, I'm sure Moss will understand."

"No, really," I argued, standing. "I'm fine. But thanks, guys."

I resumed my post by the entrance door, feeling a lot better, knowing I had the support of my colleagues.

An uneventful hour later, Sebastian's mother strolled up to me. "I do hope that when you're out with my son in public you don't slouch as you're doing now." She stood tall and regal, demonstrating the posture she had in mind.

I felt like wrapping my hands around her bejeweled neck. But I didn't want to jeopardize my job, so I straightened up.

"That's better," she said. "Always stand like a lady, with your head up and shoulders back. Poise and class should show in your stance, my dear, especially when you're wearing an evening gown."

I stifled my anger at her bossy attitude and just stared straight ahead.

"Of course," she added, "it takes more than posture to be a real lady."

She strolled away to mingle with the guests, leaving me standing there with my mouth open. I wanted to call Sebastian that instant and tell him all about it, but I was on duty. Besides, there was no point in making him mad at his mom. So I gritted my teeth, did my job, and prayed that Mrs. Stokes's attitude toward me would change.

The next night we were in New York for another formal fund-raiser. I wore the same black gown, thankful the hotel had a one-hour cleaner. The event was even more crowded than the one in Detroit.

When Kelly told me it was my turn to take a break, I sighed in relief. I'd been standing quite a while and my leg was bothering me a little.

I checked my cell phone in the ladies' room, hoping Sebastian had called. I had a message, but it was from Max. I decided to ignore it.

Before I could put my phone away, it vibrated in my hand. I answered and heard Max's cheery voice.

"I'm going to change my number," I threatened in a whisper as I walked to a quiet corner.

"Then why haven't you? You must like me callin' you."

"Don't get so full of yourself. I just haven't had the time. I've been busy."

"You don't say."

When I heard footsteps enter the bathroom, I said, "I've got to go, Max. I'm working."

"Okay," he said, "but I'll call you tomorrow. I really need to talk to you."

Just to get him off the phone, I promised I'd call him the next day.

The following afternoon I was lying in my hotel bed, reading a novel, when my cell phone rang. It was Max.

"I have to see you before you leave New York," he insisted.

"Max," I said, "I'm not going to go out with you."

"I'm not asking for a date," he claimed. "Just let me take you to dinner."

"No," I responded, setting my page-turner on the nightstand.

"Please," he begged. "I've got some things I really need to talk to you about."

"Oh, really?" I said. "Like what?"

"I have some information about Eden that I think you need to know."

All of a sudden he had my attention. I repeatedly begged Max to tell me what he knew, but he refused to discuss it over the phone.

"All right," I finally said. "But this is not a date, so don't try to impress me, all right?"

"I understand," he said.

That night, I surveyed the few outfits I'd packed to determine which one would be most suitable for a friendship dinner with Max. I considered wearing blue jeans and a tee shirt, just to reinforce the message that this was not a date. But Max had made reservations at an upscale restaurant called Finesse. I chose a coral-colored, spaghetti-strap dress that ended below the knee and wrapped a silk scarf around my shoulders. The scarf, I decided, would be good for modesty as well as warmth, in case the air became too cool or Max got too hot.

After the cab dropped me off in front of Finesse, I gave the maître d' my name and he led me to a corner table, where Max was all decked out in Bill Blass.

"Dang," he said approvingly as he stood to help me into my seat. I gave him my *don't go there* look and he quickly sat down.

The maître d', promising that our waiter would be there momentarily, gave us menus. After he left, Max said, "You look really nice tonight."

"Cut the chitchat," I said abruptly. "You said you had something to tell me about Eden."

"I do," he said. "You see, she and I had a long talk recently, and she explained everything to me."

"What did she explain?" I asked. I hadn't talked to her in a month, so my curiosity was definitely piqued.

A young black waiter came to take our orders. Max told him we weren't ready yet.

Max looked into my eyes. "Eden helped me understand how much damage I did to you for not forgiving you for the abortion back in college."

The pain of that terrible time in my life made me ache, but I managed to conceal it from him. "Come on, Max. That's been over for years. Let it go."

"I should have been there for you," he said. He took a plain white envelope out of his breast pocket and handed it to me. "Here, I want you to take this."

"What is it?" I asked, looking at the envelope in my hands.

"You should not have had to pay for the procedure. I heard you had to get a job and all to pay back money you borrowed."

Max placed his hand on mine and I looked up. Our eyes met, sending me back to the day I ended our child's life. I vividly recalled wearing the white robe, lying on that cold table with my feet in the stirrups, screaming and crying on the inside but refusing to utter a single sound.

The grief I'd kept bottled up for years suddenly exploded. I pulled my hand out from under his and fled to the bathroom, not caring that everyone in the restaurant was staring.

When I burst through the ladies' room door, I felt relieved to find it was empty. I went into a stall and cried until I couldn't cry any more. All of the pain and regret that I'd felt during and after the abortion came out in a flood.

Eventually, I left the stall and stood in front of the mirror. My eyes were puffy, my makeup ruined, and my hair a mess.

I looked at the envelope still scrunched in my fist. Curious, I opened the unsealed flap. Inside I saw five one-hundred-dollar bills.

I stared at the money, knowing I couldn't accept it. After fixing my hair and makeup the best I could, I returned to our table. Two glasses of burgundy were sitting near our place settings.

I tossed the crinkled envelope onto the table between our plates. "I don't want your money," I said calmly.

"But I want you to have it," he insisted, pushing it to my side of the table.

"The abortion cost three-fifty, not five hundred."

"I know. Eden told me. Consider the extra as interest for all the pain and suffering you went through."

Did he really think that $150 could compensate for killing a baby? "And what am I supposed to do with this money now?" I snapped at him.

"You could go buy yourself a beautiful dress like the one you're wearing now." He grinned at me. I could tell he was really trying to do the right thing, even though it was totally inappropriate.

When I saw that he wasn't going to take no for an answer, I shook my head and put the envelope in my purse. What harm could it do? He wanted to repay me. Fine! We ordered our food, made small talk about our jobs, and when the food came, we ate in silence.

During dessert, Max said, "Chris, I need your help."

"I knew this was leading up to something."

"I want to get into politics."

I nearly choked on my caramel cheesecake. "You want to run for office?"

"No," he said. "I just want to be a political player. Just so I can expand my business."

"How do you plan on doing that?" I asked, amused.

"I'd like to start by donating money to Stokes's campaign. The polls show he's climbing in popularity, and I believe he stands a strong chance of getting the Democratic nomination. Maybe it's time for a black president, after all. And if that happens, I want the most powerful brother in the country to know me by name."

"And how do you think I can help?"

"I was hoping you could get me an invitation to one of those political events you're always going to and maybe introduce me to Stokes personally."

I gave him a stern look. "I don't get involved with his business. I mean, it's not like we're friends."

"Yeah, right," he said, curling his lip. "You're just screwing around with his son."

"How dare you make a comment like that!"

"I'm sorry," he said. "I didn't mean to imply anything bad."

"Well, you did! Can't you show a little class? Don't go talking down about people when they haven't done anything to you, especially when they're not even here to defend themselves." I stood and tossed my napkin onto my plate. "I am not going to hook you up with Reverend Stokes," I said. Then I stormed out of the restaurant.

Agent Hold and I stood guard outside the hotel conference room. On the other side of the open mahogany door, I could hear several political figures arguing with Reverend Stokes. The only reason I knew who they were was because we were given their names, clearances, and political affiliations in the briefing before the gathering.

"I told you," Stokes said in a voice seething with anger, "I am not on board with that."

Georgia's governor Mike James and Governor Thomas Birks from New York debated for a few minutes. Stokes's campaign manager, Jack Applebee, argued with the staff people representing the governors.

I glanced at Agent Hold and shook my head. "Can you believe they're fussing like this?"

Ryan rolled his eyes. "They might as well not be talking at all 'cause nobody's hearing a word anyone else says."

"Next thing you know," Agent Pitts joked through our headset, "we'll have to protect them from each other."

Ryan and I laughed. Suddenly, another politician came down the hall. We immediately went back to our stiff professional positions.

More bits and pieces of heated conversation filtered out from the other side of the door.

"Look, Steven," Governor James said in his distinctive southern drawl, "I told a lot of my supporters that you were going to help get casinos legalized. Why do you think you're so far ahead in the polls?"

"I'm ahead in the polls," Stokes yelled, "because the people believe in me and my stance on the issues."

"If you're telling me you won't endorse gambling after you're in office," Governor Birks said, "we've got serious problems."

"That's for sure," Governor James added. "For one thing, you can forget about that two hundred thousand dollars you were expecting me to raise to help you get ready for the Democratic convention."

"Gentlemen," Jack Applebee said, "don't be too quick to take away your support. I'm sure we can reach a mutually satisfactory agreement on this issue."

"No, Jack," Reverend Stokes said firmly. "I didn't need their money three years ago when I let James win the race for governor by pulling out my nomination, and I sure don't need it now."

"You pulled out of the race because you knew you couldn't win," Governor James hollered. "You'll never make it to the White House without our support."

After a long pause, Reverend Stokes said quietly, "I know I can't become president without calling in a lot of favors. But I am not going to say that I will support something I'm adamantly against. A casino on the river in Savannah would be almost as bad as the one you want to put in the ocean surrounding New York City."

"Why are you so against these casinos?" Governor Birks asked. "Don't you realize they provide jobs for people?"

"From what I've seen," Stokes replied, "casinos are built primarily in poverty-level, African-American communities. Those people would have to move out of their neighborhoods to make room for the casinos, and where are they supposed to go?"

"Come on, Steven," Governor Birks retorted. "The homeowners will get paid to move. Probably more money than they've saved up their whole lives. It's a win-win situation."

"No, it's not," Stokes asserted. "Those people won't get a fair price for their property and you know it. Besides, gambling can easily become an addiction, and I won't do something that will help people get hooked. If that means losing your support . . . then you do what you have to do."

I couldn't help but smile. I felt proud to protect a man who had integrity and was willing to sacrifice his dreams for his beliefs.

I heard the scraping of chairs on the hardwood floor. The

two governors and their entourage stormed toward the elevator. Stokes did not come out, so I remained at my post.

"This isn't good, sir," I heard Jack Applebee say. "You shouldn't
rattle their cages like that."

"If I want to be president," Stokes said, "I'm going to have to
show some backbone."

"But, sir, you just took our biggest contributors out of the
game. How are we supposed to win if we're broke?"

"I'll find other contributors," he said.

I could hear Jack sigh. "Forgive me, Reverend, but I don't
see a lot of people lining up to contribute to your campaign."

"You're right," Stokes said. "but that's where you come in.
You're supposed to be out there looking for people who will
support me."

"Maybe we can find a compromise with those gentlemen,"
Jack suggested.

"I disagree," Stokes said. "Unless they back me for what I stand
for, there can never be a solution." Reverend Stokes paused. "Jack,
my first campaign manager didn't understand that sometimes
you have to bend the rules, not break them. That's why I fired
him and hired you. But now you're sounding like you don't
think I can win this election without the likes of them."

"It's not that," Jack replied in a deflated tone. "I just think it
would be a lot easier with the clout and contributions those
gentlemen have to offer."

The room was silent for a long moment.

"I have to get ready for tonight," Stokes said finally. "You can
leave now."

When Jack came out of the room he looked at me like, *Can
you believe that guy?*

I maintained my stoic stance, knowing I wasn't supposed to
respond. Jack shook his head and walked past me toward the elevator.

I entered the room and saw Reverend Stokes sitting alone at
the conference table. His face looked haggard, like a dried-up
prune. Though it wasn't my place, I touched his shoulder and
said, "Sir, are you okay?"

"I hope so," he said, looking up at me with tired eyes. "But thanks for your concern."

That evening my supervisor told me that a New York fashion designer had offered to donate outfits for all of the agents to wear at Reverend Stokes's formal fund-raising affairs.

Early the next morning, I met with the designer in his studio and we picked out a full-length, red sequined gown with a slit up the back that showed a little cleavage. I also bought a pair of red, ankle-strap pumps that matched my dress. He put a rush on the order so I'd be able to have it for the banquet that night.

If the gown was supposed to help me blend in with the crowd, it failed miserably. As I stood at the entrance to the dining hall, everyone who entered complimented me on my dress. I wished Sebastian could have been there to see me.

"Dang, you're hot!" a seductive voice behind me said.

I turned around and saw Max leering at me.

"I can't talk to you right now," I told him. "I'm on duty here."

I then turned away from him and looked around the room for Reverend Stokes.

"Look," Max whispered in my ear, "all I need is an introduction to Reverend Stokes. If I come to him on my own, he's not going to think I've got the money to help him. You know me. You can tell him I'm on the level. Come on, Chris. Please?"

Before I could answer, Agent Moss called me on the headset. "I need you to report to me immediately."

"I have to go now," I said to Max. I walked away and left him standing there.

"Yes, sir?" I said as I approached my supervisor.

"Agent Sawyer just called in. He's not feeling well, so your assignment has changed. I need you near the protectee."

I took a deep breath. Standing guard at the front door was much less stressful than directly guarding the candidate. Last time I'd done that, I'd almost gotten myself, and my protectee, killed. But I was determined to get back to full duty as quickly as possible, and apparently Agent Moss felt I was ready.

I moved toward Cool Falcon, watching everybody shaking

his hand, chatting with him, walking around him. I had to consider everyone a potential threat. Since no one had been apprehended yet for the explosion, the bomber could be among today's gathering.

When Jack Applebee came by, Reverend Stokes motioned to him and excused himself from the crowd around him. I followed the two men to a quiet alcove.

"We need to get more funds," Reverend Stokes said, "to replace those two governors who pulled out on me today. Have you found any new money connections here tonight?"

"Sir," I said, easing into his view, "I don't mean to be presumptuous, but a college friend of mine is the vice president at a bank here in New York, and he told me he'd like to contribute to your campaign. He says he knows some other folks who want to donate as well. I don't know how much money he's talking about, but he is here this evening. May I introduce you to him?"

Reverend Stokes's face lit up. "That's what I like. A guard who is beautiful, dependable, and comes through in hard times. Yes, by all means, go get this young man."

"Sir, I've been assigned as your personal bodyguard for this evening, so I can't leave your side. But I'm sure my friend will find his way to us."

"I'll count on that," Reverend Stokes said. "And thank you. Even if he only gives five dollars, that's five dollars more than we have now."

I resumed my post a few steps to his left and continued surveying the surroundings.

Back when I was working behind my desk as an FBI agent, I'd always thought about the glamour and intrigue of politics, but never realized how dangerous and nerve-wracking it was. The weight of the world on your shoulders. Your personal life on hold because you're constantly on the job. I now realized that politics was not the life for me.

At eight o'clock, dinner was served. Reverend Stokes sat at a large, rectangular table while waiters served what looked like very dry chicken.

When I spotted Max walking toward the rest room, I called Agent Moss on my headset and asked for a break. As soon as Agent Hold came to take my place, I hurried into the hallway, hoping to catch him.

I found him standing near the front entrance, talking to three dark-haired men. They looked a lot like the well-dressed criminals I'd seen in movies and on television.

One of the men poked Max in the side and pointed at me. When Max turned and saw me, his face turned bright red.

Agent Pitts came up behind me. "You think we need to get those guys out of here? They could be a potential risk—something about them doesn't look right to me. How'd they get past security, anyway?"

"I don't know, but those men are cool," I said. "That's an old friend of mine. I'm sure the guys he's with are fine."

"Oh. Well, that's different. Guess I'll go back to hallway patrol, then."

After Pitts left, Max sidled up to me. "Did your buddy want to throw me out?"

I pointed to the shifty-looking men. "Who are those guys?"

"Just some of my colleagues at the bank. They want to invest in Stokes's campaign, too." Max winked at his friends, then turned back to me. "So, can you hook me up?"

"Actually, Reverend Stokes is extremely interested in meeting you. After dinner, when you go through the receiving line, I'll introduce you."

"Great." Max rubbed his hands together like an eager child.

True to my word, when the meal ended, I introduced Max Cross and his friends to Reverend Stokes, who appeared intrigued with the group. When one of the men said he and his associates had come with cash, the candidate's face registered surprise, then joy. Reverend Stokes quickly told Jack Applebee to meet with them to discuss their contribution.

I smiled. It felt good to help the man I'd begun to admire.

When I got back to my hotel room, I checked for messages, but had none. I began to wonder about Sebastian. I hadn't heard from him in a week. Perhaps he thought I was too loose a woman.

I breathed a deep sigh of relief when I walked through the door of my apartment in D.C. I'd been away from it for far too long. Kicking off my shoes, I smiled at the cheerful sight of the artificial flowers that decorated my place. With my schedule, live plants would never survive.

Though I had checked my answering machine daily from the road, the digital display on my home phone indicated I had twenty-four messages. My heart leapt when I thought they might be from Sebastian. But he had my pager number and my cell phone number, and I always left my hotel numbers on his machine. So I didn't figure he would leave me messages at home.

The first seventeen calls were from Troy. The messages said he desperately needed to talk to me. I rolled my eyes. Couldn't he get the hint that I didn't want to go out with him?

My mom had called, saying she was worried about my sister. Message nineteen was from Eden and the next two were my mom again. Then Max, thanking me for the introduction to Reverend Stokes.

The last four messages were from Troy. His voice sounded increasingly desperate, the last one saying that if he didn't get in touch with me soon there might be some serious consequences. I called him at home, but got his answering machine.

"I'm back in town," I said. "I'll try your cell."

As I dialed his cell phone number, I told myself that no matter what he said, I was not going to let him back into my life.

When he answered, I set him straight right off. "Troy, I don't know what story you've concocted for us to get back together this time, but—"

"It's cute that you're flattering yourself, but I really do need to talk to you about something important, and it's not about the two of us. It concerns the case I was working on before you left our office."

"The high-school drug thing?"

"Yeah, I just wanted to tell you we're about to do a big bust on a guy who graduated from C. J. Douglas High about four years ago."

"That's my old school. And my sister is a junior there now."

"I know. A big drug dealer named Stone is running the school now."

Mom's frantic messages about my sister rushed to my mind. *Lord,* I thought, *what was my sister into?*

"We found out where Stone's base operation is located, and we're getting ready to reel him in. I'm casing the place right now."

"Does this have something to do with my sister?"

"It might. About a month ago I saw a girl who looked like Crystal hanging out with this guy. Last week I confirmed it was definitely your sister."

"What are you telling me?" I said, collapsing onto the bed.

"Crystal could go to jail if somebody doesn't intervene. You know, I could lose my job over this, but your sister's a good kid. I need you to get her away from Stone tonight."

"Do you know where she is?"

"Stone dropped her off at Queenie's Beauty Salon on Twenty-third Street about a half hour ago."

"All right, I'll go down there and tell her not to hang around with that guy anymore."

"What? No, Chris, you know better than that. The Secret Service done erased the way we operate from that FBI brain of yours. You know better than that. You gotta do it on the low."

"But that's my sister!"

"I understand, but if she knows he's in trouble, she'll probably tip him off and the whole investigation will be blown. I'm trusting you to handle this discreetly."

"What should I do?"

"Pick her up. Take her somewhere to eat. If she mentions Stone, try to get her to talk about him. I think they've got plans to get out of the country soon."

"Crystal's only fifteen. Surely they wouldn't try to take her with them."

"Chris, your sister's in this up to her ears, but if she's not there when the big bust goes through, I'm sure we can work out some kind of deal. Hey, I've gotta go. Stone's on the move again."

"Thanks for looking out."

"Please," he said, "I owe you much more than this."

"Stop feeling that way. I did my job," I said, hoping to get him to stop feeling like he owed me. "Will you call me and let me know what happens?"

"Definitely."

The line went dead. I grabbed my keys and headed out the door. On the way to the beauty salon, I called my mom.

"Christian, I haven't seen your sister in the last five days. Her principal says she hasn't been in school. I know she's been home, because every day when I get back from work there's a note on the counter that says, *Don't worry, Mom.*' How am I not supposed to worry? I'm sure she's doing something she's not supposed to."

Revealing to my mom what Troy had told me undoubtedly violated my promise to be discreet, but I couldn't just keep quiet. This was my mother's baby. I had to tell her enough to keep her from having a heart attack. "Mom, I think I know where she is."

"You do? Then come pick me up so we can go get her together."

"I think it would be better if I tracked her down alone. I'll call you as soon as I find her."

"Well, if you don't bring her back tonight, I'm gonna call the police."

"All right, Mom. I've got to go now."

"Thanks for handling this, baby."

As I sped down the road, I wanted to kick myself for getting so busy that I hadn't been checking in on my sister like I used to. With Mom working nights, Crystal didn't have enough parental supervision, so I'd always tried to fill in the gap. But my job had kept me away and busy. So my little sister had turned to a drug dealer for comfort and security. The thought of that made my stomach boil.

When I met Stone months back, I knew he was no good. However, I never dreamed he was a criminal. I wished I would have called the cops on him for rape. He's four years older than Crystal and taking her out of the country . . . this can't happen.

I saw three hair salons on Twenty-third Street, but only one that looked like it specialized in the kind of bright-colored hair and crazy hairdos my sister had gotten into lately. Then I saw a fluorescent sign with QUEENIE'S on it and I knew I had the right place. I found a parking spot right outside the tinted glass door.

When I walked inside, I saw my sister sitting in one of the loud orange chairs. Behind her a tall, skinny stylist was spraying oil sheen on her hair. Crystal was wearing a super-tight outfit that made her breasts look bigger than mine.

"Hey, sis!" she called out when she saw me. "Nay-Nay, this is my big sister."

"Is she the one that is an FBI agent?" her stylist, Nay-Nay, asked, popping her gum.

"Yep, but now she's doing this job protecting the president." Crystal beamed with pride. "I told her all about you," she explained to me.

"Nice to meet you, Nay-Nay, but I don't protect the president, yet—I've just got the back of a person hoping to be elected president," I said, never wanting to misrepresent myself.

"You still the woman, carrying a piece and all," Nay-Nay said as she reached out to give me dap.

"Whatcha doin' here?" Crystal asked.

"I've got a big surprise for you," I said, with what I hoped was an enticing grin.

"What is it? I don't need no money. You know my man's got a job."

"It's not money." I grabbed her hand.

"Wait," Nay-Nay whined. "I ain't finished."

"I'll bring her back," I promised. "Besides, her hair looks perfect."

"It does?" Crystal checked herself out in the mirror.

"It can't get any better than that," I lied. "Now, come on."

As we walked out of the salon, Nay-Nay hollered, "What you want me to tell your man when he comes back?"

"Tell him I'll be right back," Crystal called as I dragged her to my car.

"I don't want him breakin' no more mirrors like he did that time when he saw a guy talking to you."

"Tell him I'm with my sister," Crystal instructed as I shoved her into the passenger seat.

The worry in my sister's voice over what her guy would think frightened me. I didn't know how I was going to do it, but whatever it took, I was determined to get her away from Stone.

Chapter 10

Rocky

As I pulled out of the parking spot in front of the beauty shop, the phone in my sister's Gucci purse started ringing.

"When did you get a cell phone?" I asked, also wondering where she'd gotten the money to pay for that expensive pocket-book and the top-end hair job.

"My man gave it to me," Crystal bragged, pulling out a tiny silver phone and flipping it open. The thought of my little sister running around with a hood rat like Stone made my flesh crawl.

"Hey, baby," she purred. "I'm glad you called."

I took a long look at my sister as she gabbed on the phone. She looked like she belonged in a hip-hop video, with her fitted clothes and wild hairdo and tiny waistline. It made me sick to think of what her life was really like.

Crystal turned her head away. I knew she was saying something she didn't want me to hear. I felt like snatching the phone out of her hand and throwing it out the window. But if she said something that might clue me in to Stone's plans, maybe I could find a way to get that information to Troy.

"Tonight?" she said into the phone.

I gulped. I had to stop her from getting together with that guy tonight without tipping her off about why. If Stone got sus-picious he might deviate from the plan, which would ruin

Troy's bust. "Tell him your big sister wants you to hang out with her," I suggested, hoping she'd go for it easily.

She held her hand over the phone. "But my man's already got plans for us tonight."

"Let me talk to him," I said, reaching for the phone.

"No!" She pulled away from me. "Get out of my business." She spoke into the phone again. "That was my sister," she told Stone. "I don't know what she wants. She said she's got some big surprise for me." Crystal gave me a curious look. "You want to talk to her?"

I yanked the phone out of her hand. "Listen, man," I said, trying to sound cool, "Crystal tells me she's all hung up on you. But I haven't seen my sister in a long time. How about I take her out and get her all cute for you, huh?"

"She just got her hair and nails done," a gruff, deep voice said. "I know 'cause I paid for it."

"Well, yeah, but I wanted to take her to get a massage. Get her body all silky and sweet-smelling. You know what I'm sayin'?"

Crystal stared at me like she thought I'd gone crazy.

"Crystal told me her big sister ain't down with no sexual stuff."

"Hey, man, I ain't her mama. What she does is her own business."

"Oh, yeah?" he said, his voice suddenly smooth. "Then maybe you can get yourself one of them massages, too, and come have some fun with us tonight."

My initial instinct was to curse him out, but I restrained myself. "You got it," I said seductively. Crystal glared at me, obviously wondering what in the world we were talking about.

"All right, then," Stone said. "Go on and get yourself and my girl all dolled up for me. I got some big money coming my way today, so I can take you both out somewhere real special."

"It's a date. Where should we meet you?"

Stone gave me directions to a club called Playa's. I hung up and handed the phone to Crystal. She stared at me, speechless. I drove on toward the spa, praying they would be able to fit us in without an appointment.

When she finally got over being irritated that I was accompanying her on her date, Crystal started talking about her relationship with Stone. She went into far more detail than I felt comfortable hearing, but I pretended to be interested to encourage her to open up to me.

"One of my friends from school introduced me to him," she explained. "I told him I wanted to work the streets for him at night, but he told me he wanted to keep me for himself." She said it like it was a big deal, like she'd won a big prize. Like this scum Stone was a movie star or something.

"He has four gold teeth in the front. He's an inch shorter than me, and he's got dreads. One night he let me wash them for him. He's so cute!"

I clenched the steering wheel and bit my tongue. How could my sister be so blind? We'd both grown up with parents who spent most of their time at work and didn't have much left over for their daughters. Maybe if I'd focused more on Crystal and less on climbing the ladder in the Agency and trying to get a man for myself, I could have made a difference in her life. But I couldn't go back—I had to try to move forward.

Lord, I prayed, *help me get my sister out of this situation. I want to tell her about You and make sure she gets it. 'Cause You're the one she needs, not this jerk.*

Thank You, Lord, I prayed as the masseuse rubbed my shoulders and I saw a peaceful smile on my sister's face as she lay on the table beside me, getting an oil treatment. She looked so innocent. I had successfully kept her away from Stone during the drug deal.

After our massages, I suggested we get a bite to eat, hoping to prolong our time together.

"I don't know," she said. "My baby's planning to take me someplace special for dinner. Besides, you've already done enough for me. That massage was awesome!"

"Hey, I've got an idea," I said. "Why don't we go to Akido's for dinner. I know how much you love Japanese food."

"That does sound great," she said, then bit her lower lip. "Let me just call Stone and make sure it's okay."

"What you gotta check with him for?" I said as I pulled open my car door. "Can't you make your own decision about having a meal with your big sister?"

She got into the passenger side and started rummaging through her purse for her cell phone. "I just gotta check in, that's all. You know what I mean?"

"No, I don't," I said firmly. "That's totally unacceptable, Crystal, and you should know better. Don't you remember anything I told you about domestic violence? I'm sure you remember Mama's boyfriend, Mr. Smith. The one that came to the house all drunk and knocked her around a couple of times."

She stared at the closed phone in her hands. "We kept wondering when we would be next," she said softly.

"Uh-huh. And you and I both vowed that we would never go through anything like that."

"But Stone ain't slapped me around hard or nothing. He just likes to know where I'm at, that's all." She opened her phone, and I snatched it away from her.

Her eyes grew wild. "Give that back! I need to call Stone."

"No." I shoved her cell phone into my purse. At the same time, I furtively pressed the Record button on the handheld tape recorder I always carried in my purse.

"That creep shouldn't be sleeping with you. You're only fifteen. That's child molestation, girl!"

Her eyes grew cold. "I knew this was too good to be true. You acted like it was okay that I was dating him."

"Where do you think he gets all his money, Crystal?" I said. "Have you thought about that?"

"I know what he does," she admitted. "I know he makes drugs. So what? Half of America is doing the same thing. It's called survival."

"Have you seen him do it?"

"Sure," she said with a shrug. "He's got five boys that work for him at this warehouse he owns."

"And he's a pimp, too, huh? That must bring in some good cash."

"He gets ninety percent of whatever the girls make. Most of them are my age or younger. One's in middle school."

"How many girls does he have?" I asked, feeling more revolted by the minute.

"I think about fifteen."

"Do you even know what his real name is?"

"Shavaric Dollar."

"No wonder he calls himself Stone."

"What's with all the questions? He in trouble or somethin'?" she joked sarcastically.

"Ha ha," I downplayed her phony question. "I'm just trying to see how well you know this guy."

"Well, I'm through being grilled about him. Take me home."

"I thought you wanted to go to Akido's," I said.

"I changed my mind."

I didn't know what else I could say to get her to stay with me. So I decided to tell her the truth. "Crystal, the FBI has been investigating Stone. The cops are busting his warehouse tonight. He's probably on his way to jail right now."

"They got my baby?" she screamed. "How did you find out?"

Before I could answer, my cell phone rang. It was Troy.

"We got him," he announced. "You still with your sister?"

"Yeah," I said, watching her shoot arrows of hate at me with her eyes.

"Did you get any information out of her?"

I pulled the tape recorder out of my purse. It was still running. "Sure did."

"You taped me?" Crystal shrieked.

I gave her an apologetic shrug. "We're on our way to the station," I said into the phone. "She'll talk."

"That's what you think," she grumbled, her voice strained.

"That's what I know," I said as I hung up the phone.

I drove straight to the precinct, with Crystal screaming at me the whole way.

Mom was waiting there with two FBI agents when we arrived.

One was my supervisor, Agent Hunter. With a worn-out smile, he headed up to me.

"Good to see you again, Ware,"

"You, too, sir. Thanks for being here with my mom and for even calling her a while back and telling her about my accident."

"Your life is never dull," he said. "We miss you in the office, but with your heroics, Secret Service might try to keep you."

"You know that saying about the grass isn't always greener," I said as he nodded and chuckled. "You don't have to worry about that. I'll be back."

"Well, good," he said as he pointed over to my mom and sister. "Go take care of that."

"Yes, sir."

"Crystal, honey, are you all right?" my mom asked, hugging my sister.

Crystal didn't even return the hug. "I ain't saying nothin' to nobody," she declared.

Our mother pulled out of the hug and glared at her teenage daughter. "Oh, you're gonna talk, little girl. You're gonna talk real good." Mama grasped Crystal's slender arm and dragged her into one of the empty interrogation rooms.

Since I was an FBI agent, I was allowed to watch my sister's interrogation from behind the two-way mirror. She told them everything she knew, which thankfully turned out not to be that much. I didn't even have to play the tape. Fortunately, the agent realized she'd been brainwashed, so he didn't take her into custody, and since Stone hadn't clued her in on his goings-on, Crystal might not have to testify.

When they emerged from the interrogation room, my mother had a look of satisfaction on her face. Crystal looked scared out of her wits. My little sister shot me a hateful glare. "Mom, will you take me home now?" she said without taking her eyes off me.

"Of course, baby," Mom said.

"I will never speak to you again for as long as I live," she cried. Then she turned around and stormed out of the precinct.

I swallowed hard, trying to keep from crying. I knew what I'd done was for her own good. One day she'd thank me.

Troy came up and threw his arms around me. "You did the right thing," he assured me. "If she'd been there tonight, she would have been arrested for sure. Now it looks as if she wasn't involved at all."

"Thanks," I told him as tears escaped down my cheeks. "Thanks for saving my sister."

Troy grabbed my hand and led me into the interrogation room where my mom had convinced my sister to talk. "Chris," he said as we sat at the table, "I care for you. Being away from you has made me realize that we had something really special. I thought I wanted to be single forever, and the whole baby thing really scared me. But now I wish you were carrying my child so I'd say the right things."

"Oh, really?" I said. "And what would you say now?"

"That I want to have a family with you," he said without hesitation. "I see kids all the time who are messed up because they don't have a loving home and parents who take care of them." He took my hand. "I want to change that. I know we can't just jump right into marriage or anything. But do you think we could start dating again?"

I immediately thought about Sebastian. I hadn't heard from him in weeks and I had no idea where we stood with each other. But Sebastian wasn't the real issue.

Troy didn't know the Lord. He was a good man, and I was glad he was finally getting some decent values. But my relationship with God had been growing, and I knew I couldn't be with someone who didn't share my faith.

I took my hand out of his. "I've missed you, too, Troy. But—"

"Don't turn me down," he said.

"I'm sorry," I said, wiping a tear from my cheek. "I appreciate what you did for my sister, and it's great that you want to start a loving, caring family. But I don't want to date you again."

He lowered his head into his hands and just sat there for a while.

"I don't want to let you out of my life, either," I assured him. "I'd like us to be friends."

"I understand," he said, looking up. "Go on home and be with your sister. She really needs you."

He kissed my forehead and walked away.

As he was walking away, I called his name. He turned around and came back to me and I asked, "Troy, do you have a relationship with God?

"I haven't really thought of God in a while, Christian. Why?"

"Well, lately I've been working on getting closer to Him and trying to live the way He wants me to. I guess I wanted to know how you felt about Him. Troy, you're a good man and would benefit greatly from knowing Him."

He stood there for a moment and just looked at me; then he said good-bye and walked away without answering.

As I watched him leave, I thanked God for working in my life.

Lord, I can't believe I turned down a gorgeous guy just because I want to be with You for eternity. I shook my head as I headed for the exit. *My life sure is bumpy right now, but I'm glad to see You're straightening it out.*

The Democratic Convention was only a month away, and Reverend Stokes's campaign had escalated. He accepted every single invitation he received for a speaking engagement, no matter how big or small. I was ordered to return to Atlanta immediately.

Besides the busy schedule, two things made me apprehensive about going to the Peach State. It had only been a couple of weeks since Crystal had given the cops all the information she had on the guy she loved. On my nights off I stayed with her at Mom's house. The poor thing cried herself to sleep every night. Leaving her at such an unstable time was extremely unsettling.

And I still hadn't heard from Sebastian. Not even a message on my answering machine. I had called him a few times because

dealing with my sister had gotten me down and I needed someone to talk to. He never answered my calls. I thought about
leaving him a message saying, "It's over," but I never got the
courage.

Troy had continued reaching out to me, but I didn't want to
turn to him. So I brought all my fears and concerns to God instead, and He had given me peace.

I knew I couldn't avoid running into Sebastian, because I
would be stationed at his parents' house. Maybe it would be
better to confront him face-to-face and tell him it just wasn't
going to work out between us.

I was a strong woman. I'd never had to beg for a man's attention, and I never had trouble getting a boyfriend. My problem was keeping one. Men didn't want to settle down with me.
Sure, Troy had sounded interested in marrying me, but I knew
in my heart that if I tried to take him up on his offer, he'd back
down.

Maybe Sebastian's mom was right. Maybe he would never
think of me as anything more than a pretty bodyguard.

On my first day back in Atlanta, I stood at my post just inside
the entrance to the Stokes mansion. Part of me wanted Sebastian
to walk through the door; another part hoped I would never
have to see him again.

That night, as I was doing surveillance in the van, I saw a
limo pull into the driveway. I stopped breathing for a second. I
wanted to open the van door and run into his arms and say,
"Baby, have you missed me as much as I've missed you?" But I
was on duty.

The limo driver got out, popped up an umbrella, and opened
the back door. Sebastian emerged, looking just as handsome as
ever. He took the umbrella from the driver, then turned back
to the car, bent down, and held out his hand. I saw a pair of
shapely legs. Even through the black hose, I could tell the legs
were white!

I blinked, wondering if the heavy rain was clouding my per-
ception. I grabbed the binoculars and focused in. A tall, slen-

der blonde stood beside Sebastian, her long, straight hair blowing in the wind. He put his arm around her waist and they hurried inside the house.

I dropped the binoculars on my foot. Stifling a squeal, I picked them up and tossed them onto the seat beside me. "I gotta go to the bathroom," I said to Agent Hold.

I opened the van door and dashed across the dark, two-lane road, squeezing through the front door right behind Sebastian. His mom shut it before any more rain got into her home.

I caught a glimpse of my reflection in the full-length foyer mirror and almost didn't recognize myself. My eyeliner had smudged so badly, it looked like I had a black eye. My black pants, black blazer, and white shirt were drenched. My hair hung loose around my face, dripping water. A small puddle was forming at my feet.

I looked up at Sebastian, hoping my love for him would show through my rumpled appearance, and that his feelings for me would melt the distance between us.

"Christian," he said, giving me a warm smile. The girl beside him glared at the back of his head.

Instead of replying, I walked down the hallway to the bathroom.

God, I thought, *it's not supposed to be like this.* I stared at my sorry reflection in the gilt-edged mirror above the marble sink. *I love this man, but now he's with another woman. If things can't work out between us, You've got to help me forget him!*

I stood in the bathroom for several minutes, trying to fix my hair and makeup so I wouldn't look so bad. Although I was mad at Sebastian, I kept hoping to hear a knock on the door, and my man's voice saying, "Hey, baby, I'm sorry. Let me explain." It never happened.

After several deep breaths, I finally managed to control my anger. I twisted my shirttail over the sink and got out as much water as I could before tucking it back in. After pressing my palms against my pant legs to get out some of the wrinkles, running a brush through my tangled hair, and slopping on some foundation and mascara, I stood up straight and took another deep breath. Then, after two long minutes, I opened the door, ready to return to my post.

Before I got two steps down the hallway, Sebastian stopped me.

"Get out of my way," I said as the anger began to erupt again.

He reached up and gently touched my chin. His nearness almost made me melt into his arms.

He lifted my face, and I looked into his beautiful eyes. Before I could get lost in their depths, I pulled back and gave him a piece of my mind. "What are you doing? You think you can just walk up to me after all this time and I'll just fall for you all over again? I'm here to do a job, not to socialize with you. Now, let me go and get back to your date."

Sebastian gripped my waist, stopping my escape. "Yes, Jenny is my date. But just for this evening. We went to Harvard together. She's helping me with my campaign."

"Why haven't you called me?" I demanded.

"I just got back from South Africa."

"What?"

"I went over there to take some medicine, food, and supplies to a village my church has been supporting for years. I got so caught up helping the people there, I caught meningitis. I apologize for not calling you, but I was pretty out of it."

"You really expect me to believe that?" I seethed. "I've been with your dad off and on for the last month and a half, and nobody told me you were sick in South Africa. And you couldn't have called me when you got well enough to fly home? Now you've got a white chick on your arm? I don't buy it." I pushed him off to the side and stormed back out to the van.

When I got in, drenched again, I got a hearty chewing-out from my supervisor.

"Where have you been, Agent Ware?" he barked from the front seat. "You can't leave your post like that. It wasn't your turn to take a break. Your behavior was completely unprofessional. I know you're only temping for us, but if this neglect continues I will be forced to relieve you of your duties."

"Yes, sir," I said. His tirade had little effect on me. There wasn't anything he could say that would make me feel worse than I already did.

At that moment my career didn't seem very important, but I sucked it up and said the right things. I went back to doing my job, scoping out the house I desperately wanted to be in. But I was on the outside looking in, and that was probably the way it would stay.

The next night there was a big campaign party at the Stokes estate. The rain had stopped, and the night sky held only a trace of wispy white clouds.

The grounds were beautifully decorated with bright flowers and six large canvas tents. Each tent was filled with a different country's unique artifacts and food. I didn't have to wear my uniform, but I decided not to wear the black gown Sebastian had bought me. Instead I'd gone out and bought myself a sexy cocktail dress.

The royal blue satin covered only one of my shoulders, fit tightly to my waist, then draped outward. I'd had my nails done in a squared American manicure and pulled my hair up into a sweeping style that hid my earpiece. I wanted Sebastian to see what he was missing.

But when I saw him, my heart broke again. He was with a different girl this time—Penelope, the one from Christmas, the "friend of the family." She looked perky and cute, and it made me sick just looking at her. I backed up and blended into the crowd.

It was a grand party. Political notables, movie stars, and three gospel performers all mingled, chatted, and laughed together. I wandered about from one spot to another, shadowing my protectee. I spotted Sebastian far too often, always having fun. He certainly didn't seem to be looking around for me.

I went to the bar and ordered a soda. As the bartender handed me the glass, a warm hand touched my waist and rubbed it sensually. My instinct was to splash my drink into the face of whoever was touching me. But to my relief, when I turned around, I saw Max grinning from ear to ear.

"Hey, baby," he cooed.

I gave him a blank stare. "What are you doing here?"

He pointed to a group of guys gathered around the Jamaican table. They were the same friends I'd seen with him in New York.

"Thanks to your introduction, we're really in with our next president," Max said as he popped some chicken seasoned with West Indian spices in his mouth.

I grinned. "So you think Reverend Stokes is going to win."

"Oh, yeah," he said with confidence. "Who do you think paid for this whole shebang?" He spread his arms, almost spilling his glass of wine.

"You helped pay for this party?" I asked, wondering if he was bragging or just drunk.

"You bet. My little group paid for the whole thing. Two mill."

I whistled. "That's a lot of money. Is it all legal?"

He smiled. "Don't you worry about that." He leaned over and started to give me a big kiss on my lips, but I pulled away when I realized what he was doing.

"What do you think you're doing? I'm working here, chump."

"I'm sorry," he said, wiping his slobbery lips. "You look so good I forgot you're here in a professional capacity."

"Agent Ware," Agent Moss called through my earpiece. "Cool Falcon has left your vicinity. Do you think you can stop talking to guests long enough to do your job?"

"I gotta go," I said to Max.

Before I could walk away, he grabbed my hand. "I want to get together."

I pulled my hand free, then took off to find Reverend Stokes. He was usually easy to pick out in a crowd, because people were always gathered around him, trying to shake his hand and push their political agendas. But there were so many celebrities at this party, there were little groups of fans all over the place.

I couldn't get on the radio and say, "Hey, guys, where's the man we're supposed to be watching?" That would make me look incompetent. I searched everywhere, but couldn't find

Reverend Stokes. I did, however, find his son. I strode up to Sebastian.

Before I could ask him about his father's whereabouts, he said, "So, I guess I'm not the only one who's been dating other people."

"What?" I said.

"I saw that man kiss you."

I rolled my eyes at him. "Look, I don't have time to entertain childish insecurity. I need to—"

"I know I got you all confused," he interrupted, "but I really want to get together with you. We need to talk so I can explain. I've . . . I've missed you."

"Well, you've got a great way of showing it," I countered. "Now, I've got work to do. And I'll start by asking if you know where your father is." He made me so mad I didn't even want to ask him where his father was, yet that was my duty. Sebastian silently pointed across the way. I quickly bowed my head to him as a way of saying thanks. Then, I left him standing there in a daze.

As I crossed the courtyard, I looked up at the beautiful Georgia sky and thanked the Lord for giving me back my integrity.

After praying that prayer, I spotted Cool Falcon on the other side of the courtyard. I eased up behind my protectee as if I'd never left his side. Once again God was blessing me.

The party was still going strong at two A.M. No one seemed to want to go home. The evening just got livelier, which meant my job was getting tougher. When people consumed alcohol, they often became impossible to control.

One guy spilled his drink on the Reverend Stokes, and when he lunged forward I had to jump in front of my protectee to make sure it wasn't a ploy to stab him. Two of my colleagues escorted the drunken man to the bar and made him drink some coffee.

A few minutes later, I heard a series of pops. I stood by the protectee, but through my earpiece I could hear several agents running toward the pool area.

"False alarm," I heard the detail supervisor announce. "Just folks playing with firecrackers. Everybody go back to your post."

We need to end this party, I thought. *It's getting dangerous.* But that wasn't my call to make.

When the agents left the front gate to investigate the rowdy disturbance, the paparazzi slipped through. Dozens of tabloid reporters swarmed in and started interviewing guests.

I quickly led Reverend Stokes into the house. As we neared the door, I heard one reporter say to another, "This is quite a spread. Wonder how the good reverend's paying for it."

My colleagues tried to clear out the unwelcome guests, but they weren't having much luck. All of a sudden several reporters started surrounding Max and his associates.

"What's going on?" I heard one say to another as they rushed to join the throng.

"Those guys are criminals," the other informed him. "Organized crime money funded this party!"

Reverend Stokes's face turned pale.

"The mob?" Jack Applebee, Stokes's campaign manager, looked like he was about to choke. "Is that true?"

Press Secretary Dan Greenville put his arms on the shoulders of Jack Applebee and Reverend Stokes and said, "Let's not lose our heads here. You know how those magazines distort the truth. We need to clear everyone out and shut down the party as quickly as possible."

"Is it true?" Reverend Stokes asked his men. "Is my campaign being funded illegally?"

"We're . . . not completely sure," Jack stated. "We did a preliminary background check on those guys, but nothing extensive. You seemed pretty comfortable with them, so we didn't go any further."

"I'll go talk to those men myself." Reverend Stokes took a step in Max's direction, but Dan Greenville stopped him.

"Sir, go inside. We'll take care of this. We'll find out exactly who these men are and what their motives were for giving you so much money."

What had Max gotten me into? The main reason no one checked his guys was that they came highly recommended by me, one of the agents on the detail. Clearing people and checking them out carefully was a part of this job.

When we got the candidate safely inside, the legitimate press started calling. Everyone wanted to know why Reverend Stokes was accepting money from the Bambino crime family from New York.

"We are not in a position at this time to answer those questions," Applebee and Greenville told all the callers. "A full statement will be given at dawn tomorrow."

As soon as my shift ended and I was cleared to leave, I went looking for Max.

Several guests were standing at the end of the driveway, waiting for their limos. I searched carefully and finally found Max standing beside a white stretch limo with his Italian-looking friends. "I've been looking for you," I said in a frantic tone.

Max shook his head and said, "This party's getting crazy, isn't it?"

"Max, I'm nervous," I said, looking around to make sure none of my fellow agents saw me with him. "Can you meet me in the lobby of my hotel in thirty minutes? I'm at the Ritz downtown."

"It's four o'clock in the morning," he whined.

"I know, but this is important."

"All right. Calm down. Everything's going to be fine." He looked over his shoulder at his friends.

"Thirty minutes," I repeated. "Don't be late." I heard him laughing with his buddies as I headed for the nearest exit.

Agent Moss met me at the gate. "You're keeping some interesting company lately."

"Just saying hi to a college friend. That's not a crime, is it, sir?" I didn't mean to sound nasty, but it was four in the morning and I was extremely stressed. Still, I should have known better than to taunt my supervisor.

"Agent Ware, I saw you conversing with a known crime family."

"Sir, only the black gentleman I was speaking to is a friend of mine. I don't even know those other guys."

"One of the first things you learned in basic training was to maintain a proper image. Being seen with the wrong people isn't good for the Agency. Or for you."

"Yes, sir," I said meekly. "Can I go now?"

He rubbed his hands together. "Ware, I've already written you up for your behavior over the last couple of days, and I've tolerated you interacting on a personal level with the protectee's family. Because you've proven yourself a capable Secret Service agent by saving Reverend Stokes's life, I've looked the other way about you leaving your post, losing your protectee, and showing up late to work. You don't have any more chances. One more screw-up, and you're out of here—understand?"

"Yes, sir, I understand," I said, struggling to maintain my composure.

I climbed into the van and rode with my unit back to the hotel. No one asked what Moss had talked to me about, and I didn't offer the information.

The other agents went to their rooms, but I took a chair in an isolated corner of the lobby facing the double glass doors. There was very little movement in or out of the hotel at that hour. I desperately wanted to find out the status back at campaign headquarters, but could think of only one person who might know, and be willing to tell me. I called Sebastian.

"Things were so wild when I left," I explained, "I wanted to touch base and see how everything was going."

"The phones are still going crazy, but my dad's got good people to put out fires like this. So there's nothing to really worry about."

I wanted to shout, *But this might be my fault!* How could I tell the man I loved that I might have ruined his father's chance at the presidency?

I saw Max coming through the door and waved at him. "I'll let you go. You sound pretty busy."

"I'll call you tomorrow, okay?"

"I'd like that," I said softly.

" 'Bye." He spoke hesitantly, as if he didn't want to get off the phone any more than I did.

"Good night," I said, hanging up as Max approached.

"Hey, was that your boyfriend?" Max teased.

"Don't worry about who that was," I attacked angrily, grateful that the hotel lobby was empty so I could lay into him. "What have you gotten me into, Max?"

"Don't make a mountain out of a molehill, Chris. We had an agreement."

"What kind of agreement?"

He looked down at his hands. "All I know is that Skip Bambino has some things he wants Stokes to propose to Congress if he gets elected. Supposedly, Stokes agreed. Then all of a sudden tonight he changes his mind and says he's not going to do it. Well, Skip already invested a lot of money in the good reverend's campaign, so now the Bambino family is putting a little heat on to make him honor their agreement."

"What does this guy want Stokes to propose?"

Max shuffled his feet. "They want to divert some of the funds that are being used in the war on drugs."

"Max, how do you know this Skip Bambino?"

"He's the president of the bank where I work."

"Are you helping him launder money?"

"No," he said firmly.

"You know you're working for a criminal."

"You're assuming he's guilty."

"Hey, I got chewed out by my superior today just for talking to you. I don't want to lose my job over this! Besides, a man's presidential hopes could be ruined here." I had to restrain myself from reaching over and strangling him. "Max, I care about the Stokes family. If you're hurting them—"

"Oh, I see now. That Sebastian kid is your boyfriend, isn't he?"

"No," I argued meekly. "Look, I can't talk about this anymore. I need some sleep. My job is crazy. My love life is a mess. Everything in my life right now is upside down."

I went upstairs to my room and sat on the bed and started to pray aloud. "Dear Lord, please bestow upon me Your strength, wisdom, and grace. I made a mistake by even dealing with Max. I'm so sorry for this. Lord, don't let Reverend Stokes's campaign suffer because of something that wasn't his fault. He's a decent man who should not be penalized for something he didn't do. Please get him out of this mess. It's too rocky."

Chapter 11

Avalanche

I woke up the next morning with the covers nestled tight around me. The hotel room wasn't cold, but I was shivering anyway. Beautiful music was playing on the radio station I'd left on all night. A gospel group was singing a song about the Twenty-third Psalm.

I'd been frightened and confused about what might happen next. Reverend Stokes's hopes of getting into the White House might be snatched away from him simply because I had connected him to corrupt people. But the song on the radio calmed my nerves as it assured me that God was in control.

He was my Shepherd, my Protector, and my Guardian, and He knew what the day was going to bring. I didn't need to worry about anything. All I had to do was put my life in God's hands, because He would make me lie down in green pastures. That meant that some way, somehow, everything was going to be all right. Leading me beside the still waters meant that I didn't need to fear, that raging waters would carry me into the sea. The Lord would renew my strength and restore my soul so I could face anything.

Things might get crazy, but I didn't have to be afraid because God would be with me. He'd give me whatever I needed to make it through. He would comfort me, even in front of those who might want to harm me. I could rest in the fact that God was with me and I would be with Him in eternity. That's what the Christian life is all about. Not my circumstances changing, but my mind-set adjusting so I could see God in the good times and the bad.

I grabbed my Bible off the nightstand and read the Twenty-third Psalm, asking the Lord to help me claim every verse of that passage. If something drastic was about to happen, I knew the only way I could survive it was with Christ guiding my steps.

I set my Bible on the bed, went to the bathroom, and brushed my teeth. Then I looked into the mirror and said to my reflection, "Maybe I'm getting all worked up over nothing. Max is big-time trouble, but the whole world isn't concerned with his business."

I left the bathroom and turned on the TV. In spite of the positive statements I'd just made to myself, every local channel was broadcasting a live press conference at Reverend Stokes's headquarters. The presidential candidate was getting barraged with questions. I'd never seen the man look so frail and nervous. It was clear he hadn't slept much the night before.

"So can I quote you as saying," one reporter commented, "you didn't know the Bambino family was under investigation for mob dealings when you accepted money from them?"

"That is correct," Stokes replied.

"Then do you mind telling us how you came to know this notorious family?"

I'd never been the type to bite my nails, but at that point I was gnawing on them like they were corn on the cob. How was Stokes going to answer that question? If the Agency found out I'd abused my position, I could be seriously reprimanded. Or worse.

"I was introduced to them," Reverend Stokes said, "by someone working with the campaign."

A reporter from *USA Today* shouted, "I know you're gonna give us that name." I bit my finger so hard I pierced the skin.

Stokes glanced at Jack Applebee. Jack took the stand. "There will be no more comments today. We will release another statement later this afternoon. Thank you."

Reverend Stokes hustled off the platform and out of the

cameras' view. The local affiliate reporter stepped into the screen. "Reverend Stokes, practically a shoo-in as the first African-American Democratic nominee for President of the United States, has apparently bumped into a mountain. If he doesn't tell the truth, that mountain may prevent him from making it into the White House."

"Lord, what have I done?" I moaned as I licked my finger to stop the bleeding. I stayed in my hotel room all day, flipping channels and watching Stokes's misstep go from local to regional to national coverage. I tried calling Max several times, but he wasn't answering his cell phone. When I didn't even get through to his voice mail, I panicked even more.

My phone jangled, and I answered it on the first ring.
"May I speak to Christian Ware?" asked a sweet, feminine voice.
"This is she."
"I'm Kathy Hemmings, Jack Applebee's assistant. Jack asked me to call you and ask if you could come to campaign headquarters immediately."
"My shift doesn't start for another three hours," I argued.
"Reverend Stokes would like to see you, Ms. Ware. Can I tell him you'll be here in thirty minutes?"
This isn't good, I said to myself, but I answered, "Sure."

Agent Moss ushered me into the Stokes mansion through an entrance I had never seen before, then led me down a set of concrete steps to a large room full of cherrywood furniture. Tall bookshelves, polished to a high shine, lined two of the walls. Reverend Stokes and Jack Applebee were seated at a small conference table. They stood when we entered.

"This is my secret getaway," Reverend Stokes said. "I can even hide from you guys here." He chuckled.

"Will that be all, sir?" Agent Moss asked.

"Yes, thank you," Jack Applebee said as he waved my detail leader away.

When Moss left the room, Stokes and Applebee started whispering back and forth. I stood in the corner, barely breathing, wondering what I was supposed to do. I looked around, wondering if Moss had personally secured the room since no one else seemed to even know about it.

A sculpture sitting on a nearby bookshelf caught my eye. It depicted what appeared to be black slaves standing in the middle of a river watching a baptism. That image calmed my spirit. I felt good that the Savior was with me.

Finally Reverend Stokes said, "Agent Ware, do you know why we're here?"

"I assume this has something to do with me introducing you to my college friend, sir."

"That's right," he confirmed. "We have a serious problem here."

"Yes, sir. I'm aware of what's going on, and I want you to know I'm truly sorry for any problems I might have caused. I had no idea Max was involved with corrupt people."

"Ms. Ware," Jack Applebee said, "there's something we need you to do." He walked over to me and leaned against the polished wood conference table. "We want you to tell the press that you're the one who introduced Reverend Stokes to the Bambino family."

"But I didn't," I said. Sure, I'd connected Stokes with Max, but Max was the one with ties to the Bambinos, not me.

Jack Applebee asked me to take a seat. When I did, he went on and on about how much it would help the campaign if I did this one little favor for Reverend Stokes. "If you want to do something to ensure victory for the first African-American president, you need to tell the press that you knew the Bambino family was bad and that you put them together with Reverend Stokes because you wanted to ruin his campaign."

"What?" I cried out, standing so abruptly I nearly toppled the chair. "No way." I turned to Reverend Stokes. "I'll tell the truth about introducing you to my college friend, sir. But I won't say I hooked you up with the Bambino family to sabotage your campaign. I care about your family, sir—you know that."

Reverend Stokes stood and walked over to me. "Then if you care, you need to consider taking this bullet for us."

I stood there, staring at his face, panting for breath. He could tell by my frigid disposition that I wasn't giving in. I saw Applebee give him a mean glare.

He placed a warm hand on my shoulder. "I don't want to pressure you," he said. "However, some things I can't control, and if I can't . . ."

I cut in, brushed his hand away, and said, "What if you can't control me? Will things get ugly?"

"Maybe. I'll be honest with you. This is hard for me. You saved my life. But like I tried to say, some things are out of my control."

He looked more serious than I'd ever seen him. I knew this was not a game I could win. But I had to play my hand and my gut told me not to give in.

As he was walking me to the door, Reverend Stokes said, "Are you sure you know what you're doing?"

I shook my head. "I must stay true to myself, and I'm about truth. I'm disappointed because I thought you were, too."

Dropping his head to hide the disappointment in himself, it was clear I'd hit a nerve. He told me under his breath that he understood my decision. I was thankful Stokes wasn't angry about me refusing to lie for him. But when I looked at the sneering face of the white man standing behind him, I knew this was far from over.

Later that day, when I showed up at the Secret Service headquarters in the Stokes home, everyone in my unit seemed to be looking at me strangely. What had they heard?

Agent Moss called me into a back room. "Agent Ware," he said, closing the door, "I have to ask you to hand in your weapon and your badge."

"What?"

"As of right now, you're on suspension pending an investigation." He sounded disappointed, but I wasn't sure if he was upset with me or with what he was being forced to do.

"An investigation of what?" I questioned.

"I have no more details than that. The orders came from the top, and I just have to carry them out."

I looked at him with pleading eyes. Sure, I'd made some mistakes, but Moss knew what a good agent I was. Surely he could have fought for me.

"I'll do what I can to resolve this as quickly as possible," he assured me. "The best advice I can give you right now is to go back home to D.C. and take your mind off all this. When I know more, I'll call you."

"You said go back home—am I free to go back to my FBI cases?"

"Unfortunately not. You're off everything until this is rectified," he said in a contrite, but not rude, manner.

I placed my gun and badge on his desk and shuffled to the door. Before I walked out, he said, "Agent Ware."

I turned.

"I am sorry," he said. "We gave you a hard time at first because of the different-agency issue, but you proved you're an elite agent in your own right. Hang your hat on that."

"Thank you, sir."

Agent Hold helped me collect some of my things from my locker.

"What have you heard?" I asked, filling a duffel bag with my personal things.

"Something about you being involved with illegal campaign funds. Is it true?"

"Ryan, I don't know anything about all that."

"If there's an investigation, I'll probably be called in to testify at the review board."

"Good," I said. "You can be a character witness for me."

He stopped, took a deep breath, then looked at me and said, "Chris, I was told that you were at the benefit banquet in New York with some suspicious-looking guys. Someone heard one of them say that he had brought the campaign contribution in cash in a briefcase. No legitimate businessman would bring cash in a briefcase to a benefit banquet. Then I heard you told another agent that you could vouch for them."

"I did, sort of. But I didn't know there was major cash on them," I argued. "And really, I only vouched for the guy I knew in college. I introduced Max to Reverend Stokes, but I don't know anything about the Bambinos."

I shoved the last of my things into a duffel bag and slung it over my shoulder.

"This is so wrong. Don't worry. I'll keep you posted on the inside," Ryan said, his voice cracking a little.

My buddy was tearing up. I gave him a hug. I could tell my show of affection threw him off guard, but his kindness meant a lot to me and I wanted him to know it.

Walking toward the front door of the Stokes mansion with a duffel bag over my shoulder was humiliating. Nonetheless, I held my head up high, hoping to get out of there without a scene.

I'd almost made it to the door when Mrs. Stokes showed up. She stood in my way and glared at me. "I hear you're responsible for my husband's campaign being ruined."

"No, ma'am. You were misinformed."

"Oh, I think I have the facts. I'm so thankful that Sebastian finally realized you can be nothing but trouble for our family. You know, with people like you holding our race back, we'll never be able to achieve greatness."

I figured since I was on suspension anyway, I might as well tell her exactly what I thought. "Ma'am, with people like you, we don't need white folks attacking us. You do a pretty good job of looking down on the rest of us yourself."

"Are you saying I don't know where I come from?"

"Oh, no, ma'am." With nothing to lose, I finally had the courage to tell her how I really felt. "I'm saying that you don't know where black folks come from. Not all of us have three or four generations of money to back us up. Some of your ancestors were slaves just like mine. You may think that if you get the right education, or you have the right complexion, or you know the right people, you're above a common black person from the ghetto. But your way of thinking puts more obstacles in our path than are already there. Mrs. Stokes, I wouldn't do anything to sabotage your husband's campaign. I was only trying to help. Now I don't know why I cared so much—nobody around here seems to appreciate it."

I pushed past her, my duffel bag rubbing against the wallpaper as I tried to avoid contact with Mrs. Stokes.

She snatched my arm and pulled me back toward her. "I don't want to see you at my house ever again," she seethed. "And I certainly don't want you coming on to my son. You're just a cheap, trashy whore trying to get your hooks into a wealthy man."

"That's not true," I cried, nearly in tears. "I risked my life for your husband."

She smirked. "That was your job. You didn't do it because you care about my family. You did it for a paycheck." Mrs. Stokes released my arm roughly. "Before I get through, your name will be plastered all over every media outlet in the country. You think the little damage you tried to do to my husband was something? You just wait."

Just then, Sebastian came up and handed me a tissue. "Mom, it's obvious to me that you don't know how a lady's supposed to behave. This agent lost her job, and you're making it even worse. You're kicking someone when she's down."

"She ruined your father, and you're defending her?"

"Mom, she's under investigation. That doesn't mean she's guilty." He reached for the duffel bag on my shoulder. "Come on, Chris. Let me take you home."

"You don't have to do that," I said, keeping my bag in place. "You should stay with your family. Your mom's right. I've made a mess of things, and I don't want to complicate your life even more."

Before he could say anything, I jetted out to the Agency car waiting at the curb. I threw the duffel bag into the backseat and climbed in beside it. I couldn't wait to get out of Atlanta.

The Town Car pulled out of the driveway, then came to an

abrupt halt. I looked up and saw Sebastian standing in front of the car.

"Sir," the driver yelled out his window, "please move."

Sebastian stood his ground. "Could you roll down the passenger side window in the back?"

The driver complied, and Sebastian stuck his head in.

"Go away," I grumbled, not even looking at him.

"Explain this to me. I know what they're saying isn't true."

As I looked at his arms leaning against the window's edge, I thought about how wonderful it would feel to have his strong shoulder to lean on. I looked up and saw in his eyes how deeply he cared. With tears streaming down my cheeks, I opened the car door and fell into his embrace.

He rubbed my back and whispered reassuring words in my ear. I asked him if we could go to the hotel to talk. He got my duffel bag out of the backseat and told the driver he wasn't needed. As we walked to Sebastian's car, I felt great relief that we were going to be able to clear up this misunderstanding.

When we neared the hotel, we saw dozens of reporters milling around outside the front doors. Sebastian pulled over to a curb far enough away that they wouldn't notice us.

"Do you think they're looking for me?" I asked.

"Probably," he said calmly.

I took a deep breath. "I don't know what to say to them."

"I've got an idea." He reached out and touched my cheek. "Let's go to my place. Everybody thinks I'm at my parents' house, so no one will be looking for you there."

I nodded, grateful for his calm in my storm.

During the fifteen-minute drive to his house, Sebastian assured me that God had everything under control. "There's no trial He can't see you through," he said, "no river He can't help you cross, no mountain He can't help you over. You have nothing to fear."

When we got into his house, Sebastian offered me some water.

"That'd be great," I said. As he went to the kitchen, I walked over to his fireplace mantel, which held pictures of the family. Just looking at his mom made me cringe, remembering all of her cruel words to me.

The ice water Sebastian brought cooled me off a bit, but his nearness as we sat together on the leather couch warmed me up again.

"So, I guess you want me to tell you all about this mess now."

"Only if you want to. If you don't, I understand. We can just order some pizza, watch a little TV, go to a movie. Whatever you like."

"That all sounds great. But I want you to hear the truth."

"I know," he said, slipping his arm around me. "But for now, let's just relax, okay?"

Snuggling into his shoulder, I said, "You are an absolute godsend."

He smiled, then picked up the phone. "What do you like on your pizza?"

After he put in our order, I told Sebastian I wished I could change out of my work suit. He took me to his bedroom, where he gave me a pair of his sweats to put on. Then he left the room, closing the door behind him.

The room was magnificent. The décor was black, white, and charcoal gray, which somehow had an elegant yet casual feel. I went into the adjoining bathroom and stared into the mirror at my puffy cheeks and red nose. After I washed my face I put on his sweats, which were enormous on me, but felt cozy nonetheless.

As I headed back to the living room, I heard the television.

"Dang, man," Sebastian said, staring at the TV.

I looked at the screen and saw a surveillance picture of me.

"Presidential candidate Steven Stokes has been cleared of all wrongdoing," the reporter was saying. "At a press conference this afternoon, press secretary Dan Greenville reported that a young female Secret Service agent tried to sabotage the campaign by funneling illegal funds into the campaign."

"What?" I screamed out.

The newsman continued, "This photograph, taken two months

ago, shows the woman apparently taking a bribe from a man who is also heavily involved. Words on the bottom of the screen decipher what was said in the exchange."

The screen filled with a video of Max and me sitting at the restaurant in New York. Most of the conversation was unaltered, but the part that was added somewhere, somehow, implicated me in the scandal.

The words at the bottom of the TV had me saying, "For this amount of money, you've got a deal. I'll introduce Reverend Stokes to the Mob."

Sebastian looked up at me with an astonished expression.

"I know how this looks, but it didn't go down that way," I desperately explained, joining him on the couch. "I didn't say all that."

His eyebrows rose. "But I saw you take the money. That could not have been tampered with."

This was a big deal. How could I tell the guy I was crazy about the history behind that money? That I was accepting payment for having an abortion? Though Sebastian and I had talked about that before, I never wanted to go into my awful past with him again. How understanding could I expect a man to be? Yet, I wanted our relationship to be based on truth.

Swallowing my pride and shame, I slid closer to him and said, "That guy in the video is my ex-boyfriend from college, Max, the one that I conceived a child with. He wasn't there when I had the abortion and he didn't contribute monetarily then. The money I took was his way of correcting that mistake, reimbursement for what I paid out to the clinic, plus a little more."

Sebastian looked at me as if I did accept a bribe, once I admitted to taking more than I paid out. He hastily got up off the couch and went into his kitchen. The way he leaned against his countertop saddened me. He was slumped over, dejection written all over his face.

"It was less than two hundred extra, and that money was due me for a lot more than the baby stuff. I loaned that joker tons of cash in college for one thing or another. But understand, he asked me to help him out by introducing him to your dad. At first I was against it, but then when I worked detail one day and overheard the campaign was having severe cash flow problems, I figured Max could save the day."

"You figured wrong. He ruined the day."

"You're right," I said, nearing his side. "That's my only crime. I didn't do any scheming or plotting to bring down your dad."

Sebastian turned his back away from me. Walking behind him, I placed my hand on his back and said, "You do believe me, don't you?"

The guy I loved circled around and cupped my face in his strong hands. "I do. I just can't understand why everything else is so twisted. Who taped you? Why did they alter what was said? Some major planning has gone into this whole thing, and we've got to figure it out. I don't want this to end your career." He hugged me. "My dad—where does he fit into all of this?"

Pulling out of the embrace, I said, "I wonder the same thing. I was called into a secret meeting this morning with your dad and Mr. Applebee. I was asked to take the rap for your father's involvement with that Italian crime family. I said I wouldn't do it. Your dad acted like he was cool with it, but sort of insinuated that I should reconsider saying no. When I didn't, Applebee seemed quite upset. I guess I should have copped to something I didn't do."

"You should never compromise . . ." he said, before being cut off by his ringing cell phone. "One sec, it's my dad."

I felt so hysterical inside. How could I have been set up like this? Sebastian seemed to understand, though. Deep in my gut I really didn't know if Sebastian would take my side or his father's. Unable to watch him really listen to his dad, I went to the bathroom and changed back into my navy blue pants suit. I figured I'd head downstairs and catch a cab, though I didn't know where I'd ask to be taken. I certainly couldn't go back to the hotel.

As I crept toward the front door with my duffel bag, I heard Sebastian say, "You know what, Dad? Save it for someone who cares." He slammed down the phone.

I gasped. He turned around and saw me at the front door. He ran toward me. Extremely emotional, I dropped my bag and hugged Sebastian tightly. The only question in my mind was how long he would hold on to me.

"Don't cry, baby," he said softly as he wiped the tears from my cheeks. "It'll be okay." He showered my face with gentle kisses. When his tongue found its way into my mouth, I was overcome by passion.

The kiss continued as we made our way to his bedroom. He urged me onto the king-sized bed.

"You're so beautiful," he said, pecking gently at my neck.

Starting with his forehead, I let my lips leave a trail to his neck. I made a mark there with my teeth. Hearing him moan drove me even crazier. Being so connected like this was what we wanted to avoid, but I was so frustrated that "doing what was right" didn't seem so right anymore.

In a matter of seconds, he was on top of me. "I want you in the worst way," he whispered. The next kiss sent us soaring, higher and higher. I didn't want the flight to end.

He was acting like a pro in seduction. I guess an intimate situation is like riding a bike, once you've been on one you always remember how to ride. Every inch of my body was turned on. It took every ounce of strength I had to pull away.

The brotha was most definitely doing somethin' right as he sent me into orbit when he nibbled on my bra strap.

"You can take it off now," I said as I leaned up and quickly undid the strap clearly wanting more. When he didn't make a move, I slid the straps down, bearing my breasts. I'd never felt so sexy in my life.

He stared at me, and I knew he wasn't disappointed. But I saw a tear drop from his eye. Knowing he was really wrestling inside, I covered myself up with the sheet and sat on the edge of the bed to talk.

"I'm sorry," I said. "I just can't do this."

He moved to the edge of the bed and I sat beside him.

"I love you," I said tenderly. "You love me, too. I can feel it."

"That's not the problem." He reached for my hand and gave it a gentle squeeze. "I've been wanting to make love to you for a long time," he whispered.

I gave in. "Then do it," I said. I dropped to my knees and rested my elbows on his thighs. "Let's make all the stuff we've ever dreamed about come true right now."

"Baby, step away from me. Please. This isn't honoring God."

Of course, I understood his reluctance. I even admired him for it. I mean, we were both Christians, and the Bible had a lot to say about people having sex before marriage. Yet part of me wanted so much to believe that God would be okay with this. We were in love, after all.

I unfastened his belt buckle and unbuttoned his pants. Then I reached into the red briefs that were stretched taut around his hips. His moans let me know he was in ecstasy.

He stood suddenly. "Chris, I don't want to do this," he said, "and I need you to respect that."

I really needed him right now. The only thing I could think of was how this would make us both feel better. What was wrong with a little sex when two people loved each other?

I slipped out of what was left of my sweat suit. Then I stood before him in all the glorious splendor nature had blessed me with.

"I have to take a shower," he said, then turned and walked away.

I heard him turn on the water and slide the shower door closed. Then I tiptoed into the bathroom. Through the frosted glass I could see him standing against the wall, his hands and legs spread apart as if cops were searching him. His pecan-tan skin filled my body with desire.

I opened the shower door.

Because he was standing directly under the showerhead, he didn't see me. I placed my hands on his shoulders. He flinched slightly, but didn't turn around, so I moved my hands slowly down his back. When I reached his hips, he suddenly whirled around. Sebastian gazed at me like a lion about to tear into his captured prey.

His tongue nearly touched my tonsils. His hands raked my body. Then he led me out of the shower and turned off the water.

Without even toweling off our wet bodies, Sebastian led me to the bed. It felt like the first time, and I hated the fact that it wasn't.

"I love you," he told me over and over.

"I love you, too."

Our interlude ended with a long, leisurely rest in each other's arms. Then we decided to watch a movie on DVD. After the first five minutes, we lay beside each other, then fell asleep in each other's arms. My dream was a replay of the night's intimacy.

When I awoke, I didn't feel Sebastian's arm around me. I opened my eyes and saw him putting on his clothes.

"Where are you going?"

"I couldn't sleep all night."

I sat up, allowing the sheets to fall to my lap. "Come back to bed with me," I said in my most seductive voice.

"Cover yourself up, girl."

I slid the covers over my breasts. "What's going on?"

"Last night was a mistake," he stated firmly. "A huge mistake. I'd appreciate it if you were gone when I get back."

My heart skipped a beat. "What are you talking about? Last night was great."

Sebastian strode toward the door. I hopped out of bed and beat him to it, stationing my naked body squarely in his path.

He pulled the sheet off the bed and wrapped it around me. "I'm serious, Chris."

"Please don't go," I begged. "Maybe what we did was wrong. But maybe it wasn't." I reached up to wrap my arms around his neck, and the sheet fell to the floor.

What had I done? I'd been trying to get on the right path with God. But I knew my actions with Sebastian had really disappointed the Lord.

How could the man I love behave this way? Could he really walk away from all we had? I'd already lost my job, which had practically been everything to me. If Sebastian left me, too, how would I survive?

Chapter 12

Valley

"Chris, get dressed. Please."
Sebastian bent down, picked up the sheet that was wrapped around my ankles, and handed it to me. I covered myself and stood there, trembling.

"I've got to be honest with you," he said in an irritated voice. "Last night was great, but now all I feel is sorrow. I didn't mean to do that, and I sure didn't mean to hurt you. But the fact is, I need time to think."

He walked out and left me standing there in his bedroom. When I heard the front door close, I fell to my knees and rocked back and forth, holding myself tight.

How could he change so quickly? I asked myself. *What have I done to him?*

Part of me wanted to stay there until he came back, but as I wiped away my tears, I realized that wasn't the best thing. I had to do what he asked of me.

I put on the sweats I'd worn briefly the day before because I didn't want to put on my dirty uniform. Then I hopped in a cab and headed to the hotel. The paparazzi were gone, so I was able to get my things together, make flight arrangements, take a shower, then head to the airport.

Throughout the flight from Atlanta to D.C., I thought of Sebastian. His smile when he was in a good mood, his sensual look, and his angry one. Just hours ago we were in each other's arms. I knew what we had done was wrong, but we were in love. What else were two people in love supposed to do? I was so confused. Sebastian had made me see that premarital sex was a sin. Always before, I'd had no uneasiness about my promiscuity. This time my spirit was siding with Sebastian, but my flesh was having major issues with that.

I wondered what this would do to us. After Sebastian had some time away from me, would he want me back? If he didn't, I had no idea how I was going to live.

I stared out the airplane window at the tiny world below me. The guy in the aisle seat next to me gave me a funny look, and I tried to hide under the baseball cap I'd put on in an attempt to cover my messy hair. I wondered if my fellow passenger recognized me as the girl who'd ruined Reverend Steven Stokes's campaign. But I realized that was crazy. No one really knew me. There'd been a couple of comments about me in the tabloids and one or two announcements in the local news, but nothing more.

Just when I almost had myself convinced, the guy in seat B closed the paper he'd been reading. There on the front cover of *USA Today* was a picture of me taking a thick manila envelope from Max. The caption read, "Federal agent takes bribes to ruin Stokes campaign."

Lord, my soul cried out, *why is everything coming apart around me? Why are people lying about me? I thought I was finally getting my life together. After growing up with no money and no dad, I find a good man and a stable job. I was even trying to get You back in my life. Then everything gets all messed up! I know making love to Sebastian was a sin, and I'm trying to come to grips with that. Please help my spirit win the battle over my flesh. In Jesus' name, Amen.*

I mentally kicked myself because I knew God wasn't punishing me. He was just trying to get through to me, and all I had to do was listen.

After deplaning in D.C., as I walked through the airport, I saw my face everywhere: the newsstands, magazine racks, on television. Thankfully, no one seemed to recognize me. There weren't even any reporters waiting outside my apartment complex.

Two members of the press had left messages on my answering machine, asking for interviews. The second one offered me a thousand dollars just for talking to him. Mom, Eden, and Troy had also called.

I didn't feel like getting an interrogation from Troy or a lecture from my mother. So I called Eden. She picked up on the first ring.

"I've been calling you forever, girl," she said when she heard my voice. "Are you okay?"

"I'm hanging in there," I said. "Just hoping and praying this will end soon."

"You're so strong."

"I think I'm just all cried out. Nothing shocks me anymore."

"Chris, Chyna called me today," Eden said. "She told me she was interviewed for one of those entertainment TV shows."

"Why?" I asked.

"She claimed she was your best friend."

"What? Why on earth would she do that?"

"I don't know," Eden said. "All she'd tell me was that it was her way of getting back at you."

At first I was angry. Then I remembered that God wants us to turn the other cheek, and I needed to do that with Chyna. Whatever she said couldn't make things worse. I was just glad Eden had forewarned me.

After promising Eden I'd talk to her again soon, I surfed the TV for about two and a half hours. I finally found the interview with Chyna on CNN.

"Yeah, we were really good friends in college," that liar was saying as she stood in front of the camera in a fitted black business suit. "Christian Ware has always been a backstabber. See, I was dating Reverend Stokes's son, Sebastian." She held up a photograph of herself with Sebastian. "But here's a picture of her trying to get it on with him." She showed a picture of me talking to Sebastian at the Christmas party at his parents' house.

"I didn't realize she was also trying to get to the family through the father."

"I can't believe this!" I yelled out.

I heard a commotion outside and peeked through a curtain. On the greenbelt outside my apartment, several reporters had started gathering.

I should go out there, I thought. I needed to tell people my side of the story. "Yea, though I walk through the valley of the shadow of death, I will fear no evil," I recited aloud. But it seemed evil was all around me. I wished I had Sebastian to talk to.

I need Your light right now, Lord, I prayed, *'cause I can't see my way out of this mess.*

I glanced out my window again. Someone spotted me and pointed. The next thing I knew, a fist-sized rock came crashing through the glass.

I screamed.

Lord, I pray to You, and worse stuff happens! Are You even there? If You are, You sure ain't helping me much.

I had to get out of my apartment without being recognized. I ran to my closet and pulled out an old wig that my mother had left at my place years ago. I pinned it on, then dressed in one of my church outfits, a pair of old tennis shoes, and a baseball cap. I looked like an old lady who should be arrested by the fashion police.

Donning sunglasses to finish the costume, I ventured out of my apartment, walking slowly and bent over. My ruse worked; no one gave me a second glance.

When I got to my mother's house, she held me tight. Then we sat on the couch and I leaned on her shoulder.

"Mom, I don't know what to do," I groaned. "Things have gotten way out of hand, and I know you're disappointed in me."

"Now, you stop right there," she said, turning my head to face her. "I raised you, and I know you wouldn't do what the media is accusing you of."

"Thanks, Mom," I said with a sigh.

"Since the day you were born, I asked God to lead you down the path of righteousness, and He has always provided for those who accept Him as their savior." She squeezed my shoulder. "Christian, I know that God is going to work this out for you."

I put my pity party on hold for the moment. My mom was right, I knew that God would work this situation out.

"Betsy Jones, the lady who lives two doors down from me, has been coming over here to pray with me ever since this story broke, and we know it's going to work out. Betsy would like to meet you and pray with you."

"Could that help?" I said, feeling like the bottom had dropped out of my life.

"Yes. She's a very spiritual woman. She's our church secretary. You could benefit from her wisdom and knowledge of God."

I shook my head to let her know I knew I did need spiritual counsel. My worn-out frame sank into the nearby chair.

I felt my mom's hand on my knee. She said, "I've been praying so much for you at my church and in my quiet times with the Lord. He's been talking and talking to me. You'll be all right."

"Oh, Mom." I took my hands from my face and hugged her. "Thank you. Having you in my corner helps so much. I'm glad God is speaking to you."

She helped me stand up and pointed to the ceiling. "Me, too, baby. Me and the Lord talk all the time. When your sister was in trouble, I sensed it. That young punk she was hanging around with just didn't sit right with my spirit. But with you and God working with her, I know she'll get back on track with her life."

"God can do amazing things, Mom, can't He?"

"Yes, He can. And now I know He'll help set things right for you—I know you didn't do anything wrong."

When I was a little girl, my mama used to ridicule me all the time. Whenever anyone said I'd done something wrong, she always took their side over mine. But now she was saying that God had told her I was innocent.

"Baby, you might be down in the dumps right now, but I don't think you're gonna be there long."

I smiled and hugged my mother again. God was going to end my suffering. He would see me out of this valley.

"The neighbor lady who prays with me wants to lead you to Christ, too."

It suddenly dawned on me that I had never told my mom that I'd accepted the Lord into my life.

I looked into my mother's eyes, smiled, and told her that I had accepted Christ a long time ago. "I just never let Him become Lord of my life until recently." I said. "Now I love the Lord and have a growing relationship with Him."

She smiled. "Now we've got to get your sister to know the Lord again."

"How is she, Mom? Is that guy she was hanging out with still in jail?"

"Oh, yeah. Your agency has charges on him piled so high I doubt he'll ever get out."

"Sounds good to me."

"Your sister misses him, though. She really needs to know the Lord again. She won't talk to me, so I was hoping you could get through to her."

I knew Mom was right. Knowing the Lord would give Crystal a joy no guy could ever provide. I was learning that firsthand.

"Will you talk to her?" Mom asked, tears in her eyes.

"I don't know if it'll do any good. She's probably still angry with me for playing a part in her boyfriend's demise. She's going through that rebellious stage where she resents authority. I hope I can reach her."

"Just explain to her why you did what you did. Let her know you love her and that you always will."

"I will, Mom."

"Good. I also want you to stay here with me until this mess with Chyna blows over. That's not too much for your mama to ask, is it?"

"Actually, I think I'd like to stay here for a while. Maybe Mrs. Jones has something to say that I need to hear."

"Her number is on the refrigerator," she said.

"I love you, Mom."

"I love you, too, baby. Everything's gonna be all right. You'll
see."

Three in the morning found me wide awake. The covers
were scratchy and heavy. The air was too hot. And I was still fret-
ting out about my situation.

I crawled out of bed to get a cup of warm milk, hoping it
would soothe me. As I passed my sister's door, I heard whim-
pers. Knowing my mother was at work at the factory, I knew it
was Crystal weeping. I decided to make a cup of warm milk for
her, too.

I prepared two cups, put them on a tray, then took them to
my sister's room. She was still crying. I knocked softly as I bal-
anced the tray with one hand. I didn't hear any response to my
knock, so I decided to go in.

My sister lifted her head off the pillow when I entered and
looked at me. "Warm milk?" she questioned. "It's too hot for
that. Besides, I wouldn't drink that stuff even if it was freezing."

"Look, Crystal," I said, setting the cups on her nightstand, "I
was just trying to keep you away from that guy for your own
good. He went to jail."

"All my friends at school are laughing at me because of you.
They're saying that my boyfriend and my sister are both criminals."

I sat on her bed and took a sip of the warm milk, trying to
gather my thoughts. "I was set up, Crystal. Framed."

"Yeah, right." She turned away from me.

"It's true."

She whirled around and looked at me with angry eyes. "Then
it serves you right for framing *my* Stone."

"*Your* Stone was under surveillance for a long time. I worked
on that case way before I took the Secret Service temp job. My
colleagues in the FBI knew when his big score was going down
and they caught him. Nobody planted anything on him. He just
got caught."

"I don't care if you did what they say or not. I just want you to
take your hot milk and get out of my face."

"Crystal," I said, grabbing her shoulders, "I know I haven't been around for you lately, but I want to make up for lost time."

Her eyes lit up. "Like when you took me for a massage just so I couldn't help my boyfriend? Forget it. You have no idea how badly you've ruined my life."

She turned her back to me. I tried rubbing it, but she jerked away.

"You don't understand."

"Then explain it to me," I suggested.

She jumped up and paced beside the bed. "Why should I talk to you? You didn't try to talk to me before you had my man arrested."

"Girl, you don't need to be with any guy who's doing illegal things. You should be glad he's gone."

"You don't even know what you're talking about! "There was a long, eerie silence. Then Crystal lowered her head and said with a low moan, "I think I might be pregnant." She buried her head in her pillow, as if trying to hide the shame. When she finally looked up, I wrapped my arms around her.

"Please don't tell Mom. Please," Crystal begged.

"For now, this will be between you and me, but—"

"No buts."

"All right." I wiped her tears, stroked her hair, and kissed her on the forehead.

"I thought you were gonna be mad at me. I figured you'd think I was a tramp."

"I'm not going to judge you," I said, remembering all too well my own fear of pregnancy again not long ago. "I don't agree with what you did, and you're much too young to be having a baby. But I understand how easy it is to get into a situation like this."

She threw her arms around me. "I'm so glad you're back."

"You should get some sleep. We both need it."

I headed for the door, but she called me back. "Chris."

"Yeah?" I asked from the doorway.

"I don't believe that you tried to destroy Reverend Stokes's campaign. All my friends tried to tell me you did, but I gave them a good cursing-out for talking about my sister that way."

I couldn't help but smile. "I don't know whether to thank you or to lecture you about using profanity."

She giggled. "I knew you'd be judging me sooner or later."

I shook my head and said, "Good night." Then I closed her door, returned to my room, and said a heartfelt prayer for my little sister.

The next day I drove to the New Hope United Methodist Church, where Mom had become a regular member since I entered college and she came out of rehab. I got there well before the service was scheduled to start, so there were only two cars in the parking lot. As I started to turn the car around, I saw a lady about my mama's age peeking her head out of the sanctuary door and waving to me.

That must be Mrs. Jones, I said to myself, figuring the two cars must belong to the pastor and the church secretary.

I parked the car and joined the lady at the door. "I'm Betsy Jones," she said with a smile, then gave me a big hug. "You must be Christian. I recognize you from your mama's pictures. She prays for you all the time, you know."

We bonded quickly. I told her about Sebastian and how he'd helped me get back into a right relationship with God. I even told her about Chyna lying about me on the news. She listened attentively.

"If you have the faith and belief of Moses," she advised me, "God will part the sea for you and let you walk to the safe side. You need the courage of Daniel to be in the lion's den or to go through a fiery furnace, like Shadrach, Meshach, and Abednego, and know that you won't get burned."

This woman was amazing. She had a love for the Lord that I lacked.

"Tell me about your relationship with God," I asked.

"The Lord has been so good to me, I can't begin to tell it all. He showed me there's more to this life than just what we see here. He's got a place for me, and for you that we couldn't comprehend if we wanted to. And that gives me unexplainable joy, so deep in my soul that I walk fast everywhere I go. I've got the pep in my step from the heavenly Father pushing me along every inch of the way."

"I hope I walk with the Lord like that when I'm as old as you." Realizing what I'd just said, I added, "No offense."

She smiled from ear to ear. "None taken. I'm proud of my sixty-two years on this earth. Of course God wants new Christians to grow up in Christ. Christian faith is not something that comes easy. You have to be able to trust Him and believe that you can do nothing without Him. It's all about relinquishing control of your life to Him and depending on Him for everything. Once you let Him lead and live your life as He commanded, He will bless you. Now, there will be some trials and tribulations, but you've got to continue to pray and praise God. See, the Lord will be with you in the good and bad times. Job says it best. The Lord giveth and the Lord taketh away. Blessed be the name of the Lord. Child, you need to read your Bible, pray, and ask God to guide you."

I immediately thought of the reason my boyfriend and I weren't together. I had forced Sebastian to do something he didn't want to do because he wanted to honor God. I wasn't at that level in my walk with Christ. Oh, I believed God was there, but I hadn't been tapping into what that really meant. If I longed to please God above all things, I wouldn't have been tempted to satisfy my fleshly desires.

"How do you get that kind of faith?" I asked. "I mean, I've been saved for a few months, but I still have my foot in the world. I feel more passionately about earthly things and people than I do about the Lord. But I know that's not what I need."

She nodded. "You just have to say, 'Lord, rain down Your spirit on me.' Get on your knees and talk to Him. Not because you want Him to change your circumstances, but because you need Him to change *you*. Ask Him to take you in His arms and hold you close. Tell Him not to let you go until you have the Holy Ghost fully inside you. Admit that you need Him. Let Him know you want to know Him intimately."

This was one powerful and knowledgeable sister in the Lord.

I could see how she was able to convince my mother to come to church services and why my mom had wanted me to talk to her.

"The only one who can make your life right is Christ. Don't seek friends or your job, or a man, or even the church to get you what you need. Go to the source. Beg God to fill you. When you spend time with Him, you will shine brightly, even in your darkest hours."

"I'm trying," I said. "But sometimes it seems as if I can't get anything right."

She put her arm around me. "My dear girl, God is always with you, but you can call on me, too, if you need to. Your mama has my number. You know, she's always been proud of you. I'm proud of you, too. You're doing great things."

"I'm nothing special," I said meekly.

"Don't you talk like that," she gently chided. "You've got to believe in yourself and surround yourself with folks who love God and love you." She gave me a hug.

I was almost thankful that my life was upside down, because if things were going right I would never have realized how much I needed to get my priorities straight. God wanted me to love Him completely, 100 percent. And that was exactly what I planned to do.

The week passed quickly. Though my circumstances didn't change, my attitude made all the difference.

I decided it was time to go back to my apartment in D.C. Being with my mom and my sister had been good for me, but I had to lean on the Lord and allow Him to get me through these tough times.

As I enjoyed what I figured would be my last breakfast at home for a while, Crystal barged into the kitchen, begging me to drive her to a clinic. "I've got to find out if I really am pregnant," she said.

I changed out of my robe and drove her to a clinic. After an hour's wait, the doctor examined her and confirmed that she was going to have a baby.

Crystal broke down and cried. I put my arms around her and pulled her close. "We'll work this out together," I promised her.

After she regained her composure, we walked out of the clinic and got into my car.

"I want an abortion," she said, staring out the windshield.

I wanted to tell her I'd been down that road before and it wasn't as easy a way out as it seemed. But I was too ashamed. My wound was still raw and I didn't want it exposed.

"Promise me you'll give this at least a couple of weeks," I begged.

She gazed at me with a look of disgust in her eyes. "I don't want this thing growing inside me."

"How does your ex feel about it?"

"Stone is not my ex. We're still talking. He calls me from jail."

"Calls from jail, girl? You told me you cut that guy loose," I cried out, slamming my hand against the steering wheel.

"I'm sorry," she said defensively.

"You should be. I can't help you if you're not honest with me."

"Okay," she said. "I won't do anything drastic until we talk again. I promise."

When we arrived home, Mom was there. Crystal gave me a warning look, silently begging me to keep her secret. I avoided her questions about where we'd been by telling Mom about my decision to move back to my apartment.

"It's a cruel world out there, baby," Mom said. "I don't want you to get hurt. Why don't you stay with me a while longer?"

I patted her hand. "It's been great being here," I assured her. "But I have to get back to my life.

"Will you call me as soon as you get in so I know you're safe?"

"Come on, Mom. You keep telling me to trust God. You can't live in fear."

"I'm just being a protective mother," she said with a sad smile. "The Lord doesn't mind if I worry just a little bit."

I gave her a kiss and headed to my place.

My apartment manager had done a great job cleaning up all

the shattered glass. I couldn't even tell the window had been damaged. After I got unpacked I noticed my answering machine light blinking. I was reluctant to listen to my messages. There were probably a lot of harassing comments on there. I braced myself, then hit the Play button.

The first message was from Eden. "Dion and I are going at it again," she said, her voice sounding distressed.

Her second message was in a much calmer voice. "We made up. Things are back to normal. Call me."

The next message was from Troy. "I heard about all the stuff being piled on you. If you need me, call. I know you like trying to solve stuff on your own, but I've got inside contacts. Let me know if you want to use them."

I was happy to hear he was still there for me, particularly after I'd let him down. Apparently he did want us to be friends. He continued, "Oh yeah, and be careful. Rudy Roberts sent me a note telling me he's watching me. Get that—he's watching me. Just be careful, because the guy is crazy and I know he wants to settle the score."

Chills went up my spine. Why won't the guy just go to jail already? Though the message creeped me out, I dismissed it quickly. My career was on the line. Roberts couldn't mess me up any worse than what was already happening.

Sebastian left the next message. His voice sounded so good. "I'm sorry I walked out on you. I care about you and I want to be there for you through all this."

The next message was Sebastian again. "I guess you don't need me after all. Please just give me a call and let me know you're okay."

Sebastian's third message said, "Okay, I'm really worried now. Please call me."

I picked up the cell phone to call him, but it rang before I could dial.

"Hello," I said, trying to sound confident.

"Hey, Chris." Hearing Max's voice instead of Sebastian's made my anger flare.

"Where have you been?" I demanded.

"Hey, don't get on my case like that. I'm majorly stressed right now."

"I don't care how stressed you are," I said. "My life is falling apart because of you."

"Quit yelling. Your butt's not the only one in hot water right now."

"As far as I'm concerned, you could drop off the face of the earth. Every time I get involved with you something dramatic happens."

"Chris, I'm in D.C. At the hospital. With Eden."

"What?" I asked, my tirade suddenly deflated.

"It's pretty bad. You need to get down here right away."

When I got to the hospital, I discovered my girlfriend had a fractured jaw and a broken nose. The left side of her face looked like it had a small tomato inside it. She was unconscious and badly bruised.

"What happened?" I asked Max as we stood beside her bed.

"She and her husband have really been getting into it lately. I thought they'd worked things out, until Dion called and told me I'd better come to the hospital. I think he's on drugs."

"So why didn't you call the cops?"

"He's my friend. I don't want to get him locked up."

"How come he's not already in jail?" I asked.

"She didn't press charges."

"The police didn't arrest him anyway?"

"Yeah, they did. But he got out after a couple of hours."

I looked at my battered friend. "How long has she been here?"

"Almost twenty-four hours. But the doctor said she's going to be all right."

"She won't be if she goes back home with that fool of a husband of hers."

Just as I said that, Dion walked in with a bouquet of roses in a crystal vase. He set them on the table beside the bed.

Like roses are going to undo the damage you did.

When Dion said hi to me, I snapped. I grabbed his neck and tried to choke him.

"Girl, you're crazy," Dion said, trying to pry off my fingers.

"If you want to fight, try beating up on someone who can hit back," I screamed, pelting him in the chest with my fists.

"Get your girl off me, Max."

Max just watched and stayed out of it.

"You'd better stay away from my girlfriend," I said as I slapped Dion's face.

Max finally pulled me off of Eden's husband.

"You'd better take her away before she gets hurt," Dion said to Max, who dragged me out of the room.

In the hallway, he said, "We need to talk."

"Please, I'm so through with you." I walked straight to the parking lot, feeling Max right behind me.

Finally he caught up with me and tugged at my arm. "Come on, Chris, where are you going?"

"To my apartment—leave me alone. I said this earlier but I guess you didn't hear me, I'm through with you."

"I didn't try to set you up with Stokes," he said, looking me squarely in the eyes. "You've got to believe me. Somebody's framing both of us."

When he kept persisting, I capitulated. I really did need to get to the bottom of this, and Max had information I needed. He followed me home, then began to tell me all he knew.

"There's been a lot of heat on me lately. I've found notes in my apartment warning me to keep my mouth closed or I'd have an accident. My stuff gets moved around when I'm not there. I think my phone's bugged. And I got fired last week," he told me, clearly shaken.

"Why would someone be harassing you?"

"I don't know, but it's all political. Someone high up wants to control Stokes. And whoever it is wants the allegations against you to stick."

My phone rang, and Max jumped. When I answered, I heard the voice of my apartment manager.

"Hey, Jose, thank you so much for fixing up my place."

"Oh, no problem, no problem," he said in his thick Latino accent. "I got a package for you. You want me to bring it up?"

"I can come down and get it."

"Okay," he said.

"Someone brought a package for me to the manager," I explained to Max after I hung up.

"Are you expecting something?" he asked, his eyes narrow with suspicion.

"I did leave some things in Atlanta. Maybe the bureau is sending them to me here." I touched his hand. "I believe you didn't set me up."

He stood up and rubbed my shoulder. "Thanks, Chris, I don't want you mad at me. I didn't know things were going to turn so crazy. But I'm real scared."

"We'll figure a way out of this," I said, lightly pushing him down. "Relax. I'll be right back."

I ran down to Jose's apartment. As I walked back up, I looked at the box. There was no return address. I put my ear to it, praying it wasn't a bomb. Thankfully, I didn't hear any ticking.

When I opened my door, I didn't see Max. I called his name, figuring he must be in the bathroom.

I put the package down on my dining room table. Then I noticed a .357 magnum sitting on my couch.

I picked it up and headed down the hall toward the bathroom. "Max, why did you bring a gun into my house? You know how I—"

I opened the bathroom door, but Max wasn't there.

I went to my bedroom. There was Max, lying on the bed, his back to me. "What are you doing in here?" I complained, strutting up to him. "I have no intention of—" As I got closer I saw a dark red liquid on my bedspread. I rounded the foot of the bed and had to stifle a scream. Max was lying in a pool of blood. I dropped the gun.

I almost blacked out. I wanted to scream but no sound came from my throat. Though this was what I was trained for, this guy was my friend. We were just talking, and now he was dead. I was terrified.

Who could have done this? Was the perpetrator still somewhere in my apartment? Or in my room, even closer?

I stood beside the bed, frozen in place. Was someone trying to frame me for murder? How was I ever going to get out of this?

Chapter 13

Slope

I should have listened to Max. Someone really was following us, and now Max was dead. But who, and where, was the murderer?

I knew I should call the police, but there was an awful lot of evidence that would point to me as the killer. I had touched the murder weapon. I had motive: everyone knew I was angry about being put on suspension. Witnesses had seen me leave the hospital with Max hot on my tail. And he died in my apartment.

I had been framed, but had no idea by whom. And I didn't know who I could trust. There was no way that I was going to trust the local police to find out who framed me. I made a decision then and there that I had to remain free to find out who was behind this, and why.

I called the apartment manager. Just as Jose answered the phone, my guest bedroom door opened slowly.

"Is anybody there?" Jose asked. I couldn't answer him. I didn't even want to move.

"Hold on," I finally whispered.

I saw a black shadow inching slowly against the wall. Though I'd been trained to protect myself and others, I wasn't wearing a bulletproof vest. For all I knew, this lunatic might decide to shoot me and then put the gun in Max's hand so it would look like we'd killed each other.

Instead of trying to confront the intruder, I quickly screamed into the phone, "Jose, help me!"

The guy stepped out of the shadows and I held the phone as he started toward me. He wore a black ski mask, so I couldn't see his face. But his physique was muscular. He didn't say anything. We stared at each other for a moment, then he tried to grab the phone. I jumped on the bed with the cordless and ran to the other side of the room, screaming, "Jose! Call—"

The guy pulled a knife out of his boot and charged at me. I dropped the phone and picked up the gun that I had dropped on the floor. Though he kept swinging his long blade at me, I aimed it at his heart. I pulled the trigger and heard the shot echo.

The guy hollered, dropped the knife, and grabbed his shoulder. Then he glared at me and pulled a two-foot length of rope out of his pants pocket.

"What did I do?" I asked as he stalked toward me. "If you're gonna kill me, at least tell me why."

He ignored my request and continued toward me.

"Stay back or I'll shoot," I screamed. He kept coming.

I grazed the top of the black ski mask to scare him. It worked. He stopped. When the blaring sirens grew louder, he quickly opened the front door of my apartment and dashed out, leaving a trail of blood. I dropped the gun and fell to the floor.

I knelt there, trembling with fear. Not only had I almost been killed, but my friend was dead. Who was behind this? Would he be back?

In my emotional state I started scanning the room for more trouble, and my eyes rested on the package I'd picked up from Jose. When I opened it, there was nothing in it. It must have been a diversion sent by the murderer.

Lord, I prayed, *I need You to help me out here. What should I do? If I stay and try to explain what happened, will the cops believe me?*

The sirens were getting louder. I had to make a decision quickly.

With a murderer on the loose, maybe jail was the safest place

I could be. Then again, I'd be there for the rest of my life if I was convicted of murder.

My eyes landed on my suitcase—it was still packed. I grabbed it and flew out the door. I bumped into Jose on my way down the stairs.

"I heard shots," he said.

"I didn't do it, Jose." I shoved past him and continued down the steps.

"Señorita, wait! The police will be here soon."

I suddenly noticed the sirens had stopped. I heard quick, heavy footsteps on the stairs below me.

Turning back to Jose, I whispered, "I need your help. You've got to stall them."

He frowned at me for a moment.

"Please," I begged.

"Follow me," he mouthed. He led me to the fourth floor and unlocked the first apartment on the right. "Go in here and escape through the window," he said. Then he handed me a set of keys. "You can take my truck."

I wanted to grab him and hug him. Instead I pulled my keys out of my pants pocket and handed them to Jose. It probably wasn't safe for me to drive my own car, anyway.

I ran through the apartment, fear pulsing through my veins. What was I going to do? Where could I run? I didn't have time to think it all through. I'd have to discover a solution along the way. The murderer was still out there and my friend was dead. I wasn't safe.

I grabbed my purse and the suitcase that I hadn't unpacked and climbed out the window onto the fire escape.

As I ran through the security gate I could see police cars heading toward me. I prayed they wouldn't see me as I scanned the parking area, looking for Jose's green pickup truck. When I found it, my shaky hands unlocked the doors. To my surprise, it started right up.

The stench of Jose's truck made my stomach queasy because it smelled like he had been smoking in the truck for years without ever cleaning it, so I rolled down my windows. Loud sirens reminded me of the danger I was in.

I drove the speed limit through the city, my heart pounding. I turned on the truck's air conditioner, but it only blew warm air at me. Jose's dirty truck was littered with empty soda cans, cigarette packs, fast-food containers, and old clothes. It smelled like a locker room, but I was grateful for the means of escape.

Before I could get to the interstate, a gray van appeared behind me, driving a bit too fast. Before I knew it, its front bumper hit me from behind. I sped up but he bumped me again, harder.

I sped up more. The van kept up with me. I jerked the steering wheel hard to the left, making the tires screech. I crossed the center divider and moved into the path of oncoming traffic. The cars swerved and honked, trying to avoid hitting me head-on.

The van pulled up beside me. I glanced at the driver. It was that same horrifying man in the black ski mask!

We raced down the wrong side of the road. Three or four cars at a time were appearing every few seconds, barely missing my truck, the van, and each other.

Figuring there was a good possibility that I was going to die, I started praying out loud. "Lord, please help me find a way out of this. Help me survive somehow and not hurt anyone else. Give me the strength to find my way."

The van rammed the side of Jose's truck, knocking me over half a lane. I turned the steering wheel sharply, digging my right fender into the van's driver's-side door. He hit me again and I hit him back. The sound of metal crunching, the squealing of tires, and the smell of gas and burning rubber heightened my fear.

We rounded a bend in the road and I saw a black Honda coming straight toward us. There was no place for me to go. I was blocked between the van and the Honda.

I glanced at the driver of the van, trying to plead with him to get out of the way of the oncoming car. He lifted his ski mask. It was Rudy Roberts. He sneered at me as my heart raced with fear. Even more questions came to my terrified brain. Who hired

Roberts, a known hit man? Or was he working independently. Whatever his motives, I had to remember all I'd been taught and somehow get myself out of this.

I pressed the gas harder and turned the steering wheel left. When the van turned toward me, I jerked the steering wheel right so hard I sent the van careening off the road. It screeched over the concrete blocks of a small parking lot and rammed into an office building. The van flipped over, slid across the asphalt, then crashed into a wall of glass.

I slammed both feet onto the brakes. The truck must have skidded for half a mile before it stopped. The black Honda swerved a little but was unharmed.

I sat in the car on the shoulder of the road, staring back at the overturned van. *Roberts wanted me dead!* I watched the van for several moments, wondering if Roberts was dead. When no one climbed out, I thought, *I've got to go back. I have to make sure.*

I put the truck into reverse, and the motor died. I turned the key in the ignition but couldn't get the engine to turn over. I hit the steering wheel. "Don't quit on me now."

I turned the key again and heard nothing but a long, low rumble.

"I'm losing it here, God," I said aloud. "You've got to help me get this stupid truck started. I have to get out of here before that guy crawls out of the van and comes after me!"

I tried once more to start the truck. It sprang to roaring life. "Finally," I cried out. "Thank You, Lord!"

I looked back at the van. Still no movement. I put the truck into reverse, but before I could move, the van burst into flames.

I put the car in drive and sped off. Cars on both sides of the road came down the street, slowing down when their drivers saw the fire.

I couldn't think about what was going to happen next. I simply put as much distance between me and that van as I could, thankful that I was alive.

I suddenly realized that God had delayed the starting of the truck so I would not be in harm's way when the van exploded. *Thank You, Lord!*

I looked at my watch to check the time and saw blood all over it. I didn't know where it was coming from, but I knew I had to find its origin so I could stop the bleeding.

A neon sign along the side of the road flashed into view, indicating a gas station. I checked the gauge—it was just above the Empty mark.

I went into the rest room to wash off the blood and saw that a piece of glass from the truck window had cut my hand. I applied pressure on the wound with paper towels and it stopped bleeding.

I went back to the truck and filled the gas tank, then found a pay phone. In my rush to leave the apartment, I had neglected to pick up my cell phone.

With trembling fingers, I tried calling Troy's house, but he didn't answer. I dialed his cell phone number. When I heard his voice, I was so elated I almost dropped the receiver.

Troy told me to take a few deep breaths. When I calmed down enough to speak, I told him everything. He didn't seem very surprised to know that Roberts had come after me. "I don't think he was working on his own, either. Your friend lives in New York. That's where we've tracked Roberts to. This was a setup."

"But why? Who's behind all this? I can't believe Stokes wants me dead."

"Whoever it is, has connections on the inside. Turn off your headlights and stay put. I'll be there in forty minutes." He gave me a secret headlight code so I wouldn't get out of the car for the wrong person.

Twenty-nine minutes later, Troy's black Montero Sport zoomed into the gas station parking lot.

"The cops are going to arrest you for reckless driving," I teased him as we got out of our cars and hugged. "And I don't have the clout to get you out of jail."

"Here's some money." Troy handed me what looked like around five hundred dollars in twenties and fifties.

Not touching the cash, I said, "I can't take this. You can't help me this way. You'll lose your job."

"You saved my life, remember? I owe you. Shoot, I wouldn't have a job if I was dead."

Trying to hand me the money again, he said, "Plus, you'll need it to get somewhere safe and stay there till I can find out what happened and figure out how to get you out of this mess."

I took the money.

He asked me to give him my credit cards and checks so I wouldn't use them. "Too easy to trace," he explained as I handed them over.

"Every law-enforcement agency in the country is looking for this truck," he said. "Give me the keys."

"It's not mine."

"I know. It belongs to your apartment manager."

"How do you know that?"

"Your apartment manager told the police. They put out an APB on the truck."

We traded keys. "If you get caught driving this truck, you'll be in trouble. Or if I get caught with your car, you could go down, too."

"Don't worry about me. I'm gonna take this truck to an informant friend of mine who owns a place where they chop cars up and sell them. No one will find it." He gazed at the dilapidated truck. "And it looks like I'll be doing Jose a big favor."

"Come on, let's sit over here on this bench and talk. Chris, I want you to tell me everything. Don't leave out any detail."

I told him all I could think of.

"You're being set up," he said.

"I agree. But how can I prove it?"

"We've got to find out who sent Roberts to kill you."

"But he's dead."

"I can still find out who he was working for. We tracked his movements off and on. We thought he was lying low. I'll just have to relook at those tapes to find the connection between him and Max."

"All this started after I introduced Max to Reverend Stokes, and word got out about the money for the campaign. Maybe the bank where he worked is involved."

Troy handed me a cell phone and a gun.

"What's this for?"

"I want you to be able to get in touch with me, and you need to be able to protect yourself if the people who are setting you up locate you," he said. "Do you know where you'll go?"

"I have no idea."

"Maybe that's best."

We sat there on the bench in silence for several moments, lost in our thoughts, neither of us wanting to separate any sooner than we had to. "So, when is the FBI gonna promote you?"

I remembered that he had been waiting on a promotion in the FBI.

"I don't know. Maybe if I crack this case—"

"Oh, so you have an ulterior motive for helping me," I said with a smile.

"Yeah, Roberts has been a thorn in all our sides for far too long. Something good needs to come out of my dealings with that bastard."

I joked, "You're right, and I agree—if you solve this, you should be the highest-ranking officer in the FBI."

"Get on the road," he smirked, "and stay alert."

"Thank you."

I kissed him on the cheek. Then I headed to the black Montero Sport as he walked toward Jose's truck.

I drove down the road without even looking at the signs to see what direction I was headed. When the interstate ran out, I hopped onto another one.

I drove aimlessly for hours, stopping only when I needed gas, food, or the bathroom.

When I couldn't keep my eyes open any longer, I found a rest station, locked the doors, reclined my seat, and closed my eyes. I desperately needed to get some sleep, but my nerves were too on edge. Everything around me was pitch-black and spooky-looking.

Eight days passed that way. Besides telling the gas station attendants what pump number I wanted, the only person I talked to was myself.

I longed for a bath and a comfortable mattress, but I couldn't risk being seen at a hotel. Then again, with my clothes being so dirty and smelly, and my hair all greasy, probably no one would recognize me. I looked more like a homeless street person than an ex-agent wanted for murder.

I found a diner just off the interstate and enjoyed the first decent meal I'd had in over a week. Then I checked into a tiny motel. I had just finished bringing my luggage in when Troy's cell phone rang.

"I've been trying to call you for days, girl," he said in a panicked voice. "Are you all right?"

"I'm fine," I assured him.

"Why haven't you been answering the phone?"

"I've been driving constantly. I've got to watch the road, so I turned off the ringer," I told him.

"Well, keep it on from now on. I've been worried sick."

"What's happening back there?" I asked, settling onto the hard mattress.

Troy said, "The FBI identified the remains of the guy who tried to kill you."

"That's great."

"Not really. The guy we found in the van had been dead for ten years. Roberts is still out there."

"What? How can that be?" I exclaimed, really confused.

"About three years ago when I first got on the Roberts case, we found a body that was burned beyond recognition and had to use dental records for identification. The dental records identified that guy as the deceased so we naturally assumed it was him, but apparently they were wrong because the guy in the van was actually the guy we thought was dead ten years ago."

"Is that enough for the cops to think I'm innocent?"

"It's not enough to clear you, but it tells me we're on the right path. There's something else, too. About two million dollars was stolen from the bank Max worked at. The FBI thinks your friend Max may have embezzled the money. They're saying that might be part of the reason you killed him," Troy said.

"Great. So now they've got a motive."

"Just be careful. Keep that cell phone with you all the time, and leave it on, so I can get hold of you if something happens. Get as far away from D.C. as possible. Where are you now?"

"I don't know."

"What's the area code on the telephone?"

I went around the corner to the pay phone. "It's 615."

After a lengthy pause, he said, "That's Tennessee. Are you in a big city?"

"No, just an isolated little town."

"Good. The more isolated, the better."

"Hey, thanks for the credit cards and the money."

"You just take care of yourself. All this stuff is going to get figured out eventually, but you've got to keep yourself hidden for a while or you won't be around to see yourself cleared."

"Troy, you're an agent. You could make me turn myself in."

"If I thought you'd be treated fairly, I would. But I don't trust the system right now. We need to get some hard evidence."

"How can we do that? Max, the only person who could have cleared me, is dead."

"You're a Christian, right? Well, find a Bible and start reading it. You can't go crazy on me. I need you to be strong, all right?"

"Okay."

After hanging up the phone, I opened the drawer on the bed table. Sure enough, there was a Gideon Bible. I'd never been more happy to see the Word of God.

"God, I'm too tired to read," I said aloud. "I just pray that You will help me find the answers. Keep me strong. And be with Troy, my mom, my sister. And Sebastian, too. Keep him safe in Your arms because mine are too far away."

Suddenly it dawned on me. "I'm not that far away. Tennessee is only a few hours from Atlanta."

I started coming up with a plan to allow me to see Sebastian. Before I could figure out all the details, I fell fast asleep.

The next morning, I realized there was no way I could see Sebastian. I took a long, hot shower, changed into clean clothes, put on makeup, styled my hair, and got back into the car for another long day of driving.

A day later I checked into a motel in Atlanta. I wanted desperately to see Sebastian, to feel his arms around me and his lips on mine.

"Lord," I said as I knelt beside the motel-room bed, "I pray that You will allow me to see him. If I see him, Lord, please let him believe me and support the decision that I made to go on the run. Please don't let my situation ruin his chance of being elected as lieutenant governor, because Georgia needs a good man whose aim is to help its citizens. Also, keep me safe until I am cleared of these charges, Amen."

"Keep doing what you're doing right now," I sensed Him telling me. *"Seek Me, pray and believe in Me."*

Tears flowed down my cheeks onto the paisley-colored bedspread. "I don't even know if Sebastian wants to see me again. He might even turn me in. But I'm so close."

I got up off my knees and found that the fear that I had before I prayed was gone and was replaced by a peaceful feeling. As I picked up my small suitcase, I felt certain that I was supposed to go to Sebastian. I got in the car and drove toward his place.

With knots in my stomach, I used Troy's cell phone to call Sebastian's apartment. I got his answering machine. I wanted to leave a message, but didn't feel it was safe.

He'd have to come home sooner or later, so I decided to go to his apartment and wait for him. I thought about trying to find a way to sneak into his building without being seen.

I considered trying to find his car and then getting into the backseat.

No, I can't do that.

When I arrived at Sebastian's apartment building I parked across the street, but I didn't see his car so I sat in the Montero for several minutes and waited. Then I saw Sebastian's car pull into his apartment complex. Rather than driving into the gated parking structure, he parked at the curb and ran to the front entrance. He got out of the car with a department-store bag, and I noticed that he was wearing a tan tailored suit with tan shoes, tan shirt, and a tan-and-beige tie.

A few moments later, Sebastian returned to the car without the bag and went to the passenger side. He opened the door and pulled out a briefcase from the backseat. I saw a pair of shapely brown legs in the front. My heart skipped a beat.

He exchanged a few words with his companion, then got in the driver's side and drove off. I followed at a discreet distance. *Why am I doing this?* I asked myself. *I have really hit rock bottom. This is crazy. I wouldn't want him to do this to me.*

But I couldn't force myself to turn around. I slowed down a little so he wouldn't spot me, even though I knew he wouldn't recognize Troy's car.

I followed Sebastian to a cozy little cafe. When he opened the passenger door, a woman in a short, clingy black dress stepped out. When she turned around, I recognized her. It was that Penelope chick. The one who went to school with Sebastian's sister. The woman Mrs. Stokes wanted to be her daughter-in-law.

A few moments after they entered the restaurant, I went in, too. I looked around the place, as if trying to locate some friends I'd planned to meet. I found Sebastian and Penelope in a secluded corner booth.

I took the booth next to theirs and sat with my back to Sebastian's.

"I'm twenty-two, Sebastian," I heard Penelope say. "I have to get my life in order. I can't date forever. With the election just months away, you need to do something to get more votes. A big wedding would certainly make the world stop and take notice."

Sebastian cleared his throat. "Actually, Penelope, that's what I wanted to talk to you about today."

My stomach did a somersault. He was about to ask this girl to marry him. I knew he didn't love her. He was going to take a bride as a career move!

I felt like standing up and screaming, *"Don't do it! If you want to get married, do it right. I'm the one you love, not her."* But he was a grown man. I didn't need to tell him what to do.

Then again, I didn't need to sit there and listen, either. If I moved quietly, I could get out of there without him seeing me.

Just as I started to stand up, a waitress came to my table. She handed me a menu and asked what I wanted to drink. "Just water," I said as quietly as I could.

"You want to hear about our specials?" she asked.

I shook my head, and she went away.

"Penelope," I heard Sebastian saying, "you're a beautiful woman. You're smart and extremely classy. I'm sure there are a number of guys who would love to be with you."

What a tacky proposal. Just ask her, already.

"That's so sweet," Penelope said in a sugary voice. "But I want you."

"You don't need to settle for somebody who's not in love with you."

I almost choked on my water.

"Oh, darling," Penelope said, "we can grow into that. My dad wasn't in love with my mom when they got married."

Man, that girl is really desperate.

"I don't think so," Sebastian said quietly. "My heart belongs to somebody else."

My heart started beating wildly.

"Who?" Penelope's soft voice gained a sharp edge. "Is it that girl who used to guard your dad?"

I almost fell out of my chair as I strained to hear his reply.

"Yes," he said.

I felt like jumping up and planting a big, wet kiss right on his lips.

"Oh, please," Penelope scoffed. "She's wanted for murder, you know."

"I'm aware of that," he snapped.

Does he think I did it?

"But I know she's not guilty," he added.

Wow—he believes in me.

"That doesn't matter," Penelope argued. "Being with some-one like that would ruin you."

Penelope chattered on, but I didn't pay any attention. Sebastian loved me, and he was concerned about me. He missed me. He was scared for me.

"Fine," I heard Penelope say. "Don't bother taking me home. I don't need to waste any more time with you."

She stormed right past my table. To my relief, Sebastian didn't go after her.

"Oh, Chris," I heard him groan, "where are you?"

I stood, turned around, and said, "I'm right here."

"Chris?" He stood. I jumped into his arms and he twirled me around. He kissed my forehead, then my cheek.

"How long have you—?" he asked happily. Then his face fell. "You heard all that, didn't you?"

"Yeah." I laughed. "I thought you were about to ask that girl to marry you." I jabbed him softly in the stomach.

He stroked my face with his fingertips. "How could I marry her when I'm in love with you?"

I kissed him on the lips and embraced him tightly and said, "She's right about one thing."

"About what?"

"Loving me might not be the best thing for you."

"Since the first day I laid eyes on you, I was warned to stay away. But something in my spirit keeps drawing me to you."

We sat in the booth, sharing a bench. "So, fill me in."

"On what?"

"Everything."

I whispered my story to him, nervous about being overheard but eager to tell him my side of the story. I could tell he believed every word I said.

"Follow me to my place," he suggested.

"I don't think that's a good idea. I wouldn't want you to get in trouble for harboring a fugitive."

"Trust me, Chris. I promise you'll be safe with me." He reached for my hand and looked deeply into my eyes. "I've been wor-

ried about you for too long. It's time for me to take care of you
and make sure you're okay."

Leaving the Montero in the parking lot, he drove me to his
place. Sebastian distracted the bellman while I slipped inside
unnoticed.

Being in his apartment felt strange. In one sense, I was perfectly comfortable. But I kept thinking about our last time
there, when our relationship took a downward spiral. I had to
be stronger this time. Sebastian loved me. I wasn't going to ruin
it by trying to satisfy my lust.

"I know you've been scared," he said as we sat on his couch,
"but you don't have to run anymore. I've been praying for you,
asking God to get you to call me, and you did," he said in a concerned tone. "I promised God that if you got in touch with me,
I'd do my best to convince you to turn yourself in."

I pushed off his chest with my hand. "What are you talking
about?"

"Chris, listen to me. God's Word says we're supposed to obey
the law of the land."

"But I didn't do anything wrong. My close FBI friend Troy
said that if I turn myself in now, I could get life in prison without the possibility of parole. He thinks we should try to get evidence first, to prove my innocence."

He exhaled heavily. "Chris, God will honor you and protect
you if you do the right thing."

"No. No way." I stood and walked to the window.

He came up behind me and wrapped his arms around me.
"Baby, you can't live the way you have been. Just turn yourself
in. Get a good lawyer. Hire a private investigator to figure this
out. The longer you stay in hiding, the harder you're making it
on yourself."

What he said made sense. Maybe this was why God urged me
to see Sebastian.

"I don't want to die," I whimpered.

He tightened his embrace and kissed the back of my neck. "I
don't think God's going to allow that to happen."

My life had gone crazy. My fate was out of my hands, and I didn't like that one bit. Would turning myself in get everything back in control?

I walked to the window and looked at the azure sky. I was tired of running. Tired of sliding down this crazy slope.

Chapter 14

Slant

I stood in my dismal cage and stared at the iron bars. Blood gushed from my mouth as a result of a squabble I'd had with one of my cellmates. She was a big, rugged woman, at least six feet tall. She had corn-rolled braids, saggy jeans, and high-top tennis shoes. She'd asked to borrow a couple of dollars from me, and when I said no, she punched me in my jaw. Then a buddy of hers hit me in the gut. I was so numb I couldn't move. I just kept staring at the bars, thinking about the presiding officer in her black robe chanting, "Guilty!" My body went limp and fell to the cold, dirty cement floor.

"No!" I screamed. I opened my eyes and looked around Sebastian's bedroom.

I heard a door open. Sebastian ran to my side from the family room and shook my shoulder. "Chris, wake up," he said. "It's just a dream."

I'd had such a rough night. Sebastian and I agreed that we didn't want to tempt each other, so separate sleeping arrangements were best. Though I agreed, as I smelled him through his sheets I wished he was beside me. I wanted his comfort. When that wasn't an option I just tossed back and forth, thinking I was never going to be cleared. The next thing I knew I was in the midst of a horrible dream.

As my head cleared, I realized I'd been having a nightmare.

"I can't turn myself in," I told him, sitting up in the guest bed. "Don't make me do it. I just can't."

"I love you," he said softly. "I wouldn't ask you to do this if I didn't believe it was best. I promise I'll be with you every step of the way."

"I need more time," I said.

"You said you'd be ready to do this today. I can't let you back out now."

I got out of bed and looked out the window. "It's not your life, all right?"

"Oh, but it is." He stood up, came over to me, and put his arms around my waist. "If you disappear, do you think my life will go on?"

"I don't know," I said as I laid my head back on his chest.

I turned around in his arms and looked into his eyes. "In my dream, there was blood all over the place. The bars wouldn't go away. The presiding officer said I was guilty."

Sebastian placed his hands in mine. "Will you pray with me?"

I hesitated. I knew what God would tell me if I asked Him. But I didn't want to hear it. I wanted to stay at Sebastian's place forever, hidden from the rest of the world. Why couldn't it be that way?

I finally decided I really did need divine guidance. So I slid my hand in Sebastian's. We bowed our heads.

"Lord," Sebastian said, closing his eyes, "we're in a lot of chaos right now. We're filled with confusion, anxiety, and uncertainty. I ask You right now to send Your angels to calm things down. Please confirm Your will for Christian. Give me the right words to say to comfort her. Help us both through this. I don't want to see her hurt anymore, but I know she's Your child and You've got her in Your hands. She's nervous and scared. She's had no peace and little sleep. Lord, I praise You right now, in advance, for helping us to work through all this. In Jesus' name. Amen."

Sebastian squeezed my hand and opened his eyes. "You don't have to fear, Chris," he said. "The same God who helped Moses free the children of Israel from Egypt can help you now."

I threw my arms around him. He'd said exactly what I needed to hear. God wasn't going to leave me. He was in control. And even if I ended up in jail, there was hope. After all, in the book of Acts, when Paul and Silas went to jail, they sang until the walls came down. Sebastian's prayer helped me see things more clearly.

He went to the CD player and put on a song of praise. Then Sebastian and I danced around the apartment, praising God and thanking Him for who He was.

"You look so beautiful when you're praising God," Sebastian said as we stopped dancing long enough to catch our breath. "I love you."

His words meant a lot, but praising God felt even better.

Sebastian and I both agreed that I should surrender myself to someone I knew, so I called Troy.

"Troy, this is Christian."

"How are you doing?"

"I'm okay—I'm in Atlanta with Sebastian."

"What! Are you crazy?"

"It's okay, Troy. He knows that I'm innocent and we've decided that I should surrender, but only to you."

"Are you sure that this is what you want to do? You know you've been charged with first-degree murder, don't you?"

"I understand that, but I feel I must surrender. I'm tired of running. Plus, now that I'm a fugitive, the FBI is all over this case. Because of our past history, I know they'll let you bring me in. Also, you need to come down here anyway to pick up your Montero," I said jokingly.

Troy agreed to fly down to Atlanta that afternoon. Sebastian and I met him at the airport and when he looked at us together, I saw a look on his face that said he knew we were more than just friends.

Sebastian called a press conference for first thing the next morning. He didn't tell the media what it was about, he just said he had an important announcement. Then Troy called our FBI office, talked to Supervisor Hunter, and told him I would surrender peacefully immediately following the press conference.

When the two of us arrived at the Atlanta Police Department, a large crowd had gathered. As reporters mumbled and cameras flashed, Sebastian and I wound our way through the crowd, hand in hand. We stood at the top of the concrete steps, still holding hands, and faced the group. The crowd immediately hushed.

With a dozen microphones and videocams pointed at us, Sebastian announced, "This is Christian Ware. She is a very important person in my life. There is currently a warrant out for her arrest, but she is innocent, and there are several people working hard to prove it."

I stared at Troy, talking with two FBI officers. He was standing nearby, waiting to take me to D.C. after Sebastian and I were finished.

"Turning the woman I love over to authorities for a crime she didn't commit breaks my heart. But I believe in doing the right thing, even when the consequences are risky."

Sebastian glanced at me to indicate that it was my turn.

"My life has been crazy these last few weeks. Everything I thought I believed in, everything I stood for, everything good that I've ever done, was stripped away from me. The world thinks I'm a killer, but somebody set me up and made it look like I killed Max Cross. Then that same person tried to kill me."

I looked at Sebastian. His smile gave me the confidence to keep going.

"Whoever is behind this plan to discredit me has also tried to damage Reverend Stokes's reputation by saying that I am responsible for introducing him to known felons. But I never tried to sabotage his campaign."

A barrage of lightbulbs went off in my face, but I kept my cool.

"Politics can be a dirty game. Some people are willing to pay any cost, or promise impossible favors, even stoop to illegal activities, just to get elected. Well, I'm not running for any political office. I don't owe anyone anything. I'm not trying to get anything from anybody except the truth. Because when the truth comes out, everyone will see that I'm innocent. However, I have decided to turn myself in until that can be proven."

The reporters raised their hands and started blurting out questions, but I didn't have a chance to answer them because Troy grabbed me roughly, slapped handcuffs on my wrists, and escorted me to their black van waiting at the curb. Sebastian tried to come to my aid, but other FBI agents stopped him.

Troy turned to my guy and said, "Man, don't worry, I'll make sure she's treated right."

Sebastian nodded, but I could tell by the solemn look in his eye he was second-guessing this decision.

When I felt the cold handcuffs on my wrists, I instantly wondered if I'd made a mistake. Maybe I should have run after all.

"I love you," Sebastian screamed, giving me comfort to hang in there.

As I was being shoved into the van, I heard a reporter say, "This is going to ruin his chances of being elected lieutenant governor of Georgia."

During the ride to the jail, I tried talking about sports and politics with the black cop who was in the seat beside me. We ended up having a pretty good chat.

"You're pretty cool," he said to me. "I've got good instincts, and my gut feeling is that if you did kill that man, you would've stayed around and said, 'Here I am. I did it.' "

"That's right," I told him.

The car took me to the airport where I boarded a commercial plane. Once on board, I was handcuffed to Troy, who said that he had to make it look like he wasn't giving me special treatment. I smiled and waved to the guy in the car as they drove away.

When the plane landed at the airport in D.C., I saw Sebastian standing by the hangar, waiting. Beside him stood a tall black man in a navy blue suit. Sebastian introduced him as Greg Smith, my attorney.

"Don't you worry, Ms. Ware," Mr. Smith assured me. "You're not going to spend one night in jail."

"Greg went to Harvard with me," Sebastian said. "He's one of the top African-American defense attorneys on the East Coast."

Unfortunately, the police took so long booking and charging me that no presiding officer would come out that late. The arraignment was scheduled for first thing the next morning.

Sebastian, Greg, and I sat down in an interrogation room and I told my entire story. We decided that I should plead not guilty. Greg would argue for bail, and if bail was granted, Sebastian would pay it.

When the police officers told Sebastian he had to leave, he pulled me close, hugged me tight, then looked deep into my eyes. "I won't be with you tonight, but God will. I'll be praying for you." Tears fell from his eyes and his voice cracked. "I love you with all my heart, and I'll see you through this. Together we'll prove your innocence to the world."

I wiped the tears from his face. "Shhh, baby, don't cry—have faith in God. I know God will see us both through this ordeal. I love you."

We began to kiss passionately but were interrupted by an officer who told us it was time for me to go.

"Sebastian, I'm scared," I said as a female guard slapped handcuffs on me again.

"Just pray, Christian. God will bring us through this. You have to be strong, baby."

"Come on, man," Greg said, tugging on his arm. "You'll see her tomorrow. I promise."

The guard took me to a room where my fingerprints and mug shots were taken. Then I had to take off my clothes and allow every cavity of my body to be searched. My clothes were put in a clear plastic bag and I was given orange overalls to put on. Then I was taken to a cell block that smelled like urine and smoke.

The cells were the size of a small bathroom, with little space for anything but sitting down on one of the two narrow bunk beds. A sink and a toilet were the only other furnishings.

"Hey, wait a minute," I hollered when I noticed that two women occupied each cell. The guard turned around and looked at me with raised eyebrows. "I'm a Secret Service agent," I explained to her. "I'm supposed to be segregated from the regular inmates."

She laughed heartily, shoved me into a cell, and closed the door with a loud, metallic slam. Memories of the dream I'd had about being in jail suddenly filled my mind.

"This is your cellmate, Mrs. Willie Mae," the chunky woman guard said smugly. "She requested that you be put in her cell, though I sure don't know why."

The guard laughed as she walked away down the hall. I could hear the soles of her shoes slapping the concrete floor—the sound echoed through the row of cells.

I stared at Mrs. Willie Mae. She looked to be in her late fifties, with heavily wrinkled eyes and thick, salt-and-pepper hair. She was a heavyset, strong-looking woman, more muscular than fat.

"I been in prison for thirty-two years," she said in a rusty voice. "They put me in here 'cause I stabbed somebody."

She sat on the lower bunk and looked up at me. "I ain't gonna lie to you, honey. I did it."

"Why?" I asked, barely breathing.

"A teenage boy raped my baby and killed her. Wouldn't nobody do nothing about it, so I found him myself and made him pay. I realize now that vengeance is the Lord's, and I feel bad for what I done. But at the time it seemed like the only thing I could do."

"I'm so sorry," I said, sitting beside her on the bunk.

"Everybody in here has been talking about you for weeks. Rumor has it you've been on the run."

"That's right."

"Why?"

"I didn't do what I'm accused of. I was trying to gather evidence to prove it."

"Guess you didn't find any, or you wouldn't be here."

My shoulders slumped. "I don't know that any will ever be found."

Mrs. Willie Mae picked up a Bible from under her pillow.

She turned to Psalm 10 and read verses one through six to me. Then she started breaking down what the passage meant.

"In them first two verses, we can see that David was angry. Mighty angry. He kept asking the Lord what he'd done to deserve such a fate."

"I can understand that," I grumbled.

"In verses three and four, though, he realized that maybe there was something God was trying to get through to him. David realized he was blocking his own blessing.

"David got himself right with the Lord, and verses five and six record his praises to God. David didn't worry about his circumstances. He just praised the Lord. And the next thing you know, he got what he wanted."

She closed the Bible and put it back under her pillow. "So don't you worry about getting the evidence you need. Just think about how good God is and start praising Him. Even if you never step outside this jail cell, God's been good enough for you to praise Him. Shout praises so loud until it gives you a headache."

I couldn't help but laugh. She was so passionate and so right. God had brought Sebastian back to me. He had given me a great relationship with my sister. More important, He gave me Himself.

"I can do that," I said.

She started singing some old hymns and I sang along with her. "Thank You, Lord," I cried loudly, "for sending Your Son." I waved my hands high. "I love You, God," I shouted.

For two days I spent most of my time singing and shouting praises to God. I wrote a list of all that I had to be thankful for. I loved my carpet, my car, fresh air. I was thankful for the telephone. The two days passed quickly.

On day three, the guard came to my cell and said, "Ware, you got a visitor." She led me down a series of hallways and into a small room divided in half by a glass wall. On each side of the wall were little booths, each with a chair and a phone. When the guard shoved me into one of the booths, I was shocked to see Dion sitting on the other side of the glass partition.

I looked at Eden's husband through the glass. We both picked up the phone. "What are you doing here?" I asked gruffly.

"I have something to say that you'll want to hear."

"All I want to know from you is how Eden's doing."

Ignoring my attitude, he said, "She's fine. I've found the Lord through that whole ordeal. And now I'm a changed man."

I couldn't believe what I was hearing. But his mannerisms were more relaxed, the cold expression on his face gone. He even talked with humility. Was he really saved?

Quickly I said, "I don't believe you, and anyway, I'm sure you didn't come here to tell me that."

"Whether you believe me or not isn't the issue. You'll see in time that my heart has changed. I feel reborn and though I know my past sins are forgiven, I'm still hurting from them. So I came here to tell you something that I think can help your case."

Still reluctant, I listened on.

"You remember I was with Max a few hours before he died?"

"Yeah, that's who called me to tell me you sent my girl to the hospital. He said he had to see you," I said.

"When he came to visit Eden in the hospital, he told me that if anything happened to him, I was supposed to get a package he'd left at my house a month ago and give it to you. If you weren't alive, Max said, I was supposed to take the package to the cops."

If it weren't for the glass between us, I'd have slapped Dion for sitting on this information for so long.

"I asked Max why he couldn't go get the package himself. He told me somebody was after him. I thought he was just para-noid—now I wish I had listened. Maybe I could have saved his life."

"I did the same thing," I admitted. "Just a few minutes before I left him that day, he told me someone was after him. Don't blame yourself." I took a deep breath, finally feeling Dion's pain. "Did you get the package?"

"Yeah," he said, lowering his eyes.

"Have you opened it?"

"Max told me it would be better if I didn't. Considering what happened to him, I wanted to honor his request and just give it to you."

He leaned down and picked up a large, bulging manila envelope from the floor beside him.

A guard on his side of the glass partition came up and took the envelope. "You'll get this later," he assured me.

"So," I asked Dion after the guard resumed his position in the corner, "how are things between you and Eden?"

"I messed up with her big-time," he said, massaging his forehead. "But she's giving me another chance."

"How did you get so out of whack, Dion?"

"I didn't have God. I always swore I would never be anything like my father. But as soon as I took a wife, his characteristics started to surface."

"And why the change now?"

"God broke me and showed me why I needed a Savior. I can't explain it—it's just like I heard Him calling my name. We had a chat and I agreed to His terms. Plus, Eden and I have been in counseling. Besides, now that my best friend's gone, she's all I've got."

I stared at the broken guy before me. Though I couldn't completely forgive him for what he'd done to my girlfriend, I knew I had to pray for him. I hoped this change he spoke of was real and would last.

The guard, who was still holding the envelope Dion had brought for me, tapped him on the shoulder and told him his time was up. I thanked Dion for bringing me the package. He told me to let him know if there was anything else I needed.

Back in my cell, I stared at the package the guard had brought to me. I could tell it had already been opened and searched. Was this the evidence I needed to get me out of this horrible mess? I decided to wait for my lawyer to arrive, hoping this was the break we needed.

"The package contained a tape and several documents," Greg said, looking at me with a solemn face. Sebastian reached out and took my hand. The three of us sat at a table in a small room that was used for defendants to meet with their lawyers.

"We haven't verified everything," Greg said, "but one of the pieces of paper had a phone number on it. It belongs to a private investigator, the one who rigged Max's office three weeks before he was shot."

"Go on," I said impatiently.

"Apparently Max hired him because he was afraid for his life—he was trying to find out who was threatening him and why."

"He told me that much."

"The security cameras at the bank where he worked taped the proof he was looking for," Sebastian said. "The bank president talked to four goons in slick suits and dark glasses, about how he was going to frame you for something, and if Max didn't cooperate in bringing you down, he wouldn't live too long. Rudy Roberts is one of those men." Sebastian squeezed my hand. "When Max asked why he was doing this, the guy told him the orders were coming from a much higher place."

"What does that mean?"

"I'm afraid I don't have a clue."

"What happens now?" I asked.

"We're going to turn this stuff over to the FBI and see if they can come up with the missing pieces of the puzzle."

"I have a good friend who's an FBI agent. Troy Evans. I'm sure he'd be glad to help."

"Max gave the stolen money to his buddy Dion. He's turning it in to the authorities today."

"So is all this enough to clear me?"

Greg shrugged. "The district attorney has to assess the evidence. Your fate is in his hands now."

The guard came to escort me back to my cell. As I was led from the room, Sebastian and I gazed at each other, our eyes expressing our love—and our desperation.

As I took each step down the narrow corridor, I realized my fate wasn't in the hands of the D.A. It wasn't even in my hands. God would have to clear me. I just had to focus on the blessings He had bestowed upon me. At least we had some evidence now.

Even before the guard slammed my cell door shut, I had decided to adopt a new motto for my life: Too blessed to be stressed! Even though I wasn't free on the outside, I was free within. Nobody could take away my joy.

Moments later, the guard came back. She slapped handcuffs on me and escorted me to the fourth floor of the jailhouse.

When the elevator doors opened, the guard handed me over to a security officer who took me to the assistant D.A.'s office, a large room with tall shelves filled with books. The prosecutor was a pale, balding, middle-aged man who sat behind an antique desk with a Tiffany lamp on it. He was holding a phone against his ear and looking out the window.

"Have a seat," the officer said. I settled into a small chair near the door. As I waited for the man to get off the phone, the door opened and Sebastian walked in. My heart leapt. He sat in the chair next to me, held my hand even though I was in handcuffs, and whispered that everything was going to be all right. The guard at the door motioned for us to quiet down.

When the assistant D.A. finally hung up, he folded his hands on the desk and looked at me. "The evidence brought in by your lawyer indicates that you were indeed framed."

I stared at him for a moment, hardly believing what I had just heard.

"One of the four people on the tape is the infamous Rudy Roberts, whom you shot months back, and who has made threats to the FBI office. Your buddy Troy Evans has been working around the clock to locate this man. Finally, he's been arrested. Since his fingerprints were found in your apartment, your story has credibility. Now, with Roberts trying to plea to lesser charges because we have so much on him, he's agreed to take the stand. He says he reports to the bank president. We know someone else even higher up has hired him. Though he says he knows no more, he will testify that you were not the murderer."

I jumped out of my chair and screamed.

"We're dismissing all charges."

Sebastian picked me up and twirled me around. I went over to the guard and held out my manacled hands. When he unlocked the cuffs, I grabbed Sebastian's hands and held them tight.

Sebastian drove me to FBI headquarters, where I answered more questions that I hoped would help them solve the case. Then we drove to a classy hotel where Sebastian promised I could relax and unwind. On the way to the hotel I told him that I thought the guy in the van was dead because I saw the van explode with him in it. Sebastian said that Troy found Roberts because he kept going back to a local hospital for treatment for injuries and burns. However, he managed to get out of the van with his life, then flee with his buddies.

"I want to go to my place and pick up some things," I said as Sebastian checked us in.

"Can't do that," he said. "Your apartment is still a crime scene, remember? It's off-limits."

The desk clerk handed Sebastian a key. "Will there be anything else, sir?" he asked.

"Not right now," Sebastian replied. "Thanks."

I followed him to the elevator. "I need to call my mom and tell her everything's okay."

"You can do that later," he said, punching the highest number on the elevator's keypad. "First you need to get some rest."

The elevator stopped at the top floor. When the doors opened, I saw a huge room with a fireplace, chandelier, oil paintings, and antique furniture. A dozen roses and a bottle of wine sat on an ornate side table.

"Is this the penthouse suite?" I asked.

"You've been in jail for too long," he said, leading me into the room. "Now you need to be treated like a queen. Since I can't get you a castle, the penthouse suite will have to do."

He strolled to a door in the left wall. When he opened it, a bunch of people poured out and screamed, "Surprise!"

My mom, my sister, Eden, Dion, Troy, and my fellow FBI agents all surrounded me with love and affection.

I thanked Sebastian for the party, then mingled with everyone and had a wonderful time. When things settled down a bit, I noticed my sister sitting alone on the couch. I invited her to go out on the balcony so we could talk privately.

"Have you thought about what you want to do with the baby?" I asked quietly.

"Yes," she said, staring into her glass of punch. "I've decided I have to do what's best for me."

I took her onto the balcony and closed the door. "Listen, I didn't want to have to tell you this, but . . ."

"What?" she asked.

"I had an abortion."

Her eyes grew wide.

"I still have dreams about my baby. I wonder if it was a boy or a girl, and how old he or she would be. Sometimes it hurts so bad I get a crampy feeling in the pit of my stomach." I placed my arm on her shoulder. "Crystal, I made the wrong choice by having sex with a guy I wasn't married to. But then I committed an even worse sin when I ended a human being's life just because it wasn't convenient for me. It was a selfish act, and I don't want you to walk down that road. Your conscience will eat at you every time you lay your eyes on a child for the rest of your life."

"Chris, I can't raise a child," she said as tears started to stream down her face.

"I agree. You're too young to be a mother. But there are plenty of people who want to adopt a baby. Why not give them a chance?"

"How would I know that my baby would go to a good family?"

"Why don't we ask God?"

She shook her head. "If God were watching over us, you wouldn't be in the mess you're in."

"Don't say that. If it wasn't for Him, I wouldn't have gotten out of jail so quickly. Only the Lord could have caused all that evidence to show up when it did." I took a deep breath. "Crystal, I'll go with you to the adoption agency if you want."

"My child will hate me when he finds out I gave him up because I didn't want him."

"That child will be thankful that you gave him a chance to live, and that you gave him to parents who loved him and could help him grow into the best person he could be."

She tilted her head slightly. "You sure have given me something to think about."

"Well, take all the time you need. It's a big decision."

"Thanks," she said as she gave me a hug.

When I opened the door, I saw Eden coming down the hall toward the bathroom. As my sister walked out of the room, I pulled Eden in.

"You're looking better," I said. The swelling on her face had gone down completely. "How do you feel?"

"I'm fine," she said.

"Really?" I asked, probing for details on more than just her physical condition.

"Chris, I know you think I'm wrong to stay with a guy who beat me. But ever since his best friend died, he's really changed. I guess Dion realized that it could have been him."

"How so?" I asked.

"I could have shot him or stabbed him. I could have hired somebody to kill him."

"Were you really at that point?" I asked.

"I'm not sure. I was close. At least, Dion thought I was." She breathed heavily, and I knew she was emotional. "But ever since his friend died, he's become a changed person. He realizes that what he did to me was wrong, and we're going to counseling at our church to help heal our relationship. He's really growing in his walk with God. Chris, he's changed and has not looked back once."

"Just be smart," I cautioned her. "Pray like crazy, and keep God at the center of your marriage."

"I will," she said. "I'm glad to see things are looking up for you."

"I still don't have a job."

"That will come. You've got peace, the kind only God can give. You may not be on top, but you're definitely on the upper part of the slant."

Chapter 15

Altitude

In September, I moved out of my apartment to a smaller one. I still didn't have a job, and my paid leave of absence was running out.

I'd been cleared of all charges, but the Agency wanted to conclude their internal investigation before a decision would be made about whether I kept my job or not. In the interim, I volunteered at church helping the homeless: feeding them, giving them clothes, and teaching workshops.

My sister had decided to give birth to her baby, but on the adoption agency application she insisted that she be allowed to approve the family seeking to adopt her child. She wanted to make sure it was the right family. I prayed she wouldn't change her mind if she didn't find a family that was up to her standards. I could only imagine how devastated an adoptive mother would be if the birth mother changed her mind at the last moment and decided to keep the baby.

Crystal was not ready to be a parent. I hoped that when her boyfriend got out of jail, he wouldn't demand that she keep the baby. I always hated that some gang guys looked at the number of children they fathered as notches in their belts, so I wouldn't have put it past Stone to try to bully her into it.

My mom was doing well. She even had a boyfriend, an older guy named John Flowers. He sold fresh flowers on a street in downtown D.C. Mom met him while she was standing on the corner, waiting to take the bus.

Sebastian was back in Georgia, working on his campaign. After finding some serious discrepancies in his opponent's campaign, he had begun to take his race for lieutenant governor seriously. He was still in second place but gaining support every day. I was proud of him. We talked three or four times a day. One day while we were talking on the phone, he said that he missed me so much that he was flying to D.C. from Georgia to see me the next day.

I stood in the airport baggage claim area, waiting for Sebastian to come down the escalator. When I saw him, my heart leaped. When the escalator finally reached the bottom, I ran to him and melted into his arms. "I missed you," he said softly. Then he kissed my forehead.

"Did you check any luggage?" I asked, noticing the carry-on bag over his shoulder.

"Yeah," he said as we proceeded toward the conveyor belt. Sebastian couldn't stop grinning.

"What are you so happy about?" I teased him.

"I'm just glad I have a woman who loves me, and I can look into her eyes and know that what she feels for me is real." He grabbed my waist and pulled me close to him. "Oh," he said, suddenly releasing me, "there's the luggage."

I watched him lift two large, black Samsonite suitcases off the conveyor and arrange them on a carrying cart. "What in the world is all that for?" I asked. "I thought you were only going to be here for a couple of days."

"I am," he said, shattering my hopes that he'd be staying longer. "This," he said, gesturing at one of the bags on the cart, "is for you."

"What?"

He smiled. "I want you to travel with your own fine luggage."

I touched the beautiful black case. "There are some surprises inside the bag. I took the liberty of purchasing an outfit that I can't wait to see you in. I also got you this gift certificate," he said as he took it out of his pocket.

"What is all that for?" I asked, amazed at this man's generosity.

"I miss you and you've been through a lot—you deserve a few perks. Plus, election day is near, and the race is close. I've got a couple of important functions coming up, and I need you to be with me, cheering me on."

I stared at him, confused. "What are you talking about?"

He gazed into my eyes. "When I leave on Wednesday," he said, pulling something out of his jacket pocket, "I want you to come with me." He handed me an airline ticket. I stared at it, blinking stupidly. "My sister says you can stay with her for a couple of weeks. What do you say?"

I looked up at him, not knowing what to say. He kissed my left cheek, then my right. Then he kissed my neck.

"Okay," I said, giggling. "I'll go."

We drove to Sebastian's hotel and ordered sandwiches from room service. After we ate, we watched the news for a while, then I headed home.

As I drove, I thanked God for Sebastian's love. It was clearly stronger than the love I had for myself. It was scary, but in a warm, fuzzy way.

October in Georgia felt no different from August: hot and muggy. The sky was clear blue with peach clouds and hints of pinks and yellows that blended into a pretty purple.

Sebastian was driving me straight from the airport to his sister's house. He had a meeting to attend, but he wanted to get me settled in first. I'd only met Savannah once, and that was in an official capacity. She seemed like a brat, always sucking up to her dad and whining to her mom. I couldn't see how my visit with her was going to be pleasurable. I wished I could get out of it, but Sebastian thought it would be good for me to get to know his sister. Since it meant so much to him, I'd reluctantly agreed.

"What are you thinking?" he asked as I gazed out the car window at the beautiful sky.

"I wish I could be up there."

"What do you mean? Like an angel in heaven or something?"

"No," I said, giggling. "That sky just seems so appealing. Like it holds a whole precious world of promise."

He squinted into the sunshine. "I never thought about it like that."

"The skies in D.C., Chicago, Detroit, and New York are all dark and dirty. But this is almost surreal."

He grinned at me. "Do you think you could make this city your home?"

I gave him a huge smile. "Is that a hint?"

He smiled back. "Could you hand me my cell? It's in the glove compartment." I gave him the phone and he pressed a few buttons. "Hey, sis, we're almost there." He winked at me. "Oh, yeah, she's real excited." He mouthed, *I love you* to me. "Okay. We'll see you soon."

I wondered if Sebastian's sister was anything like his mother. If so, I knew I couldn't stay with her without a war erupting between us. I said a silent prayer, asking the Lord to give me the strength I would need to deal with her if she was difficult.

Apparently noticing my concern, he asked, "Are you uncomfortable about staying with Savannah?"

"How'd you guess?" I said sarcastically, biting my bottom lip and twitching my nose.

"You don't need to be. Vannah's cool. I think you'll really like her."

"You call her Vannah?"

"Her nickname used to be Muffin Bread."

"What?"

"My little sister can really cook."

"She didn't strike me as the domestic type."

"She spent a lot of time in the kitchen with my grandmother before she died. Maybe she can teach you a few things."

I hit his arm. We both laughed.

Sebastian parked in front of an apartment complex. I looked at him with a very uncomfortable stare. He ignored me and we both got out of the car. When he lifted my bag out of the trunk, he said, "Your bag's pretty light. You're not leaving tomorrow, are you?"

"Don't joke—I don't like the idea of being dropped off at your sister's so she can babysit me while you go off to your meetings. Maybe I should have stayed in D.C."

He put my suitcase down on the sidewalk and held me close. "I won't be gone long. And tonight we'll go to dinner at the governor's mansion with all the other candidates. That should be fun."

I rolled my eyes. An evening at the governor's mansion didn't sound very exciting to me. "I don't know if I should," I said, backing out of his arms. "That's a pretty high-profile event."

He put a finger over my lips. "Hush, baby. I don't want us hiding out. I love you, and the whole world knows it. There's no reason you shouldn't be by my side."

"All right," I said, putting my hands on my hips. "But I'll need to get my hair and nails done."

He laughed. "Savannah went to cosmetology school one summer."

"Are you serious?"

"She'll take good care of you."

We walked up the sidewalk to the red brick town home. The small yard was neat and manicured, with perfectly cut hedges lining the building. Lively purple flowers grew in stone pots on the porch.

We didn't even have to knock. The door flew open, and there stood Savannah. Her hair was in tiny braids on top of her head. When I'd met her at the Christmas party, her hair was down. I loved the more casual style. She was very cute. Savannah looked just like I could imagine their mom looking twenty-five years earlier.

"Welcome," she said warmly, surrounding me with a tight embrace. She wore a long blue denim skirt with a beige pull-over that fit loosely. The choker on her neck had a small turquoise in the center of it. When she hugged me, I could smell her light herbal cologne.

She turned to Sebastian, who was carrying my heavy suitcase. "You can put those around the corner in the guest room."

After getting me settled in, he said, "I have to go now but I'll see you at seven." He kissed me on the lips, then his sister on the cheek, and left.

I turned around and looked at Savannah. "So, what should we do for seven hours?"

She gave me a huge smile. "Don't worry. I've got our day all planned out."

"Oh, you don't have to entertain me," I said.

"Nonsense." She grabbed my hand and led me into the living room. "We're sisters. Well, practically, anyway." She gave me a sweet smile. "From everything my brother told me about you, I think we're going to get along great."

Savannah gave me a tour of her place. The apartment had three bedrooms and two full baths. Each room was decorated with fabrics and trinkets from a different country, yet they all felt perfectly homey. The guest room where Sebastian put my suitcases was decorated in an African style. Wooden masks graced the walls, hand-carved statues of wood and ivory sat on the dressers, and the king-sized bed was covered with leopard-skin bedding and throw pillows. The adjoining bathroom was stocked with everything a guest might need or want, including a new toothbrush and lavender-scented candles.

"After you freshen up," Savannah said, "we can go shopping at Phipps Plaza. You've got to see this great dress at LaRue's. When I saw you at our Thanksgiving dinner, I could just picture you in it."

"Good—I love to shop, and your brother gave me a gift certificate I can use it at one of the stores."

I took a quick shower and put on capri pants, a short-sleeved blouse, and sandals. Then Savannah and I hopped in her Expedition and drove to the mall, jamming to an upbeat CD as if we were longtime best friends.

When we got to the mall, Savannah headed directly for LaRue's. Along the way, I noticed that just about every name-brand designer had a store there. This was not the kind of shopping mall I was used to. This place was for people who had a lot of money.

Upon entering LaRue's, Savannah spoke with a saleswoman, who then left with a smile and brought back an adorable dress, handing it to me. It was a black Donna Karan original with spaghetti straps that showed major cleavage and came down to the ankle but had a split up to the thigh.

I checked it out, practically drooling. Even on the hanger, it looked amazing. When I looked at the price tag, I nearly choked.

"You know what?" I said, hanging the $1200 dress on the nearest rack. "Your brother bought me a nice dress. And my gift certificate won't cover this. I'm sure I can find something suitable for way less than that."

Savannah giggled. "I know. I helped him pick it out. But that dress won't do for the event you're going to tonight." She touched my arm. "My brother's running for lieutenant governor," she said quietly. "As his girlfriend, you have to dress the part."

"I don't know," I whispered, looking back at the adorable dress. "It's just so . . ."

"Don't you like it?" she asked, her eyes wide.

"I love it," I assured her. "But it's awfully . . . expensive."

Savannah laughed. "Don't you worry about the price. I told Sebastian about this dress. He gave me his credit card to pay for it if you decided you liked it."

"I don't want to take his money for a dress I probably won't wear more than once."

Savannah smiled. "You'll be wearing a lot of dresses just like this one. There will be reporters taking pictures at every event you attend with my brother. Every newspaper in the state will have photographs of you, and women everywhere will be checking out your clothes."

I hadn't even thought that I would be in the limelight because I was Sebastian Stokes's girlfriend. Suddenly the shopping spree was unsettling. "Look," I said, "I appreciate the gesture, but no thanks. The dress is gorgeous, but it's just too much money."

"Okay." She turned away from the saleswoman and whispered,

"Don't sweat the price—I told you we can use a credit card to buy the dress. You wear it to the governor's dinner tonight, and tomorrow one of my girlfriends can bring it back and get a full refund. We do that all the time."

I giggled. "My friend Eden and I used to do the same thing, but we don't anymore. Girl, that's wrong, and now we just buy cheaper dresses."

We left the expensive dress on the rack, and the saleswoman frowning, to see what else we could find. As we strolled through the mall I saw a Parisians store. "Let's look in here," I suggested.

Savannah hesitated, but followed me in. As I searched through the racks of clothes, Savannah stood behind me, glancing around as if she didn't want to be seen by anyone.

I found two breathtaking outfits: a conservative black blouse with an ankle-length skirt that had slits on both sides, and a long, red, form-fitting gown with a bare back, also slit above the thigh. I asked Savannah what she thought of them.

"They're really nice," she said.

"Let's both try one on," I suggested, handing her the black one.

We tried on the dresses, then walked out of the dressing rooms to check each other out. We smiled and nodded, complimenting each other on how we looked.

"See?" I said. "You don't have to spend a lot of money to look good."

She checked the price tag and shook her head. "I had no idea a great dress like this could cost so little."

We changed back into our street clothes and got in line at the counter. "Thanks for showing me this store, Christian," she said. "All my life my mother taught me that women had to pay a lot of money to look good, but she was wrong. You just have to know how to shop."

"That's right," I said with a grin.

When our turn came to pay, I pulled out my wallet.

"No way," Savannah said. "Since you showed me how to get

the most for my money, I want to buy this dress for you. With Sebastian's credit card, of course."

"Now, I can afford to pay for this," I said. "It's only a hundred and sixty dollars."

"But Sebastian told me to get a dress for you with his credit card."

"I've got the gift certificate," I said, pulling it from my purse.

Savannah gently guided the gold-foiled envelope Sebastian had given me back to my handbag. "Save that for another time. Besides, thanks to your shopping expertise, we can get two dresses for less than the price he was willing to pay for one."

I reluctantly let her purchase the dresses, but insisted on buying her lunch. Savannah suggested we go to a Caribbean restaurant and I eagerly agreed, though I'd never been to one before. She drove to downtown Atlanta and parked in front of a place called Reggae.

To my surprise, Reggae had moderate prices. Soft Jamaican music played in the background, and people from all walks of life were dining there.

We seated ourselves and were given menus by the waitress. I asked Savannah what she recommended and she said the jerk chicken was great. I ordered the chicken, a beef patty, and a cola. Savannah got the same thing. When I took my first bite, I thought that I had died and gone to heaven.

Between forkfuls of food, Savannah filled me in on the family background.

"Most people don't realize this," she said, leaning close and whispering, "but my dad is a real player with the ladies."

"Reverend Stokes?" I said, dumbfounded, realizing that there was much about the man I protected that I didn't know.

"It really hurts my mom," Savannah added. "She's from the old school where women tolerate their men's infidelities, and she's afraid to give up all her luxuries. Besides, she really wants to be first lady."

"Is that why Sebastian is so adamant about not having sex outside marriage?" I asked.

"That's part of it," she said, "but the main reason is that my older brother, Steven, was diagnosed with HIV a year ago. I probably shouldn't be telling you all this, but since you're practically family, I figure you ought to know all the dirt."

I raised my eyebrows. I loved Sebastian, and I wanted to take our relationship further, but I wasn't sure a proposal was in our immediate future.

"His wife asked for a divorce as soon as she found out about the disease."

I stared at my beef patty, then I told her that Sebastian had already told me a little about that.

She looked a little surprised, then said, "You and my brother are really close. He tells no one about family stuff."

I smiled, knowing deep inside that I did have a special bond with Sebastian that meant so much to me.

Savannah then said, "Steven convinced her to see a doctor. They checked her out and said she's fine. He promised to be faithful from then on, even though the two of them couldn't have unprotected sex again. They seemed to be getting along okay, but then last month Steven used my apartment when I wasn't there. I came home early and caught him with a woman."

"Did you talk to him about using your place to cheat on his wife?" I asked.

She shook her head. "He's got something on me that I don't want to get back to my mom."

"What did you do?" I asked, enjoying the close friendship developing between us.

She blushed. "It's not that bad. But my mom would flip if she knew. When I was at Spelman, I had a boyfriend who went to Morehouse."

"Isn't that where your brother went undergrad?" I asked.

"Yeah. But my boyfriend transferred to Morris Brown. He wanted to go out for pro football after he graduated, and Morris Brown has a better sports program than Morehouse. He didn't make the pros, but he's a great player, so he took a job as a college football coach."

"That sounds good."

"My mother wouldn't think so. She wants me to be with someone whose family has money. So we told her that his family is wealthy and he just coaches because he wants to. If she finds out the truth, she'll probably get him fired. So, whenever we go out with my family, we pick a really nice restaurant and my brother Steven lends us the money to pay for it."

"Savannah, if you really like this guy, you're going to have to be honest with your parents sooner or later."

"I know," she said, exhaling deeply. "But it's not easy. I'm used to the finer things in life. I mean, when you've been eating caviar all your life, it's hard to settle for hamburger."

Though I couldn't relate, I could sympathize. I felt sorry for her. She was trapped by what her mom wanted, what she wanted, and what her boyfriend could offer. "I don't know what to say."

"That's okay," she said. "It feels good just talking about it. Thanks."

After we finished our lunch, I told Savannah I needed to get my hair and nails done. She offered to give me a manicure and style my hair for me. I accepted her offer, and we went back to her apartment.

Savannah decided that my hair would complement my spicy red dress best if I wore it up. She pinned it up, leaving a few curls dangling around my face.

I was in my room putting on my makeup when I heard Sebastian calling my name. Savannah came in and told me he was anxious to see me. I put on the full-length wrap Savannah had loaned me for the evening and followed her to the living room.

When I walked down the stairs, Sebastian gasped. "You're beautiful." Without tearing his gaze away, he added, "Thanks, sis. She looks fabulous! It's a little revealing, but you wear it well."

As Sebastian drove us to the governor's mansion, I wondered what he really thought of my dress. I'd searched hard to find something nice. Did he hate it and not say anything just to keep peace? From that moment on, I was self-conscious. Wearing clothes that accented my body was certainly my thing; however, he was my guy and if I'd overdone it, I'd feel bad. Searching for words to break the silence, I told him how much I'd enjoyed my day with his sister.

"I'm glad," he said. "I spent most of the day thinking about you and hoping you were having a good time."

"It was great. I really like her," I said, pleased that he didn't seem angry.

As we drove up the long driveway to the governor's mansion, I hoped the night would go well. I was nervous, wondering how I would be received by his supporters and campaign workers.

When the car stopped, a valet opened the door and took Sebastian's keys. As we walked to the house, I noticed the other couples going in were dressed more conservatively than I was.

An African-American butler offered to take my coat at the door. As he deftly lifted the wrap from my shoulders, I smiled at Sebastian, waiting for his response. His face seemed to pale, but he didn't say anything as he ushered me into the room.

The party was rather boring. I met a lot of politicians, danced, had a few watered-down drinks, and listened to Sebastian talk about politics all night. Throughout the evening he seemed a little uncomfortable, and I wondered whether he always acted this way at highbrow political affairs.

On the way home, Sebastian's lips were pressed tight and his forehead furrowed. After several moments of more uncomfortable silence, I said, "Sebastian, what's wrong?"

He hesitated. Then, finally, he mumbled, "I was taking you to the governor's mansion, not a nightclub."

Knowing I read him right earlier, I said, "Are you telling me I look like a—"

"Don't even talk like that," he interrupted. "A Christian woman wouldn't—"

I cut him off. "Wouldn't what? Look cute for her man?"

"You're dressed like one of my dad's girlfriends. Wearing devil red to a conservative function. You want to stand out."

My temples started to throb. "The other candidates found me charming. You were the only one acting stupid."

"I thought we were ready to move to the next level. But if you want to be with me, you're going to have to change."

"Then maybe I don't want to be with you."

He stared at me with a look of anger and disbelief.

We drove the rest of the way to his sister's house in silence. I prayed silently, *Lord, if I'm dressing wrong in Your eyes, open mine.*

For the next two days, Sebastian kept himself busy during the day and I spent time with his sister. He invited me to a couple of stiff-sounding engagements, but I declined his lukewarm offers, so he just went without me.

"Christian, what happened between you and Sebastian?" Savannah finally asked as we sat in the den talking.

"Your brother was embarrassed by the outfit I wore," I burst out, glad she'd asked so I could get it off my chest. "He said I looked like one of your father's women, and that if I was going to be with him, I had to change."

"He didn't!" she exclaimed, her hand over her mouth.

"Yes, he did. So now we're not communicating at all. I am seriously thinking about going back to D.C."

"Have you told him that?" she asked.

"No," I said. "Why should I? Since I'm obviously not the woman he wants me to be, it shouldn't matter if I'm here or not."

Placing her hand on my shoulder, she said, "You really should talk to him before you just up and leave."

"Forget it," I said. "And I want you to promise me you won't tell him."

"Okay," she said, "if that's the way you want it."

That night, Sebastian came over while Savannah and I were watching TV. "I need to talk to you before you do something drastic," he said.

I turned and looked at Savannah. "Thanks," I grumbled.

She shrugged. "Sorry. But I didn't want you to leave." She turned off the television and stood. "Why don't you two just kiss and make up," she said as she left the room.

Sebastian sat on the couch next to me. I got up and moved to a chair.

"Sorry I haven't been around much," he said, massaging his temples. "This campaign is making me crazy."

"You don't have to apologize," I said coldly. "Just take care of your business and don't worry about me."

He got up from the couch, pulled me from the chair, and grabbed my waist. "I've missed you," he said softly.

I took his hands off my body and flung them back at him. Then I walked to the couch and sat down.

He stood there, staring at me. "So it's like that, huh?"

Picking up a magazine, I mumbled, "Yeah, it's like that."

He sat beside me. "I have another event tonight."

"That's nice," I said, flipping pages.

"I think you'd be comfortable at this one. It's at a dance club called Altitude."

"Oh, so you think I'd be in my element hanging with the nightlife instead of in a refined setting like the governor's party? Is that supposed to make me feel better?"

Before he could answer, Savannah's phone rang. A moment later, she yelled out, "Christian, it's for you."

"Excuse me," I said, standing.

I walked past Sebastian to get to the phone. He stopped me by grabbing my wrist. Without looking up, I proceeded to answer the phone.

"Your hearing's been moved up to tomorrow afternoon," Troy said without a word of small talk.

"I'll be there," I promised.

After I ended the call, I went back into the living room. "I have to go back to D.C. right away. My hearing's tomorrow afternoon."

He grabbed my hand. "You can still go to the club with me tonight and fly back in the morning."

"I have to get packed."

"Please," he begged.

I made the mistake of looking into his eyes. He looked so forlorn, so repentant, I almost melted into his arms. I turned away and took a deep breath. "Fine," I said halfheartedly. "But I'm gonna wear whatever I want, you got it?"

"Got it," he said. "Thanks."

I went upstairs and put on a pair of tight red pants and an

off-the-shoulder top with long sleeves that showed part of my belly button. It was the sexiest outfit I owned. I planned on showing him the difference between an outfit that was sexy yet conservative and a hootchie club outfit.

The parking lot of Altitude was full of expensive cars. A line of people wrapped around the building, waiting to get in. Everyone was dressed in the latest fashions.

Sebastian opened the car door for me, then took my hand and escorted me to the front door. All the people in line murmured when we were allowed in.

Inside, the club was dark and the music was jammin'. I smelled a little reefer but I didn't see anyone smoking it. The huge dance floor had a DJ booth above it, a long bar alongside it, and several small, round tables around it.

A tall, bald man dressed in a Rocawear jean outfit showed Sebastian and me to a small group of tables. There was a private bar just to serve these few tables, and one of the tables had a card with Sebastian's last name on it.

The owner of the club came up to Sebastian and they started talking. As I sat at the table, watching the people dancing and mingling, a guy came up to me and asked for a dance. I looked at Sebastian. He was too busy talking to even notice the guy approach me, so I said yes and went out on the dance floor. I stared at Sebastian the whole time, but he never once looked my way.

When the song ended I thanked the handsome guy I danced with and went back to Sebastian's table. He was still talking with the club owner and several other people who had joined them.

Sebastian and the owner walked to the DJ platform, and the music stopped. The two men announced that it was time to cut the ribbon for the club's dedication. The crowd cheered and clapped. I checked my watch, wondering how much longer this was going to take.

When the ribbon-cutting ceremony was over, the music blared again and people resumed dancing. Sebastian continued mingling with his friends and ignoring me.

Another guy came up and asked me to dance. After I boogied with him, seven other guys asked me to dance, one right after the other. I was happy to oblige the fine-looking brothers.

When a slow song came up, I excused myself and returned to my table. I found Sebastian there, frowning at me.

"What's the matter?" I asked, my hands on my hips. "Don't you like it when men look at me?"

"I wish you hadn't worn that outfit."

"What's wrong with it?" I did a fashion-model twirl for him. "Everyone else seems to like it."

"It's not really the image I'm trying to portray."

"Then you should have said something before we left the house," I snarled. I took off and left him sitting there. I thought about calling a taxi, but I didn't know his sister's address. So I just strutted to the long bar by the dance floor.

After ordering a drink, I turned around to see if he'd followed me. Instead I saw him walking toward the exit. Before he could leave, a girl who was dressed even raunchier than I was slipped up to him and started talking. I stood a few feet away and watched.

He was trying to be polite to the girl, but I could tell it was just an act. I noticed him looking around, trying to find me. After a few awkward moments, I entered their conversation. "Oh, Sebastian, you two make a great couple. And to think, your mom thinks you should be married."

The girl placed herself between me and Sebastian. "Dang! Are you his sister?"

I laughed.

"She's my girlfriend," Sebastian said firmly. "She's just mad at me right now."

She grinned. "Well, if she doesn't want you, I'll take you."

I spread out my arms, letting her know she could have him.

She stared at me even harder. "Aren't you that girl that went to jail?" Before I could respond, she yelled out to her friends, "Hey, y'all, this is the girl this guy forced to turn herself in."

A crowd of people circled around us. Sebastian and I were pushed into each other's arms.

"You two ought to just kiss and make up," the girl said.

"Yeah," a guy shouted from the crowd. "Kiss her!"

Sebastian grabbed my waist, pulled me close, and kissed me passionately.

Though my eyes were closed, I noticed a bright flash of light. I looked up and saw the reporter who'd filmed the ribbon-cutting. He had taken a picture of our passionate kiss. I hoped our public display would be beneficial to the last few days of his campaign, because people tend to vote for a man who has a stable personal life. The DJ put on a slow song. "Go on, Mr. Stokes," he said. "Dance with your lady. Show the brothers and sisters here what you're made of."

I expected Sebastian to decline. He hated being put on the spot. But he slipped his arm around my waist and escorted me onto the dance floor, to the cheers of everyone in the place. We danced with a rhythm that rocked my soul.

When the song ended, he took my hand, lifted it up, and waved to the cheering crowd. We made a grand exit to a standing ovation.

We cuddled in the backseat of the limo all the way back to his sister's place.

He walked me to the door, our fingers locked together. When he opened the door for me, I did a double take. Sebastian's mom was sitting on the couch.

Savannah jumped up. "I tried to get her—"

"Sit down," Mrs. Stokes lashed out. Savannah sat immediately.

"Why are you here?" Mrs. Stokes asked me coolly. "I came over to see my daughter," she said with an evil glare. "Imagine my surprise at seeing your bags in the guest room." She then turned and glared at Sebastian and said, "I can't believe you'd allow your sister to be a part of this."

"A part of what, Mom?" he asked, his jaw twitching angrily.

"This rendezvous with your little hooker."

I could have reached across the room and slapped her.

"You can't talk about her like that," Sebastian yelled.

"Look at those clothes." She pointed at me with a long, tapered finger. "She's showing off her flesh like she's ready to be sold off to the highest bidder. I'm utterly ashamed that my son would allow his chances in the polls to be ruined by such a scandal."

She stood, flounced over to him, and cupped his face in her hands. "Son, we don't expect you to win. But everyone's quite pleased with how you've been conducting yourself in this campaign. If your father does get the presidency, you'll be able to write your own ticket. But you've got to be careful who you associate with."

"Maybe your mom's right," I said, my eyes filling with tears. "Don't worry, Mrs. Stokes. I won't be bothering your children again." I started toward the door.

Savannah grabbed my arm. "What are you doing? My mom can't tell you who to see or where to go."

"Savannah Stokes!" her mom yelled.

"Mother, this is my apartment." Savannah strode to the front door and opened it. "And I want you to leave."

Mrs. Stokes stood there in shock. Savannah stomped over, grasped her mother's elbow, and pushed her out the door. The slamming of the door echoed in the room.

I sat in the sterile conference room, still thankful that no one from the press was allowed inside. Greg Smith, my lawyer, stood in a corner of the room, talking quietly on his cell phone.

The jury had been in deliberations for about an hour. Since there was nothing for me to do but wait, I looked around the room. The wooden furniture looked old and scratched up. The walls had paintings of presidents. A U.S. flag flew behind the huge presiding officer's chair.

Agent Barrington, the third-highest-ranked Secret Service agent in the country, came into the room and sat at the officer-presenting-charges table. Greg got off the phone and joined me at the table where we'd sat earlier. We both stood and faced the presiding officer.

"You've argued a very good case, Agent Ware," Barrington said. "However, the Secret Service is not ready to allow you to come back to work at this time."

"What?" I lashed out. "Why not? I was cleared of all charges."

"We understand that," Barrington said, "but the claim by your protectee, which sent you on a hiatus in the first place, is still outstanding. There has been no evidence provided in this hearing to prove that you did not inappropriately introduce Reverend Stokes to a group that wanted to give him illegal campaign funds."

"But I never—"

"Until those claims are proven false, you will remain on suspension."

I looked at Greg and asked how they could do this to me. His silence and look of dejection gave me no hope.

"Thank you for your time," Barrington said, then left the room.

I had been flying high the last few months—I had a new place, I was back with my man. All I needed was my job, and I'd been certain I would get that back. Until the Secret Service cleared me, I was on suspension with all federal agencies. I couldn't even go back to my old job. Now it seemed as though my flight had hit some heavy turbulence. My ears could not take the changing altitude.

Chapter 16

High

Greg Smith and I stood in the empty conference room, shocked at the unfair decision that had just been handed down.

He touched my shoulder. "We can appeal."

"You don't understand," I groaned. "This is like being released from the army with a dishonorable discharge. I can't believe this is happening."

I sat on the wooden table. It was cold and hard, like my heart. After giving my all on this detail and even saving the protectee's life, my superiors didn't believe me or support me.

Greg's eyes suddenly lit up. "I'll be right back," he said. "There's something I want to go check on."

He left me alone in the quiet room, but that was fine with me. I had nothing to say to anybody.

A few minutes later, the door opened and Agent Hold came in. I smiled when I noticed his mustache was finally growing in. I remember that he had always wanted to look older, and I had suggested that he try growing a mustache. I was happy to see that the new look was working.

"How are you doing?" he said as he walked up to me.

"I'm okay," I lied.

He shifted his weight from one foot to the other. "I just got the word that they denied you permission to come back. I miss you. I've been an agent for five years and you're the best partner I've ever had."

"Oh, don't worry about me," I said, taking a deep breath to keep myself from crying.

"I want you to know that none of us on the team thinks this is right, including Agent Moss. It's totally unfair, and we realize it could easily happen to any of us."

Hearing him say that blew me away. I wasn't officially one of them, but after Hold's comment, I guess I was. It felt good to know that others were willing to do something for my cause. The coldness within me started to warm up. Maybe God was moving the mountain after all.

"We want to help," he said.

"I really don't know what you can do," I told him. "No one has been able to find any evidence to prove that tape was altered."

His face brightened. "I heard you had a private investigator who found some evidence that cleared you in the murder case. What about getting back in touch with that guy? I mean, if the tape was altered, there's probably a production company that has to know about it. Maybe that investigator of yours can trace the origin of the tape."

"You know, that's worth a try." I got up quickly and headed toward the exit.

"Where are you going?" Ryan asked.

"You gave me an idea."

I burst out of the conference room door and ran smack into my attorney. "Sorry."

"No problem," he said. "I was hoping to bump into you, just not literally." He chuckled. "I've got a call for you on my cell phone." He handed me the phone.

"Hey, baby," I heard Sebastian's sexy voice say. "I just heard. I figured you'd be pretty down, so I wanted to call you right away."

"Listen," I said, glossing over his attempt to comfort me, "I'm going to follow up on a lead my colleague came up with."

"I have some ideas, too."

"Don't worry about me. You just take care of your campaign."

"I'll check on you tonight then, baby. I love you."

"I love you, too," I told him.

The next day I contacted the private investigator's office and we went over all the information he had uncovered so I could decide what to do next. Glenn O'Malley was a short, balding man in his fifties who wore wrinkled suits and bow ties. He was so pleased to be able to work on such a high-profile case, he offered to work for me pro bono.

Together we called every newspaper that had written about me previously and told them my side of the story. The articles they published generated so much public interest that the agency reluctantly decided to give me another hearing.

Days later, sitting again in front of the committee, I hoped Mr. O'Malley could clear my name. Greg was still my lawyer, and to me he seemed confident. Agent Barrington frowned at O'Malley. Since he was on the other side, anything that irritated him was a good thing for me. A few reporters and FBI agents I liked from my D.C. office were in the room as well, sitting behind me. The three men and two women who helped to make up the committee with the head prosecutor were checkin' me out.

The head of the Secret Service investigative committee, also known as the presiding officer, said, "We understand you have some information that could clear Ms. Ware of the charges against her."

"Yes, sir, I do," O'Malley replied.

"Then let's hear it."

He reached into his inside coat pocket and pulled out a cassette tape. "This is a copy of the video recording that made Ms. Ware appear guilty of taking a bribe to set up Reverend Stokes."

The men and women on the committee nodded.

"I took it to five different production companies and asked them to analyze the film. They all came back with the same report." He leaned down and opened the tattered briefcase on the floor beside him. He pulled a folder full of documents out of it, waving the folder in the air. "That tape was altered. It was so well done that most people viewing the tape would never see it. But minute computer alterations were found."

The crowd started whispering. The committee members leaned forward with anticipation.

O'Malley made eye contact with each member of the committee. "None of the production companies could decipher exactly what had been done to the tape, but knowing it was altered spurred me on to find out."

Agent Barrington objected, asking the presiding officer where Mr. O'Malley's statements were leading. The presiding officer told the prosecutor to stop interrupting.

Glenn O'Malley smiled. "I contacted several more production companies and finally found the one that worked on the tape. At first the owner would not admit he'd altered it, of course. Until I told him that I saw the company's hidden trademark. Then he sang like a bird."

A few snickers of glee came from supporters behind me. The presiding officer gave them a stern look.

"I told this man," O'Malley continued, "that if he didn't cooperate, I was going to call the detective involved in the case and have him come by with a search warrant to look at all of their tapes. The owner then told me that one of his former employees had altered the tape and had been fired for it. I convinced him to give me the former employee's name, home address, and phone number."

Mr. O'Malley paused for dramatic effect, then continued. "That former employee, a young man named Kurt James, denied altering the tape. When I told him the owner of the production company was willing to testify against him in court, Kurt confessed that he was paid a large sum of money to alter the tape. Here is his bank statement showing the deposit."

The committee members started whispering to each other.

"I have Kurt James's signed and certified testimony," O'Malley said, pulling a document out of his file folder and handing it to the presiding officer. "He admits that Skip Bambino gave him some video footage and told him to doctor it so it would incriminate Miss Ware. If necessary, the committee can contact Mr. James at the address given in the statement to confirm its validity."

When the officer presenting charges chose not to question Mr. O'Malley, the presiding officer told him that he could step down from the witness stand. My lawyer then stood and addressed the committee.

"In light of this new evidence," Greg said, "I am appealing to the committee to reinstate Agent Christian Ware."

The presiding officer dismissed the committee, and they all filed out of the room. For the next ten minutes, Greg and I discussed the possible outcome of these proceedings. He thought I'd get off. I wasn't too confident. My heart wanted to believe him, but my brain dared not.

When the committee came back, my hands were sweaty. All of them stood as the presiding officer said, "We need more time to deliberate."

My head dropped. I wanted this to be over. I was totally stressed out.

I tried to call Sebastian, hoping his voice would calm my nerves. But I couldn't locate him, so I called Eden. She wasn't home, either. So I sat back in my seat, tapping my feet in a nervous rhythm.

Greg saw I was uneasy. "You're going to be fine."

After two hours, the committee finally came back into the courtroom. I rose to my feet and so did the few other folks who had stayed.

The spokesman stood and faced me. "We do not feel that this new evidence is sufficient to overturn Agent Ware's suspension," he pronounced.

I put my hands over my face and started weeping. *Lord,* I cried out. *What happened? I thought You were with me!*

Immediately, God spoke to my troubled mind. *I am here, My child. And I am in control. Not your lawyer. Not your investigator. Not you. Trust Me.*

I felt like a load had been lifted off my chest. I inhaled, lifted my head, and dried my eyes with my sleeves. *I'm so sorry, Lord,* I confessed from my heart.

Just as I did, the doors swung open. I turned back and saw Sebastian striding in.

"I've got more evidence," he announced, holding a brown envelope in his hand.

I sat on the edge of my seat.

Greg went to the presiding officer and got special privilege to allow Sebastian to present material. I sat back and held my breath as my guy walked before the committee.

"I was dating this lady at the time of the alleged incident with my father, and I know beyond a doubt that she is not guilty of the charges against her. I also respect my father, so I had a hard time believing that he would stoop to destroying her life in order to get ahead. So I decided to come right out and ask him what was happening."

The conference room crowd began their side discussions. Sebastian pulled a small tape recorder out of his coat pocket and set it on the railing in front of him. The oversized room became silent.

Sebastian said, "This is a recording of our telephone conversation last night."

Agent Barrington stood up. "Objection. Inadmissible. You can't tape without the person's knowledge."

Greg said to the committee, "Please allow the witness to speak. He'll explain."

"Make it quick please," the presiding officer said to Sebastian before he spoke to Agent Barrington. "Overruled—we need to get at the truth here."

"The tape is legal. At the beginning I let my father know that I was taping him. As the conversation goes on, you'll hear that my father is so upset, he is not even thinking about a tape."

He pushed Play. As the tape spun, I heard Sebastian's voice. "Dad, why are you letting Christian go down for something she didn't do? You said yourself she was a great protector. She was almost blown to pieces trying to save your life."

"You're right, son," Reverend Stokes's voice said clearly. "But I figured the Agency would give her job back after she was cleared of the murder charges. When that didn't happen, I realized that this case was keeping my name in the national media and even portrayed me in a positive light. Voters feel bad that I was framed. So members of my campaign staff convinced me to implicate her."

"You've been tailing my girlfriend."

"Of course, son—actually, it was your mom's idea and I supported it. You're a political figure. We had to make sure this agent girl had nothing in her past to kill your future."

"And when you found nothing damaging about her, you had the video altered and created something to promote your presidential hopes."

"Yes and no, son. Listen, I pissed off the wrong people, and when I agreed to get back in their good graces they said they could fix the mess they put me in and asked for the tape and they changed a few things."

"They . . . who is *they?*" Sebastian said, sounding upset.

"Never mind all that—I've learned the hard way that to win in politics you must play dirty. I'm sorry," Reverend Stokes said without regret. "It wasn't personal. Your girlfriend just could help me with my business. She'll be cleared."

"How? Have you sent a letter to the Agency telling them all this?"

"Have you lost your mind?" Stokes's booming voice maxed out the volume level on the recorder. "I can't publicly admit my involvement in all this."

"You could have gotten her killed, being connected to those goons."

Reverend Stokes said, "I knew nothing about what else they had planned, and that's why I have to carefully pull myself away from them. You understand, son—they're dangerous people, and I told Agent Ware she should take the fall for this or I couldn't control what might happen."

The room was silent. Sebastian clicked the Stop button on the tape recorder.

Sebastian stared at the committee. "That should be enough to clear Christian Ware of all allegations of campaign fraud."

"Can we have a copy of that tape?" asked the presiding officer.

Sebastian took the small tape out of the recorder and handed it to him. "I have the original in a safe place," he added.

The committee went off to deliberate again. Sebastian, Greg, and I walked out into the busy hallway. We talked about the possible outcome. Sebastian guided me to a bench away from everyone, where he kissed me and told me that God would make everything all right. We then joined hands and prayed that God would allow the committee to see the truth.

Greg motioned for Sebastian and me minutes later, when the committee came back. Once again, I stood and faced the presiding officer. "We are pleased to report that Agent Ware is cleared of any accusations of wrongdoing and her Federal Agent status will be reinstated. However, because of this case we have no choice but to relieve Agent Ware of her temp Secret Service position. We cannot have her protecting a man who set her up."

I jumped up, shouted, and hugged Sebastian. Then I hugged Greg and thanked him for doing such a great job.

After lots of hugging and screaming, people finally started filing out of the conference room. When everyone else had left, I turned to Sebastian. "You just proved that your father lied so that I would be reinstated as a Federal Agent. What will you tell your father when this information gets out? How will this affect your relationship with him?"

He didn't answer, but just held me tight.

Lord, I prayed, *I hope the price he paid doesn't end up being too high.*

I felt lighter than an air balloon. Outside the conference room, many reporters tried talking to me. Agent Barrington came over to me first.

Since the Agency knew I could sue them for slander and unfair termination, they tried to appease me by having Agent Barrington tell me that I would be paid for the time I was suspended, and even though I wasn't going to be protecting Cool Falcon, they'd love to forward me to another detail. In addition, I could take more time off with pay, plus a bonus, and start working again at the beginning of the new year, in the Secret Service or FBI.

Sebastian pulled me over to the bench where we'd prayed earlier. "I need another favor."

"Anything."

"Come back to Atlanta with me."

"Why?"

"Well, since you are on vacation and I'm trying to win this campaign, I thought that you could come with me on the campaign trail so we could spend some time together."

"If you're sure that's what you want, I'm there."

"I'm sure."

"Can we visit my mom first?" I asked.

"Oh, I think it's about time I met your mother," he said with a smile.

My mom welcomed Sebastian warmly, and thanked him about a million times for sticking his neck out for me.

"Mrs. Ware, I love your daughter," he said, holding my hands as we sat close on the living room couch. "I didn't do anything heroic."

My mom just looked at me and smiled.

"I apologize for whisking her back and forth between D.C. and Atlanta," Sebastian continued. "I know you haven't seen much of your daughter lately."

Mom grabbed his hand. "My dear young man, you didn't exactly twist her arm. Don't let her fool you. She likes being whisked about."

We all laughed.

"You're good for my daughter," Mom said. "Since your father is 'The Reverend Stokes,' I've watched you since you were a little boy. But I never would have thought I'd see you two getting married someday."

She squeezed him with a bear hug. He peered up at me and blushed.

* * *

As our plane took off, Sebastian sat beside me in silence. He seemed deeply burdened. I took his hand and squeezed it tight. We were having such a great time with my mom, and all of a sudden he'd turned sullen. What was wrong?

Finally he opened up and simply said, "I can't believe what lengths my dad would go to, to become president. Could anyone stoop lower?"

"I'm sorry—really I am. I hate that you have to go through this with your family."

He didn't say a word, just squeezed my hand back and offered one of his smooth smiles.

Lord, I need You to help me support Sebastian. Thank You for putting our relationship back on track. Our relationship has had its ups and downs, but because of You, we were able to choose the right path and commit to doing things the right way, which is Your way. Now I want to help him through whatever lies ahead for him. Please help me do that. In Your name I pray. Amen.

Sebastian leaned his head on my shoulder. "The election is next week. I'm still behind the two Democratic front-runners in the polls, so I probably won't win. It's a long shot, I know. Maybe that just sounds crazy."

"No, it doesn't," I assured him. "You're the best candidate, and Georgia needs you." I rubbed his cheek with the hand that wasn't holding his. "Besides, with God all things are possible."

"Yeah, I know," he said, giving me a half smile. "But my dad has always wanted to become the first black president. I hope I haven't ruined his chances."

"Shhh," I said, lifting his chin. I kissed him gently on the lips. "If it's God's will, it will happen. The Lord doesn't want us to worry about tomorrow. We got through today victoriously. Let's just relax while we can and rest in the knowledge that God can do anything. Except fail."

Sebastian lifted my hand to his lips and kissed it. "Thanks for seeing me through this."

"You're welcome. Now let's get some sleep." He rested his head on my shoulder and within minutes started snoring quietly. I drifted off to sleep, believing that nothing bad could come to Sebastian and me that we couldn't work out. With the help of our Lord, of course.

When the plane landed in Atlanta, reporters were waiting for us at the gate.

"How did they find out when we were arriving?" Sebastian whispered.

I shrugged, gritting my teeth in disgust, wondering whether they were for me or against me.

Sebastian grabbed my hand and we briskly started walking away from the reporters before they spotted us.

"Where are we going?" I asked.

"To my parents'. I need to talk to my dad."

"Why don't you take me to your sister's place first," I suggested.

"I want you with me. This whole thing involves you, and he needs to apologize."

"I'll feel uncomfortable. Plus, an apology isn't necessary," I assured him.

"Yes, it is." Determination set his face like stone. "We just got back in town, and his campaign workers have already started calling me. I need to see him face-to-face."

"Sebastian, I know that you want to clear the air with your father, but I think it's too soon. I would love for the two of you to discuss the situation and mend whatever damage has been done to your relationship, but please give him a few days to digest the information."

"I understand that you care about me and my relationship with my father, but this is something that I need to do now with you by my side."

As we walked past a magazine stand, I saw our picture on the front page of the *Atlanta Journal-Constitution*. One side had a picture of Sebastian and me hugging at my courtroom trial. Beside that shot was a photo of Reverend Stokes, looking like his life was over. The headline read, SON CHOOSES FLESH OVER BLOOD. I pointed it out to Sebastian. "That explains why those reporters were waiting for us at the gate when we arrived."

When we pulled into his parents' driveway, I suddenly felt cold all over. My hands started trembling. With everything I'd been through, I should have been able to handle this, but I simply couldn't calm down.

Sebastian grabbed my hands and gave me a kiss. "It's gonna be okay." He helped me out of the car and walked me to the front door of the mansion.

A housekeeper I'd never seen opened the door before Sebastian had a chance to knock. She frowned at him, and turned her nose up at me.

"Sadie, I missed you," he said to the gray-haired black woman who looked to be in her sixties. "How are you feeling?"

She smiled at him slightly, seemingly happy that he cared. "The cancer is in remission. I needed to get back to work. Almost a year off from this family, and you all have torn each other apart."

She looked at him with disapproval. Though I was sorry she'd been ill, I was almost sure I wasn't her favorite person. Being at the Stokes mansion had been hard enough, taking the mean stares from his mother. Two women hatin' on me would have been too much to bear.

"Don't give me that look," he said, kissing her on the cheek.

"I hope she's worth it," the housekeeper said with a sly smile. "Your momma's been fillin' me in."

"Sadie," Sebastian said with a grin, "she's worth it and then some."

"Your father is in the library and your mother isn't here," she informed us.

As we entered the room, Reverend Stokes was sitting at his desk, reading a legal document. When he saw us, he glared.

"How could you do this to me?" Stokes bellowed, slapping the desk.

"That's what I came here to ask *you*."

Reverend Stokes stood and started pacing around the room. "Why didn't you destroy that tape of our conversation once things escalated?" he yelled. "You've probably ruined me.

"We could have made it to the White House," Reverend

Stokes continued ranting. "I was at the top of the polls as of last week. Then you had to go and do this. If my own son calls me a liar, how is the rest of the country supposed to believe me?"

"I asked you to come clean, Dad," Sebastian said, "but you refused."

"After I won the election, I was planning to have her cleared."

"You never mentioned that to me," Sebastian said. "Dad, if you have to destroy someone else in order to achieve your goals, there's no point in pursuing them. If the only way to get the presidency is to throw your morals out the window—"

"I could have won," Reverend Stokes moaned. "I could have won."

"You still might, if people vote for what you've accomplished and what you want to do for this country."

"I'm doomed," Stokes said, looking at his son with disgust.

I grabbed Sebastian's arm and tugged him toward the door. He hesitated.

"Come on," I said softly. "Talking isn't doing any good."

Father and son stood there for a few minutes, staring each other down. Then Sebastian turned and left the room, his shoulders slumped. I shot Stokes a withering look, then followed my man out of the house.

As we drove to Savannah's apartment, Sebastian didn't say anything. He just stared at the road.

When we got there, she wasn't home. We found a note on the fridge, though. "Chris," it said, "help yourself to anything. I'll see you sometime tomorrow."

I was kind of glad she wasn't there. Sebastian needed to let out what was pent-up inside him. I grabbed his hand and started praying aloud in the kitchen.

"Heavenly Father," I said, "we're so sorry if anything we've done in this situation with Reverend Stokes was wrong. It seems the relationship between a father and son has been irreversibly broken. Your Word says that You will come through for us when we need You. And we really need You to help us out right now. Please be with Sebastian's parents. Only You can work this out.

Sebastian and his dad both need to be at their best right now. Amen."

We opened our eyes and I held him in my arms. As we embraced, I knew God was going to work all this out for the good. So I rested my head on Sebastian's chest and enjoyed the moment.

On Halloween night, I dressed up as Tina Turner. I wore a leather skirt and ankle boots that laced up in the front. For a finishing touch, I wore a large afro wig.

When Sebastian came to his sister's house to pick me up, his mouth dropped open. After he finally composed himself, he placed a corsage on my wrist, then kissed me sweetly on my cheek. "You look ravishing!"

"You don't look too bad yourself, handsome," I said, admiring his black tux, 1800s-style.

"Just think," I said. "Our ancestors were slaves during the time these outfits were popular. But tonight we're going to party with white folks, eat what they eat, use the same rest rooms. You'll even be giving a candidate's speech. Black people sure have come a long way. Our great-great-grandmothers would be proud, don't you think?"

"I know they would be." Sebastian stroked my cheek with the back of his hand.

"I could just stay here all night with you."

"That would get us into a lot of trouble," he teased.

"You're right. We'd better get going."

As we opened the door, Savannah walked in with a handsome, muscular young guy, light-skinned like the Stokes family. *This must be the destitute boyfriend Mrs. Stokes doesn't approve of.*

Sebastian introduced me to Bruce, referring to me as "the love of my life." My heart melted.

"You guys look so cute," Savannah said. "I've got to get my camera."

Bruce watched Savannah leave the room with a fondness in his eyes that no money could ever buy.

Savannah came back and snapped a couple of pictures of us. I felt like I was going to my senior prom.

"What are you two planning to do tonight?" Sebastian asked.

"Just stay home, answer the door for trick-or-treaters, and watch TV," Savannah answered.

"Well, don't have too much fun," her big brother said with a grin. Then we hopped into his car.

"Will there be a lot of reporters there?" I asked as Sebastian drove down the road.

"I expect so," he said with a glum face.

After the valet took the car, we walked toward the entrance of the building. Several reporters took pictures of us.

The ballroom had red-brick walls and old wooden beams. The lighting was dim and the decorations gaily spooky. People mingled at the bar, danced, and sat at long, rectangular tables.

Sebastian guided me to our table near the stage. I was told by a sweet lady sitting next to me that we would be eating a buffet-style breakfast at midnight. Since it was early evening, I nibbled on the snacks in front of me.

From the moment we were seated, people came up to Sebastian to say hello and discuss politics.

The governor of Georgia complimented me on how lovely I looked. Then he asked if he could borrow Sebastian. I nodded gracefully. Sebastian kissed me on the cheek, then headed to the governor's table.

I noticed several agents follow the two men discreetly, all camouflaged in Halloween costumes that made them blend in with the crowd. But I could tell they were watching Sebastian like a hawk.

Actually, when I looked closer, I saw Agent Sawyer. He was now guarding Governor James. He was dressed as a turkey and it fit him so well. He didn't even acknowledge me. Not that we were ever chummy, but he could have said something. I wondered why he had changed details.

I then wondered how everyone else was doing. When I was at Sebastian's house, I didn't see any agents I knew. My detail unit was on vacation. I really missed my job, though. I couldn't wait to go back to work. I wanted to saunter up to one of them and say, "If you need a break, come get me."

I watched a couple of agents move in closer to the governor. Sebastian saw them, too. His shoulders tightened.

When Sebastian came back to the table, I asked, "What was that all about?"

Sebastian gritted his teeth. "The governor asked me to withdraw from the race."

"Why would he want you to do that?"

"He says the scandal with my dad is making me a joke, so I should bow out. All I'd be doing is taking votes away from the two front-runners, he said. The governor said I didn't have a chance of winning, anyway."

"He said that?"

"Not in so many words. He offered me a job as a cabinet member if I withdraw my candidacy."

"What did you tell him?" I asked, practically holding my breath.

Before he could answer, the event coordinator came to the table and told Sebastian it was time for his speech.

"Guess you'll find out when I tell the rest of these people," he said.

Sebastian strolled up to the platform, where he was announced and welcomed.

"Good evening, ladies and gentlemen," he said calmly, leaning against the podium. "Thank you for inviting me tonight." He looked out across the crowd of listeners. "Over the course of my candidacy, many people have asked me why I want to be lieutenant governor. I've always answered that I want to help the people. My father always taught me that politicians have a huge responsibility to govern and protect the rest of us. And I used to think, *I want to be one of those politicians someday.* My goal is to make sure that everyone in this great state of Georgia, rich or poor, has the chance to succeed. I want folks to know that the government works for them. If I am elected, I don't want it to happen because people did me political favors that I had to pay back after I got into office. And I wouldn't want to try to ruin people to get there."

Sebastian locked eyes with me for a moment, then continued to pan the crowd. "I figured I would do it the right way, God's way, or not do it at all. I'd want to earn the people's trust. I'd make them glad they chose me to serve."

While Sebastian was speaking, I looked at the faces of the people. Every eye in the room was on my man.

"I recently found myself in a position where I had to choose between family and a lie, and the truth. It was an extremely difficult decision. But I believe I made the right choice."

He looked across the room at me, and it was as though he was standing next to me, looking deeply into my eyes. "Having passed that test, I have the confidence to believe that I can be a great leader. I'm not going to compromise my dignity for anybody. In fact," he said with a barely perceptible glance at the governor, "I was asked tonight to resign from the race for lieutenant governor."

People gasped.

"If I had any doubt that I could serve the people of Georgia well, I would have withdrawn my name from the race. But I believe God has called me to do this. Whether I win or lose, I'm standing for something with my campaign—integrity."

The room erupted with applause. When the crowd calmed down, he continued. "There has been too much bullying and corruption and self-centeredness in our state. I want to get back to the dream I had as a little boy. In two days you will all be going to the polls to vote. I don't know what the outcome will be, but I promise you my name will be on the ballot."

He received a standing ovation. I sprang to my feet and joined in the applause. My only regret was that I didn't live in Georgia, so I couldn't vote for this amazing man.

When he came back to our table, I hugged him tight, the crowd still cheering.

*   *   *

Election day was crazy. Calls came in constantly from all over the state, including reports of the poll results in various counties. Reporters from television stations, magazines, and newspapers were calling to get interviews.

Sebastian granted a few interviews, then returned to campaign headquarters. Together we prayed that whatever the outcome, God would get the glory. He was still a long-shot since he had just been involved in a national scandal. But he wanted this, and he wanted it badly.

He paced the large ballroom, passing by his campaign staff and friends. We were all watching the election results on TV. His assistant and the campaign manager and other supporters and staff members wandered in and out. I stood in a corner and prayed all day. I hoped my presence was helping him get through this.

Every now and then he'd glance at me with those warm eyes that said things his mouth couldn't because we were in a public place. I could tell that my being there for him relieved some of his anxiety.

I tried calling my mom but just got the answering machine. I called Eden. Same thing. As I began leaving a message for her, she picked up and started sobbing hysterically.

"What's wrong?" I asked, trying to sound calm.

"The doctor just told us we can't have children because I have endometriosis."

"What's endometriosis?"

"It's a condition in which tissue resembling the uterine lining is growing in my abdomen."

"Oh, Eden, I'm so sorry," I said.

"Don't be—it's not anyone's fault. It just happens sometimes."

"Can't they do surgery or something to allow you to have children?"

"No, there's no cure—only treatment."

Everyone around me erupted into loud cheering.

"What's going on?" I hollered with my mouth away from the phone.

"The preliminary polls came out," replied one of the campaign workers. "The margin's a lot tighter than anyone pre-
dicted. We're only down by three hundred votes, and the
African-American precincts aren't even in yet!"

Sebastian rushed over to me, his face radiating joy. He picked
me up and twirled me around, kissing my cheek. "I might have
a real shot," he cried, not even seeing the phone in my hand.

I was happy for him, but devastated for Eden. When Sebastian
took off, I put the phone back to my ear. "I'm back now. Sorry
about that."

"Sounds like there's good stuff going on over there."

"Yeah, there is. But what about you?"

"Oh, don't worry about me. I'll be fine. God knows what
He's doing."

I was shocked by Eden's statement but glad she was trying to
deal with the situation. "I love you," I told her.

"I love you, too," she said.

After hanging up, I hurried over to the TV to join the others.
More votes were coming in for Sebastian. His numbers were going
up rapidly. With forty-five percent of the votes in, the independent candidate dropped off the charts. I grabbed Sebastian's
hand.

Three intense hours later, the votes were confirmed. Sebastian
won with fifty-seven percent of the votes. The crowd went crazy,
blowing on party whistles and throwing confetti in the air. Everyone yelled and screamed, celebrating the victory. His acceptance
speech was excellent.

A little later we went upstairs to his hotel suite with his press
secretary and campaign manager. We all sat down and watched
the presidential election on television. It took a little longer to
get the presidential votes in. Reverend Stokes lost with only
nineteen percent of the vote.

"I'm so proud of you!" I exclaimed.

"I want to call my dad," he said quietly, obviously torn.

"Then do it," I suggested.

"What should I say?" he asked, touching the hotel phone.

"God will give you the right words."

Before he could use the phone, it rang. A campaign worker called to ask him to come back downstairs. As soon as we got downstairs, the press barged up to us. Loyal supporters streamed in behind them, eager to congratulate the new lieutenant governor of the state of Georgia.

Sebastian put on a happy face, but I could tell he was sad because his family couldn't be there to share in his victory.

During his interview with the reporters, Savannah walked in. Sebastian's eyes lit up—he ended the interview and hugged his sister.

"Congratulations," she squealed, giving him a big hug. "You made history. The first black lieutenant governor of Georgia."

"And the youngest, too," he added.

"I knew that you could do it," she said. "Hey, I brought some people with me who want to see you."

Sebastian followed her gaze. There in the doorway stood his parents. Mrs. Stokes held her arms out. After the briefest moment of hesitation, Sebastian ran into her embrace, and they cried together.

"We're proud of you, son," Reverend Stokes said, patting him on the back.

Tears flowed all around the room.

"Speech!" the crowd chanted.

As my man took his rightful place as the center of attention, with his mom and dad on either side of him, I thanked God for bringing them back together.

"You know, God is good," he said.

Several people shouted "Amen!"

"He has worked a miracle, done the impossible. No one thought I could be the next lieutenant governor of this state, but it seems like it's the Lord's will. Thank you, voters!"

Everyone in the place shouted.

Sebastian thanked everyone who'd helped in his campaign, including every person who had voted for him. Then he gave a passionate description of some of the initial things he was going to do in office. "Integrity at its best, working for the people, produces great results."

As the crowd cheered again, I saw Sebastian looking around. When they had settled down a little, he continued. "Most of you have been following the romantic adventures between myself and Miss Christian Ware."

"Where is she?" someone hollered from behind me.

"That's what I'd like to know," he said with a chuckle.

Everyone looked around. I raised my hand and waved. Someone nudged me forward and the crowd moved out of my way.

When I reached the platform, Sebastian took me into his arms.

"This lady has captured my heart," he announced. "She's given me back something I had lost: belief in myself. She gave me something to fight for. Thanks to her, I know I am where the Lord wants me to be. I could not have won this election if she hadn't encouraged me."

The people in the room started shouting and clapping for me.

"You know, I was so sure I'd be defeated tonight that I had planned to do something special with this young lady to take my mind off of my loss."

Everyone laughed and clapped again.

"But my plans seem even more appropriate now." He looked deeply into my eyes. "Because the only way I want to be lieutenant governor is if I have this woman by my side as my wife."

I gasped.

He reached into his pants pocket and pulled out a small black box. When he opened it, I saw a gorgeous diamond sparkle. "Christian Ware," he said, kneeling, "will you marry me?"

The crowd held its breath. I was so choked up I couldn't speak right away. I just stared at that beautiful ring.

He stood, smiling into my eyes. "I know you've been on your own for a long time, but I think we make a pretty good team. I don't want that to end. So I'm asking you to step out in faith. If you say yes, you'll make me even happier than the voters of Georgia did tonight."

I couldn't get the words out of my mouth because I was so choked up and shocked.

Everyone started cheering. Someone called out, "Say yes!" A women hollered, "If you don't, I will!" Everyone laughed. Several other voices shouted encouragements.

"Go ahead!"

"Do it!"

"Go for it!"

A few people whistled.

It all felt like a dream. Sebastian Stokes had proposed to me! Just thinking about it sent me on a natural high.

Chapter 17

Peak

The crowd was waiting for my answer. I just stood on the platform in a daze. I tried to snap out of it but couldn't. It was as if I were watching it all happen to someone else.

Sebastian reached for my hand. Everyone was silent, waiting for my answer.

He slid closer, still bent on one knee, and kissed my hand passionately. "I love you more than my next breath. You know me better than any soul on earth. I simply must spend the rest of my life with you. Say you'll be my wife?"

With tears flowing down my cheeks, I moved both my hands to the sides of his face, bent forward, and kissed him hard on the lips. The crowd cheered our public display of affection.

A woman from the crowd grabbed the mic. "So, what's your answer?"

I gazed deep into his eyes. "Yes," I whispered. Then I yelled, "Of course I'll marry you!"

Sebastian picked me up and twirled me around.

"Thank You, Lord!" I cried out, but my voice was nearly drowned out by the joyful screams of the crowd.

Sebastian grabbed my hand and raised it in the air with his. I felt like we could do anything together. I looked at his parents, sitting straight up in their chairs, glaring at me. Their expressions of disapproval, disgust, and downright displeasure couldn't have been more obvious.

What in the world had I agreed to?

I'm not marrying them, I thought. Or was I?

The television camera got up close, and Sebastian kissed me again as the crowd cheered us on.

Sebastian looked into the camera. "This lovely lady has always had obstacles in her way. She has overcome them, and she's taught me how to be an overcomer, too. We both know there's nothing we can't do as long as God is guiding our way." He took my hand. "The Lord put this union together, and with Christian's help, I'm going to be the best public servant you've ever had."

The crowd went crazy again.

"We'll be around here until dawn, so I want every single one of you to come up and say hello, let me thank you personally, and allow me to introduce you to my fiancée. Enjoy the evening!"

As the group applauded, Sebastian hugged me again. Then everyone started talking and dancing to the soothing sounds of the funky jazz band.

A local deli donated food and sodas to the campaign headquarters to help us celebrate Sebastian's win and our engagement.

As we were in the middle of enjoying our delicious sandwiches, Sebastian's parents came up to us. "Son, I need to talk to you," Reverend Stokes said. He did not look happy.

Sebastian kissed my cheek, squeezed my hand, got up, and led his father into his office. Mrs. Stokes stood there and glared at me, her mouth a thin, tight line.

"Well, I guess I'm going to be marrying your son," I said politely, using a napkin to wipe my mouth. "I know you don't like me very much, but I think it's best if we try to get along—for Sebastian's sake, if nothing else."

"My son simply isn't thinking straight right now. If he were, he would not even consider marrying a girl like you. You're hardly his caliber."

I stood and faced her down. "Mrs. Stokes, if you try to come between us, you'll lose."

"I am his mother. You just remember that. If you give me the proper respect, we might just be able to get along." Mrs. Stokes pointed into the crowd. "Now, do you know that young man my daughter is talking to?"

I looked where she was indicating and saw Savannah talking with her boyfriend, Bruce.

"Nice-looking fellow," I said, messing with her.

Just as Savannah and her boyfriend were about to kiss, Mrs. Stokes left me standing there and stomped up to them. I stayed where I was and watched, hoping there wasn't going to be a big scene.

"Hello," she said in a high-pitched voice. "I'm Vivian Stokes, Savannah's mother." Bruce took a step away from Savannah and gave Mrs. Stokes his full attention.

"You must know my daughter quite well to be kissing her in public, but I haven't had the pleasure of meeting you."

Poor Savannah. She had hidden him away from her parents for so long, not letting any of her family know how much her heart belonged to him. She must have gotten swept up in the moment and forgotten that her parents were present.

"What is your name, young man?" Mrs. Stokes asked.

"Mom," Savannah interjected, "this is a good friend of mine from school."

Bruce looked at Savannah with disappointed eyes.

Mrs. Stokes gasped and put a hand on her chest. "You went to Morehouse? Are you in graduate school somewhere locally then?"

"No, ma'am, I coach football at Morehouse."

Mrs. Stokes's excited face fell like a soufflé. Bruce pretended not to notice. He started telling Mrs. Stokes about his hopes and dreams. Personally, I thought he was a very articulate and charismatic speaker. And I was impressed by his desire to be a football coach. He was teaching young men how to be leaders. Taking responsibility for the future is a noble job.

"Anyone need something to drink?" he asked. Savannah requested a soda, and Bruce went to get it. Mrs. Stokes grabbed Savannah's arm. "What do you think you're doing?" she seethed.

"Mom, don't you think you need to be with Dad right now?

He just lost the biggest election of a lifetime by a landslide. You should be with him, making sure he's okay, not worrying about what's going on with my love life."

"So, you have a love life now?"

"Yes, Mother, I do," Savannah said, rolling her eyes.

"Coaches don't make any money. I bet he can't even afford to pay his rent."

"He makes twenty-nine thousand a year," Savannah said.

"That kind of salary couldn't cover half of your mortgage payment."

Savannah looked like she was about to cry. "Mom, can't you just be glad I have somebody who loves me?"

"No," Mrs. Stokes shouted. "What good is love if you have no money to pay the bills? Darling, I know you think you're in love with this man, but there are several delightful gentlemen here this evening that I'd like to introduce you to."

"Don't you understand?" Savannah yelled, tears streaming down her face. "I'm not interested in meeting someone else."

Noticing that people were staring at them, Mrs. Stokes pulled a handkerchief from her bag and handed it to her daughter. "Let's not talk about this now," she said quietly. "We can get together tomorrow for tea and discuss this further."

"I don't want to have tea with you," Savannah cried.

Mrs. Stokes turned to me. "You may join us if you like."

I raised an eyebrow, surprised she even knew I was still there, and shocked that she would invite me to tea with her and her daughter.

"Please," Savannah begged me.

"Sure, sounds great," I said.

"I'll make reservations at the Ritz Carlton restaurant for one o'clock."

I thanked her for the invitation and she took off as if she had a very important meeting to attend.

"Thanks," Savannah said to me. "There's no way I could get through that tea tomorrow without you there for support."

"It's my pleasure," I assured her.

Bruce came up with Savannah's soda. There was a thin layer

of water on top where the ice had melted. He must have been standing by, waiting for Mrs. Stokes to leave. The two of them gazed into each other's eyes.

"Well, if you two are okay now, I'd like to find Sebastian."

"Go for it," she said with a mischievous smile.

As I searched for my man, several people stopped to congratulate me on the engagement. As one woman babbled on about the best bridal stores and florists, I noticed what looked like a heated conversation between the governor and Reverend Stokes.

Hoping to find out more, I excused myself from the babbler and moved a little closer, being careful to stay out of their line of vision.

"Pity you lost that election, Stokes," the governor said.

"No thanks to you," Reverend Stokes replied gruffly.

"Don't blame me, my good man. You did this yourself, with your lying, cheating, and stealing."

"Did you come here just to gloat over my failure?"

"No, no," the governor said. "I had to congratulate my right-hand man. After all, your son was part of our gimmick for you to run for president. Who would have thought he'd win?" He gave an arrogant chuckle.

"We were both fooled on that one," Reverend Stokes said.

The governor's tone became serious. "If you think you're going to have a say in how I run this state just because your son is lieutenant governor, forget it."

"If you think you're going to run my son, you'd better think again. If he stood up for what I did wrong, he'll find you out and expose you as well."

The two men started laughing. Did Sebastian know what he was getting into?

The next morning, Sebastian and I were having a fun breakfast in Savannah's kitchen, happily discussing what type of ceremony we wanted, how many guests, and where to go on our honeymoon. Then he pulled a day-planner out of his coat pocket and said, "So, when are we gonna set the date?"

For some reason I started to panic.

"How about Christmas Day?" he suggested, before taking a bite of his Belgian waffle.

I almost choked on my orange juice. "You mean Christmas next year, right?"

He smiled. "I want us to be married before I take office."

"That's only two months away," I argued. "There's no way we can put together the kind of wedding we want that quickly. What's the rush?"

He leaned over the table and kissed me. "I want you to be my wife when I become lieutenant governor. Besides, I love you too much to wait. If we could get married today, I would. I called a wedding planner on my way over here this morning. She's been a friend of the family for years. She's gonna call you later today to start going over some details."

I stood and walked to the window, which provided a beautiful view of Atlanta. I could see myself calling this place home someday. But my home was in D.C., and I wasn't ready to make that change just yet.

When I felt Sebastian's presence behind me, I turned around. His eyes were filled with concern.

"I love you," I said. "And I know that putting off the wedding means waiting on certain . . . other things. But I just don't feel ready to—"

He cut me off with a chuckle. "I wasn't talking about sex, silly."

"I know," I said with a shy smile. "But that's a big part of it, right?"

His face grew serious. "I thought being married was something we both wanted."

"You just proposed to me last night," I reminded him.

"You never thought about being my wife until last night?"

"Oh, I did," I said. "I guess I just didn't really think about moving to Atlanta."

"If you had a problem with it, why did you say yes?"

"I don't know," I said, my strained voice revealing my frustration. "Maybe because you asked me in front of three thousand people."

"Well, it's just me and you now. You want me to ask you again so you can change your answer?"

"I'm not saying this right. I do want to marry you. The way you proposed was extremely romantic, and I'll never forget it."

"Then what's the problem?"

"I just didn't think we'd be getting married so soon. I'm set to go back to my FBI office and start working again in D.C. come January," I told him.

"I know, baby," he said, wrapping his arms around me. "But if we get married you won't have to go back."

"What are you saying?" I asked, pulling away from him. "I'm in the best office in D.C., and I don't want to transfer."

He reached out and started playing with my hair. "I mean, you won't have to work at all. I can take care of you."

I couldn't believe what I was hearing. As hard as I'd fought to keep my job, surely he couldn't be implying that I should give it up now. "I don't want to quit," I said, planting my hands on my hips. "Besides, there's a lot of other things going on in my life right now." I started pacing as I thought about all the stuff in my life that was up in the air. "My girlfriend Eden just found out she can't have any babies. My sister's pregnant and I promised to help her choose the adoptive parents. I've tried calling my mom several times, but all I get lately is her answering machine, so something's going on there." I placed my hands on the kitchen counter to steady myself and glanced down at the beautiful engagement ring on my finger. It sparkled in the sun coming in through the window, which softened my heart but not my resolve. "Besides, baby, I have to show off this fantastic ring to my mom and my best friend."

He stared at me with a blank look.

"Look, there are just a lot of things in D.C. I need to take care of right now."

"So what were you thinking when you accepted my proposal? That we'd agree to get married and then live in separate states?"

"Of course not," I said softly. "I figured I could go back and forth between here and D.C. until things settled down." I put my arms around his neck. "I wish we could get married tomorrow, too," I whispered in his ear. "But there are some things I need to tie up first. Please try to understand."

He returned my embrace, then asked weakly, "When do you have to leave?"

I kissed him passionately. "I'm having lunch with your mom this afternoon, so I booked a flight back tonight. Your life's going to be awfully busy for a while, anyway. You probably won't even notice I'm gone."

"I'll notice."

I could tell he was crushed, and I felt bad about that, but I had to be honest. There was more to my life than just him and he needed to understand that.

"You ready to go?" Savannah asked as she tapped on my door at noon that day. She peeked through the open door and saw me packing. "Wait a minute. Are you leaving?"

"I've got to go back home for a while."

"I was hoping you two could go on a double date with me and Bruce."

"I won't be gone forever," I said. "There are just some things I need to take care of back home."

"I understand," she said. "I'll miss you."

"I'll miss you, too," I said as we hugged. "By the way, I think Bruce is extremely handsome. And very attentive."

"You could tell he loves me, huh?"

"Yeah, I really could."

She gave me a sly grin. "My brother loves you, too."

"I wish your parents didn't hate me so much."

"They'll come around," she assured me. "You'll see. You'll win them over when they see how much you two love each other."

"I'm sure Bruce will do the same for you," I said.

Savannah looked at her watch. "We'd better get going. I don't want to keep Mom waiting. Wouldn't want to do anything else to make her more angry at us."

I scoffed. I didn't really care if Mrs. Stokes got peeved because I was a few minutes late for tea. I mean, I wanted her approval, but I didn't need it.

We arrived at the restaurant. I gazed all around me.

"It's beautiful," I said.

Savannah shrugged. "You'll get used to places like this after you marry my brother."

I couldn't imagine ever taking a place like that for granted.

I stepped gingerly across the white marble floor to the hostess's counter. A huge arrangement of birds of paradise and gladiolas stood in an exquisite red vase behind the woman, who looked like a model. Her auburn hair sparkled under the enormous crystal chandelier that hung from the high ceiling. I'd eaten at some nice restaurants with my job, but I'd never been able to just relax and enjoy the atmosphere. *I might just enjoy this tea,* I thought. Until I saw Mrs. Stokes.

She was standing on the other side of the door, talking to an elegant-looking lady wearing a long leather coat and boots. When the lady turned around, I realized it was Sebastian's old flame, Penelope. She gave me a once-over, then glanced at my ring finger. I clasped my hands behind my back.

Mrs. Stokes made a point of looking at her watch when she saw us. "Look who I ran into while I was waiting on you girls," she said pointedly.

"Sorry we're late, Mom," Savannah said as she kissed her cheek. "The valet took forever."

"Well, I've got to skedaddle," Penelope said, turning to leave.

Mrs. Stokes grabbed her hand. "But we have so much catching up to do. Surely you have a few minutes to spare while we wait on our table."

"Sure, okay."

I excused myself to go freshen up and headed for the bathroom. When I returned, I overheard Mrs. Stokes telling Penelope, "I'm absolutely devastated. I thought you were going to be the one to marry my son."

I stopped just around the corner from the two and lingered, wondering what more I might hear.

"The way that girl destroyed my husband's presidential campaign, I'd have thought he would prefer you over her, but apparently that's not the case."

"Stokes, table for three," the maître d' announced.

"Well, I'd better not keep you, dear," Mrs. Stokes said sadly.

As Mrs. Stokes was ushered to our table, I saw Savannah pull Penelope aside. "Listen," Savannah said. "You're my friend, and I'm sorry things didn't work out for you and my brother. But his girlfriend—"

"I know she's been staying at your apartment," Penelope interrupted in an angry voice. "How could you choose her over me?"

"Come on, Penelope. I couldn't make him like you more."

"Whatever."

"So now you're angry at me?"

"Payback's coming," Penelope retorted as she stomped out of the restaurant.

"What was that all about?" I asked, pretending I hadn't heard their conversation, as I walked up to Savannah.

"She's just mad because Sebastian wants you and not her."

"Well, too bad for her," I mumbled.

When we got to the table, Mrs. Stokes glared at us. "It's about time you two got here," she said. "The tea is getting cold."

As soon as we sat down, the waiter approached us for our orders.

Savannah spent most of our teatime trying to convince her mother that her boyfriend was likable. I sat back and just enjoyed the chai tea and finger sandwiches. The caviar and salmon on rye was scrumptious.

When the conversation switched to me, I almost choked on my sandwich.

"Sebastian said you set the date for next month," Savannah said.

Mrs. Stokes practically gagged. "Surely you aren't getting married that soon."

"Actually, I told him this morning that I don't want to rush into the marriage."

"Oh, smart decision," she said, patting my hand.

"Mom," Savannah said, "they're in love. Even if they got married tomorrow, it wouldn't be rushing it."

"Well, it takes a lot more than love to make a successful marriage. You don't want to struggle to make ends meet from month to month. That may sound appealing, but you won't think so once you try it. I'm sure you understand, don't you, Agent Ware?"

"My name is Christian," I corrected her.

"Sorry. As you know, Christian, my son will be hosting many important events. He needs the right wife, one who's capable of helping him."

I nodded for her to continue, wondering what this was leading up to.

"Take attire, for example. If a wife doesn't know when to wear what, she might do her husband more harm than good. Love is simply not enough."

"Hey, look," Savannah said, interrupting her mother's discourse. "There's Daddy at the hotel lobby desk."

She picked up her cup without even glancing at the lobby. "Just finish your tea, dear."

"I want to say hi real quick." Savannah started to stand, but her mother placed a hand on her arm.

"Don't be rude, darling. After we finish our meal, then we'll go see your father."

When teatime was over, I thanked Mrs. Stokes for allowing me to come. She instructed Savannah and me to wait in the lobby while she strode up to the desk and spoke in hushed tones to the hotel manager. She then came back to where we were and asked us to go upstairs with her. On the walk to the elevator she told us that the desk clerk told her the Reverend Stokes had checked into the penthouse suite.

Mrs. Stokes rapped on the door. "Room service," she said in a high-pitched voice, feigning a Mexican accent. "Compliments of the hotel."

A giggly female voice rang out, "Coming!"

To my amazement, the door was opened by Penelope, draped

in a man's white dress shirt. Her mouth hung open when Mrs. Stokes walked in and marched right past her.

Savannah and I followed like a couple of pet poodles. I couldn't believe my eyes when we walked into the bedroom and saw Reverend Stokes lying in the bed, wearing nothing but his birthday suit. He quickly sat up when he saw us, pulling the white sheet over his body.

"Oh, don't cover up for me," his wife said. "You have nothing I haven't seen."

"How did you know?" he asked, his lower lip trembling.

"Penelope's mother called me," Mrs. Stokes explained, her voice filled with an emotion I'd never heard from her before. She was obviously deeply hurt. "She saw your private number on her caller ID. I guess now I know why you told Sebastian you didn't think Penelope was right for him."

"Mrs. Stokes—" Penelope said, coming into the room.

Savannah stepped in front of her former best friend and said, "Don't say anything. Get your stuff and go. I don't ever want to see you around my family."

Penelope looked upset, got her belongings, and left.

When the door shut, Mrs. Stokes looked at her husband and yelled, "I know you've been running around for years, but I never thought you'd do this with such a young girl. Now that the election is over, I don't have to pretend any longer."

She turned around and walked out, leaving her husband sitting there, speechless. I followed her, but Savannah stayed behind with her dad.

"I don't know what to say," I told Mrs. Stokes when we got into the hall.

"I don't care what you say," she said. "You can go tell this to the press, for all I care."

"I would never do that," I assured her. I held out my arms and she fell into them. She just started sobbing right there in front of the door.

When Savannah came out she saw me consoling her mom. "It's going to be okay, Mom."

Mrs. Stokes lifted her head from my shoulder. "You know,

girls, maybe I was wrong. Perhaps love *is* the most important thing in a relationship."

Savannah and I hugged her. I guess in her own weird way, Mrs. Stokes wanted Savannah and me to accompany her to the penthouse for support.

"I should never have put up with his infidelities. Now that I've caught him red-handed, I think I've got the strength to walk away."

She strode down the hallway, holding her head up.

Our "teatime" had lasted so much longer than I anticipated, I barely had time to get my luggage and drive to the airport. I didn't even have a chance to say good-bye to Sebastian.

The first thing I did when I got home was call Eden. She came over immediately. "Let's see that ring," she said, before I even had a chance to close the door behind her. I obliged her request. "It's gorgeous," she said, ogling the diamond. She looked up at me. "You're going to have an incredible wedding, girl."

"If there is one," I said under my breath, crossing to the couch.

"Now what does that mean?" she asked, joining me. "You just got engaged yesterday."

"Yeah, and he wants to get married tomorrow."

"Seriously?"

"Well, before the new year, anyway."

"I take it you have a problem with that," she said.

"I just don't want to rush it," I said, twisting the ring on my finger.

"I was wondering why you came back here the day after you got that amazing proposal."

I smiled at my friend. "Well, I wanted to be here for you. I know you're going through a lot right now."

"Shoot, girl," she said, "we could have talked by phone. You didn't have to fly all the way out for me."

"It wasn't just for you," I admitted. "Sebastian and I needed some time apart."

Eden sat quietly for a while, her lips pressed tight. I could tell she was trying to figure out how to say something serious, so I gave her time.

"Max's death really changed Dion," she finally said. "He kept saying things like, 'Tomorrow's not promised to us' and 'You never know what will happen in life.' But he didn't mean it in a negative way. He started coming alive, living every day to its fullest."

"Dion? Your husband? *That* Dion?" I asked, trying to imagine her drunk and abusive husband being positive and happy.

"Yes, my husband, silly," Eden said, laughing. Then her face became serious again. "I just don't think you should put off becoming this guy's wife. I mean, if you don't want to marry him, then don't. But if you love him, don't waste time. You don't know how much time you've got. None of us know."

The thought made me uncomfortable, so I changed the focus back to her. "I still can't believe you'll never be able to have kids."

We talked and cried over her loss for a while. Then a loud knock at my door interrupted us. Someone started banging on my door like a crazy person.

I opened the door and found my sister standing there. "Crystal, what's wrong?"

"Nothing much, I just wanted to see you." She barreled in and made herself at home. I was a little taken aback by the sight of her big belly. I mentally did a quick calculation. She was about seven months along.

"You got something to eat in here?" she asked, going straight to my kitchen.

"I haven't been to a grocery store yet," I explained. "My cupboards are pretty bare."

"You've always got something," she said, rummaging through my refrigerator. "I'm sure I can scrounge something up."

As she shuffled through my pantry, Eden whispered, "I didn't know your sister was having a baby."

I looked at her shocked face. "I guess with everything going on in my life, it must have slipped my mind."

"How old is she?" Eden asked quietly.

"Almost sixteen."

"Girl, you don't have nothing in here except tuna," Crystal said, coming out of the kitchen carrying a small can.

"You can have that if you want," I told her.

"How are you going to take care of a baby?" Eden asked.

"Oh, I ain't keeping it," Crystal said, pulling a can opener out of the silverware drawer. "I'm gonna place it for adoption."

"Where's the baby's father?" Eden questioned.

Crystal finally got the lid off the tuna can and tossed it into the wastebasket. "Oh, he's in jail."

"I thought he got out," I said.

"The cops found something else on him, so they took him back in."

"Sounds like you're a lot better off without that loser," Eden commented.

Crystal grabbed a fork and started eating right out of the can. "If I don't find an adoptive family soon, I may have to raise this baby myself. I don't want to do that. I'm not ready to be a mama. Besides, my mom would get attached and then she'd have a real hard time giving up her grandbaby."

Crystal tossed the empty tuna can into the trash. "Well, I'll let you two go back to catching up. Talk to you later, sis."

After she left, Eden and I sat on the couch and went back to talking about her situation. All of a sudden Eden said, "Wait! Your sister's looking for parents for her baby?"

"Yeah," I said hesitantly.

"Why couldn't Dion and I adopt Crystal's baby?"

"I don't know," I said.

"If you're concerned about Dion, don't be. He's changed."

"Really?"

"Yeah. He's been going to AA meetings and working for the pastor of our church."

"That sounds like a good start, anyway," I said.

"Pray about it for me, will you?" she asked, getting up. "I can't wait to tell Dion about this."

I walked with her to the door. "Thanks for trying to help my sister."

"Your sister could be helping me out, too," she said, beaming. "Tell Crystal to take care of herself. If she needs food, tell her I'll be happy to cook something for her."

"I love you, girl," I told her as I watched her practically skipping to her car.

Two weeks went by. I really missed Sebastian, but I didn't call him. I wanted to stay tough. I guess he was taking the same stance because he didn't call me, either.

Mom took me to church with her and I got to sit with Mrs. Jones, the lady who'd helped me understand how important my commitment to Christ was.

My mother had bragged to all the church members about my engagement to the newly elected lieutenant governor of Georgia. After the service, lots of people came up to me, telling me about their cousins or ex-boyfriends or high-school friends who lived in various small towns in Georgia. I didn't want to be rude, but since I didn't live in that state, the names of the places meant nothing to me.

Trying to learn how to be a politician's wife, I just said things like, "Oh, that's wonderful. I'll be sure to tell Sebastian." I knew I would never remember the names of the towns they mentioned, much less their friends' or relatives' names.

After everyone had gone, Mrs. Jones came up to me. "You're representing your man quite well." Apparently she'd been watching me. "There's just one thing I don't understand, my dear. Why aren't you by his side?"

"I honestly don't know," I admitted. "Everything's perfect, but I now don't know if I want to go through with the marriage." I sighed. "Am I an idiot?"

She smiled briefly, then asked, "What are you afraid of?"

I stared at my hands, digging deep inside myself for the answer. "Mrs. Jones, I just recently started developing a relationship with the Lord. He speaks to me and I hear His voice. I love that. I guess I'm afraid that if I get married, I'll have to submit my will to someone, and that might become a wedge between me and God. I don't want to have to go through Sebastian to talk to the Lord, and I don't want to stop hearing directly from Him."

Mrs. Jones chuckled a bit. "Oh, my. Your mama always said you were a strong cookie. Not many young women would hold up a wedding just because they wanted to keep their independence."

"So, what do I do?" I asked, hoping she'd have a clear answer for me.

She took a deep breath. "Christian, darling, being married to a godly man isn't about losing anything. You gain a loving man who leads you, but I don't think you really understand what that means."

"Can you break it down for me?" I asked.

She smiled. "God will speak through and to your man, but He'll still talk to you as well. You don't have to worry about him leading you astray. If you've got a man who loves God, Christ is calling him to love you. You won't mind following him, serving him, submitting to him, and helping him because without you, he wouldn't be able to become all that God wants him to be. You've heard that behind every great man there's a great woman? Well, it's true. God created Eve to help Adam."

"Yeah, but tempted him to fall," I pointed out.

"That's true," she said. "And we're all now paying the price of pain for what Eve did. But you don't have to make the same mistakes Eve did. When God tells your husband to do something, follow it, even if you feel led to do something else."

"That sounds like a tough thing to do," I said.

"You're right," she said. "When you're single you can totally focus on God. But if the Lord gives you a husband who loves Him, you'll have so much joy, you can't even imagine it." She threw her hands up. "You won't believe all the things you two will be able to do together to worship God. Just pray and ask God to give you guidance."

After Mrs. Jones left I sat in the pew and thought and prayed. I soon realized that I didn't want to live without the man I loved.

I rushed home and called Sebastian.

"I've missed you," he said.

"I love you."

He asked about my Thanksgiving plans.

"I wanted to be with you," I said, "but I'm not sure I can come out there."

"Actually," he said, "I've been thinking I'd like to get away from Georgia for a while. Maybe I can come up there. If that's all right."

"That'd be great!"

"We'll plan on it, then," he said, sounding relieved.

"How are your parents doing?" I asked.

"Not good," he said, the excitement in his voice disappearing. "Mom moved out for a while, but then she decided that since she wasn't the one who did anything wrong, Dad should leave. So she kicked him out."

"Where'd he go?" I asked, searching my kitchen cabinets for something to eat.

"Believe it or not, he's staying with me. That's why I'm trying to get a break from here."

"Gee, and I thought you just wanted to see me," I teased him.

"I do," he assured me. "But my dad really is driving me crazy. He keeps trying to tell me what I need to do when I get into office."

"At least you two are talking."

"The line of communication is open between us, and I'm thankful for that. So what are your family's plans for Thanksgiving?"

"I'm sure my mom will cook a big dinner. Now, we don't have fancy china and crystal or anything."

"Oh, I can't come, then," he joked.

I laughed. "Will you be able to stay long?"

"The governor has given me a vacation as an engagement

gift. He even offered to let me stay at his cabin at a ski resort in Tennessee. Think you might want to join me there for a couple of days?"

"I'd love to."

"We could head up there the day after Thanksgiving."

"Sounds perfect."

We sent each other hugs and kisses through the phone. Our relationship was back on track, and it felt so good. I still wasn't ready to set a date for our wedding, but I figured another two weeks would give me time to decide.

On Thanksgiving my mom's house was full with my sister and her friends, Eden and Dion, and, of course, Sebastian and me. Dion and Sebastian hit it off right from the start.

The next day, Sebastian and I flew to the ski resort. The governor's wood cabin had a high ceiling, a large brick fireplace, and antique furniture. It was beautiful and cozy, and I relished the thought of just relaxing for a change. Too bad I was going to be staying in the nearby lodge and not with Sebastian in the cabin. Since I had started my walk with God, I knew that we should not sleep in the same cabin because things may get out of control like they did in the hotel room. I figured that we could hang out in my room in the ski resort or the cabin but I was definitely sleeping alone in my room.

Sebastian wanted to take to the slopes right away. I asked if he'd mind if I just sat by the roaring fire and spent some time alone with the Lord. "I'll go skiing with you tomorrow," I promised.

He came out of the bedroom dressed in his dark yellow snowsuit. He looked so adorable all bundled up. Before leaving, he gave me a long kiss. I appreciated it, but it was like he was going off to the army or something.

"What was that for?" I asked him, very uneasy with his strong good-bye kiss. "You'll be right back."

"Yes, I will, but I don't want to take you for granted. I want every kiss we share to be special," he said, leaving my side to grab his skis and poles.

I felt much better after hearing his sweet explanation. He was so silly as he put on his gloves and then blew me kisses. Gosh, I loved him.

As soon as he left, I settled in the recliner by the fireplace. I was so cozy, curled up in an afghan. I read a few chapters in Proverbs and then fell asleep.

My peaceful solitude was interrupted by Sebastian's cell phone ringing. I let the voice mail pick up. Since it rang again right away, I decided it might be Sebastian trying to reach me, so I picked up.

When I said hello, I heard a deep sigh, but no words.

"Can I help you?" I asked.

"Christian, this is Reverend Stokes."

"What can I do for you?" I asked coolly.

"Is my son there?"

"No, sir. He's out skiing."

"He's on the slope already?" Stokes asked, his voice sounding strange, almost panicked. "How long has he been gone?"

"About twenty minutes. Is something wrong?"

"Christian . . ." Reverend Stokes paused. "The governor offered to let Sebastian stay at his cabin because . . ."

His uncharacteristic nervousness had me scared.

"He sent Sebastian out there to get rid of him," Stokes blurted out.

I sat bolt upright. "What are you talking about?"

"Governor James doesn't believe Sebastian will support him in his bid to get the casino approved. That deal is worth millions of dollars, so he and his people are willing to do anything to get it. And I do mean anything."

I sucked in my breath, trying to take in his implications.

"Christian, you have to go out to the slopes and find him. You've got to save my son!"

"I'll do my best, sir," I said. The second after I hung up, I called the ski patrol and told them what Reverend Stokes had said. "Sebastian told me he was going to the Deer Run slope."

"That's the most dangerous one, this time of year," the ranger said. "It's very close to the deer-hunting side. Stray bullets sometimes fly through there. We've tried for years to get the park to close it down."

Since the slopes were less than a mile from the cabin, Sebastian had walked, leaving the rented four-wheel-drive Jeep in the driveway. I drove as fast as I could on the icy roads to the ski patrol building.

When I pulled up, I saw a patrolman mounting a white snowmobile with a forest ranger emblem on it. "Are you going after Sebastian Stokes?" I hollered over the rev of the engine.

"Sure am," he said. "Are you the one who called?"

"Yeah," I said. "Can I come with you?"

He handed me a helmet. I hopped on behind him, my heart beating like crazy.

Lord, please don't let anything happen to him, I chanted over and over as wet snow assaulted my cheeks. The patrolman's broad back offered me some protection.

The snowmobile slowed down and I peeked around the patrolman's shoulders. I saw a guy in a black ski mask and black clothes pointing a gun at a skier coming down the hill. As the skier slid past us, I recognized the bright yellow of Sebastian's ski suit.

A loud booming sound rang out across the snow. I turned around and saw the man in black skiing down the far side of the slope. I quickly looked back at the skier who'd passed us. All I could see was a yellow suit lying in the white snow.

"Sebastian," I screamed. I pounded on the back of the ski patrolman and pointed. He called for backup and steered the snowmobile toward the yellow lump in the snow. As we drew closer, I noticed some of the white snow was turning pink.

Even before the snowmobile came to a complete stop, I hopped off and tramped through the deep snow to get to my injured man.

"Stay here," the patrolman ordered. "I have to make sure the area is clear of danger."

"What about Sebastian?" I asked, furious that he would leave a wounded person.

"Ma'am, if that gunman is still in the area, we could get shot, too."

I saw his point. This was definitely a no-win situation.

"I've called for backup," he assured me. "The medics will be here soon." He turned the snowmobile around and zoomed off.

What was happening? How could things get so bad just when they were at their peak?

Chapter 18

Heaven

"Please don't go to heaven yet," I screamed with my knees buried in the snow. I held Sebastian's head in my lap as if my protecting his head would make him better. Blood was gushing from his left side, so I took fresh snow and put it on his wound, hoping it would stop the flow. I begged Sebastian to say something to me. He didn't utter a word.

I kept pressing snow against his side. Finally I heard him moan. "Thank You, God," I cried.

A blue-and-white vehicle that resembled a large snowmobile slid up to us. Three paramedics climbed off, carrying first-aid bags. "Is he breathing?" the larger one asked as they trudged toward me.

"Yes, but he's lost a lot of blood."

"His pulse is faint," the female paramedic said, her bare hand against Sebastian's neck.

"We've got to get him to the hospital stat," the tall paramedic said. He radioed for a helicopter.

"We're losing him," the woman called out.

"Don't let him die," I screamed. "Please don't let him die."

The large guy ripped open Sebastian's snowsuit and started CPR, alternating between pressing my man's chest and blowing into his mouth while holding his nose closed.

I was trained in CPR but forgot everything I knew because I

was panicking. I yelled, "He's bleeding. Are you supposed to press his chest?"

The lady looked up at me and said, "Basic first aid says that you have to get the guy breathing first before you attend to his wounds. Unless you want us to attend to the wounds of a dead guy."

"Janna, don't say that," the tall guy responded.

Janna said, "Well, it's true, and she's got to let us do our job."

Horrified by the thought that Sebastian could be dead, I knelt in the snow and held on to hope.

One of the ski patrol guys got a portable defibrillator from one of the jet skis. He turned on the machine, instructed everyone to move back, put gel on the paddles of the defibrillator, yelled "Clear!" and put the paddles on Sebastian's chest. He then pressed a button on the back of each of the paddles and they sent an electrical current to Sebastian's heart, which caused his whole body to jerk. He then checked Sebastian's pulse and said that there was a faint pulse.

Lord, I prayed, *I'm not ready to let him go, but it looks like he's in a lot of pain, and I don't want him to be hurting so much. Just take him.*

Though the last thing I wanted was for Sebastian to be gone, God's Word said it was far better for him.

"He's going," the female paramedic yelled.

"Let's shock him one more time," the tall guy responded. The awful procedure was performed again.

"There's a pulse," the female reported, "but it's faint."

Just then I heard helicopter blades whirling above us. We all looked up. As the chopper landed nearby, kicking up snow in all directions, the paramedics put Sebastian on a stretcher. They carried him to the waiting aircraft.

The EMT in the helicopter told me I could ride in front with the pilot. I quickly thanked the paramedics and jumped in. As the chopper lifted, the EMT started Sebastian on an IV and dressed his wound.

When we landed at Gatlinburg Memorial Hospital, the doctors rushed Sebastian to surgery. I prayed aloud in a quiet corner of the hospital chapel. Though my whole body was shaking, I had a peace in my heart that came from God.

I went to the waiting room. When I dug in the pocket of my jeans to get money for a cup of coffee, I found Sebastian's cell phone in my pocket. *I should call his parents.* But what would I say?

Apparently, the governor of Georgia had invited us to his cabin to have Sebastian assassinated. But why? Did Sebastian know something that Governor James wanted to keep hidden? It made me pretty sick to think that this was connected to the attempt on my life.

Opening the cell phone, I punched the button to display the last number called. When I recognized the number as the one for Sebastian's parents' home, I pressed Send.

"Hello?" Reverend Stokes answered, though he had moved out.

"This is Christian," I said in a tone that hated to be making the call. "I've got some bad news about Sebastian."

"Dear Lord."

"He was shot. We're at Gatlinburg Memorial Hospital."

"Is he all right?"

"He's in surgery. I don't know anything yet."

"I'll call his mother, and we'll be there as quickly as we can," his worried father promised.

I went to the waiting room. A nurse came in and updated me on the progress of Sebastian's surgery. She advised me that he was doing well, the surgery was going fine, and that they should be finished soon. A few minutes after the nurse left, Detective Hart came in and asked me questions about what happened. I told him everything that I knew and he said that he would keep in touch with the hospital to check on Sebastian's progress so he could question him when he was awake.

His parents chartered a plane and arrived in two hours. When they spotted me, his mother rushed up and hugged me. A tear from her face touched mine.

Feeling and sharing her fear, I eagerly returned her embrace. "I still don't know anything yet. He's been in there for hours."

Mrs. Stokes slowly pulled me away and looked me in the eye. "Everything will be all right," she said in a loving mother's voice.

A distinguished-looking man in a green surgical gown entered.

"Dr. Barber?" I asked.

"You must be Christian," he said. "And of course I've seen Reverend and Mrs. Stokes before." He shook our hands. "Sebastian made it through the operation successfully," he informed us, "but at the moment he's unresponsive."

"What does that mean?" I asked.

"He hasn't woken up yet. A few of his arteries were ruptured. We had to fix them and get the bullet out. We've moved him to ICU and put him on a ventilator."

I felt nauseous.

"What do we do now, Doctor?" Reverend Stokes asked, his arm around his wife's shoulders.

"The only thing you can do is wait and pray," the doctor said.

"Can we see him?" I asked.

"Sure," he said, "once his vital signs are stable. A nurse will come and get you in about twenty or thirty minutes." We then thanked the doctor and he left.

"I need to talk to the police," Reverend Stokes said, "and see if they found out anything about the sniper." Stokes turned to his wife, who looked harried. "Do you want to go to the hotel and rest for a while?" he asked her.

"No, I want to be here when he wakes up."

"We've been up for over twenty-four hours and we both need some rest."

"What if something should happen to him while we are gone?"

"Christian will call us if anything happens." He turned to me. "I've been a preacher of the gospel for over thirty years, and when I entered politics almost ten years ago, I lost a little part of my Christianity. Watching you go through so much, yet staying connected with God, has shown me that I want back what

I've lost along the way." He touched my shoulder. "I'm trying to say I'm sorry for putting you through so much misery. I'm going through my own hell now, and I'm . . ."

"I know what you're trying to say. It's okay. I'm learning that this Christian walk ain't easy. None of us will get it exactly right. I just know that God helps me through. And I know he's gonna help your son. Now you guys go get some rest."

They both smiled at me. Mrs. Stokes hesitated to leave. Reverend Stokes promised her they would come back to the hospital first thing in the morning, and she finally agreed. Before they left, he looked at me with grateful eyes. "Thank you for looking after my son."

Mrs. Stokes took my hand in both of hers. "I want to thank you, too. I hate to think what would have happened if you hadn't called the police right away."

Tears filled my eyes. I couldn't speak. I was glad to have finally gained their respect, though this sure wasn't the way I would have picked for it to happen.

A few minutes after they left for the hotel, the nurse called me to go see Sebastian. When I entered his room, I saw that he was hooked up to a monitor that measured his blood pressure and heart rate. He had an IV in one arm, a tube in his other arm, and his face was pale. I also noticed that the room had a place for another bed, but it had been removed so Sebastian could have the entire room to himself. Being wealthy and a political figure did have its perks.

For a moment, my tears fell nonstop. It was hard seeing him so still and lifeless. When I'd composed myself a bit, I kissed his forehead and pulled a chair up next to his bed.

"Hey, baby," I said, hoping he could hear me. "I love you." I held his hand so he would know I was there with him.

In the morning when his parents came back, I went to the ski resort to get a bite to eat and give his parents some time alone with their son. I also packed a bag of clothes and personal items to take with me. When I returned to the hospital, I asked if I could sleep on a cot in his room, but the nurse said no. She did say I could sleep in the waiting room, though.

Reverend Stokes told me he had spoken to the officer investigating Sebastian's shooting, and the officer was going to stop by the next day to question me further and see if Sebastian had regained consciousness so he could question him.

I sat by Sebastian's bed for eight days, crying and praying. I struggled to keep my faith as I sat there day after day, looking at the man I loved lie there so unresponsive. His face became thinner, as did the rest of his body. The tubes in his nose frightened me. The IV concerned me even more because I had to be careful each time I hugged him. I had never felt so helpless. One of the nurses told me that I should touch his hands and feet occasionally to see if he would respond.

I started thinking, *I need to talk to him.*

On the sixth day I brought in a Bible that I'd found in the hospital chapel and started reading in the Book of Jeremiah. I must have fallen asleep and unknowingly turned the pages, because I woke up with my head in the middle of Job. I heard Sebastian's parents talking outside of the door.

"I wish we had that kind of love," Mrs. Stokes said.

"Me, too," I heard Stokes say. "I'm sorry I messed up."

Mrs. Stokes said, "My mother was wrong. She always told me status was more important than love. But when I think about the way Sebastian has defended the woman he loves, I realize that the two of them have experienced more love than you and I have in thirty-five years."

"You're right about that," he said.

As they opened the door, Mrs. Stokes whispered, "Look at her, sleeping by his side. She should go to the hotel and get some rest. She's been here constantly."

"She's not going to leave him."

I moved a little, then acted as if I was just waking up. I didn't want them to know that I'd been listening to their conversation. I lifted my head and said hello. Then I pulled down the covers and touched his hands and feet to see if he would respond, as the nurse had told me to do. He didn't respond, so I pulled his covers back up over him.

"Christian," Mrs. Stokes said, "why don't you go to the cabin to get some rest."

"No, ma'am," I said. "I want to be here if he wakes up."

"We'll stay with him," Reverend Stokes said. "If he wakes up, we'll call you at the hotel."

I finally agreed to go to the Marriott so I could freshen up and get some sleep. Reverend Stokes gave me the key to their room and the rental car key because the Jeep was still at the ski patrol station. After he gave me directions to the hotel, I grabbed my bag and went to the Marriott.

I took the elevator to the fifth floor and found the room. When I opened the door I found myself in a large suite with a black leather living room set, fireplace, large-screen TV, and wet bar. All three bedrooms had king-sized beds. Two of them had clothes in them—his in one, hers in the other. I made myself comfortable in the third one. I took a long, hot bath, put the cell phone on the nightstand, and climbed into bed. I was asleep in seconds.

Sebastian's cell phone rang, startling me from sleep. I looked at the clock on the nightstand. It said six o'clock. Light streamed in from the windows. How long had I been out?

"Father, give me strength," I said, bracing myself for the news that Sebastian had taken a turn for the worse while I was away. I picked up the phone with a trembling hand.

"Ms. Ware," a woman's voice said, "this is Nurse Washington from Gatlinburg Memorial."

"Yes?" I said, wondering why the nurse was calling me and not Reverend or Mrs. Stokes.

"You need to come to the hospital. Sebastian—"

I hung up before she had the chance to tell me he was gone. I sped to the hospital.

When I saw Savannah, Steven, Steven's wife, and Mrs. and Mrs. Stokes talking quietly in the waiting room, tears began falling again. The whole family gathering like this could only mean one thing. I had to start imagining my life without Sebastian.

Savannah rushed up to me and hugged me. Then she grabbed

my arm and pulled me close. Her heart was beating wildly. "Isn't it wonderful?" she said.

What? I thought. I know death for believers is supposed to be a celebration, but I was way too sad to think that his going home was *wonderful.*

"Look," I said, "I know I'm supposed to be happy about him being in heaven and all, but I just can't do that right now."

She smiled. "Didn't the nurse tell you? Sebastian is awake!"

I stared at her for a moment to make sure I'd heard right. Her huge grin told me I had. I immediately rushed to Sebastian's room.

When I walked into the room, his eyes were closed but his color looked better. I whispered his name. His eyes opened and he smiled at me.

"There you are, beautiful," he said, his voice weak and scratchy. "My parents told me you never left my side, but when I finally woke up you were gone."

"I'm so sorry, I—"

"Come here," he interrupted.

My tears of sadness turned to tears of joy. I rushed over and kissed him. "Thank You, Lord," I cried out. "I love you, Sebastian. I love you so much."

"I'm sorry," he said.

"For what?"

"My dad told me about the governor. I can't believe he hired someone to kill me. Dad said the police caught the guy who shot me. The police are trying to get him to admit that he was hired by the governor and to help them expose the governor's hand in it."

"I never should have gone to the hotel," I said, shaking my head. An awful lot had happened while I was asleep! I gently rubbed his hand. "How are you feeling?"

"Now that I see you, I feel good. Mom told me you read almost the whole Bible to me."

"Not quite. We were going to start on the New Testament today."

"Well, then," he said, "you'd better get to reading."

At first I thought he was kidding, but when he told me he really wanted to hear the Word, I opened the Bible and started to read.

Before I got very far, a man came into the room. He was thin and balding, dressed all in black, and he introduced himself as Chaplain Burke, the hospital chaplain. I asked if he could pray for Sebastian, then suddenly had a crazy thought.

"Sir," I asked, "do you marry people?"

Sebastian gave me a confused look.

I took his hand. "I don't want to wait any longer. I almost lost you. If I could be your wife tonight, I'd marry you right now."

"Really?" he said, his eyes twinkling.

I turned to Chaplain Burke and asked, "Is that possible?"

He asked, "Do you have a marriage license?"

I said, "No."

"My father has a friend who's a presiding officer," Sebastian said. "I'm sure he can arrange that." I was thrilled to hear him so excited about my idea.

"You'll have to get blood tests," Chaplain Burke added.

"We're in a hospital," I said, my smile getting broader by the minute. "Can't get much easier than that!"

Burke shrugged. "When do you want the ceremony?"

"Tonight," I said, my heart pounding with anticipation.

"Do you really think we can set everything up?" Sebastian asked. "What about all the plans we made for our big, fancy wedding?"

I laughed. "As long as I marry you, who cares about fancy? You just relax. I'll make the arrangements." I turned to Chaplain Burke and said, "How's eight o'clock for you?"

"Great for me," he joked. From the grin on his face, it seemed he was almost as excited about this as we were.

"Thank you, sir," Sebastian said as the chaplain left the room.

When Sebastian's family came back in, we told them about our decision. His hospital room was so spacious and nice that even with all his family in there, we weren't cramped.

To my surprise, his mom gave me a great, big hug. Then she stood back, her eyes wide. "We've got so much to do!" She grabbed my arm and Savannah's, then tried to drag us out of the room.

I stopped her and said, "Mrs. Stokes, I can't leave Sebastian when he just woke up from his coma. I can get married in what I have on."

Before Mrs. Stokes could answer, Sebastian said, "Christian, I'm going to be fine. Go with Mom and get a beautiful wedding dress and my dad will stay here with me to make sure that I'm okay."

"I can't leave you now!"

"Yes, you can. Dad will be here, along with the doctors and nurses. If my condition changes, they will call you on my cell phone. Go, Christian. I want you to be the most beautiful bride ever."

"Okay, but I'll call to check up on you."

The first thing Mrs. Stokes did when we left the hospital was to announce the wedding to all the press who were gathered outside. The reporters all asked if they could have an exclusive. I told them no media would be allowed to attend, but that we would be happy to provide them with pictures after the ceremony.

Mrs. Stokes ended the impromptu press conference and escorted Savannah and me to her rental car. While she drove, I called my mom on Sebastian's cell phone. "I've got great news," I told her. "Sebastian is awake, he's doing okay, and we're getting married tonight."

"Praise the Lord," she said. "Congratulations, honey."

"Can you and Crystal come? I know it's short notice, but I really want you both to be here. D.C. has flights leaving every day— you could fly into Atlanta and catch a connecting flight to Nashville, then I'll have someone drive you to Gatlinburg. It can be done, Mom. Come."

"Honey, Crystal is seven and a half months pregnant and the doctor told her that she couldn't fly after her sixth month. Besides, I wouldn't want my first grandchild to be born in an airport or in the middle of your wedding. But I'll be there if I can get a flight. What time is the ceremony?"

"Eight o'clock," I told her.

I gave her my credit card information to pay for the flight, knowing how expensive last-minute arrangements could be. "Call me when you've made the reservations so I can arrange to have someone pick you up at the airport. And book a room at the Marriott in Gatlinburg with my credit card, too."

"Have you told Eden yet?" Mom asked.

"No," I said. "I'm planning to call her next. I'll have her call you so the two of you can come out together."

"That sounds wonderful, dear," she said.

Mrs. Stokes pulled into a parking structure and my connection started to break up. "I've got to go, Mom," I said. "I'll talk to you later. I love you."

"I love you, too, baby," she said. "I'll see you soon!"

I had been in Tennessee for almost two weeks, but this was my first time in historical downtown Gatlinburg. The city was quaint, cozy, and cute. Cable cars and horse-drawn carriages traveled on cobblestone streets between old restored buildings. Since it was Christmastime, the streets were decorated with antique nativity scenes, old-fashioned sleighs, and millions of dazzling Christmas lights.

The three of us strolled down the street, looking into all the boutique windows to see if anything caught our eye. Finally, one shop had a gorgeous dress I just had to try on. It was made of white lace, had a three-foot train, the sleeves had pearls woven into the fabric, and the bodice showed a hint of cleavage.

When I put it on in the dressing room and looked in the mirror, I was stunned by how beautiful the dress looked on me. I knew this was the dress I would marry Sebastian in. When I stepped out of the dressing room, Mrs. Stokes and Savannah gasped. When the salesperson told me how much the dress cost, it was my turn to gasp. But Mrs. Stokes insisted on taking care of the bill.

As the salesperson rang up the purchase, my soon-to-be mother-in-law said, "Christian, I was wrong to treat you the way

I have, and I want to apologize. You taught me that love is more important than social status. And you've made my son the happiest I have ever seen him."

"Thank you," I choked out. The salesclerk handed me the huge plastic bag with my wedding gown in it, and I looked at Mrs. Stokes with misty eyes. "Thank you so much."

We went to several more stores to buy shoes and accessories, then returned to the hospital. Mrs. Stokes stopped at the nurse's station to see if they had a room available for me to change in.

The nurse took me to a small room three doors down from Sebastian's. She asked, "Will this do?"

I said, "Yes, this will be just fine. Thank you very much."

As I was putting on my makeup, my mom walked into the room. She must have gotten on the first plane coming to Tennessee.

"You made it!" I screamed as I gave her a hug.

"I wouldn't miss this for anything." She gave me a kiss on the cheek.

"How's Crystal?" I asked.

"She's very excited for you. And for herself, too. Just yesterday she signed the papers to let Eden adopt her baby."

"Really? I know Eden will be a great mother, and Crystal can be at ease because she knows Eden will take good care of the baby."

I stood in front of the mirror in the bathroom, putting on a pearl necklace and earrings while my mother spoke to me from the bathroom doorway.

"Did Eden come with you?"

"No, she couldn't get off of work and she didn't want to leave Crystal, but she was sad that she is missing your special day. She sends her love and she wants you to call her as soon as you can. But I did bring someone with me," Mom said. "I hope you don't mind."

Mom went out of the room and I racked my brain to figure out who she might have brought. She came back in with a man about her age. He had short gray hair, a dark brown complexion, and was dressed in slacks and a long-sleeved dress shirt.

"Hello," I said politely, because I thought that she had brought her new boyfriend.

"Hey, baby girl," the man said in a raspy voice.

"Honey," Mom said, her voice strained, "this is Mr. Flowers."

I smiled and said, "Hello."

He hugged me like he'd known me all of my life.

She gave me an apologetic look, silently begging me to understand and accept this man.

"I've been watching you on the news," he said, looking back and forth between my mom and me. "I told your mom that I wanted to meet you, but she didn't think it was the right time. When she told me you were getting married, I begged her to let me come."

"That was sweet of you, Mr. Flowers," I said.

He touched my shoulder and said, "You're not upset that I came?"

"How could I be upset with the man who makes my mother happy? I haven't seen her this way since she and my dad split up. Just make sure that you treat her right, okay?"

He smiled and said, "Baby, your mother is the best thing to happen to me in a long time, and I plan on treating her like a queen."

My mother looked from me to Mr. Flowers with a big smile and said, "I don't even know why I was worried about you two meeting. I can see that you are going to get along just fine."

Shortly after Mr. Flowers left the room, Savannah came in to see if I was ready. I told her what had happened with my mom and Mr. Flowers and she told me how thrilled she was for them.

Then the doctor came in and said, "I heard that you guys have planned a wedding in the chapel tonight."

"Yes, we have."

"Well, Mr. Stokes isn't well enough to go down to the chapel for the ceremony."

"Oh my God, what are we going to do now?" I said as I sat on the hospital bed.

Savannah said, "Don't worry about anything—it's going to

work out. I'm going to go and speak to Sebastian. I'll be right back."

The doctor left the room and I sat there praying that the Lord would provide a way for us to be married tonight. I was also glad that Savannah had volunteered to speak with Sebastian, because I didn't have the heart to tell him.

She returned and said that Sebastian didn't want to postpone the wedding.

"Let's just have it in his room." I suggested.

Savannah bit her lip. "But that's so small and—"

"I know it's not a chapel, but God will bless it. That's the room where the Lord restored him. It's a perfect place for me to give myself to him in marriage. Will you go ask him if that's okay?"

"Sure," she said, then left the room again.

While she was gone I paced the room, wondering what he would say.

Moments later she returned with a big smile. "Sebastian said he'd marry you in jail if need be, but he is definitely marrying you tonight!"

I thanked God for sending me such a wonderful guy. Then I asked Savannah to go to the chapel and tell everyone about the change of plans and bring them up to his room.

While she was gone I put on my dress, veil, stockings and shoes, and made a final inspection of my hair and makeup. Under normal circumstances I would have had someone to assist me, but these weren't normal circumstances! Savannah came back in the room and told me that everyone was in Sebastian's room, all ready for me. Mr. Flowers stepped from behind her with my bridal bouquet in his hands. He told me that he had purchased it from the hospital florist. The bouquet was lovely, composed of roses and baby's breath. He said that he wanted to get me something for my special day.

"You look gorgeous," Savannah said as she kissed me on the cheek, pulled my veil over my face, and headed out the door.

Mr. Flowers gave me a fatherly kiss on the cheek. "Your soul mate is waiting for you." He held out his arm for me. I took it and we walked down the hall to Sebastian's room.

When we entered the room, I saw that it was crowded. Chaplain Burke stood at the foot of the bed. The people in attendance started humming the bridal march, and Steven was taking pictures. I also noticed that everyone in the room carried a single red rose.

Sebastian was still hooked up to monitors and IVs, but in addition to his hospital gown he wore a top hat and a black bow tie. It looked pretty silly, but that didn't matter to me. He was so handsome, and he was soon to be my husband.

Mr. Flowers kissed my cheek and put my hand in Sebastian's; then he stepped aside.

I stood beside Sebastian's bed, holding his hand. Never could I have imagined that my mom and his parents would be happily present at our wedding. Also in attendance were Savannah, Steven and his wife, nurses, doctors, and the clergyman. It was a tight fit but we managed to get everyone into the room.

Sebastian and I said the traditional wedding vows, and his mother sang "Endless Love." When the chaplain said it was time to exchange rings, I suddenly realized I hadn't bought him one. But Reverend Stokes opened his suit jacket and brought out two platinum bands. He gave the thinner one to his son and the wider one to me.

"Consider this a token of my approval," he said.

After we placed the rings on each other's fingers, the clergyman pronounced us husband and wife. We kissed passionately, in spite of all the medical machinery that got in the way.

Everyone applauded and congratulated us.

A nurse announced that one of the waiting rooms had been set up as a reception hall. Everyone applauded again, then left to go celebrate.

When our family and friends were all gone, Sebastian pulled me close. "Hello, wife," he said.

"Hello, husband," I replied.

We laughed. But when our eyes locked we began to kiss the way we had when we first started to make love. Sebastian tried to maneuver me onto his lap and ended up wincing. I hurried out of the room to get the nurse, and when we returned I saw a pained look come over his face.

The nurse gave him some morphine and said it would make him sleepy in just a few minutes.

"I'm sorry," he said to me.

I stroked his hand. "Hey, we've got a lifetime to be intimate. I'm just glad to be married now."

"Me, too," he said, already starting to sound groggy. "After this, I know we can make it through anything."

Three weeks later, Sebastian and I were back at his place in Atlanta. It was Inauguration Day, and my mother-in-law had helped me pick out the perfect outfit. It was a red suit, tapered at the waist to show off my figure. The skirt came to my knees and had a slight split up the back. I wore matching red shoes and a diamond brooch Sebastian had given me for a wedding present.

Sebastian was still not one hundred percent. He complained of pain occasionally, especially when we tried to be intimate. Though I'd slept in the same bed with him for the last three weeks, our marriage still hadn't been consummated.

The inauguration was held in the coliseum on Georgia Tech's campus. Banners, flags, and balloons waved in the breeze, and thousands of people sat in the stands. Sebastian's parents, who were still working through their reconciliation, were seated in the front row.

My mom was there, sitting next to Sebastian's parents with Mr. Flowers. He was wearing a well-cut gray suit, pink shirt, pink-and-gray striped tie, and gray shoes.

Before the ceremony started I went to my mom, Mr. Flowers, and Sebastian's parents and thanked them for coming, then hugged them all.

As I hugged Mr. Flowers, I whispered in his ear, "I've been hearing how good you are to my mother."

He kissed me on the cheek and said, "Baby girl, I gave you my word."

Steven and his wife were also in attendance. The brothers had a nice chat before we arrived at the building.

Steven said, "Sebastian, I just wanted you to know that I'm working on the problems in my life—in fact, my wife and I are going to counseling. When you were shot it made me realize that I haven't been a good brother or husband. I also wanted you to know that I'm proud of you and the man that you've become."

When Steven turned toward me, all I could say was, "I love you and I'm proud of you for realizing that it was time to make some changes." I hugged him tightly.

Sebastian would tell me later that this was the first time his brother had ever expressed pride in him.

Savannah and Bruce were also in attendance. I spoke with them and she pulled me over for a brief chat.

"Girl, I sat my parents down and told them about my relationship with Bruce and instead of getting mad, they invited him over for dinner."

"Well, after Sebastian got shot it seemed as if they reevaluated their beliefs in terms of love and relationships."

"I want to thank you for that, because your love for Sebastian showed them how it could be."

"You don't have to thank me—just be happy that you don't have to sneak around to be with the man you love."

They finally had her parents' support. I looked forward to having Bruce as my brother-in-law.

Eden and Dion were seated in the front row in front of the stage with the rest of our families. They couldn't make the wedding, but I was elated that they came to the inauguration. Crystal stayed in D.C. with church members since she was due any day.

I hugged Eden and she said, "Look at us—you've just become a wife and I'm going to be a mother as soon as Crystal gives birth."

"You're going to make a great mom to your son," I told her. "Mom told me Crystal's having a boy. Congrats."

"Dion is thrilled. He can't wait to get a basketball in his hand." We laughed.

"Is everything okay with Stone?" I asked.

Eden smiled. "Dion went to see him in jail. You know he got fifteen years for selling drugs."

"Wow," I said.

"He signed the papers that said that he willingly forfeited all parental rights, and he thanked Dion for adopting his child. Stone told Dion that his father wasn't in his life when he grew up, and Stone wanted his son to have a good father."

"Are you coming to D.C. when the baby is born?"

"I promise Sebastian and I will be there," I said as we hugged.

I went backstage with Sebastian, and when he was introduced, we came out on the stage and sat down.

Since the governor could not be there because he was still under investigation, a presiding officer swore Sebastian in.

Presiding Officer Mathis said, "Ladies and gentlemen, I would like to welcome you to the inauguration of Sebastian Stokes as lieutenant governor of Georgia. Normally, the lieutenant governor is sworn in by the governor, but since the governor is indisposed at this moment, I will be swearing in Sebastian Stokes."

When my husband took the platform, I felt so proud. He gave a speech, telling the people how much he appreciated their support. He thanked them for all the concern they'd shown during his recovery, and he vowed to serve them with dignity and honesty, and to make Georgia a better place to live. My heart was overjoyed when he also thanked God for the good times and bad that helped prepare him for this great endeavor.

There were more flags and balloons at the reception. In addition, there was a huge banner that proclaimed Sebastian as lieutenant governor. As we mingled with the guests, the presiding officer came over and asked to speak privately with us.

Presiding Officer Mathis said, "I have some really great news. I was just told that the governor resigned. Sebastian, you are now the governor of Georgia. Congratulations—you've became the lieutenant governor and governor on the same day."

Sebastian's mouth fell open and he squeezed my hand. Suddenly he turned to me and hugged me.

"Presiding Officer Mathis, you have made me one of the

happiest men in Georgia. Besides marrying this lovely woman, this is the proudest day of my life. Thank you so much for telling me."

I said, "This is the greatest news. I know that you will be a superb governor."

The presiding officer then told us that my friend Troy and several other FBI agents had found a connection between the Mob's attempt to frame me and the shooting of my husband. He added, "He discovered that Governor James partnered with Governor Holmes of New York to get the Mob to help him build a gambling dynasty. Both of these men were behind all that happened to you with the money scam. Whenever someone got in their way, they did whatever it took."

The presiding officer congratulated us and left.

"You're going to be the first lady of the state." Sebastian picked me up and twirled me around in the air.

"And she's going to make a fine first lady," his mom said as she came up and gave me a big hug.

"I wish I had your class," I ventured.

"Oh, you've got more than class," she said. "You have integrity—and heart."

"Having your support means so much to me."

"Don't you worry, my dear," she said, straightening the lapels on my suit jacket. "I'll get you ready for the big house in Georgia."

"Thanks."

Everyone in the room crowded around my husband to interview and congratulate him.

The next thing I knew we were back in Gatlinburg, Tennessee, in our own rented cabin. We sat on the floor in front of a crackling fire, sipping sparkling cider.

"Eden gave me a wedding present," I said, tracing Sebastian's lips with my fingers. "Would you like me to try it on?"

His eyes lit up, giving me my answer.

"I'll be right back." I went into the bedroom and dug into my suitcase for the one-piece white lace teddy my best friend had given me after the inauguration ceremony. When I posed in the doorway between the bedroom and the living room, my husband smiled appreciatively. He joined me in the bedroom, where he gently but passionately removed my lingerie.

After we made love, we lay in bed holding each other. I couldn't believe such a wonderful man was all mine.

"So," he said, stroking my arm, "what have you decided to do about your work?"

"I don't want to quit," I said.

"Oh." His voice sounded sad and disappointed.

"But I could request an assignment protecting the new governor of Georgia. He's quite young, you know, and incredibly handsome. So he's going to need some very close and personal attention."

He sat up and looked me in the eyes. "You really love me, don't you?"

"Yes, I do." I kissed him briefly. "If you want me to be your first lady full-time, I'll gladly turn in my gun for you."

"I'll only be governor for two years."

"If you run for office after that, I'm sure you'll win," I assured him.

He pulled me closer.

I didn't know where life would take Governor Stokes and me. but I'd always lived in the valley and wondered what it would be like to be on the hilltop, enjoying the good life. Now I had fame, fortune, and a wonderful husband, but none of that came close to the joy I felt in my relationship with Christ. My husband and I prayed together and thanked God for all of our blessings. Then I thanked my husband for loving me so much.

He put his arm around my waist. "I hope you're happy."

"How could I not be? My mom's got a good man, my sister is a believer and has a great family for her baby, my husband is the governor, your parents like me, and though my earthly dad walked out on me, my Heavenly Father has healed my wounded heart. I'm ecstatic!"

He played with the platinum band on my finger. "I know we can't stay on this mountaintop forever. Every life has its ups and downs."

For so long, I'd been chasing something, unable to put my finger on just what I was searching for. As I listened to my husband proclaiming of life's uncertainties, it was clearer than a shining goblet that I had been searching for true peace, hope, and love all that time. Now that search was over. On my journey, I found the Lord is the only One that can fill me. Since I've let Him into my heart, I have total faith that everything else will work out fine.

So with my index finger I covered his lips, then kissed them, "Wherever we go, though, God will be with us. We've got everything we need. And I want you to know, my love for you won't ever change. 'Cause no matter what happens, being with you is like a piece of heaven."